Courting the Country Miss

by

Donna Hatch

Courting Series, Book 2

This is a work of fiction. Names, characters, places, and incidents are either the product of the author's imagination or are used fictitiously, and any resemblance to actual persons living or dead, business establishments, events, or locales, is entirely coincidental.

Courting the Country Miss

Cover Art by *Debbie Taylor*

The Wild Rose Press, Inc.
PO Box 708
Adams Basin, NY 14410-0708
Visit us at www.thewildrosepress.com

Publishing History
First Tea Rose Edition, 2017
Print ISBN 978-1-5092-1580-5
Digital ISBN 978-1-5092-1581-2

Courting Series, Book 2
Published in the United States of America

Dedication

To my husband,
whose love and unswerving support
always sustains me.

Acknowledgments

My thanks to Airial Hot Air Balloons and their pilot, Bill, for giving me an unforgettable ride in a hot air balloon and tons of information about the history of balloons to help me research this book.

Also, I thank Lynda Crispino at the Albuquerque International Balloon Fiesta for providing more information regarding hydrogen gas balloons similar to those used in Regency England.

I would be remiss without thanking my editor, Cindy Davis; my amazing critique partner and all around cheerleader, Jennifer; and Julie, Liz, Charlotte, Laura, and Nichole for dropping everything to do a final proof read for me out of the kindness of their hearts.

And I want to thank Vicki, who begged me to write Tristan's story.

Chapter One

England, 1817

Leticia Wentworth was twenty times a fool. Richard Barrett never cared for her beyond a childhood friendship, and Leticia had been naive to believe he would love her as she loved him. With savage ferocity, Leticia squelched the cry of pain her heart made every time Richard turned a gaze of adoration upon his wife—the kind of look he never gave Leticia, not even when she'd been certain he'd approach her father to ask for her hand in marriage. She'd pinned all her hopes and dreams of love and family on a man she would never have.

Stupid, stupid girl.

Here she stood, watching Richard kiss his wife's fingertips—the way she'd always imagined he'd do with hers—at a house party much like the one last year when her future had crumbled to dust.

Of course, Richard had never looked at Leticia the way he looked at his wife. He never loved Leticia—not really. That thought lessened the heartache that he'd been snatched from her.

Or so she told herself as she left the party for the quiet serenity of the garden.

She bolted down the gravel pathway and stopped as she came upon a garden fountain—very much like the place where it all started. And where it all ended.

"Weary of the noise inside?" drawled Tristan's familiar voice.

Leticia didn't turn around. Instead she sank onto a nearby stone bench and inhaled the sweet, fresh scent of roses. "I need a moment away from all that." She made a loose wave toward the house.

Tristan's clothing rustled as he sat with her. "Makes you want to move to the continent, doesn't it?"

"What does—the house party?" She looked up at Tristan Barrett, his handsome face and midnight hair so like his brother Richard's. Tristan's presence filled her with the warmth of childhood friendship.

His grin turned sardonic as his coal-black gaze slid her way. "The lovebirds inside."

"It's lovely." Did her voice sound as devoid of sincerity as she felt?

Tristan let out his breath in a huff of amusement. "Admit it; it's nauseating."

"I'm happy for them. They have what marriage should be." Softer, she added, "It's what I've always wanted." She stiffened, cursed herself for her confession, and looked away before her long-time friend saw too much. They used to confide in one another; it had been so easy, so comfortable. But everything had changed.

He fingered his signet ring. "Sorry, Tish. You must hate me for making a muddle of your future."

She sifted through possible replies. "He's happier...with Elizabeth than he would have been with me."

"You don't truly believe that." He paused. "Do you?"

"Of course I do. He never loved me the way he loves her."

"Then he's a fool."

She wound her fingers together in her lap.

He laid a gentle hand over hers. "You'll have that with someone else."

She let out a sharp exhale that doubled as a mirthless laugh. "I think not. I have no prospects."

"That's what the London Season is all about, isn't it? You'll meet a duke or some other stuffed shirt and there you go." He snapped his fingers. "The problem of spinsterhood solved."

She shook her head. "I'm no longer in the first bloom of youth, and my dowry is unremarkable; I have little to offer. Besides, I'll never love anyone else. And my sister Isabella is out now, and will have her first Season this year. We can't afford a Season for us both."

"Never love anyone else?"

Leave it to Tristan to pick up on what she least wanted to discuss. She pretended not to hear him. "Besides, the money I might have spent on clothes for a London Season would be better used helping educate the poor. Have I told you about Elizabeth's and my newest project?"

"Never love anyone else?" he persisted.

Tristan could be annoyingly relentless at times. She adjusted her glove. "I don't wish to discuss it."

He made a *tsking* sound. "Since when won't you discuss your thoughts with me?"

Long-suppressed anger roiled up inside her. "Since you ruined a duke's daughter and forced my intended to wed her to save you from a duel!"

Tristan stared as if she'd slapped him, blinked, then

3

hunched over and rested his elbows on his knees.

She turned away, her anger fading at the obvious sign that she'd hurt him. "Pray, forgive me. I didn't mean that."

"Of course you meant it. All of it." He pushed out a breath. "I've known it all along. You've barely said a word to me since then. I deserve your hatred."

"I could never hate you, Tristan."

"Then you're kinder than I deserve. I made an enormous mistake on so many levels. I should have dueled her brother and spared all of you the heartache."

"No!" she almost shouted. Catching herself, she softened her voice. "No, you most certainly should not have dueled. You might have been injured or killed, or done the same to her brother." She affected a tone her mother would have used. "Perhaps what you ought to be telling yourself is that you should never have lured an innocent out to a secluded garden."

"How could I have known some of London's biggest gossips would have a sudden need to go for a walk?" He trailed off. "You're right. I shouldn't have been alone with her."

No, he most certainly should not have coaxed a gently bred lady out for a moonlit kiss. No young lady should be unchaperoned in the company of a known libertine such as Tristan.

She halted that line of thought. No need to agonize over the past. Tristan had the wisdom to learn from his mistakes, she hoped. As her life-long friend slumped, clearly so full of regret, she had to say something. "It all worked out for the best."

"Except you still hate me."

She attempted to laugh lightly but it sounded as

forced as an old key in a rusty lock. "I don't hate you. I haven't been avoiding you—I've been in Suffolk helping my sister Luciana with her new baby."

He said nothing, his usual smile absent. "I didn't mean to hurt you, Tish. I'd only pursued Elizabeth as a flirtation, an interesting diversion. I never dreamed it would go that far, to feel…" He shrugged. "A mistake in many ways, all of it."

Had Tristan formed a true attachment for Elizabeth? Leticia reached for the brother-sister-like banter they'd used so much of their lives. "Yes, well, the last several years, you've had a terrible time behaving as a gentleman and have taken a great many things too far."

He feigned outrage. "I'm always a gentleman."

She opened her eyes in mock wide-eyed innocence. "Since when is the word rake synonymous with gentleman?"

"Oh, you mean a gentleman by behavior and not by birth? Well, now, that's another matter." A touch of that familiar, teasing smile tugged at his expressive mouth, a mouth with full, kissable lips so like his brother's, a mouth Tristan had probably used on dozens of women. How could two brothers be so alike in appearance and yet so different in behavior?

Unable to keep up the banter, Leticia turned her knees toward him. "What happened to that sweet, dreamy boy who loved poetry and clouds? You didn't used to be so dissipated."

Some inner pain passed over his expression so quickly that she might have imagined it. His grin flashed in the near darkness. "Merely living well, Tish."

"Men can live well without becoming debauched."

His mouth pulled to one side. "Yes, well, my dear brother is perfect enough for the both of us."

"So, since you'll never reach Richard's level of perfection, you'll be the perfect *roué*?"

He adopted a Byronic pose. "But of course."

His fears of not measuring up to Richard didn't touch that inner pain she glimpsed earlier. What secret did he hide? Had it been there all the time?

"Is it because you dislike women?"

He choked. "How can you say that after calling me dissipated, a rake, and a *roué*?"

"I'm not suggesting you don't like to be in a woman's arms, so to speak." She cleared her throat while she blushed with such heat that she wished for a fan. "But no man who cares for the heart or sensibilities of a woman would use her in such a casual manner."

"Trust me, none of the women I *use*, as you say, are innocent, or pretend to have true feelings for me. None of their hearts are involved."

She let out a noise of disgust. "So it's meaningless to you."

"Well, there certainly aren't any pretenses or promises."

Fury at his nonchalant attitude brought her to her feet. "This is an improper conversation to have, even between us."

He rose to his full height, like a cat uncurling after a nap, his smile lazy. "You brought it up."

"Well, I'm ending it. Please don't ruin anyone else's life with all your *pleasures*, you heartless cad." She turned and marched deeper into the garden.

His clothes rustled as he stood and his footsteps trailed after her. He caught up to her, matching her stride. He spoke in a voice as soft as silk on her skin. "Tish."

She kept marching.

"Leticia." He took her arm firm enough to halt her strides. "I'm sorry. For everything."

"For being who you are?" she shot back.

"For disappointing you." True regret rang in his tone and in his expression.

His contrition smoothed the edges of her anger. Honestly, the infuriating man knew how to raise strong emotions in her, sending her from one extreme to the other.

"'Tis of no consequence." She resumed her march back to the house.

Still keeping pace with her, he said, "I'm troubled that you believe you'll never love or marry. Someone like you should not live as a spinster."

"Someone like me?" she echoed.

He made a helpless gesture. "You have much to offer. You're gracious and constant and…well…you'd make a good wife and mother—not run off when life gets dull or when your children misbehave."

She stopped walking and stared at him. That same pain returned in Tristan's eyes but this time it lingered as he stared out into the darkness. *Not run off*…the way his mother had. Is that what haunted him? Did he feel that no woman would ever love him enough to stay with him, that she'd leave him as his mother left when Tristan was a child?

She went deeper with that thought. Perhaps he believed his mother left because of something he'd done to drive her away. She'd heard of that happening. This, then, might be the source of that pain. Perhaps the source of his debauchery.

He seemed to catch himself. With a self-conscious smile curving his mouth, he pulled his gaze back to her face. "There are other dull stuffed shirts like Richard all over England. You have only to find them."

She smiled. "Dull, stuffed shirt, eh? I'd almost believe that, except I know that you would die for your brother."

Memories flitted through her mind of the daring rescue Tristan and Captain Kensington and one of Elizabeth's reformed servants had orchestrated when Richard had been held captive during the peer trial last year. She'd prayed for Tristan when she'd heard he had been shot freeing his brother. To her regret, she'd been too far away at the time to offer assistance for his care.

Tristan shrugged as a sardonic smile played on his mouth. "Taking a bullet for my brother doesn't mean I like him."

She almost laughed. "I see."

He cleared his throat. "I think all you need is to meet a new crop of eligible bachelors. Surely you'll find one who can steal your heart."

Leticia had no desire for anyone to steal her heart. She'd rather willingly give her heart to someone who loved her. She shook her head. "I'm going to dedicate my life to helping the poor. Elizabeth and I are planning to open a charity school for girls. Won't that be wonderful?"

He narrowed his gaze at her. "Is that what you want?"

"Of course. There are a lot of fine minds out there that don't have the advantages of education. Reading and mathematics is crucial to any skilled profession. An education will help them better themselves."

"I mean, is educating other people's children what you want? Do you aspire to be an old maid?"

She flinched. No, of course she did not, but what choice did she have? She would never love another as she'd loved Richard. She couldn't remember a time when she didn't love him. That didn't matter anymore. "I want to make a difference…"

"Getting married and having children won't make a difference?"

She huffed in exasperation. "I told you, I have no prospects. I'm not likely to find one, nor do I want to try. They would all be compared to the ideal and fall short. And I will never, ever, open up my heart to that kind of pain again."

He tilted his head. "I wager a hundred guineas I can find you a husband by Christmas."

She waved her hand. "Pish! You'd lose that wager."

"Don't be so sure."

"Besides all the reasons I listed, it'd never work because you'd introduce me to your dissipated comrades, and I refuse to marry someone one like that."

"Someone like me, you mean?" Did she imagine that his smile faded a little?

"You've always been a good friend, Tristan. Well, *mostly* a good friend," she teased. "But you'd make a terrible husband."

"I would, I really would. Which is why I'll never marry. I wouldn't want to break my wife's heart. No one deserves that." His gaze drifted over the night scene, his expression growing solemn.

She squeezed his hand. When did Tristan become

so enigmatic?

Her touch seemed to bring him back to their topic. "Very well, I will not introduce you to any of my associates. Tell me what you require in a suitable husband and I will search for him."

Taken aback, she stared. "You're serious?"

"Absolutely. How do you define the perfect husband?"

Amused, she shook her head but decided to play along. Perhaps his search for a good husband for her would do him good. It might, at least, put him in respectable company, which may temper his wildness. "Well, to begin with, he must be capable of monogamy. Contrary to current trends, I refuse to love a man who chases light skirts or keeps a mistress."

He nodded. "Monogamy. A worthy virtue."

"A *crucial* virtue."

"Point taken. What else?"

"He must be a man of integrity."

"Of course. I wouldn't expect anything less for you."

"Are you mocking me?" She folded her arms.

"No, ma'am. Agreeing. Monogamy, integrity. Please continue."

"He must have some means of supporting me. Nothing in excess—a vicar's salary would be sufficient so long as he can afford to buy essentials such as food and candles."

"Won't let you starve or sit in the dark. Sensible." He smiled.

"Now you are making fun of me." She unfolded her arms and stepped forward so he might feel the full force of her glare.

"Why is it when I agree with you, you assume I'm mocking you?"

"Because you do it so seldom."

"Mock you or agree with you?" A grin played around the corners of his eyes.

"Agree with me!" Exasperated, she almost stomped her foot.

His teeth flashed in the darkness. "I vow to agree with you whenever you are right. Pray, continue. Any other virtues you require?"

Her ire faded. She thought for a moment, the silvery tinkling of a fountain breaking the garden's stillness. "He must be both kind and gentle. No selfish bully who thinks wives should be ignored or kept under his thumb."

He shivered. "I'd never introduce you to such a boorish brute. So your paragon is faithful, a man of integrity, has a respectable fortune, and is kind-hearted. Is that all?"

"A sense of humor and some wit. He cannot be dull or stone-faced all of the time."

"Of course not. A lively young lady like you must have someone with whom to converse and remind her not to take herself too seriously."

She chuckled softly. "Do I take myself too seriously?"

"Perhaps on occasion. So, the wager is, if I fail to find you this paragon in possession of all these fine virtues before Christmas, I will give you a hundred guineas."

"It won't happen. First of all, you don't know anyone who matches that criteria. However, if you're itching to give me a hundred guineas, I'll take it in the form of a donation to our school for the poor."

He grinned. "Done. Now, what remains to be seen is; what will you give me if you lose?"

She thought a moment. "If I saved all my pin money for a decade, I could never come up with a hundred guineas."

He waved it away. "Not your money. No, it must be something more personal. Hmm…." He stroked his chin, exaggerating his pensiveness. Then he snapped his fingers. "I have it. If you marry a man I find for you before Christmas, you must name your first son Tristan."

She laughed at his vanity. "Very well."

She'd never lose this silly wager. After all, who could measure up to Richard? And if she did meet this paragon, he'd never marry her, the daughter of a country gentleman with a paltry dowry.

Nor would she risk her heart to such a risky venture as love.

Chapter Two

Tristan grinned as Leticia tasted her future victory, so certain she'd win. She must have forgotten how tenacious he could be. Or perhaps she thought him incapable of rubbing shoulders with the kind of men who'd make an appropriate husband. But all he'd have to do is arrange to introduce her to some of Richard's acquaintances. Surely among them, one would make a suitable husband for a prudish lady such as Leticia.

And if not, he'd play dirty and enlist Elizabeth's help. His sister-in-law would no doubt feel obligated to help the girl who'd once planned to marry Richard. Elizabeth had been a willing participant in that kiss resulting in the challenge that set the rest of the events in motion. No doubt she still nursed some guilt over Leticia's plight enough to help Tristan's quest. Although, truth be told, Elizabeth would help him out of the kindness of her heart.

Tristan resisted the urge to rub his hands together, picturing his victory. He'd find Leticia a husband. Then maybe at last he'd stop feeling so confoundedly guilty about the whole sordid affair.

Leticia rubbed her arms and folded them tight.

"Chilled?" he asked.

"A little."

He removed his superfine tailcoat and placed it around her shoulders. "Let's return."

She nodded and they turned, passing a fountain similar to the place where he'd been caught alone with Elizabeth, which had started all the trouble. Leticia stiffened and quickened her steps. Another bolt of guilt shot through Tristan.

Yes, he'd find some way to atone for his crime. Although, Richard so clearly loved Elizabeth, more than he had ever cared for Leticia, that Tristan couldn't truly regret his actions. Once he found Leticia the love of her life, all would be well. Then he could return to enjoying his bachelorhood without a squirming conscience.

Before they reached the terrace, Leticia returned his tailcoat and stepped inside the ballroom. After donning the coat, Tristan entered, scanning the room for potential husbands for Leticia. More than the house party attended; all the families in the area had also come for the ball, including a few prospects for Leticia. He'd have to give them some thought.

Leticia gave him a knowing smile and moved to her mother. Tristan looked Leticia over with a critical eye. She'd grown from a knobby-kneed, freckle-faced little tag-along into a lovely young lady. Her figure, a bit fuller than strictly fashionable, curved in all the right places. Her brown hair held a touch of red that shone almost auburn in the ballroom lamplight. Her features were pleasant if not striking, but her expressive eyes had an arresting quality that made men take a second look, eyes the color of...hmmm. What color, exactly, were her eyes?

Frowning, he sifted through memories. Odd that he'd known her all his life and yet couldn't recall the exact color of her eyes. Lightish, he thought. No matter, he'd look again when next he conversed with her. Still, she had much to offer a man. Her dowry might be a deterrent for some but would prevent fortune hunters from sniffing around her like hungry dogs.

Tristan cast a casual glance about the room and moved in the direction of a group of bachelors in the corner, all holding glasses of brandy. He joined them, greeting the two he knew.

"Rowley, Seton." He nodded.

Rowley clapped him on the back. "Ahh...Barrett. Good of you to join us. Jolly good hunt today, eh?"

"Yes, indeed." Tristan accepted a glass from a passing tray. "I thought the hounds would actually climb the tree."

They chuckled at his poor joke. Tristan sized up the men, searching his memory regarding their worthiness as a potential husband for Leticia.

Rowley gestured at the man Tristan didn't recognize. "I don't believe you know Wynn, here."

"No, I've not had that pleasure."

"Tristan Barrett, meet John Wynn."

After inclining his head in greeting, Tristan looked Wynn over. Well-heeled, tall, lean. Wearing a knot in his cravat preferred by the Corinthian set and a tasteful evening tailcoat. Nothing unattractive about him. Leticia didn't say it, of course, but Tristan knew enough about women to know that she wouldn't want to wake up every morning to a hideous face.

"Yes, I believe I saw you at the hunt this morning," Tristan said. "Do you live in the area?"

Wynn grinned. "Not when I can help it. Don't much care for the country, unless there's a steeple chase or a hunt."

A pity, that. Leticia preferred the country to the city. "You'll attend the ball tonight?" Tristan probed.

"Of course. Couldn't offend the host or hostess, you know." At Tristan's searching gaze, he lowered his voice. "Very well, if you must know, my sister threatened to tell my mother about a little indiscretion I had if I didn't come even out the numbers."

Ah. Debauched. Wynn was not for Leticia.

Wynn glanced around. "Although, I must say, I'm not sorry I came. Quite a selection of delectables. The one at the head of the line looks promising. What's her name?"

Tristan looked over his shoulder. He choked. Leticia danced at the head of the line.

"Miss Leticia Wentworth," supplied Seton, who'd been silent until now. Did he detect a note of longing in the diminutive man's voice?

"Leticia Wentworth," Wynn repeated as if testing her name on his tongue. "Care to introduce me to her?"

"She's not your type," Tristan snapped. Chuckling at the sudden and unexplained protectiveness surging through him, he softened his voice, grinning. "I mean, she's a lady. Not a delectable with whom you can dally." A wicked thought entered his mind. "Her father is the one who made the kill in the hunt today."

"The crack shot?"

"The very one." There. That ought to make the rogue think twice about pursuing Leticia.

While Wynn digested Tristan's information, Seton narrowed his eyes at Tristan. "She's not your sister, you know, Barrett."

Taken aback, Tristan raised a hand. "No, of course not. Still, I've known her longer than most so I can't help but feel a bit brotherly toward her."

A challenging gleam entered Seton's eyes, his usual mild expression almost fierce. "Still, it isn't your place to decide who may and may not stand up with her."

Tristan shrugged. "Never claimed it was. Good heavens, Seton, if you're mooning over her, go ask her for a set."

Seton drew himself up to his less than impressive height. "Perhaps I will."

Wynn brushed an imaginary speck off his sleeve and touched his cravat. "Right after one of you introduce me to her."

Tristan glared at Wynn before looking away. He shook his head at his own reaction. It wasn't his place to warn off men unworthy of Leticia. Besides, what harm would there be in a dance? And if men vied for her company at a ball, it might prove to her once and for all that men found her attractive. If nothing else, gentlemen's attention might get her mind off Richard. It had the added advantage of bringing her to the notice of other, more suitable gentlemen. Men were always interested by women who intrigued other men. Must be the competitive nature of the beast. Or a desire to solve the mystery. Still, if a rogue like Wynn showed too much interest in Leticia, Tristan would warn him off.

Tristan searched for Leticia among the dancers. Her eyes sparkled and her cheeks flushed, painting a lovely picture.

"Pretty thing, isn't she?" Rowley said.

"Perhaps you each should ask her for a set," Tristan suggested in a nonchalant tone to no one in particular.

Wynn straightened further, Rowley looked thoughtful, and Seton appeared to be bracing himself for battle, gulping and tugging at the hem of his waistcoat.

Wynn glanced back at the others, his gaze resting longest on Tristan. "Deuce take it, lads, I cannot approach her without an introduction."

"You could ask the hostess," Tristan suggested.

Wynn looked around. "I don't see her."

Tristan growled under his breath. He'd rather introduce Leticia to a bug than to Wynn.

Wynn pinned Tristan with a look. "If you'd be so kind."

Tristan sighed. "Very well."

Flanked by Wynn, Tristan ambled toward the dance floor as the music ended. A laughing Leticia and her partner—a true dandy in a bright yellow and blue brocade waistcoat with a green tailcoat—left the floor. Her partner left Leticia with her mother, bowed, then pinched some snuff as he wound through the crowd.

"You've developed a liking for peacocks, I see," Tristan teased Leticia.

Leticia gave his arm a playful swat. "Mr. Pottinger is a fine dancer and a pleasant conversationalist."

Green. Her eyes were green—the exact shade of a new leaf in spring, moments after it opens. How could he have missed such an intriguing shade of green all these years?

"Uh huh." Tristan raised his brows as if he didn't believe a word of her assessment of the dandy. Which he didn't. Before Leticia got tempted to do something unladylike such as crack her fan over his head, Tristan turned to Wynn. "Please allow me to introduce you to

Mr. John Wynn. He's here with his family, including a rather *spirited* sister, I understand." He hoped Wynn heard the warning in his voice.

Wynn flashed a debonair smile, but at the last second, his gaze flitted toward Tristan as if he feared Tristan might reveal a secret.

After a last look of challenge, Tristan said, "Mr. Wynn, meet one of my oldest and dearest friends, Miss Wentworth."

"A delight to make your acquaintance, Miss Wentworth." Wynn bowed low.

Leticia smiled as if she'd found a missing puzzle piece. "Wynn? Oh, yes, I met your sister. Spirited, indeed."

Wynn wasted no time. "Miss Wentworth, if I may be so bold, will you do me the honor of standing up with me?" He gestured toward the dance floor where dancers lined up for the next set.

"I'd be delighted." As she placed her hand on Wynn's proffered arm, she glanced at Tristan as if to say, 'I know you've put him up to this.'

Tristan would take the earliest opportunity to ensure she knew he did not put Wynn up to it and that the scoundrel failed to meet the criteria for a suitable husband, by Leticia's own list. And his own.

Perhaps this matchmaking business would be a greater challenge than he first supposed.

Chapter Three

The following morning, while seated at the breakfast table, Leticia spread Devonshire cream on her scone as if she were attempting a fine watercolor, and set the knife at the edge of her plate.

"You seem thoughtful today, dearest." Mama stirred her tea. "Thinking about last night's ball?"

"I was remembering a discussion I had with Elizabeth—er, Lady Averston," she corrected out of respect for Mama's sense of propriety, "regarding our plans to raise money for the school."

Mama smiled indulgently. "It seems a daunting prospect but so kind to try to uplift the poor in London."

"Perhaps, but we mean to go forth with our plans."

"Speaking of plans, we've had a change."

Leticia looked up at the odd tone in her mother's voice. "A change?"

"About all of us going to London…"

Leticia's thoughts raced. "I understand, Mama. T'isn't necessary that I go this Season. This is Isabella's time to—"

"That's not what I'm saying." Mama sipped her tea and set down the cup as if she feared she might shatter the china.

Leticia gave Mama her full attention. Mama glanced around, but they were alone in the breakfast room. Few of the other guests had risen yet, and most of the gentlemen had already left for another hunt.

Still, she lowered her voice. "I will be unable to attend as Isabella's chaperone."

Leticia blinked. "I don't understand."

Mama sighed. "'Tis unexpected, but excellent news. A bit later than I'd hoped…"

"Mama, don't keep me in suspense. Have out with it."

"It appears that I am in a…er…rather…delicate condition."

Leticia blinked. Did she mean…

"The doctor has recommended that I not travel any long distances. He allowed this visit because it's a scant few hours' drive. Once I return home, he advises that I stay abed for the duration."

Leticia put her hand on her cheek. "A baby?"

Mama beamed, her eyes shining, and said in an excited whisper, "Isn't it wonderful? Perhaps I'll give your father a son, at last. Of course we'd love another daughter, as we love all you girls, but a son…" She stared off into some distant view only she saw.

After five daughters, a son would be a blessing for Papa, not to mention that an heir would keep the property in the immediate family and assure the family line. And yet…

"Why must you stay in bed?"

Her mother put a hand over her stomach as if cradling the unborn child. "Due to my age, and after losing the last one, we can't be too cautious."

Leticia's mouth went dry. She leaned in, touching her mother's hand. "Are you in danger?"

"Oh, good heavens, no. Well, you know, not any

more than normal—merely a precaution to help the baby not come too soon."

Leticia gave her mother's hand a squeeze. How Mama endured childbirth all those times posed a mystery. "So, since you cannot accompany Isabella, are we to cancel the trip?"

"Of course not. Isabella will go to Town this Season—she's the perfect age and besides, we've already let a house in Town."

"Then you want me to be her chaperone."

Mama choked on her tea. "Leticia, I wonder about you sometimes, I really do. You aren't old enough to be a proper chaperone. Believe it or not, you aren't as long in the tooth as you seem to think." Her eyes twinkled.

Leticia spread her hands in a helpless gesture, warming at the indirect assurance she wasn't a complete spinster—a silly thought, since she no longer wished to marry. Spinsterhood lay in her future regardless of her wishes. "What do you plan to do?"

"Aunt Alice offered to chaperone Isabella in my place on one condition; she wants you to go, too. She insists that sisters always make a bigger splash than one girl. She's still crowing about how both your older sisters received proposals when she launched them together four years ago."

"She wants me to go, too?" Leticia's thoughts tumbled. "But my wardrobe is unfit for a Season in London. Papa already explained he cannot bear the cost of a wardrobe for me in addition to Isabella, especially since I've already other Seasons." Her face warmed at the reminder that, while her older sister married after one Season, Leticia had not received a proposal in two. That might have been because everyone thought she and Richard had an understanding...or perhaps she was even plainer and less interesting than she supposed.

It didn't matter. She had a school to which she planned to devote her life and her energy. She didn't need a husband or children to make her feel worthwhile.

Mama's voice broke into her thoughts. "I've given some thought to your wardrobe issue. I think if we make over your best gowns from two years ago, we'll manage. Perhaps not quite as spectacular as a London *modiste*, but I'm sure if we study the latest La Belle Assemble engravings, our own town dressmaker can modify yours and come close to something fashionable."

"I suppose she could," Leticia conceded. She need only look fashionable enough not to embarrass her sister in front of London's *grande dames*.

"If we make over a few of Isabella's things, too, we ought to be able to get you at least one ball gown from London."

"Mama, that's not necessary. Make Isabella's gowns the very finest. Mine aren't important. I won't be going to London to search for a husband, I'll be going to satisfy Aunt Alice's stipulations...and to help with our cause."

"Cause? Ah, of course—the school." A mysterious gleam entered Mama's eye. "Then you must look fashionable if you are to garner some commitments from those who have deep pockets."

"My relationship with Lady Averston will help with that. A duke's daughter who marries an earl has few doors closed to her."

"Thanks in some part to you, I think."

Leticia toyed with her napkin. "Certainly not. Her reticence adds to her charm, and she's toasted as a beauty everywhere she goes. Everyone admires her."

"I know all about how you helped quell the rumors regarding the origin of her betrothal to Lord Averston. That was most admirably done, dearest."

Her mother smiled with such fondness that a lump rose to Leticia's throat. She had tried, whenever possible, to protect the couple from rumor but not for the unselfish reasons Mama supposed.

As guilt wagged its finger, Leticia glanced at her mother. "I did it for Richard, not for Lady Elizabeth. At least, not entirely."

"Still, both benefited."

Leticia nodded. "Well worth the effort if it spared Richard any discomfort. Besides, it led to a partner in my venture for the school and to an unexpected friendship with Lady Elizabeth—er, Lady Averston."

Who would have thought she'd become friends with the very girl whose actions had torn Richard away from her? Still, she couldn't truly blame Elizabeth; Tristan's allure had spiraled into the stuff of legends. Few could resist his shocking good looks and silver tongue. The scoundrel.

Then again, no one knew the real Tristan, not the way Leticia did. Why did that knowledge make her feel smug?

Isabella and Maranda came in together, both fresh and bright as spring daisies. The one Wentworth daughter blessed with raven hair, Isabella wore it down in long curls in the back with the sides swept back, and it showered in glorious array around her trim figure. Two years Isabella's junior, Maranda had tried to duplicate Isabella's coiffure, but her lighter brown hair lacked the thickness to succeed. The youngest sister of the Wentworth brood, Maranda had come out this week, a maneuver Leticia suspected had more to do with allowing her to attend this house party with the family than her age. Beforehand, Maranda had shed stormy tears about being left behind. Though Mama worried the family would receive criticism for having three daughters out at the same time, no one had voiced disapproval.

Leticia exchanged greetings with her sisters as they served themselves from the dishes laid out on the sideboard table. Other guests entered, their chattering filling the breakfast room and ending any personal conversation. While the others gossiped, Leticia fell silent, content to listen.

Maranda blurted out, "Mama, *why* can't I go to London, too? I don't expect to do everything with you; I know it's Isabella's moment to shine so I won't expect to attend all the balls and soirees as she, but I cannot abide remaining behind in the country while the rest of you go off and enjoy all those parties and *soirees musicales* and everything else without me."

Leticia and Isabella smiled at each other over Maranda's head. Isabella held up three fingers. She had wagered Maranda would bring up that old complaint during the house party at least five times. Leticia had hoped her youngest sister would be mature enough to limit her complaints to two.

Mama patted Maranda's hand and cast a meaningful look at the others filling the breakfast room. "For now, rest assured, you shall not be abandoned."

"But—"

Mama raised her hand. "That's all I will say on the matter for now."

Maranda opened her mouth again but Leticia sent her a quelling look. Maranda closed her mouth with a snap and sat pouting. "I always get left behind."

"Not for this house party, you didn't," Leticia reminded her.

Maranda sighed. "True. That would have been intolerable."

A footman walked by with a steaming pot in one hand. "Chocolate, anyone?"

Maranda perked up. "Yes, please."

Her mood brightened by the cup of chocolate, she clearly forgot her pique and began conversing with the others again.

Leticia smiled at Isabella again, then excused herself from breakfast and went off in search of Elizabeth whom she hadn't yet seen this morn. An early riser, Elizabeth had probably gone for a walk. Or maybe she'd wandered into the music room where a harp resided. As Leticia meandered through the rooms, the faint, heavenly strains of a harp sang to her as sweetly as a dream. A pity her family didn't own one; Leticia had always wanted to learn to play but harps were far too extravagant a purchase. She'd had to make do on their old pianoforte.

Following the sweet strains, Leticia pushed open a door to the drawing room partitioned off to make a smaller music room.

Elizabeth painted a lovely picture, her graceful hands fluttering over the harp strings, her face serene. Her emerald morning gown swept around her, moving as her feet made adjustments to the pedals at the base of the harp each time she played an accidental or key change. Leticia stilled, hardly daring to breathe lest she give away her presence. Leaning against the doorframe, Leticia closed her eyes and immersed herself in the music, imagining a garden where fairies danced with butterflies and flowers nodded in approval.

The music stopped. Elizabeth's voice rang with surprise. "Leticia. I didn't hear you come in."

Opening her eyes, Leticia smiled. "I knew you'd stop if I gave away my presence."

Her cheeks pink, Elizabeth moved the pedals into their natural position and leaned the harp forward until it rested on its feet. Standing, she shook her head. "Shame on you for eavesdropping."

"I've never met anyone with a worse case of stage fright—which is a pity considering your remarkable talent. In all those *soirees musicales* I attend, I seldom hear anyone play with as much proficiency or emotion as you."

Elizabeth's mouth lifted on one side but her gaze lowered as if she didn't believe Leticia. She stood. "How kind of you to say. Pray, tell me what brings you to me, besides the call of my 'considerable talent,' that is?"

"I wondered if you'd received a reply to any of the letters you sent."

"Not since you asked me last night." Elizabeth's mouth curved into a gentle, teasing smile.

Leticia laughed at herself. "Of course not. Perhaps we should see if Lord Ellerton or Mrs. Bateford are still entertaining the idea of lending their support."

"I mentioned it to Lord Ellerton last night, but he failed to commit. I asked Richard to give him a nudge.

We ought to seek out Mrs. Bateford. She seemed interested."

"I saw her at breakfast, so I know she's arisen."

"Perhaps we can invite her to take a turn about the gardens this morning." Elizabeth tapped her lower lip with a finger. "Then again, she may feel overwhelmed by us both. She is a bit of a recluse. I can't imagine how the Colonel and his wife coaxed her to attend the house party. Should I speak with her alone, or do you wish to?"

"You seem to have a better rapport with her than I."

Elizabeth nodded. "Very well. I shall seek her out. Pray, walk with me until we find her."

"Certainly." Leticia fell into step with the countess as she moved toward the breakfast room.

Elizabeth glanced at her. "You danced quite a few sets last night. You appeared to have captured the attention of some fine gentlemen, many of them unattached."

Leticia offered a self-deprecating smile. "Tristan put them up to it."

"Tristan? Why would he do that?"

"He seems to have it in his head that he owes me a husband." She cleared her throat. Had she stepped on Elizabeth's emotional toes?

Elizabeth only nodded as if she understood Tristan's motives.

"So," Leticia continued, "he's appointed himself my personal matchmaker. What's more, he bet a hundred guineas to our school that I'd receive a proposal from a worthy man by Christmas." She gave a little laugh. "Ridiculous, of course. I humored him so that he might spend some time in respectable company during his search for my so-called future husband. He agreed not to introduce me to any of his usual associates, thank goodness."

Elizabeth's smile faded. "I don't know his friends well. Are they so disreputable?"

"Most of his closest cronies are. But he's become quite chummy with Rhys Kensington since his return from the continent, and from what I know of Kensington, he's a decent sort."

"Richard thinks highly of Captain Kensington."

"Yes, they've known each other forever. I'm sure Richard was relieved when he came home from the war whole and hale."

"Yes. Very. He came to our wedding, which meant a lot to Richard. And without Captain Kensington and his military experience, they might not have gotten Richard out alive when he was held captive."

Leticia shivered, thinking of Richard overpowered by thugs and killers, but the idea of them shooting Tristan turned her cold. If only she'd been here to nurse him back to health. "As to your question, I admit I don't know many of Tristan's acquaintances. However, I gave him high criteria for a husband in the hopes that he'll seek out better company than gamblers and philanderers. Perhaps he'll make friends with respectable gentlemen for a change. Plenty of that kind like to race and box and hunt, so he can still pursue the diversions he enjoys while seeking better company."

Elizabeth had stopped walking and stood staring at her. "You don't have a very high opinion of Tristan, do you?"

Leticia put her hand on her cheek. "Good heavens,

do I give you that impression? No, quite the contrary. I love him like a brother." She paused. "I do wish he were more like the sweet, poetic boy he used to be—the one who'd never break a lady's heart, or risk his neck in a race, or bet a fortune on the turn of a card."

"He is very different from his brother." Elizabeth wore a serene expression with no sign of the infatuated miss she'd been a year ago.

"Yes, indeed. Richard has always been more serious and dependable, and Tristan has a zest for life. He sees beauty and poetry everywhere. Richard could ponder something and unlock its secrets, but Tristan had to take it all apart with his hands and find some analogy for life in the process." Leticia's gaze moved to the window. "The last few years, he's grown so...so lost."

"I don't think he's as lost as you seem to think," Elizabeth said. "Perhaps your plan to lure him into more respectable company is exactly what he needs. Or perhaps the approval of those closest to him would go a long way."

"Approval? With his lifestyle?" Leticia said, aghast.

"Not of what he does—of who he is. I respond to approval and love far better than to criticism." Again that brief flash of pain passed through Elizabeth's eyes. Had growing up under the rule of the daunting Duchess of Pemberton been terrible? The intimidating duchess made Leticia want to hide her face. Fortunately, the ducal family had failed to attend this house party.

Leticia nodded. "I'm certain I respond best to encouragement, too." A thought came to her, a wonderful, delicious thought. "Perhaps you can help. If

I know Tristan, he'll come to you for advice—for recommendations of gentlemen to whom he might introduce to me. When you make those suggestions, bear in mind gentlemen whose presence will be good for Tristan rather than those you think would be a husband for me. We'll see if we can match Tristan with good friends while he's trying to match me with a husband."

Elizabeth laughed. "I foresee a merry chase for us all."

Leticia joined her laughter. "Let us hope a grand prize is caught."

Perhaps in her crusade to save the poor, she could save Tristan as well.

Chapter Four

Tristan strode alongside his brother, Richard, and slapped his riding gloves against his buckskin breeches. He had to admit, the country life provided invigorating diversions. The pleasures of Town life were varied and enjoyable, but there was something about the simplicity of the country that left him feeling almost wholesome.

Richard removed his beaver hat, brushed it off, and set it back on his head, looking every inch a perfect English earl. "I daresay, the colonel has the finest hounds in the county, and his hunts always prove entertaining."

Tristan smirked. "And seeing Seton almost lose his seat proved a bit diverting, as well."

Richard chuckled. "Poor lad. He does try."

"He should stop trying. I'm sure he has other skills. Of some kind. However hidden."

"He had some rather kind words in your behalf."

"Did he?" Tristan frowned. "Can't imagine why."

"Did you know his father is a member of the House of Commons?"

Tristan shrugged. "Of course. That's why he's invited to these parties."

Sobering, Richard turned a rather discomfortingly piercing gaze on Tristan. "He said someone with a fine mind like yours should consider becoming an MP."

Groaning, Tristan held out a hand. "Oh, no. Not the

you need to grow up and start doing something worthwhile with your life speech again."

Richard sighed. "Not a speech, a plea. Grow up. Choose a worthwhile occupation—something better than the next race or card game or light skirt."

Anger simmered in Tristan's stomach. First Leticia and now Richard. One would think they'd decided ahead of time to beat him with the whip of responsibility during the house party.

Tristan fisted his hands. "For your information, I have nobler pursuits."

"I have something more meaningful in mind than fencing and shooting and fisticuffs."

Tristan reined in his temper and smirked. "One never knows when one may need to use those skills."

"I mean a calling, a profession—anything."

Tristan's last attempt to hold on to his humor collapsed. "Face it, Richard, I will never measure up to your level of perfection, so stop trying to make me over into your image."

"That's not what—"

"Stop." Tristan wheeled around and strode toward the stables. With each step, his frustration heated, speeding his steps, until he reached a boiling point. Veering away from the stables, he headed for the open fields. He broke into a run, his long strides taking him far from the stables, far from the house, out toward solitude.

Dodging hedgerows and bracken, he flew over the ground, trying to leave all thought behind him. Still he ran, pushing himself harder until his lungs burned and his legs ached. No matter how fast he ran, he couldn't lose the demons that always lurked nearby, nor all their insidious whispers that he'd never be good enough, never be worthy enough. Never be loved.

When he could run no more, Tristan slowed to a walk. He stripped off his tailcoat and loosened his cravat, then lifted his face to the sun. The image of Mama's back as she left him burst into his memory along with his own child's voice begging her to come back.

After receiving a paddling for not correctly conjugating his Latin verb, he'd fled his tutor in the nursery. Seeking Mama's comfort, he'd raced into her sitting room. He'd found it empty. The house was empty. From that moment, his heart was empty.

A glimmer of life had sparked when he'd met Elizabeth, but that extinguished. Just as well. She and Richard were disgustingly happy.

And so he excelled as a debauched bachelor. Or he would be as soon as he cleared his conscience regarding Leticia. Then he could focus on getting Richard off his back. Perhaps it was time for a Grand Tour. The continent would take him far away from Richard, responsibility, and maybe his demons. He might pay a call on his sister Selina, try to coax her into coming home. Surely, she'd painted all of Italy by now.

Tristan headed for the river and strolled along its sun-dappled surface. Idly fingering his signet ring, he watched the sunlight shimmer on the water like thousands of prisms.

His stomach's rumbling drove him back to the manor house. As he arrived at the edge of the outer garden and rounded a topiary shaped like a peacock, he almost collided with Leticia.

She put an arm out. "What's amiss?"

He shook his head.

Leticia linked arms with him, and he slowed his step to match hers. She said nothing while they strolled in companionable silence.

After a pause, she offered, "You've been running again."

He pushed his fingers through his hair but no doubt needed a comb and mirror. "Richard gave another speech about how I ought to do something meaningful with my life. He doesn't understand. I'm not like him."

"No of course not—you're much more charming."

He looked up at the exaggerated serious tone in her voice. As he suspected, her voice had been a mask for humor; her eyes twinkled and that mischievous smile tugged at the corner of her mouth. Her teasing soothed like balm over his wounds.

"I suspect you're mocking me, Miss Wentworth."

"Now, why would I do a thing like that, Mr. Barrett?" She batted her lashes, all innocence except for that gleam in her eye.

She probably agreed with Richard. She usually did, though gentler in her approach.

She touched his brow. "My, what a scowl. Either Richard gave you a proper whipping or you're hungry."

He laughed as the comfort of her companionship soothed the last of his ruffled feathers. "Do you know me so well?"

"We'd best feed you lest you start tearing into the roses."

"I'd settle for a tree branch."

She steered him back the way she'd come. "We had luncheon *al fresco*. I'm certain there's plenty left."

"*Al fresco* this time of year?"

"We decided to take advantage of the fine weather today, although it is a bit cooler than I prefer for outdoor dining."

Voices drifted on the garden-scented breeze, guiding them to a wide lawn underneath a lilac tree. A few guests remained lounging on chaises and chairs, nibbling at cheese or fruit or drinking wine, all the while chatting with Colonel and Mrs. Sherwood. Neither Richard nor Elizabeth mingled with the diners.

At Tristan and Leticia's approach, a servant brought them a basket. Within moments Tristan devoured ham, grapes, apples, bread, and cheese.

As he reached for a meat pie, she said, "Those have mushrooms in them."

Only a good friend like Leticia would think of such a detail as warning him off from a food he disliked. Another knot in his stomach unwound and relaxed. He shook his head. "I don't understand why people would ruin a perfectly good dish with such nasty little things. My thanks for the warning."

"They were delicious; I had two." Leticia smiled at their old debate and smoothed her skirts. "You missed a fascinating walk."

With his mouth full, Tristan raised his brows.

"Miss Wynn tried to feed the ducks but they overwhelmed her and nearly knocked her down. Then the geese got involved, and when she ran out of food, they started pecking her, on a, er…rather embarrassing location. Her mother started shrieking and waving so madly to chase them off that she ran into her daughter and they both fell into the pond."

Tristan snickered.

"Miss Wynn's brother started laughing so she

whacked his arm with her reticule. He said, 'What do you want me to do, challenge the goose to a duel?' And she said, 'Yes, that, at least would have been gallant. That goose is the very devil!'"

Tristan chuckled.

Leticia leaned back on her hands and smiled up at Tristan with such an impishness to her expression that it transported him back to their childhood when Leticia wasn't quite so pretty.

She cocked her head to one side. "I don't have brothers, of course, but I'm certain you'd shoot the goose who, er, goosed me, instead of laughing at my discomfort, wouldn't you?"

Tristan choked and swallowed his mouthful. "I'd laugh first. Then I'd shoot the goose that dared defile you, and I wouldn't let you fall into the lake."

"That *is* gallant."

"Would you rather be sopping wet, or the object of laughter?"

"I'm accustomed to you laughing at me, so I suppose I'd take that over a spill in a dirty pond filled with cantankerous geese."

"You didn't seem to mind a dirty pond filled with cantankerous boys."

She drew herself up primly and brushed a wrinkle out of her walking gown. "That was years ago. I associate with cantankerous boys on the dance floor now."

"You associated with several of them last night. Did you enjoy yourself?"

"Yes, and I didn't need your help, thank you."

Tristan held out his hands in surrender. "I didn't put them up to it. Well, maybe Seton; he was aching to catch your eye, so I made a suggestion that he might have better luck if he actually *asked* you for a set. The others did it on their own."

"I'm happy to hear you didn't have to force them to dance with a dowdy thing like me."

"You aren't dowdy and you know it, you saucy wench. By the way, that Wynn fellow is not a candidate for your future husband."

"Oh? Didn't you introduce him to me?"

"I felt obligated to do so because he asked. But under no circumstances are you to allow him to pursue you."

"Why, Tristan, you sound almost protective." Overly dramatic, she laid her hand over her head and fluttered her eyelashes like a coquette.

Tristan normally found her theatrics humorous. Today he scowled that she made light of his concerns. "He admitted to an indiscretion, so he isn't a potential husband for you."

Her brows shot up, but she looked amused rather than annoyed. "Don't I have a say in this?"

"I'm making a judgment based on your own list."

"I see." Her mouth contorted as if trying to smother a laugh.

He glared. "I'm doing this to spare you embarrassment or bruised feelings later, you ingrate."

She did laugh then. "Oh, Tristan. You can be very sweet, you know that?"

He had nothing to say to that so he stuffed a large piece of cake into his mouth.

She patted his arm. "Don't frown so. It will mar your stunning good looks for your next conquest."

He choked again. "Leticia, really."

"Oh, right. How unladylike of me to use such a word."

After finishing his cake, he leaned back and closed his eyes. Leticia's soothing mirth had eased away his tension and all seemed right again. Content with a full stomach and in the presence of a friend who'd always understood him, he drew a breath and listened to the song of birds, the gentle lapping of the pond, the shiver of wings in flight, Leticia's breathing. He always felt more comfortable with her than he had with any other female, even his sister, Selena. He smiled, recalling his sister's letter detailing how much she enjoyed her time in Italy with Aunt Fanny. Perhaps he'd join them this summer after he matched Leticia with a boring, dependable husband.

Feminine laughter broke into his reverie.

"Good day, Miss Wentworth," sang out a sultry alto.

Tristan opened an eye and peered at a cluster of ladies hovering nearby.

"Good afternoon," Leticia replied. When they didn't leave, but remained nearby, she motioned them over. "Care to join us?"

"Thank you," said another.

A moment later Tristan found himself surrounded by a flock of pretty young ladies, all smiling and fluttering like so many hens. He got to his feet to greet them as Leticia made the introductions.

"Tristan Barrett? Oh, dear, I've heard of you." The sultry alto voice belonged to a gorgeous brunette whose long-lashed eyes moved up and down his body, her come-hither tone not matching the disapproving words she spoke. "You aren't as wicked and scandalous as they say, are you?"

Tristan cast an appraising glance over her, noting that she failed to blush or lower her eyes. What had Leticia said her name was? He gave her a lazy grin. "I am wonderfully wicked and properly scandalous."

Trills of laughter erupted in all but one, a blonde who blinked and wore a bewildered expression as if she couldn't quite place the meaning of his words.

"Miss Wentworth tells me you and she are childhood friends," the brunette said.

"That's true."

"Then I suppose she knows all sorts of delicious secrets about you."

"Perhaps some of the tamer ones I kept in my youth." Wickedly, he added, "But nothing compared to those I have now."

"You don't say?" Again came that come-hither look.

Tristan gave her a heavily lidded smile. "She grew up to become proper and I grew up to become scandalous."

"Oh, my," said another girl, Wynn's sister, by her coloring and the shape of her mouth, which, at the moment, pressed into a disapproving line. Her hair appeared to be damp, no doubt from her fall in the pond after the goose attack. "You are rather proud of yourself, aren't you?"

"I'm honest, Miss Wynn."

She inclined her head as if to concede his point, but disapproval still oozed from every pore. He pictured her at odds with a flock of geese. A pity he missed that little show.

"His honesty allows for some degree of

exaggeration," Leticia said with a knowing smile.

Tristan eyed Leticia. Could it be possible she didn't believe every rumor that flittered around him? For the first time in his life, he wished all the rumors were false and that he'd been as upright as Richard. But Richard never had any fun; he always busied himself being perfectly respectable. So, Tristan would be perfectly dissipated. It wasn't like he'd ever marry. No lady would have him, and he refused to give his heart or his hand to a lusty woman who'd eventually leave him in wreckage.

The brunette sidled in closer. "Are you going to join us for bowls and nine-pins, Mr. Barrett?"

He hadn't heard that the game had been planned. He glanced at Leticia.

She came to his rescue. "The colonel has invited us all to the south lawn for bowls this afternoon, followed by an archery tournament."

Tristan nodded. "Then by all means, who am I to miss a moment of sport?" He held out one arm to Leticia and the other to the brunette. "May I escort you?"

As Leticia took his right arm, a comfortable, familiar motion, the brunette entwined her arm through his left, a sensual movement that evoked all kinds of images that shouldn't be in his head, at least, not while in Leticia's presence. Leticia glanced at him, one corner of her mouth lifting as if she knew the direction of his thoughts. But that couldn't be. She was an innocent.

He always worried that his wickedness would somehow taint Leticia. There were times when he almost decided he should stop spending time in her company lest he mar her pristine reputation. But dash it all, she was his oldest friend and the one female he trusted not to have some hidden agenda.

And he needed to find her a husband so she would be happy. Then he could be happy.

Chattering and laughing, the other ladies walked several steps behind Tristan and the ladies he escorted.

Feeling the brunette's gaze, he turned to her. "Are you enjoying the house party?"

Boldly, she looked into his eyes. "I find it hard to believe that we haven't been introduced until now, Mr. Barrett."

"Why is that so hard to believe?"

"Well…" she looked him up and down again. "I've been in London the last four Seasons, and I tend to notice"—her gaze flickered to Leticia—"tall, dark-haired men." She'd obviously amended the thoughts she would have expressed had they been having this conversation in private. "I'm certain I would have remembered you if we'd met." Again, that come-hither smile.

He laughed hoarsely and wanted to tug at his collar that the brunette came on so strong in front of Leticia. It made him feel something of a rascal to be caught by his very virtuous friend in the middle of such bold flirtation.

Leticia leaned around him to speak to the brunette. "Are you accomplished at bowls and nine-pins or archery, Mrs. Hunter?"

Ah, Mrs. Hunter. He sent a look of gratitude to Leticia as he sifted through all possible Mr. Hunters in his memory. He came up with nothing. Who was her husband? And where the deuce was he?

Mrs. Hunter let out a throaty sort of purr that

doubled as a laugh. "Please, we're all friends here. And Mrs. Hunter makes me sound so old. Do call me Georgette." She focused on his mouth.

"Yes, do," Leticia said in an even voice but Tristan recognized the mockery couched in her tone.

So did Georgette Hunter, apparently, judging from her sideways glance and amused, condescending twitch of her lips. "To answer your question, Miss Wentworth; yes, I admit, I have a fondness for both bowls and nine-pins and archery, especially in such fine company." She looked up into his eyes again. Hers were a vibrant shade of violet-blue and he found it hard to look away. She murmured, "How was the hunt this morning?"

"Splendid," Tristan said. "The Colonel has the finest hounds in the county."

Mrs. Hunter nodded. "So I've heard. I'd planned to ride with the hunt this morning but was a bit fatigued from the long journey yesterday in addition to last evening's festivities. I'll join you tomorrow."

Tristan raised a brow at her. "A woman who rides to hounds. How unconventional of you, Mrs. Hunter."

"Georgette, remember? I used to ride with my father and brothers. I assure you, I am a competent rider."

"You don't ride with your husband?" Tristan fished.

Mrs. Hunter made an elegant wave of her hand. "No. He was killed in battle two weeks after we married. He was a post captain, you see."

"My condolences."

Leticia broke in, all sympathy. "You must have been heartbroken."

Looking down, Mrs. Hunter lifted her shoulder in a

delicate shrug. "We hardly knew each other. We met while he was home on leave, fancied ourselves madly in love, married in haste. It all seemed splendidly romantic at the time." She sighed. "He's been gone more than two years, and I am moving on."

"Of course you should." Tristan glanced at Leticia, whose brows had pulled into a troubled frown and her lips puckered.

He'd never noticed how shapely Leticia's lips were. He wondered if Richard had ever been bold enough to kiss her. From their childhood, they'd always understood that Richard would marry Leticia, until Tristan's actions threw Richard together with Elizabeth, leaving Leticia alone. He must remember his goal to find Leticia a husband—someone worthy of her.

A group of gentlemen clustered around a lawn preparing for bowls and nine-pins. Tristan guided the ladies on his arm toward the game area, appraising the men as potential husbands. Four were married, two too old, three he'd already determined were unsuitable. Tristan had not yet made a determination about Rowley. He seemed a good sort. Tristan would find out if he passed muster.

Ah. Rhys Kensington. He might do. Tristan didn't remember seeing Kensington at the ball.

Georgette Hunter tightened her grip on Tristan's arm and said in a near-whisper, "I think I'd do almost anything not to spend another night alone."

She looked into his eyes with such convincing vulnerability that Tristan almost fell for it. He remained silent, and not because he remembered Leticia on his other arm. Did Mrs. Hunter intend her words as a plea for a proposal? Or did she mean to imply he'd be welcome in her bedchamber that night? Some other kind of clever trick? The brunette reminded Tristan of the mythical sirens who promised untold pleasure to sailors, yet lured them to their deaths.

"Please excuse me," Leticia broke in. "I think I'll retrieve my shawl from my bedchamber." She unwound her arm from Tristan's.

"Shall I fetch it for you?" Tristan offered.

"No, no, you two go on. I'll join you in a moment." With her head as high and regal as a queen, Leticia glided toward the manor house.

Tristan had the distinct impression he had been dismissed.

Chapter Five

At the end of dinner, Leticia kept her gaze away from Tristan as she followed the hostess and other ladies out of the dining room. Thankfully, she'd managed to be otherwise occupied throughout the afternoon, and tonight she'd sat at the opposite end of the table from Tristan, so she hadn't had to speak with him—which was a good thing, really, because being civil to him at present might pose a challenge.

Why it bothered Leticia so much to know the identity of his next ladybird, she couldn't say, yet the thought of that lewd widow entangling herself with Tristan made Leticia grind her teeth. Tristan would never change. The bounder. Still, Leticia had to save him if he wouldn't save himself. He wasn't bad; he was…lost.

As the ladies reached the drawing room closed off to create a more intimate setting, Leticia maneuvered herself next to Mrs. Seton and her daughter who seldom opened her mouth.

Mrs. Seton smiled and patted the seat cushion. "Do sit by me, Miss Wentworth."

Leticia obliged her. "Thank you."

"My, you've grown into a charming young lady—so poised compared to how awkward you were when we met years ago. I suppose there's hope for my dear Hermione, too."

Leticia barely managed not to gape and stammered out, "Er, thank you."

The young Miss Seton flushed scarlet and slumped her shoulders.

Mrs. Seton said to her daughter in a *sotto voce*, "Sit up straight, dear. Gentlemen will never look at you if you slouch like that."

The poor girl stiffened her spine, her face still red.

Leticia ached for her. "I adore your gown, Miss Seton. You look lovely in that shade of ivory."

Miss Seton made eye contact for a split second and replied in a voice barely above a whisper, "How kind of you to say."

Leticia continued, "Are you enjoying yourself, Miss Seton?"

The shy young lady stammered a reply. Leticia glanced at the girl's mother, Mrs. Seton. She had not seemed so dominant until now. Perhaps her overzealous attempts to ensure her children turn out well had worsened their shyness. Leticia cast off her discomfort as they chatted about the weather, the newest young ladies to have come out, and other social niceties. Leticia tried to include the young Miss Seton but that seemed to make her shyness worse instead of better. Eventually, Leticia steered the conversation to London.

"I assume you'll be there since your husband has a seat in the House of Commons?" Leticia asked.

Mrs. Seton's feathers bobbed as she nodded her head. "Of course. We never miss a Season. My Hermione had a delightful time last Season and is looking forward to this year as well."

Miss Seton closed her eyes and let out a long breath, clearly unhappy to be thrust into another social whirl.

Leticia gave her a sympathetic smile before returning her attention to the girl's mother. "I admit I know little of politics, but Lord Averston is hoping his brother, Tristan Barrett, will run for candidacy for the House of Commons. I understand there's a borough in one of the earl's landholdings without a representative, so Tristan could run for that one the next election, is that correct?"

Mrs. Seton nodded. "If the borough is rotten—meaning uncontested—the election would be a mere formality. I doubt anyone would bother running against him since everyone knows the earl controls the seat."

"So, all Tristan must do is decide to run."

"Probably." Mrs. Seton lowered her voice. "Don't tell my husband that I told any of this to you; he thinks I don't have a thought in my head except fashion and embroidery." An impish twinkle sparked in her eye making her look ten years younger, and her mouth twitched to suppress a smile.

Leticia placed a hand over her heart. "I vow your secret is safe with me."

The young Miss Seton met Leticia's eye and almost smiled before looking down.

"I must say," Mrs. Seton said. "I'm surprised young Barrett is considering Parliament. He doesn't seem the type to take on something so sober."

"'Tis more his brother's idea than his own, but he is considering it." Of course, every time Richard brought it up, Tristan rejected the idea, but she didn't volunteer that. "I believe he will embrace the idea soon." Which may require considerable cajoling—and time—but it would involve him in something worthwhile and keep him too busy for the gambling establishments in London or consorting with loose women.

Mrs. Seton lifted her shoulders in a resigned shrug. "Tristan Barrett has the charm to garner votes."

Nodding, the shy young Miss Seton sighed, a dreamy smile touching her mouth. Another victim of Tristan's legendary allure.

Leticia leaned forward. "Tell me, Mrs. Seton, how do you feel about reform?"

The lady raised a brow. "What aspect?"

"Helping the unfortunate raise themselves out of poverty and ignorance, and sometimes out of criminal behavior."

"I applaud the efforts of reformers. Occasionally, I make contributions to Mrs. Goodfellow's institution and have employed a few of those she has helped reform."

"Lady Averston and I also feel that helping those wishing to leave undesirable activities would be beneficial to society. We'd like to provide a way to teach them basic reading and mathematics so that they may qualify for honest vocations—shop girls, clerks, and so forth."

Mrs. Seton wore a thoughtful expression. "I believe that would much improve their chances to pursue such work."

Leticia touched the lady's hand. "As do I—most emphatically. That's why Lady Averston and I, along with a group of sponsors, are raising money to fund the opening of a school for the poor and the orphans— especially girls. We hope in particular to enroll children, to give them a better chance to be law-abiding, hard-working citizens."

"Oooh," said young Miss Seton, her eyes shining. "How admirable."

Leticia smiled. How sweet that her charity school had piqued the shy girl's interest enough to finally speak her thoughts. "I'm so glad you agree."

Her mother's brow wrinkled. "I fear not everyone will appreciate your venture."

With a resigned sigh, Leticia shook her head. "No, many don't feel it's worthwhile, more's the pity."

"It's more than that." Mrs. Seton lowered her voice, but this time no twinkle danced in her eyes. "Many of the nobility fear if we educate the poor, it will result in a repeat of the French Revolution, right here in England."

Oh, that. "I understand their concern. Still, we aren't talking about any kind of grand scale—merely a school for a few children who have fled either brothels or living in the streets. Surely anyone can see the advantage of that."

"My husband doesn't agree. He's one of those who fear the possibilities. His uncle lost his life to Madame Guillotine in the French revolution, you see."

Leticia shivered. "Dreadful."

Sobered, they fell silent. Mrs. Seton drew a breath. "Still, saving children is a most charitable venture. I assume you approached me because you'd like my help?"

Sheepish, Leticia nodded. "If it won't put you at odds with your husband."

Mrs. Seton smiled. "He doesn't need to know; I have my own money. I'd be glad to make a donation."

"Truly?" Leticia clasped her hands together. "How

generous of you." Perhaps Leticia's assessment of Mrs. Seton's character had been overly uncharitable. She might be a bit heavy-handed in her methods to help her daughter have a successful Season, but she seemed to have a good heart, at least as far as helping the down-trodden. If only she could see how badly her daughter needed gentler treatment.

The gentlemen joined them and soon young ladies took turns on the pianoforte and sang to provide entertainment and show off their skills for any interested parties. Leticia played to please her mother, although she had no real talent, while her sister, Isabella sang. Poised and beautiful, Isabella sang like an angel and Leticia's heart swelled in pride.

After the musical performances, a group of young men engaged Isabella in conversation. Leticia melted back to give her sister her moment in the sun and found a seat near her mother who sat with Mrs. Seton, Mrs. Wynn, and their daughters. "Perhaps a Season in London won't be necessary," Leticia said to Mother. "Isabella may receive a proposal sooner."

"Perhaps. But these things take time," Mother said.

Leticia admired a collection of figurines on a nearby shelf before letting her gaze drift over the other members of the party.

With the ease of a skilled dancer, Tristan mingled with the guests, reducing most of the ladies to blushing, tongue-tied fools—except the sensual Mrs. Hunter, who flirted with him in bold confidence.

Colonel Sherwood announced a game of Whist. As servants set up tables, partners paired off.

Mr. Rowley bowed to Miss Wynn. "Will you do me the honors, Miss Wynn?"

She inclined her head, all signs of her goose adventure erased from her expression. "Of course."

Tristan and a handsome, dark-haired gentleman strode to Leticia. She cocked her head. Why did he seem familiar?

"Leticia, do you remember Rhys Kensington?" Tristan said.

She smiled. "Of course. Richard and Tristan often speak of you."

"It has been a long time, Miss Wentworth. I am delighted to see you again." He made a polite bow, his smoky gray eyes sweeping over her as if trying to make up his mind about her.

She curtsied. "A pleasure, Captain Kensington."

A third voice joined in. "A sea captain?" Mrs. Hunter sidled up to them.

Captain Kensington's eyes danced in amusement. "No, Mrs. Hunter. Captain was my rank in the cavalry. No ships or pirates or anything exciting."

"Just war," Leticia added wryly.

He made a brief gesture of acquiescence. "There was that. Exciting isn't the word I would have chosen, however."

Tristan glanced at a group of ladies clustered nearby. After excusing himself, he moved to the shy Miss Seton, and extended a hand, executing a half bow. "Would you do me the honors of partnering with me for Whist, Miss Seton?"

Miss Seton turned the color of a ripe tomato and let out a choking sound, looking two parts terrified and one part smitten. She managed a nod, took his hand, and let him bring her to her feet. A surprising turn of events. Leticia had been certain he'd choose Mrs. Hunter for a partner. His choice in the wallflower, Miss Seton, left Leticia reeling. What drove him to it? Pity? Kindness? Some game he played with Mrs. Hunter? Or worse, did he view her as a challenge, the way he'd viewed—and hurt—Elizabeth last year at the house party? A surge of protectiveness toward the shy young girl arose in Leticia. He'd better not break her heart the way he'd broken Elizabeth's!

Captain Kensington offered Leticia an apologetic, if somewhat uncomfortable smile. "I believe that leaves me in need of a partner as well. Would you be so kind?"

Leticia faltered. "Of course." Leticia caught Tristan's eye and shot a knowing glare that all but screamed, 'I know you arranged this.'

Tristan, curse him, looked the picture of innocence except for a smirk playing around his mouth. He returned his focus to his partner and shuffled the cards.

"Shall we join them?" Captain Kensington gestured to Tristan and his blushing partner.

Leticia nodded. "As you wish."

As she sat across from Captain Kensington, she scanned the room for the sultry Mrs. Hunter. Sitting with Mr. Wynn, Mrs. Hunter laughed, her gaze moving to Tristan. Whether she longed for his presence, or reminisced about a tryst they'd already had, Leticia couldn't be certain. Not that it mattered. Leticia deliberately avoided looking at him. Scoundrel.

She turned her attention to the game. Captain Kensington proved a skilled ally in whist, but Tristan and Miss Seton were downright dangerous. Leticia had to admire Tristan's skill at drawing Miss Seton out and getting her to talk. The shy young woman even revealed a witty side to her Leticia had never seen before. Engaging in her own quiet way, when Miss Seton smiled she transformed into a pretty girl. Hopefully, others would see that in her as well.

Regardless of his motives, Tristan gave the sweet girl a memorable evening. Perhaps now that such a well-connected and handsome gentleman had paid her special notice, others would take an interest in her and realize what a kind heart and charming wit lay under her shyness.

As the last game ended, Leticia smiled at Captain Kensington. "A worthy showing, sir, but I fear we were outwitted."

"Luck did not favor us, I fear," the captain said.

Tristan smoothed a wrinkle from his sleeve. "All skill, my man. No luck needed." He turned to Miss Seton, who'd gained a measure of poise. "My thanks to you for partnering with me, Miss Seton. I daresay we make a formidable team."

Miss Seton's smile turned mysterious. "Indeed we do, sir."

Leticia suppressed an amazed chuckle. Leave it to Tristan to draw out the most reticent girl. Perhaps she should enlist his aid in garnering pledges for their school. He could coax a few guineas from the tightest purse with a mere twitch of his roguish lips.

Now that she thought of it, Tristan's kindness came as no surprise. He'd always had that soft spot for those he viewed in need of rescue. As children, she'd often had to be the lady in distress while he played the gallant rescuer. How like him to still fulfill that role…unless he truly harbored an interest in the girl. Leticia frowned. Surely not.

Did Tristan find Miss Seton attractive? Did this attraction motivate his interest in the wallflower?

Why did that thought inspire a sudden disliking for the girl, who, only moments ago, Leticia wished to champion? As the evening games ended, many guests bade goodnight, and the group dispersed. Leticia joined her mother and sisters who chatted with the hostess, Mrs. Sherwood. Other guests gathered in clusters to talk and drink. Tristan sauntered to the far end of the room. Mrs. Hunter wandered to him, trying to make it appear as if she'd been taking a turn about the room and happened to pass by, but Leticia knew better. Mrs. Hunter had no apparent qualms about approaching a man instead of waiting for him to approach her. By the evening's end, their heads were close together. Mrs. Hunter let out a sultry, throaty laugh and touched his arm—just Tristan's type, curse him. Curse them both. And curse her for letting it irritate her.

Unable to watch another moment, Leticia turned away in disgust. "I believe I'll go to bed now, Mama."

Her mother nodded. "Good night, dearest. I'm sure to follow soon."

Isabella arose. "I will, as well."

They bade good night to the others. Leticia raised her chin and searched for pleasant thoughts to replace her annoyance about Mrs. Hunter's clear motives toward Tristan, who would willingly succumb, no doubt, if he hadn't already, and her fear of Tristan's motive in showing an interest in Miss Seton. Was it kindness? True interest? A repeat of last year? She barely managed not to groan.

"A diverting party, is it not?" Isabella said as they headed toward the grand staircase.

Leticia sighed. Surely she could find something positive to say about the evening. "Mrs. Seton made a pledge to our foundation."

"Have you made any new friends?"

"Yes, indeed. I must say, I find it odd when people such as the Sherwoods and the Einsburghs have house parties at this time of year. Of late the weather seems to have obliged them."

"It does. This is the warmest spring I've ever seen." Her brows raised, Isabella glanced at her. "Is something amiss?"

"No, of course not."

"You seem a trifle out of sorts. Didn't you enjoy partnering with the very handsome Captain Kensington?"

"I worry about Tristan. He's so reckless. I fear he'll get himself into trouble."

"He's already been in a great deal of trouble over the course of his life, I'd say."

"Yes, and one of these days it will be something that destroys him." The thought of Tristan coming to any kind of harm tied her stomach into knots.

"What concerns you?" her sister asked.

"The way that Mrs. Hunter woman fawns all over him. And he lets her." She threw her hands up into the air. "He can't resist a pretty face."

"It seems that a great many men have that failing."

"Not to his extreme. It's more than the women, it's the drinking, the gambling, the reckless living." She let out a huff. "He's become one of the worst rakes I've ever heard of."

"Have you heard of many rakes?" Isabella teased.

Leticia couldn't lift her present mood. She made a

helpless gesture. "I wish he'd grow up and take some responsibility. Richard can't go around fixing all his problems."

Isabella's smile faded. "You're quite overset by all this."

Leticia pushed out a long exhale. "It's the house party and all the memories of the Einsburghs' party last year. I don't want him to ruin anyone else's life."

"The way Tristan and Lady Elizabeth ruined yours?"

Leticia clamped her mouth shut.

"I don't blame Tristan for that scandal," Isabella announced. "I blame Lady Elizabeth. She behaved badly."

Leticia turned to her. "Oh, no, Bella, don't. A nun couldn't resist Tristan. And besides, Richard is so happy with Elizabeth now so I'm sure it worked out for the best."

"For everyone except you." Isabella glanced at her.

Leticia put an arm around her sister and gave her a warm squeeze. "Do not concern yourself with me; I am well enough."

Her mother had told her heartache gets easier over time. Perhaps time really would heal all wounds.

Leticia rather thought not.

The following morning, Leticia walked her mount at a sedate pace to cool him after her brisk morning ride. As she rounded a bend in the path, Tristan, at a canter on his favorite gelding, appeared on her path. Leticia reined. She should cut him, she really should. After all, he'd probably spent last night in the arms of that vulgar woman. Leticia's face warmed with righteous anger, and she trotted forward as if she hadn't seen him. He waved, a smile lighting his face.

Softening, she let out her breath. She couldn't cut him. He hadn't changed. He was the same rake he'd been the last four or five years. Leopards never change their spots. Just because she'd been present to witness his latest conquest didn't justify being rude to him nor throwing away their friendship.

"Good morning, Tish. Bit cold this early, huh?"

She narrowed her gaze in mock suspicion. "Who are you? You can't be Tristan Barrett—it's not yet high noon."

He grinned. "Yes, I admit, I'm more acquainted with sunset than sunrise. Must be all this clean country air having an adverse influence on me. Or maybe it's Colonel Sherwood's not so subtle hints about retiring that sent us scurrying to our beds at an unfashionably early hour."

Leticia ground out, "Yes, I'll bet you scurried to your bed early."

Tristan cocked his head at her peevish tone. "Meaning?"

Leticia let out a noise of derision. "You and that woman were very chummy."

"Ohhhhh"—amusement danced in his eyes—"you think Mrs. Hunter and I—"

"I don't care!"

He chuckled. "You sound like a jealous lover, Tish."

"I do not. I…." Why *was* she so upset? "I think you could do better." She stared straight ahead so he wouldn't see too much of her expression.

"You're right. She's not my type."

"She's exactly your type; a young widow seeking a

lover."

"Then why are you so angry?"

"I'm not angry," she lied. "I'm...disappointed. I wish you'd court someone respectable and think about settling down."

He choked. "I'm twenty-three. I don't plan to settle down for a long time, if ever."

"If ever?" She studied him then.

Silently, he stared at something far ahead.

Captain Kensington astride a bay rounded the bend and caught up to them. "Good morning." His gaze danced between them. "Am I interrupting?"

Tristan replied, "Not at all. Leticia was telling me how much she's looking forward to the Season."

Leticia choked.

The Captain focused on Leticia. "Ah, yes. The infamous London Season."

"You'll be there, I trust?" Leticia said.

Captain Kensington inclined his head, looking somehow more elegant than before. "I'll be in London on official business, but I doubt I'll attend many social events."

Leticia smiled. "By choice, you mean, of course. Surely you aren't implying that you won't receive invitations by the cartful?"

"A bit of both." His tone suggested an end to the topic.

Leticia plunged ahead. "Shame on you, Captain. Think of all those hostesses who'll need you to even up their numbers, and with a military hero, no less."

His lips curved. "I'm confident they'll survive the blow, Miss Wentworth."

As she opened her mouth, Tristan sent her a

quelling glance. She raised her brow at Tristan, who shook his head. *Later*, his look stated. Why so secretive?

She changed tactics. "To be honest, Captain, I'm not attending the Season for the reason you suppose. I'm accompanying my sister who's having her first Season, and to seek pledges to help us fund the opening of a school for the poor."

The captain nodded. "Lady Averston already wheedled a pledge out of me."

"Very sensible of you, Captain. We'd have to hound you the entire time, else."

He smiled. "Of that, I have no doubt."

A chill wind blew and they quickened their pace back to the stables, seeking the warmth of a fire. The guests gathered in the drawing room and, after enjoying some refreshment, began a game of charades.

Mrs. Hunter took a seat nearby. Leticia stiffened and managed a civil incline of her head.

"Miss Wentworth," the widow said with a low voice. "I feel I owe you an apology."

Taken aback, Leticia blinked. "I beg your pardon?"

The temptress glanced about. "I didn't realize you and Tristan Barrett had an understanding. If I'd known, I wouldn't have flirted with him."

Leticia let out a weak laugh. "Oh, no, there's nothing between Tristan and me. We're merely childhood friends."

"You don't say? Then you don't mind if he and I become…involved?"

Leticia looked down and strove to keep her tone even. "Why would I mind? It's his business, after all."

Mrs. Hunter paused, her gaze heavy on Leticia.

"Are you quite certain?"

"Yes," she ground out.

"Then why are you angry?"

Leticia drew a deep breath and let it out slowly, trying to rein in her temper that always seemed to flare at the sight of the beautiful, sultry woman. "I'm not angry." She mustered a smile and turned to the woman. "Forgive me if I haven't been friendly. I'm preoccupied."

A moment passed. The game of charades went on around them, but they ignored it. Then, Mrs. Hunter spoke. "I'm not after his money, if that's what worries you."

"No, you don't strike me as a fortune hunter." To be a fortune hunter, she'd have to be after marriage, clearly not on her agenda.

Mrs. Hunter nodded but her eyes reflected sadness. "Do not judge me, Miss Wentworth. Life can alter one beyond what you may imagine." She folded her hands together until the tips of her fingers turned white.

Something melted inside Leticia. "It's not my place to offer judgment."

Mrs. Hunter stood. "Thank you for your reassurance regarding Mr. Barrett."

Leticia glared at the woman's back, then chided herself. Tristan could conduct himself as he saw fit. If he wanted to spend time with an attractive widow, his earlier words notwithstanding, Leticia had no business interfering. Besides, the school should be Leticia's first priority. Tristan's quest to seek out a suitable husband for her might help him meet enough upright men to have a calming influence on him, but she rather doubted it. While she'd love to put saving Tristan at the top of her list, it all came down to whether or not Tristan wanted to be saved.

Chapter Six

Several weeks after the Sherwoods' house party, Tristan stood on the sidewalk and took one last glance at the bow window next to the front door of White's, one of London's most respectable gentlemen's clubs. He'd requested membership a few years ago, on principle, but hadn't entered since—too full of boring stuffed shirts trying too hard to prove their self-importance by pontificating about politics. After another bracing breath, Tristan waded through the London fog and up the stairs to the door.

Inside the club, a porter wearing a stylish tailcoat met him. He stopped short, blinked, but recovered his astonishment. "Good evening, Mr. Barrett. May I take your hat?"

"Of course." Tristan offered a weak smile, surprised the man knew him after all these years. After surrendering his hat, Tristan sauntered into the main room as if he came here every day.

A gentleman glanced over his newspaper, took a second look, blinked, and lowered his paper. A group of men in conversation abruptly stopped talking, while two others whispered, eyes riveted to Tristan.

Perhaps coming here had been a bad idea. Still, he had come for Leticia's sake and he would see this through—even if it killed him.

"Tristan." Richard's voice boomed across the

room. His brother strode to his side. "I'm….glad to see you here."

Tristan lifted a brow. "Surprised, you mean."

Richard's smile flashed. Tristan looked away, hoping Richard didn't see how much his rescue meant.

"Do join us. We were about to order beefsteak."

Richard led the way back to a circle of peers. "May I introduce my brother Tristan Barrett? This is the Duke of Suttenberg."

Tristan bowed to the young duke who had a blond streak running through his dark hair. Keen intelligence glittered in his eyes. Tristan had heard Suttenberg lauded as a paragon of an Englishman but had never met him until now. Richard launched into introductions such as, "I'm sure you remember lord thus and such, and of course you know lord so and so." And on it went with gentlemen too old for Leticia.

Within moments, Tristan dug into an excellent beefsteak as conversation roiled around him. Keeping his mouth full and ears open, he resumed his hunt for potential husbands for Leticia, ruling out those married and those too old to be suitable.

"…got what was coming. Can't go around destroying expensive equipment, after all," one lord said.

"No, but capital punishment?" Richard shook his head. "That's too much. The fellows didn't kill anyone, merely damaged some looms."

"It's the law," the first man stated.

"The damage cost the factories thousands," added a second, "in replacing the equipment and loss of business."

Richard nodded. "Yes, yes, I agree that they

committed a crime with significant losses, but execution is too harsh. After all, they didn't commit murder or treason. Besides, they are desperate; their jobs were replaced by machines. How are they to support their families?"

The first man snorted. "Not by destroying property."

"No, but how else are they to be heard? If they remain silent, no one will learn of their plight. Nothing will change for them."

Tristan stared. Who knew his brother would be sympathetic to the Luddites?

"There's a price to progress." A third man thumped the tabletop.

Tristan leaped into the discussion. "And while everyone is busy crowing about the advantages of automated looms, they fail to consider the consequences to skilled laborers. Rich factory owners get fat while their former laborers starve."

Five pairs of eyes trained on Tristan. He raised his chin in silent challenge.

Richard had never needed Tristan's help in a fight, except one year in school, when fifteen-year-old Richard had been targeted by a group of boys who had jumped him without warning. Tristan, only a first-year student, had sprung to Richard's aid without hesitation; his brother's tormenters outnumbered him, and Tristan had acted. He'd received a bloodied nose for his trouble, but Richard's surprise and gratitude that Tristan had entered the fray for his sake—against much older boys, no less—had left Tristan puffing out his chest for days.

That same surprise and gratitude also shone in

Richard's eyes when Tristan and Kensington had freed Richard from the clutches of the criminal ring run by Mr. Black. Of course, that act of heroism earned Tristan a bullet in the shoulder, but the bond it strengthened between them had been worth the pain.

Surprise and gratitude reappeared in Richard now. With luck, today's encounter would not result in Tristan losing any blood.

His brother shifted his posture and moved his gaze back to the other men. "I don't pretend to have all the answers, but if we keep our minds open to options, a better solution can be found to the problem."

The first man nodded. "Perhaps."

The second let out a humph. "Next thing, you'll be noising about how you think we should educate all the poor and free all the women in prison."

Richard gave him a cold smile. "One battle at a time, Lord Petre."

The first man nudged Lord Petre. "Averston's wife is already crusading for that."

Lord Petre made a sound of disgust. "Reformers. I thought so. Although, I'm as surprised as I am disappointed to find a reformer in a Tory. Are you trying to start a revolution here, too? Complete with Madam Guillotine?"

"No, of course not," Richard said.

Petre addressed the Duke of Suttenberg, "What do you think, Suttenberg?"

All eyes turned to the Duke of Suttenberg, who'd been quiet throughout the exchange.

The young duke sipped his wine and set down his glass as if placing it in a precise location. "Education and reform are one of the many ways we can prevent a revolution—help them raise themselves up out of poverty so the privileged and the impoverished aren't so far apart. In medieval times, landowners were duty-bound to protect serfs from invaders and ensure they had adequate crops and shelter. Today, our duty is to help raise them out of poverty. Allowing them at least a rudimentary education seems a reasonable method."

Lord Petre's face reddened and he started to rise out of his seat. "You can't be in earnest. Why—"

"Let's all agree to disagree, shall we?" Richard waved at a passing waiter. "Another round of brandy for these fine gentlemen, here."

The duke and Richard exchanged glances, and by the time the brandy had arrived, the conversation turned to less volatile matters such as stories of card games, outrageous dares and wagers, fencing, riding and the hunt. Tristan had more in common with these men than he'd assumed. Except for the overly pompous Lord Petre, they were a likable set of chaps—for a bunch of stuffed shirts, that is.

Later, as the others dispersed, Tristan remembered his reason for coming. Over two hours had passed since his arrival, and he'd actually enjoyed his time in the club. As he sipped his drink, he scanned the main room, noting those of the proper age and rank for Leticia.

Richard leaned in, a teasing smile playing around his mouth. "Why are you here? Really? Surely not to help me debate the Luddite issues?"

Tristan shifted. "Can't I enjoy food and drink with my brother and his peers?"

"Now? After all these years?" Richard's eyes conveyed disbelief.

Tristan sighed. He'd rather go for a swim in the

Thames than confess to his brother, but dash it, he needed Richard's help; he had the right kind of connections. Tristan offered a wry smile. "It appears I've taken on the job of matchmaker."

Richard gaped.

"For Leticia," Tristan clarified. "I feel after my involvement in the house party last year that I, er…well, I owe her a husband." He cleared his voice and resisted the urge to loosen his cravat.

"I…see…" Richard said.

"Since none of my friends are good enough for her, I'm searching for someone high in the instep and disgustingly respectable—like you—so she won't have to live out her life as a spinster. She seems to have made up her mind that such is her future."

A small crease formed between Richard's eyes and he stared down at his drink, his shoulders slumping ever so slightly, but enough to reveal his dismay at the future of the girl he'd once planned to marry. In a low voice, Richard asked, "What would you ask of me?"

"Not much—a few introductions so I can assess their suitability, then perhaps present one or two of them to her. She seems to think this is a game. She doesn't know how determined I am to clear my conscience."

Richard looked up then. "Your conscience will be clear once she's wedded?"

Tristan kept his tone light. "Of course. You and Elizabeth are sickeningly happy, and Leticia deserves that, too."

"Yes, she does." Richard didn't smile but rather took on an intent expression.

"I, on the other hand, consider wedded bliss akin to

a fate worse than torture, but each to his, or her, own." Tristan smirked.

A grin tugged at the corner of Richard's mouth. "Trust me, nothing about wedded bliss is torturous."

"As I said, to each his own."

"Very well, come to our dinner party Tuesday next. Perhaps you can find someone there who satisfies your requirements."

"Thank you. I shall, if you don't think that will upset the numbers."

Richard grinned. "I don't believe finding one more lady to even things up will be a problem. Getting enough men to attend is always Elizabeth's biggest concern."

"Very well, Tuesday then." Tristan stood and turned.

"Tristan."

He paused, looked back.

Richard eyed him with something like—surely not, but it appeared to be—approval. "I think what you're doing for her is admirable and honorable. I commend you for your efforts."

Tristan nodded in reply. He couldn't remember the last time he'd earned Richard's approval doing something that didn't include bleeding.

Chapter Seven

Sitting next to Elizabeth on a settee in the small parlor of Mrs. Goodfellow's institution in London, Leticia folded her hands in her lap to conceal her nervous excitement. Elizabeth looked serene as usual, every inch a countess. Though still fatigued from the journey to Town, Leticia had agreed to accompany Elizabeth as they met with a like-minded individual who might help them with their school. How, remained a mystery, but Leticia trusted Elizabeth.

Elizabeth glanced at Leticia, her eyes sparkling. "There's nothing to worry about. I'm confident Mrs. Goodfellow will help our cause."

Leticia twisted her gloved hands together, eyeing the tiny stain on the end of her index finger. "Isn't she already depending on donations to keep her agency open? How could she give us funds?"

"Not funds," Elizabeth explained. "She may have contacts who would help us."

Mrs. Goodfellow appeared. The plump, matronly woman wearing a lace cap over salt-and-pepper hair strode in with firm, confident steps. "Lady Averston, delightful to see you again."

"Thank you for receiving us, Madam. May I present Miss Wentworth?"

They exchanged greetings, and Mrs. Goodfellow poured tea. "How can I be of service, my lady?"

Elizabeth leaned forward. "Miss Wentworth and I have a new venture; we have decided to open a school."

"Oh? Do you need servants to help staff it?"

"Perhaps a few, but that's not the reason we've come to call. We're forming a foundation to fund a charity school for girls—especially orphans—to teach them to read and write and perform basic mathematics. It will be similar to your efforts, but more academic."

"Academic? For girls?" Mrs. Goodfellow's incredulity seeped out of her voice.

Leticia added, "What you're doing, is of course, of great value. But think of it; if they had a basic education, they could also work in shops—perhaps own a shop of their own someday. Those who wish to become house servants could obtain higher positions. It would give them a tremendous advantage over the general populace who cannot read."

Mrs. Goodfellow's eyes narrowed thoughtfully. "True, but you will meet with much opposition."

"We already have," Elizabeth said.

Leticia nodded. "Lord Petre called it a fool idea that would lead to our ruin."

"We're not going to let people like him stop us," Elizabeth said.

Mrs. Goodfellow set down her tea. "It's a grand idea. How can I help?"

Elizabeth leaned forward. "Introductions to a few of your benefactors who you think might support our cause as well."

"What have you tried to raise money?" asked Mrs. Goodfellow.

"Approaching people directly has worked well so far," Elizabeth said. "We will have a dinner party where we will address the whole group."

Leticia added, "We also plan to have a subscription ball with all proceeds going to the foundation."

Mrs. Goodfellow nodded. "Those are all good ideas. I'll share with you something that worked for me; I enlisted a group of young ladies to sell flowers at the open dances at the park. They carried baskets of flowers as they circulated the area. Young men who wished to impress a girl bought them and gave the flowers to the girls. Perhaps you could do something like that at your ball."

Leticia turned to Elizabeth. "We could ask Richard to make a point of buying one and presenting it to you. Then you'd gush about how lovely his gesture is, and the men might all follow suit."

Elizabeth nodded. "I like it."

Leticia straightened as an idea hit her. "What if we take it a step further? This may sound scandalous at first, but perhaps we could have ladies sell dances."

"What?" Two pairs of eyes blinked at her.

Perhaps she trod on dangerous ground, but it might also appeal to the adventurous. If Elizabeth and Richard endorsed it, others would view it as acceptable. Besides, the Averstons always invited the most respected people among the *beau monde* to their parties.

Leticia moistened her lips. "If a gentleman wishes to dance with a particular lady, he must pay for a dance. Or better yet, have an auction. We'll make it clear that it is for charity. Everyone will take note of who was the most generous and what lady garnered the highest bid."

Elizabeth paled. "Oh dear. That may be embarrassing for some. What if a lady doesn't get a high bid?"

Leticia sorted her thoughts as they tumbled out. "We could have a team of rescuers: gentlemen who have agreed ahead of time to drive up bids and ensure each lady gets a respectable bidding. You know Richard would do it, and Tristan would as well. I'd wager Captain Kensington would, too. I believe if we put our heads together, we can find enough gentlemen. Once the bidding starts, everyone will catch the fever."

Mrs. Goodfellow's eyes twinkled. "Miss Wentworth, that is a brilliant idea. I'm sure I've never seen the like, but that will force the men to compete for position as the most generous. No one will want to lose face by not getting the highest possible bid for the lady whose favor he wants to win."

Elizabeth looked pensive and her smile grew. "Yes, I do believe that will work."

"What if we have each dance be a set price and then have the auction for the supper dance?" Leticia said.

Mrs. Goodfellow's eyes sparkled. "I think you've hit on the right combination. All you have to do is make it feel exclusive and the gentlemen will line up."

Elizabeth turned to Leticia. "We need to modify the guest list."

"Indeed."

After thanking the hostess and taking their leave, Leticia and Elizabeth stood in the foyer to don their pelisses and bonnets, all the while discussing possible guests, rescuers, and ladies to approach about auctioning their supper dance.

Elizabeth's voice trailed off as her head turned to a small figure in the doorway. In a gentle voice, she asked, "What is it, child?"

A girl in the first stages of womanhood took a tentative step toward them, then hung back, her eyes on the floor.

Leticia gestured at the girl to come closer. "May we help you?"

"B-begging yer pardon yer ladyship, but I couldn't 'elp but over 'ear…yer openin' a school for the poor folk?"

"We are," said Leticia.

She took another step nearer. "I'm not an orphan and I'm no' a chil' anymore, neither but I wonder…migh' I come to school?"

Elizabeth's eyes lit up. "You wish to learn to read and write?"

"Yes'um. I want it ever so bad. If'in I could read, maybe…" The girl swallowed. "Please?" She turned hopeful brown eyes on them.

Leticia's heart squeezed. "Of course you may."

The girl offered a timid smile. "I'd like so much t' work in a dressmaker's shop. I can sew a li'le. O' course, Mrs. Goodfellow, she's teaching me t' be a maid, and that'd be fine, too. Anything tha' don't…" She folded her arms and seemed to retreat inside herself.

Elizabeth looked as if she were about to cry. "We're trying to get our school open very soon and you'll be one of our first students. I promise."

Wonder brightened the girl's eyes. She bobbed a curtsy. "Thankee kindly, yer ladyship."

Leticia smiled. She couldn't save them all of course, but she could save this one, and perhaps a few others like her. She glanced at Elizabeth. Judging by the determined set of her jaw, her friend thought the same. For this cause, Leticia would beg every lady in London to put herself upon the auction block.

Chapter Eight

Tristan sauntered to Rhys Kensington who stood apart from the other guests at the garden party gazing at the hills as if he saw something different than the landscape.

"The view is better if you turn around," Tristan quipped.

Kensington's posture straightened as he glanced at Tristan. "Oh?" He looked over his shoulder at a cluster of young ladies twittering like so many birds. "Yes, the view there is pleasant, too." His voice rose sharply, as if he were trying too hard.

Tristan peered at him. "What ails you?"

Kensington shrugged. "Thoughts unfit for such a fine day." He faced Tristan. "You look as though you have something on your mind, as well."

"What are your thoughts of Leticia Wentworth?"

Kensington blinked, clearly taken aback. "Er, she's…a fine woman. A proper lady. Witty."

"Anything else?"

His forehead creased in mild confusion. "Anything in particular you're looking for?"

Tristan shrugged. "No, not specifically." He switched tactics. "A group of us are going to Vauxhall Gardens Wednesday next. Care to come along?"

One of Kensington's black brows rose. "Is Miss Wentworth in the party?"

Tristan kept his voice causal. "I'd planned to invite her—we are friends, after all."

Kensington narrowed his eyes. "Did Richard put you up to this? Or his wife?"

Tristan raised a brow. "Put me up to what?"

"Trying to match me with Miss Wentworth."

"Er, no." Tristan resisted the urge to tug at his collar. "They haven't mentioned her and you in the same sentence. I thought a visit to Vauxhall Gardens would be a diverting evening—providing the weather holds—and wanted you to be comfortable with the others in our group. Miss Wynn mentioned she'd never seen them, which gave me the idea."

Kensington folded his arms and stared Tristan in the eye. "I'm not in the marriage mart."

"No, no, of course not. What man is?" Tristan laughed uneasily. He should have known Kensington would see the transparency of his scheme.

A muscle in Kensington's jaw twitched. "I have no plans to…marry."

Questions crowded into Tristan's mind but he didn't dare voice them and pry. Guilt stabbed him. He should have taken a more direct, honest approach with Kensington.

Conjuring a grin, Tristan held up his hands in surrender. "Not setting you for the parson's noose, my good fellow. Merely a diverting evening."

Kensington eyed him with a shrewd gaze. "I see."

"Will you come?" Perspiration dampened his back. What if Kensington rejected Leticia? Or told her Tristan had prodded him to approach her? Surely he would not do something so ungallant. Moreover, Kensington had partnered with Leticia at Whist, which suggested interest on some level, his protestations notwithstanding. At the moment, the idea of attempting to match Leticia with Kensington suggested higher stakes than he would have supposed.

Kensington glanced away. "I fear I'm not much company at social gatherings."

"You're here," Tristan pointed out.

"I couldn't refuse." He sent a sidelong glare at someone out of Tristan's range of sight.

Tristan had no idea how a man of Kensington's formidable presence could be coerced into anything, but kept his questions to himself. "Anyone in particular you'd like me to invite to join us at the Gardens?"

"No."

Tristan laughed, more uneasy than before. "It's nothing but an outing with friends—all respectable."

"Not your usual circle of reprobates, then?"

Tristan winced. "They aren't that bad."

"Not bad if one seeks gambling, racing, too much to drink, and loose women. Oh, no, they're perfect."

He was starting to sound like Richard. Unfortunately, he was right. Tristan squared his shoulders. "Most of the chaps in the Four Horse Club are not rakes."

"True. I admit, they're a bit more my speed than your usual set of friends."

"So, you like fast horses better than fast women?" Tristan said, trying to lighten the mood.

"I suppose I do." Kensington smiled, but no humor touched his eyes.

Tristan shrugged, attempting nonchalance. This conversation had been unexpectedly tense. "I'm not worried about having even numbers at the Gardens—

nothing that formal. You're invited if you care to come, or not."

He clapped Kensington on the shoulder and wandered off. Out of Kensington's surprisingly dark company, Tristan let out a breath and focused on his objective. By the end of the afternoon, Tristan had invited Rowley, Seton, and several others in a mixed group of Richard's ilk as well as a few considered respectable but not quite so stuffy. He left out the debauched Mr. Wynn, of course. Tristan also invited several young ladies, choosing those with whom Leticia would be comfortable.

That task complete, Tristan approached Leticia standing with a group of young ladies including her sister, Isabella. As he sauntered to them wearing his most winsome smile, Leticia glanced his way. Her mouth softened and the rest of the world fell away, leaving the two of them. If only he could feel this safe with another woman beside his best friend. Although that might result in love and marriage, and he'd never be reckless enough to take that plunge.

For propriety's sake, he bowed and murmured, "Miss Wentworth, Miss Isabella." He greeted the other ladies in the circle, gratified he remembered their names.

"A man with a purpose, I see." Leticia's smile turned knowing.

Why did everyone suspect him of seeking more than polite conversation today? "No, not a purpose. Er...not really. Several of us are for Vauxhall Gardens Wednesday next. Care to join us?" His glance included the other ladies. "All of you are invited, of course."

Leticia's expression turned mischievous and almost

suspicious. "Vauxhall? With whom?"

"Reputable invitees, I assure you. Mr. Rowley, Captain Kensington, Miss Wynn, Miss Seton and her brother Mr. Seton, among others." All designed to provide Leticia with potential husband candidates, as she already guessed.

She pursed her lips in a lopsided pout like she always did when she considered something. Then, with a mild shrug that stated *why not*, she nodded. "It sounds diverting. I hope the weather holds." She looked up as if she expected a cloudburst at any moment.

Her earlier suspicion still stung but Tristan inclined his head. "I'll be sure to order perfect weather for our outing."

The other ladies present murmured their assent.

Leticia smiled as if she knew a secret. "Very well, it seems we accept."

"Excellent." He inclined his head.

After providing details of when and where to meet, Tristan took his leave and headed for the refreshment table. Matchmaking made him hungry. As he sat and devoured an array of delectable treats intended to tempt the palate rather than fill a man's stomach, a cool shadow fell over him. He glanced up.

"Mrs. Hunter," he said in surprise.

"Please," she purred. "Georgette, remember?" She took a bite-sized sandwich and bit into it, each motion of her lips pure seduction. She glanced up at him from under her lashes. Her tongue slid out and licked off the crumbs from her full lips. She smiled, a sensuous movement with a clear invitation.

A rush of heat tightened Tristan's collar. She was beautiful and desirable and clearly wanted him. It would be a nice, simple affair with no promises asked or made.

He cast a guilty backward glance at Leticia who stood engrossed in conversation with an older couple. Her sweet, light laugh rang through the air. Her fresh loveliness contrasted against the foil of the sultry Mrs. Hunter. He stood torn between night and day. But that made no sense. Leticia offered friendship, nothing more. Mrs. Hunter desired an uncomplicated liaison.

He focused on Mrs. Hunter. "A fine day for a gathering, is it not?"

"A very fine day," she agreed. "Are you attending the Miller's *soiree musicale* tomorrow night?"

Tristan paused. "I think not."

She pouted prettily. "A pity. I'd rather hoped to see you again in a more…intimate setting." Her gaze swept over him from head to toe.

Tristan tugged at his strangling cravat and shot another guilty glance at Leticia. When he chose to enjoy the charms of women who propositioned him, he had always done so without an audience. Short liaisons helped to stave off his consuming loneliness. But blast it all, he couldn't enjoy Georgette Hunter's attention with the virtuous Leticia nearby. It seemed too…crass.

Besides, the last few affairs had left him empty, almost used. Which is why he'd avoided them the last several months. Mrs. Hunter was too…obvious. Wanton. Vulgar.

Affecting a proper bow, Tristan smiled politely at Mrs. Hunter. "Perhaps our paths will cross again. Good day."

He strode away before he had time to register the expression on Mrs. Hunter's face. As he walked, he glanced at Leticia. Their gazes met. Leticia studied him as if to assess his response to Mrs. Hunter. He should march over to Leticia and tell her to get out of his head and stop acting like a conscience. Her attention flitted between him and Mrs. Hunter. Then she smiled, approval shining in her leaf-green eyes.

Tristan drew himself up taller.

"You'd better rein in your wife, Averston. She and that Wentworth twit are getting too pushy in their ridiculous crusade," said a nearby voice.

Tristan slowed his steps and searched the crowd. Lord Petre confronted Richard.

Richard looked as calm as if he'd been discussing the cut of a tailcoat. Mildly, he said, "My wife is my business, Petre. I'll thank you to mind yours."

The utter stillness in Richard's posture betrayed his controlled anger.

Lord Petre's face reddened. "It's become my business because my wife has been spouting nonsense about our *duty to help the poor better themselves*. Next thing you know, the poor will start lopping off the heads of all their betters."

Tristan went on alert. Should he offer his support or let Richard fight his own battle?

Richard laughed softly, velvet over steel. "I doubt teaching a few urchins to read and find decent jobs will cause such upheaval."

"I don't want your wife nor that Wentworth chit anywhere near my wife, giving her all these revolutionary ideas that could lead to ambitious tradesmen thinking they're our equal. That may be enough to set it off. There's enough unrest already, what with all the riots." Lord Petre glared at Richard as if he were to blame for the civil discontent.

"Which Parliament is addressing, as you recall," Richard reminded him. "And there were many factors that lead to the bloodshed in France."

Perhaps Richard didn't need him, but Tristan's annoyance that the boorish Lord Petre had brought Leticia into his criticism, not to mention his disparaging remarks about her worthy cause spurred him. He took up two glasses of sherry and sauntered over to them with an external calm at odds with his irritation with the lord.

"None of these factors, to my knowledge, included teaching orphans to read, sir." Tristan handed Richard a glass and glanced at Petre, keeping his stance open and non-confrontational. If he could diffuse the other man's hostility, perhaps he could reason with him.

Lord Petre gave Tristan a dismissive glance and glowered at Richard. "I'm telling you, Averston, put a leash on your woman and that conniving little country chit, and stop spreading dangerous ideas. It will lead to no good."

The slight to Leticia's character pushed Tristan's annoyance toward true ire. He tensed, barely catching himself before he leaped at the man's throat.

Richard gripped Tristan's arm and said in a low, dangerous voice, "That so-called conniving little country chit and her family are long-time friends of our family."

"She ought to heed her betters," Petre said.

"She is the daughter of a gentleman," Tristan ground out. "I'll thank you to speak more courteously of her."

"Hmph." Petre stalked off.

A muscle in Richard's jaw tightened and his fingers drummed on his thigh, the one visible sign of agitation.

Tristan shook off Richard's arm and fought to release his anger. "Do you ever allow yourself to get truly enraged and go punch something?"

Richard lifted a brow. "About a year ago, in fact."

Right. Richard had done exactly that. Tristan rubbed his jaw still feeling the bone-cracking punch Richard dealt him when he'd been certain Tristan seduced his wife. "Other than me, that is."

A smile twitched Richard's mouth. "Why do you think I box and fence so often? And often, I run it off."

"You still do that, too?" Interesting. Richard still ran when his emotions threatened to get the better of him. Warmth enfolded Tristan. They still had that in common, at least. Tristan glanced back to find Lord Petre talking to another stuffed shirt and waving his hands. "Is he cause for concern?"

"Others may agree with him. It might mean Elizabeth and Leticia losing supporters for their school, if he keeps it up."

"Might he be a problem on any other level?"

Richard took a slow sip of his drink, a tactic he used when he needed a moment to sort through his thoughts. "I doubt it. Most consider him a windbag. I don't think he'd do anything about it except complain and try to discourage others from contributing." The corners of his mouth relaxed. "Elizabeth and Leticia have a rather unconventional manner of raising funds, however, so I doubt many will resist."

Rhys Kensington joined them. "You both look as if you're plotting a siege."

Tristan pointed with his chin. "Some take exception to the school Leticia and Elizabeth plan to open."

Kensington glanced around. "Trouble?"

Richard chuckled. "Are you both ready to grab guns and go in shooting again?"

Kensington's gun hand twitched and he grinned. "Sounds like fun. Who do we get to shoot?"

"Stuffed shirts," quipped Tristan.

Turning to Richard, Kensington smiled. "Oh? Friends of yours?"

Richard grimaced. "That windbag is no friend of mine, and we're not shooting him, only ensuring he doesn't hinder fundraising."

Elizabeth appeared at Richard's elbow and linked her arm through his as she smiled up at both Tristan and Kensington. "Gentlemen. I haven't received your response to our ball."

Tristan blinked. Ball? Had he received an invitation to a ball? He couldn't remember the last time he went through his correspondence.

"This one is special," Elizabeth explained. "It's a subscription ball to benefit the charity school. We'll have an auction for men to bid on supper dances."

"You're auctioning ladies?" Kensington sounded scandalized.

"Dances with ladies. It's respectable," Elizabeth said in a defensive tone.

"And you would know." Richard smiled at her. "You've developed a reputation for being the leader in proper etiquette. Next year, everyone will be having auctions at their balls for charity."

Tristan let out a snort. "Good luck with that one.

Most men I know would rather hide out in the billiards room than the ballroom, much less *pay* for a dance."

"Which is why we need your help." Leticia nudged her way into the circle. "If we get enough of the right support, other gentlemen won't want to be outdone." She smiled meaningfully at all of them.

Tristan groaned. "I can already tell I won't like this."

"I hope you will help us," said Elizabeth. "The Duke of Suttenburg has agreed to start off the bidding and Richard will, too, of course." She shot Richard an adoring gaze. Richard looked helpless against her subtle attack, the poor besotted fool. "The Earl of Tarrington has pledged to bid as well. Even my father agreed to be an early bidder."

An awed hush touched her tone. No wonder. If powerful men such as the Duke of Pemberton, the Duke of Suttenberg, and the Earl of Tarrington supported the auction and the school, the foundation would succeed.

Kensington nodded. "Two dukes and an earl will have enough clout to encourage others to bid."

Leticia nodded at Kensington. "Not to mention the influence of a military hero—a captain, to be precise. Also, if one of the most confirmed bachelors in England helps us, we are sure to succeed." She turned a blinding smile to Tristan that blew all rational thought out of his mind.

He almost stammered under the force of that smile. He recovered his wits and drawled, "My dear Leticia, I don't pursue women; they pursue me."

Elizabeth looked away and Richard leveled a stare on him so hard that Tristan dropped his gaze. Very well, he *generally* didn't pursue women. He'd flirted with Elizabeth at that house party last year because he liked to see her blush, and he considered her a challenge. He never expected to connect with her in so many ways. Now she belonged to Richard, leaving Tristan blissfully free from entanglements.

Leticia broke the uncomfortable silence. "Which is why you must bid, Tristan. If you of all people do, others will follow your lead."

Tristan raised a brow. "Is there an insult in there somewhere?"

With an exasperated laugh, Leticia shook her head. "Everyone knows what a rake you are, and they also know all you have to do is smile at a woman for her to proposition you. So, if you believe in the cause enough to bid on a dance, you will influence other gentlemen to follow your example."

He wanted to squirm. Instead, he raised his hands in surrender, if for no other reason than to get Leticia off the subject of his rakishness. His reputation had grown into a thorn in his side. "Very well, I promise to bid the first time there appears to be a lapse."

Leticia looked at Kensington with a clear question.

Kensington nodded, but looked less than enthusiastic. "I'll help you."

Leticia clapped her hands together. "Wonderful! I knew we could count on you both. I can't tell you how much this means to us and to the school."

With her face lit by excitement, Leticia transformed into a positively enchanting fairy princess. Tristan grinned, happy to have brought that expression to her face.

The group dispersed and Tristan turned his mind from the subscription ball and began planning the details of the outing to Vauxhall Gardens, mentally checking off the guest list to be sure he'd included enough men to parade in front of Leticia, and enough ladies to make her comfortable.

He'd never felt a greater sense of purpose.

Chapter Nine

Leticia sat next to her Aunt Alice in Madame DuBois's establishment watching as the *modiste* did the final measurements on Isabella's newest ball gown.

Leticia glanced outside at the misty afternoon. Too bad they couldn't return home and cozy up next to a fire with a novel. The day seemed suited for nothing else. She sipped her tea and wondered if Isabella were as chilled as she. Leticia finished her tea and set down her cup. "Perhaps a visit to the sweet shop would be in order as well. Isabella looks as if she is in need of refreshment."

Isabella perked up and Aunt Alice smiled. "Yes, the very thing."

Once they'd completed their shopping, they strolled to the sweet shop. A passing carriage splashed mud on Isabella, getting her feet and hem wet. Leticia wanted to shake her fist at the driver. By the time they arrived at the shop, Isabella's teeth were chattering.

They found a table as far from the door as possible and ordered hot chocolate and pastries. At the ringing of the bell, and the blast of cold wet air that accompanied the opened door, Leticia looked up.

Lord Petre with his wife and mother entered. Leticia turned away, pretending she didn't see the lord who'd renounced her cause and prevented his wife from participating.

Cradling her teacup, Isabella let out a sigh. "Ah, this is what I needed. Another four or five cups and I'll feel right again."

"We need to get you home and dry," Aunt Alice said.

The dowager Lady Petre stepped into her line of vision and shook her cane at Leticia. "You are disgraceful. Young ladies should be looking for husbands, not sticking their noses into matters that don't concern them."

Leticia gaped at such rudeness.

Aunt Alice glared at the dowager. "How dare you insult my niece? She is a perfect lady, and I'll not have you say ought about her."

The dowager rounded on her. "If you were any kind of chaperone, you'd put a stop to these vulgar activities. Humph. Selling dances. Teaching urchins to read. Bah!"

Speechless, Leticia stared. Then, finding her voice, "Vulgar activities? Lady Averston and I are trying to help orphans."

The dowager scowled. "One can forgive the Countess Averston. As a duke's daughter and an earl's wife, she's entitled to her eccentricities, but you…you aren't of high enough rank for such nonsense." She wagged her cane at Leticia again. "Leave well enough alone and go find a husband!"

Lord Petre put a hand on his mother's arm. "Come along, Mother. This little baggage isn't worth your time. Thrown over by the earl, and now embroiled in radical behavior, no respectable gentleman would have her." He turned a cold eye on Leticia. "Hussy. Go back to whatever insignificant little hole you crawled out of."

Leticia's stomach clenched and she ground her teeth. Her fingers itched to throw her chocolate into that boorish man's face. "We have a great cause, and I'll thank you to mind your own business."

"How dare you!" Petre snarled.

Aunt Alice's face reddened and she stood, staring down both of them. "You don't intimidate us. Begone, vipers!"

Lord Petre held out a hand to someone out of Leticia's line of sight. "Come. Let's go patronize a shop with a more respectable clientele."

Lord Petre's wife came to him, her eyes downcast, and put her hand in his. As a group, they turned their backs on Leticia and left together. Only Lord Petre's wife looked back with an apologetic expression before leaving with her husband and mother-in-law.

Leticia sat rigidly in her chair. Their opinions shouldn't matter. But their words cut and Leticia bled inside.

Aunt Alice huffed. "Well, I never! They shall not receive an invitation to any of my parties, and I'll be sure to cut them whenever I see them in the future. No one insults my family. No one!"

Isabella put an arm around Leticia. Unshed tears of sympathy shone in her eyes. "I'm sure their opinions aren't shared by others."

Aunt Alice patted Leticia's hand. "That's right. Though their rank should put them in high circles, no one likes Lord Petre and his draconian mother. Poisonous snakes, the lot of them. And Isabella, have no fear, they will not mar your *entrée* to society."

"I'm not worried about that, Aunt," Isabella murmured.

"Good." Aunt Alice stood. "We ought to get you home and into some dry clothes, dear. Then we must lie down and rest before we attend tonight's musicale. Oh, dear. I hope the Petres aren't in attendance. Well, if they are I'll cut them—publicly."

Rallying herself, Leticia stood and tried to put on a smile. "Yes. The musicale tonight. Isabella, have you chosen the gown you'll wear when you play?"

"The white with rosebuds." Isabella looked at her as if she feared Leticia might burst into tears.

"Good choice."

They left the shop discussing the upcoming musicale with forced cheer. Leticia weighed Aunt Alice's optimism against realism. If the crusade to fund the school met with enough resistance, it might hurt Isabella's chances of making a match. As much as she loved her cause, she'd give up anything to ensure that her sister found happiness.

Hours later, rested and dressed in their finery, Leticia, Isabella, and Aunt Alice arrived at the musicale and greeted their gracious hostess. Isabella carried her violin tucked under her arm in preparation to perform tonight in the musicale. Lovely and talented, she would surely attract attention. As long as Leticia's imperfect performance at the pianoforte didn't detract from Isabella's talent, her sister would be a triumph this evening.

Elizabeth stood near Richard, each talking to their circle of acquaintances.

"Let's say good evening to Lady Averston," Aunt Alice said. "It won't hurt for Isabella to be seen conversing with the countess."

Though Leticia understood the strategy, she

inwardly cringed at the thought of using her friendship with Elizabeth as a way of improving one's importance. Elizabeth wouldn't mind helping Isabella, of course, but it still felt wrong. Leticia glanced at her sister, but Isabella, though composed and serene, stiffened as if she were trying too hard to look pleasant. What could be amiss? Surely not nerves?

"Good evening, Elizabeth," Leticia said.

Elizabeth beamed. "Leticia, dear, how delightful to see you tonight. And how beautiful you look." She clasped Leticia by both hands.

Leticia hid her surprise at the enthusiastic greeting. "You look stunning as usual. You remember my Aunt, Mrs. Tallier."

"Of course I do. She's been kind enough to invite me to her home for dinner. It's always a pleasure to see you, Mrs. Tallier." Elizabeth clasped Aunt Alice's hand then turned to Isabella. "And Isabella, I adore your gown. I hear you are already leaving a trail of ardent admirers everywhere you go, and rightly so." Her eyes twinkled.

"Good evening, my lady." Isabella's smile tightened, her expression cool. "How kind of you to say, although whatever you've heard has been terribly exaggerated, I'm sure, as I have no knowledge of such admirers."

Elizabeth laughed. "And modest, as well. What a treasure you are."

"You're too kind." Isabella cleared her throat. "Pray, excuse me, my lady. I see someone I'd like to greet."

"Of course." Elizabeth nodded, as gracious as a queen.

93

Leticia stared after Isabella's back. Why the abrupt departure?

Aunt Alice let out her breath in exasperation. "What has gotten into that girl?"

Elizabeth sighed. "Oh dear. I'm afraid she blames me for marrying Richard and ruining your happiness, Leticia."

"No, surely not." Leticia fingered her reticule.

"She may be upset over the debacle in the sweet shop," Aunt Alice said.

Elizabeth's eyes widened. "What debacle?"

Leticia shot a look of annoyance at Aunt Alice. "I wish you hadn't brought that up. I didn't wish to alarm Elizabeth."

"Tell me what happened." Elizabeth took Leticia by the arm and steered her to a corner where they could converse without being overheard.

In a low voice, Leticia replayed the accusations, trying to minimize them.

Elizabeth put a hand on her chest, her eyes narrowed in concern. "I had no idea the repercussions would be so serious. I don't want this to hurt you or Isabella."

"It won't. It's only their opinion, and anyway, Aunt Alice says they are not well-liked among the *ton* despite their rank."

"That's true."

"Don't worry. Everything will turn out well."

The hostess of the *soiree musicale* called everyone's attention and asked the guests to take their seats. Everyone sought their companions and seats in a flurry of movement.

When Leticia found Isabella, she leaned into her

ear. "Why were you curt to Elizabeth?"

"I wasn't—I merely excused myself as quickly as possible."

"Why?"

Isabella hesitated, frowning. "I don't like her. She stole Richard from you."

"Oh, Bella, that's not how it happened."

"You can lie to yourself, but you can't lie to me. I know what happened and I don't care how high her rank is. Her behavior was inexcusable, and she doesn't deserve to marry well because of it."

"She fell in love, Bella. You may do foolish things when you find love, too."

"I won't steal anyone's almost-betrothed."

"Hush!"

Isabella's mouth tightened.

Leticia didn't know whether to weep or rejoice that her sister felt so protective of her, but Isabella's hostility toward Elizabeth was misplaced and unwarranted. How could she help Isabella see that?

They took a seat near the back with Aunt Alice. As the first young lady took the stage, Tristan slipped in, his eyes darting around as if searching for someone. When his gaze landed on Leticia, he moved toward her, but his eyes still searched. Perhaps he sought Mrs. Hunter, or some other potential amusement.

Unaccountably, her heart grew heavy at the thought.

He slipped into the empty chair next to Leticia and he grinned like the smooth rogue of his reputation. "You look ravishing."

Careful not to smile, Leticia let out a huff. "Your compliments are outrageous and too freely given."

Tristan's soft laugh touched her like a caress.

The first musician began and Leticia turned her full attention to the performance, but each breath Tristan drew distracted her. Each time he shifted, she wanted to turn and look at him.

When Isabella and Leticia's names were called, they rose. Isabella, poised and confident, took center stage while Leticia sat at the pianoforte. After tuning her violin to the pianoforte, Isabella nodded. Leticia took a calming breath and began. At the right cue, Isabella's violin joined in. Light seemed to fill the room as Isabella brought life to the violin. The usual noises of the audience disappeared until a mere whisper could have been heard.

Breathless, the crowd leaned in, straining to catch every note she played. Leticia's fingers flew over the keyboard as if possessed by some muse designed to showcase Isabella's talent. With passion and precision, Isabella played the entire piece flawlessly, and with deep emotion. Tears sprang to Leticia's eyes at the sheer majesty of it. Leticia played on, unable to see the keys, somehow without making a mistake to mar the perfection of Isabella's performance. When the final note faded away, silence enveloped the room. A spontaneous and deafening applause rattled the candelabras.

Leticia gripped Isabella's hand as they took their bows. Isabella stood with head bowed demurely. Leticia wanted to hug her.

"Brava," Tristan mouthed, nodding, admiration shining in his eyes.

Leticia straightened, her heart leaping at his approval.

When the applause died down, they left the stage. Many leaned forward to speak additional praises as Leticia and Isabella made their way back to Aunt Alice. Since they were the final number, conversation rose and fell around them.

Aunt Alice hugged them both and rocked them back and forth. "Oh, you'll be the talk of Town."

Tristan laid a hand over his heart. "You two stole my heart. Will you both marry me?"

They laughed and Leticia swatted Tristan's arm, earning a very cocky grin in return.

"I didn't realize you played that well," Tristan continued. "The last time I heard you perform, it sounded like you were torturing a cat."

Isabella tilted her head archly. "You call that a compliment?"

A young gentleman appeared, his eyes starry as he gazed at Isabella. "Miss Isabella, you were like an angel."

"You're too kind, Mr. Griffith." Isabella lowered her eyes and her cheeks pinked enough to make her appear demure but not shy.

"May I fetch you some lemonade?" the buck asked.

Before she could agree, another young gentleman approached and bowed, first to the buck, then to Aunt Alice. "Good evening, Griffith. Mrs. Tallier." He shot an admiring glance at Isabella before addressing Aunt Alice. "Please, Mrs. Tallier, I beg you, introduce me to this vision." His gaze flitted toward Leticia. "Both of them."

He failed to fool Leticia with his amended request. Still, she recognized the kindness of his gesture.

While Aunt Alice made the introductions, Mr.

Griffith's smile faded. He held out a hand to Isabella. "Please excuse me but Miss Isabella and I were about to take a turn about the room and enjoy some refreshments."

Isabella glanced between both young gentlemen and then accepted Mr. Griffith's offered hand. She looked back at the newcomer as they moved away. "It was a pleasure to meet you."

"The pleasure was mine, Miss Isabella."

As Isabella left on Griffith's arm, Aunt Alice preened. "Already a dozen suitors."

The newcomer looked alarmed. "A dozen?"

"Oh, at least," Leticia added, wickedly.

"Hmm." He moved off toward the refreshment table, but Leticia suspected he had Isabella on his mind more than the glasses of lemonade or the trays of food.

Aunt Alice rubbed her hands together in delight. "If that girl doesn't receive a handful of offers by summer, I'll eat my prized fish."

Leticia effected a mock shocked expression. "I hope not, Aunt. Those decorative fish in your pond aren't good eating."

Chuckling, Aunt Alice put an arm around her. "I'm expecting a few for you, as well."

"Oh, no, Aunt. I'm here to help Isabella make a splash."

Aunt Alice's eyes twinkled. "We shall see."

"Yes, we shall," Tristan added, the expression in his eyes growing more wicked.

A third gentleman approached and nodded at Tristan. "Barrett."

"Ah, good evening. Miss Wentworth, may I introduce Major Hawkins? Major, please allow me to introduce you to my good friend, Miss Wentworth."

The major bowed. "Delighted to meet you, Miss Wentworth. Your performance was well done." He spoke with supreme politeness, as if he were either very stuffy, or very nervous.

Leticia couldn't resist tweaking them both. "Thank you. I'm told I've progressed from sounding as if I am killing a cat."

Tristan choked and then laughed. The other man looked confused.

Leticia smiled at the very formal man. "Forgive us; that's an inside joke, I'm afraid."

"Of course." As they exchanged pleasantries, his face remained solemn as if he feared smiling might crack his face.

After he bowed and took his leave, Leticia turned to Tristan. "You forgot a sense of humor is on my list."

Tristan snapped his fingers. "Oh, that's right. I'll do better next time." The mischievous grin told another story.

Isabella returned, and after greeting a steady stream of visitors, they donned their wraps and waited for the carriage.

"I met some delightful people tonight," Isabella murmured.

"Indeed, you did." Aunt Alice gloated.

Isabella sighed. "You know, Tristan is awfully handsome. I declare, you and he make a striking couple. What a dash the two of you would cut."

Leticia barely suppressed a snort. "I view Tristan as a brother, nothing more."

"I think you're mad to overlook him."

"I'd be mad to consider an avowed bachelor and

shameless rake as anything else. Besides, I haven't forgiven him for all those years he pulled my pigtails."

Isabella let out a sound at odds with her usual ladylike perfection. "You keep telling yourself that, Tish, and maybe you'll believe it."

"What's that supposed to mean?"

"Oh nothing. The carriage is here."

Glee glittered in Aunt Alice eyes. "I must write your mother. She'll be so pleased."

As they climbed into the carriage, Isabella with her violin case tucked under her arm, Leticia let out a happy sigh. After Isabella's triumph tonight, no one would fault her for Leticia's involvement in the school.

Chapter Ten

Tristan loped into Cribb's Parlor in the center of a throng of friends from the Four Horse Club, all still whooping over Tristan's victory in the curricle race moments ago.

"Barrett's buying!" Appleton shouted.

Tristan shrugged. "I suppose, considering all I've won, I can at least buy the first round."

This announcement brought on another roar of cheers, and he settled in among his friends as he told his victory over again amidst interruptions of the others telling what they'd seen. As the night went on and the conversation dissolved into a dozen tangents, Tristan sipped his brandy. He looked down at his glass—still his first one, while the others already gulped down their third round. Strange, but he rather liked his clear-headed focus instead of stumbling through a drunken fog. Something must be wrong with him.

The others swayed in their seats and some made a game of trying to pinch the rump of the serving girl as she passed. The girl looked alarmed instead of flirtatious.

Tristan swatted away the hand of the fellow next to him. "Leave her alone, Palmer. Can't you see she isn't interested?"

Palmer made a face. "You aren't any fun, Barrett. What, are you getting all respectable on us?"

"Keep your hands off the girl," Tristan said, anger edging his voice.

"Ah, leave off," Appleton slurred, "Barrett's right. Go after greener fields or shomething."

Palmer let it go, but the longer Tristan sat there, the more he wanted to leave. His friends' language turned more and more bawdy. Instead of joining in like he used to, Tristan wanted to apologize to anyone who might overhear them.

Repulsed, Tristan stood. "I must leave you, gents. Have a grand evening."

A few including Appleton called out farewells, but the rest were too deep in their cups to notice. Palmer laughed raucously at something and swayed so hard he almost fell off his seat.

Tristan stepped out of the pub and adjusted his hat. Night had fallen since they went inside, but it had hardly passed the dinner hour. What to do with the rest of his evening? His empty bachelor rooms waited with nothing but the promise of loneliness. Perhaps he could catch Richard at White's. He often went there after a day at Parliament before going home to his wife.

Tristan arrived in White's in the middle of a high-stakes game of faro. Richard stood watching, his arms folded, his expression grave. When Tristan walked in, Richard's gaze flitted to him, then he motioned him over.

"Someone is about to lose a fortune." His searching gaze revealed his curiosity at seeing Tristan in the respectable Tory club for the second time this Season. "Come, join me in a drink."

They took a seat away from the game, but Tristan waved off the drink. "I've already had enough for tonight."

Richard's brows shot up but he made no comment. "Have you eaten yet?"

"No. You?"

"I'm going home to dine with Elizabeth soon. How goes your search for Leticia's future husband?"

"I've introduced her to several but she doesn't seem to show a preference for any of them. Other men are starting to take note of her."

Richard swirled his drink in his glass as if debating with himself. "Have I introduced you to Lord Bradbury?"

"No. Why?"

"Rumor has it he's looking for a wife. Something about pressure from his father to continue the family line." He gestured with his chin to the table where the game took place on the other side of the room. "He's the one wearing the silver-and-green waistcoat. This is the first game I've seen him play in a long time."

"So, he's not a frequent gambler."

"Not that I know of."

The man Richard indicated wore an expensive suit. A fashionably lean gentleman of perhaps thirty, he sat taller than most of the other players at the table. With mahogany hair and patrician features, he epitomized the type of gentleman ladies found attractive.

Tristan continued to study him. "Do you think she'd be interested in him?"

"The ladies seem to like him. He doesn't appear at many events, but when he does, there's always a flock of tittering females nearby, peeking at him from behind their fans."

"Do you know him well?"

"Not well. He strikes me as intelligent, articulate, and well-mannered."

Tristan asked the most important question, "Womanizer?"

Richard shook his head. "Clean reputation."

At the table where the game took place, Lord Bradbury tossed down his hand and stood. "Too rich for me."

A chorus of *ohs* followed this pronouncement. The winner let out a gleeful chuckle and the crowd broke up.

Bradbury wrote out his vowels on a slip of paper and handed it to the winner along with a calling card. "Call on my man of business tomorrow to settle up." He strode toward the door.

"Bradbury," Richard called out. "Come, let me buy you a drink."

Bradbury's gaze searched for the voice and his face relaxed as he veered off his original path and took an empty seat at their table.

As Richard made the introductions and ordered Bradbury a port, Tristan sized up the man. Confident, poised, serious. Tristan mentally went through Leticia's checklist, uncertain if the lord met her criteria. A decided gulf separated the lord's status and Leticia's, but not insurmountable.

"Not your night at the tables, eh?" Richard said.

A brief, wry smile touched Bradbury's mouth. "So it seems, which is why I seldom play."

Not a frequent gambler. Good.

Bradbury met Tristan's direct gaze with one of his own. "Have we met?"

"No, I think not."

Richard smiled. "My brother and I look enough alike that people often say that."

Tristan let out a mock sound of outrage. "We look nothing alike; I'm charming and you're stuffy."

"I'm responsible and you're dissipated," Richard shot back, though a smile lit his eyes.

Bradbury cleared his throat. Richard and Tristan ceased their banter. A waiter set down a glass in front of Bradbury. The lord sipped as he took measure of Tristan.

Bradbury turned his attention to Richard. "I received an invitation to your subscription ball. I suppose that's your lot now that you're a married man."

"Will you come?" Richard asked. "It's for a good cause."

Bradbury traced the edge of his glass with a finger. "I suppose I should."

Tristan and Richard waited, but he didn't elaborate as to his reasons.

Richard's lips twitched. "I'd be indebted to you if you would attend as well as help me with a project of my wife's. We are having a bid for the pleasure of the supper dance with certain ladies, the proceeds of which will go toward her foundation. May I count on your participation to help get things started? I'll be bidding, of course, and my brother here, and a few others, including Suttenberg and Pemberton, but in case there are a few in attendance who are reluctant to join in, your involvement may help tip the scales, and get things moving along."

Bradbury nodded. "I see what you mean. Very well, then, count on me."

"Much obliged."

Donna Hatch

Fascinated, Tristan fingered his signet ring as he watched the lord. He'd never met someone whose mannerisms and deportment reminded him so much of Richard. Leticia would find it hard to resist such a perfect replica. Tristan must find a way to introduce them.

Bradbury's gaze swung to Tristan. "Have you made up your mind about me yet?"

Tristan started. "Excuse me?"

"You seem to be trying rather hard to take my measure. Have you come to a conclusion?"

Tristan gave him a cocky grin. "No, but I might if you would be so kind as to join me and a group of friends on an excursion to Vauxhall Gardens Wednesday."

Bradbury said nothing for a moment—a methodical man, perhaps even cautious. Did the man do anything spontaneous?

"I haven't been to the gardens in some time," he said at last. "I admit I would like to see them again. It's been deuced strange weather we've had this spring, though, so you may not have any cooperation on that front."

"Then I suppose I shall have to make a request for fair weather," Tristan said. "I've heard of tribal rain dances; surely there's a sun dance, no?"

Bradbury smiled at Tristan's quip, transforming his serious visage to one of a younger, more approachable man. "I'll leave the sun dancing to you, but I'll pay homage to the sun goddess, if it would help."

A man of humor. Tristan mentally checked off another requirement on Leticia's list.

A waiter brought Tristan his meal and as he ate, he

asked careful questions and exchanged pleasantries, more and more certain that Leticia would like him, and yet, not sure he liked Bradbury—too much a stuffed shirt. Tristan couldn't see Bradbury steeple chasing or flirting with barmaids, which boded well for Leticia. Very well, he'd make the introductions and see what happened. If the man proved unworthy of her in any way, Tristan would intervene.

After Bradbury left, Tristan finished his meal and eyed Richard. "You seem thoughtful this eve."

"Elizabeth is worried. Leticia was insulted in public, and Elizabeth fears their involvement in the school may make Leticia seem unsuitable to potential husbands."

A surge of protectiveness welled up inside. "Insulted by whom?"

"Petre and his dragon of a mother."

Anger boiled in Tristan's gut. "I should go give that pompous bore a piece of my mind." Or a challenge to a duel.

"That would fuel his argument. We must expect opposition from the small-minded."

"I won't stand by while people besmirch Leticia's reputation."

Richard's mouth curved into an indulgent smile. "Ignore small minds."

Tristan quoted Alexander Pope, "*At ev'ry word, a reputation dies.*"

Richard raised a brow. "I haven't heard you quote poetry in some time."

"Come to think of it, I haven't read poetry in ages. Perhaps I should pick it up again."

Odd, how past interests seemed to be returning.

Perhaps this quest to marry off Leticia had put him in that frame of mind. Or the time he spent with a childhood friend resurrected old behaviors.

There was something liberating about returning to his former, more natural self.

Chapter Eleven

As Leticia climbed out of the hackney, she eyed a line of boats waiting at Westminster to take them across the Thames to Vauxhall Gardens. A group already gathered there. She glanced up at the blue, cloudless sky, the most pleasant day they'd had in weeks, which promised a perfect evening.

Tristan stood among the group, his tall, elegant form standing out as the others faded into gray shadows. She swallowed the lump in her throat. Tristan was too handsome by half—too handsome for his own good.

Isabella nudged her and said *sotto voce*, "Your Tristan appears to have this well organized."

"He's not *my* Tristan, you goose," Leticia murmured.

Isabella cocked her head. "Do you think he will ever give up his wild ways and settle down?"

Leticia shook her head. "He shows no sign of that."

"Perhaps if he stopped chasing loose women and got to know a lady, he'd find one he could love," Isabella said.

A man as romantic as he ought to find a true love and settle down. Instead, he wasted his time with women who never knew or appreciated what a remarkable person lay under his flirtatious exterior. Such a travesty.

Leticia led the way toward the group, keeping her voice low. "That's the odd thing. He doesn't chase them. They chase him. He's not a hunter. He's…"

Isabella watched her. "He's what?"

"At times, he seems to be a frightened little boy willing to accept anyone who might love him."

Isabella looked at her as if she'd stood on her head. "He's hardly a boy."

"You know what I mean. I think he's lonely, but afraid to open up his heart because that would make him vulnerable. So he tries to forget about his loneliness by spending time with women who promise no complications."

Isabella's stare turned pensive. "Lonely, but afraid to trust."

"I think so. But then, what do I know?" Leticia flushed. She'd speculated about something rather too private about Tristan that she ought to have kept secret. "I've been reading a great number of gothics of late, so it's possible that I'm creating a fantasy about him that has no basis in truth. Have you read *A Lady in Peril* by E.L. Windover?"

"I stayed up all night to finish it. It was her best book yet."

With a silent breath of relief that she'd diverted the conversation away from Tristan, Leticia nodded. "So, I have heard. I can't wait to read it."

"You'll love the hero. He's so wonderful! Dark and forbidding at first, but then he is so gentle inside, and capable of such passion."

Leticia smiled. "I'll borrow it tonight." Silently, she chided herself. She ought to mind her tongue, even to Isabella. Her observations about Tristan's heart should be kept in the same strict confidence he gave her.

Tristan trotted up to them. His infectious grin flashed. "Good afternoon. A fine day for the gardens."

Leticia returned his smile. "I admit I am rather looking forward to it. I've never seen them."

"No? Well, then, I'm delighted to be the first man to introduce you to such a pleasure." His voice took on a sultry tone, and she looked up sharply, but the rakish gleam in his eyes softened into one of teasing.

He offered them each an arm and escorted them to the rest of the group.

The tongue-tied Miss Seton and her equally bashful brother arrived last. Tristan greeted the shy siblings and treated them with upmost courtesy, playing the perfect host, attentive, charming, seeing to everyone's comfort.

A moment later, he called out over the group. "I believe we are all here. Shall we go?" He gestured to the line of boats waiting to ferry them across the river to the gardens.

As groups began entering the boats, Tristan offered an arm to Miss Seton, who blushed. He leaned in and murmured something to her, the word 'Whist' mingled in. Miss Seton straightened and smiled. He guided her to Mr. Rowley and said something to them both that initiated a conversation between the charming Mr. Rowley and the shy Miss Seton. They stepped into the boat together.

Tristan arrived at her side with two men in tow.

"Miss Leticia Wentworth, Isabella, may I present Mr. Finley and Mr. Dixon."

Leticia greeted the two gentlemen, both of whom appeared to be under thirty, well-heeled and without that rakish gleam that most of Tristan's friends all seemed to have. But then, he had assured her that his guests were all perfectly respectable.

If she remembered her Debrett's peerage, Mr. Finley was the grandson of a viscount, and Mr. Dixon was the third son of a marquis. Tristan seemed to be reaching high for potential husband candidates. She awarded Tristan a knowing smile, and he opened his eyes wide in mock innocence. She and Isabella exchanged greetings with the gentlemen and enjoyed polite, if a bit stiff, conversation.

They stepped into the boats and cast off. As the ferryman guided them across the river, Mr. Finley pointed out birds along the way and explained their traits to a degree that she couldn't decide if it were impressive or frightfully dull. Still, ever courteous, he asked her questions about herself. Mr. Dixon offered Isabella livelier dialogue, but his self-importance would grow tiresome. Eventually, Isabella and Mr. Dixon fell into conversation of him speaking and her nodding as if interested.

The boat bobbed in the gentle waves, but Leticia kept a white-knuckled hold onto her seat. The water lapped at the edges as if hungry to consume them. Mr. Finley's litany, though dry, helped keep her anxiety down to manageable levels.

They reached the other side of the river by Vauxhall. Mr. Finley extended a hand to help her, and they waited for Isabella and Mr. Dixon to disembark.

"That was a lovely lead up to the thrills of the gardens." Isabella exchanged glances with Mr. Dixon who grinned back at her. His air of self-importance appeared to have diminished.

Out of the group, the diminutive Mr. Seton approached Leticia, offered her a nervous smile, then examined his feet.

She curtsied. "Good afternoon, Mr. Seton."

"Miss Wentworth." The small man shot his gaze at her before returning to his study of his feet. It was a wonder he managed to ask her to dance at the house party.

Mr. Finley pointed to a branch in a nearby tree. "Oh, look, that's a blackcap—a male. Blackcaps have a jaunty little song. Many call it a Northern Nightingale."

Leticia pretended interest in Mr. Finley's description of the bird while Mr. Seton darted glances at her.

When Mr. Finley finished discussing the mating rituals of the bird, Leticia nodded at him. "I had no idea there was so much to know about birds." She focused her attention on Mr. Seton. "Are you a bird watcher, too, Mr. Seton?"

"Er, no."

She addressed them both. "Lovely afternoon for a visit to the gardens, isn't it?"

"Indeed it is." Mr. Finley continued searching the trees, no doubt hoping he'd find some new exciting specimen.

"Yes. Lovely." Mr. Seton looked up at her with undisguised admiration in his eyes, then resumed his stare at the ground.

Leticia's heart swelled in sympathy. Poor man. She couldn't help but be flattered that he liked her but she felt no attraction for him in return. Still, she couldn't leave him stranded. A tense silence fell on them.

She searched for a topic. "I understand you plan to

run for the House of Commons, as your father did."

"Yes." He opened his mouth as if to say more, but then returned to stare at the ground.

She hoped only ladies tied his tongue or he'd have difficulty getting elected to the House of Commons. Well, if Tristan could be kind to shy Miss Seton, she could do the same to the equally bashful Mr. Seton and the enthusiastic bird watcher, Mr. Finley.

Leticia took a step nearer Mr. Seton. "I'm sure you'll be a fine elected official."

He looked up again. "Do you think so?"

"Certainly. Your parents both seem well informed and I'm sure you have the good of the people in mind."

"I do, I really do. I…" he stammered for a moment. "I admire your cause to help the orphans learn how to read. I want to help."

"Do you? Oh, that would be lovely." She smiled at him and he offered a smile in return.

"I…I can't give as much as I'd like, but I'd be willing to make a pledge.

"Oh, Mr. Seton, you are as generous as you are kind. Here is the name of our solicitor who is handling the account for the school." She pulled a card out of her reticule and handed it to him. "Thank you so much."

"It's my pleasure, Miss Wentworth."

Tristan arrived last, no doubt to ensure no one had been left behind. He led the way to the garden's main entrance. As he moved so confidently among the guests, Leticia couldn't help but admire the calm, efficient way he managed everyone, seeing to their needs, making them feel heard. He would be a great leader, if he'd give himself a chance. If only he'd settle down and look for a kind, loyal lady who would love and cherish him as he deserved.

They proceeded forward, and Mr. Seton melted back into the group. Mr. Finley remained next to her, listing birds he'd seen at the gardens on previous trips. Leticia stifled a yawn. Apparently, Tristan equated respectable with boring. But then, men were often different with one another than they were with ladies so she ought not to blame Mr. Finley for his singular topic.

As Kensington walked by, he glanced her way. A touch of humor touched his mouth as if he suspected her disinterest with her walking partner's topic of conversation. "I say, Finley, I overheard Miss Wynn say she's a birdwatcher. Perhaps you ought to compare notes with her."

"Is she, now?" Finley peered around. "I was not aware of that."

"I think she's partial to geese," Kensington deadpanned.

As images of Miss Wynn's incident with a flock of geese at the house party burst into her mind, Leticia tried to hold back a laugh but it ended up sounding like a cross between a cough and a snort.

Kensington's eyes crinkled at the corners. Finley bade her a good day and went off in search of a fellow birdwatcher. Leticia suspected he would be disappointed.

Leticia gave in to her laughter. "I didn't realize you had a wicked streak."

His smile grew. "I prefer to think of it as a rescue, Miss Wentworth. I feared you'd die of boredom if I didn't intervene."

"It appears I owe you my life then."

She admired the breadth of his shoulders, the

sunlight shining on his dark hair. Captain Kensington was, without question, an attractive man.

They arrived at the gate of Vauxhall Gardens, paid admission, and moved inside. Leticia drank in the sight of the Grand Walk, a large, open pathway lined with trees and whimsical pavilions. Tristan and an unfamiliar gentleman approached. The newcomer held Leticia's gaze. He stood a few inches taller than Tristan but less broad, possessing that enviable lean figure that the dandy set adored. His clothing oozed wealth and taste, almost too opulent for an afternoon outing, but fit the sinewy grace of his every movement.

Tristan led the gentleman to her. "May I present Lord Bradbury. My Lord, Miss Leticia Wentworth."

Leticia lowered her eyes and sank into a curtsy as she greeted the newcomer. "Delighted to meet you, Lord Bradbury."

Lord Bradbury bowed. "Your servant, Miss Wentworth."

She looked up at the rumble to his voice and exchanged a rather direct stare with him. His dark hair had the faintest touches of auburn, and his blue eyes gave the impression of wisdom and kindness.

Tristan cleared his throat. "And I believe you know Captain Kensington, my lord."

Leticia caught herself staring. Her cheeks warmed and she glanced at Tristan. With his head cocked to one side and his eyes widened with curiosity, Tristan looked so impish and adorable that she wished they were children again so she could throw her arms around him. Tristan glanced meaningfully at Lord Bradbury, and her cheeks burned hotter still. No doubt Tristan wanted to crow over his victory at having introduced her to a man that piqued her interest.

Lord Bradbury inclined his head to greet Kensington. "Captain."

Kensington nodded but his posture changed subtly, as if he were preparing to spring into action.

Bradbury's gaze shifted back to Leticia with another piercing look, giving Leticia the distinct impression he viewed her as a beautiful lady rather than a dowdy country miss. Which was silly. She never claimed to be as elegant as this lord, and no one had ever called her beautiful.

"I understand this is your first visit to this auspicious garden?" Lord Bradbury said.

"Indeed it is," she admitted. Further proof of her low gentry status.

"Then allow me to show you around." He offered his arm. "If you don't mind, Captain?"

Kensington held up a hand. "Not at all, my lord."

With a backward glance at Tristan and Kensington, who both looked too thoughtful for her comfort, she took Lord Bradbury's arm and allowed him to lead her. Another glance backward assured her that Isabella stood in the middle of the group, surrounded by three men vying for her favor. Leticia returned her attention to the gardens and to her companion.

A large marble statue of a man standing in a relaxed pose, wearing slippers and a banyon-like dressing gown greeted them. He looked neither a statesman nor a soldier and his state of dress mystified Leticia.

"That's the great composer Handel," Lord Bradbury explained.

"What an unusual way to sculpt a man—in such a

state of undress."

"Indeed." His eyes crinkled in humor. "I understand that idea belongs to the man who commissioned it, Jonathan Tyers, a music lover and patron of the arts."

They walked past lush flowerbeds and arbors. Street performers stood among the guests who roamed and danced, all mingling with the aristocracy, the gentry, and the working class. Leticia verbalized her delight as they strolled through the Grove surrounded by supper boxes. The orchestra building dominated the center of the Grove. Lord Bradbury led her to a pavilion where pastoral paintings hung.

I understand you and Mr. Barrett are old family friends," Lord Bradbury said.

"Yes, we are."

"Averston asked me to encourage his brother to run for Parliament but I must say, his reputation gives me pause."

"Lord Averston's?"

"No," he chuckled. "Mr. Barrett's."

"Oh, yes, well, I'm sure he was deserving of that when he was younger, but he seems to have turned over a new leaf as of late."

At least, she hoped he had. He did seem more clear-eyed and purposeful lately. If she had to exaggerate the truth to help him get elected, she would.

"So I'm told," Bradbury said. "He seems to be genuinely interested in the working class, an admirable quality for a candidate for the House of Commons."

"Yes, he is very compassionate toward the down-trodden. He's helping Lady Averston and me with our school for the poor. I assume you've heard of it?"

"My help with her rather unconventional auction has been enlisted." Amusement colored his voice. "I found it difficult to say no."

They shared a smile, and Leticia breathed another sigh of relief that they'd gained the support of such a respected lord.

They strolled through lawns and charming groves intersected with winding paths. Around every turn, they encountered floral bowers arching over benches of wrought iron and some of stone. Trees and thatched pavilions canopied the area.

Isabella's laughter floated over the air, and Leticia glanced back. Isabella walked between Captain Kensington and Mr. Dixon while two others tried to impress her with their wit. Most of Tristan's group strolled nearby in groups of three or four. Music floated over the air, lending a magical quality to the already surreal beauty of the gardens. Lord Bradbury led her past a replica of a castle, complete with cannons, swings, and bowling greens.

"Amazing," she said.

"There are ruins over that direction." He gestured. "Replicas instead of the original, of course, but diverting, nonetheless."

While they admired the gardens, often stopping to exclaim over some charming statue or fountain or artwork, dusk deepened.

Tristan called out. "We should head back to the dinner boxes." He laughed at something Miss Wynn said. His gaze caught Leticia's gaze and grinned meaningfully at her, no doubt pleased Leticia still walked on the arm of Lord Bradbury.

Who was she fooling? Bradbury's position in

society soared above her. Tristan must be deranged to think a lord like Bradbury would make a match with a simple miss such as she.

As they returned to the area of the dinner boxes, she looked for Tristan but only found other members of their group. The two ladies Tristan had been accompanying now walked with other gentlemen. Craning her neck, she scanned the darkening gardens for him.

"Our group seems to be congregating by that fountain," Lord Bradbury said. "Shall we join them?"

"There's Isabella. I wonder how she's enjoying the gardens. Please excuse me."

Lord Bradbury bowed. "It was a pleasure to enjoy the sites thus far in your company, Miss Wentworth."

"The pleasure was mine, my lord."

He inclined his head and she curtsied before she moved toward Isabella, trying to appear casual as she let her gaze slip over the crowd, searching for Tristan.

Where had he gone?

She approached Isabella in the middle of the group admiring the fountain. "Isn't this beautiful?"

"It's magical." Isabella linked arms with her. "Tell me about Lord Bradbury."

"He's very charming." She craned her neck, looking out another direction for Tristan's form.

"And handsome."

"Yes." Where could Tristan have gone?

Isabella's smile turned sly. "I haven't seen him for a few minutes."

"Who? Lord Bradbury? He's right back there."

"No, goose—your Tristan."

"He's not my Tristan."

"So you keep telling me."

Leticia spotted him striding toward them from the main pavilion. A woman of questionable reputation wearing a rather low-cut red gown revealing most of her large bosom stepped in front of him, swaying suggestively. Leticia held her breath. Tristan shook his head. Stepping around her, he continued toward Leticia and the others with long, purposeful strides.

Leticia let out her breath to release her tension. Tristan had refused. He hadn't even seemed to deliberate. She should have known he would never associate with members of the *demi-monde*.

"Our dinner boxes are ready for us," Tristan said as he reached her side.

Kensington appeared at Leticia's side and held out an arm. "Shall we?"

"Thank you." She took his arm, mystified at the attention of so many distinguished gentlemen.

"I haven't been here in years," Kensington commented. "They've made a few additions since then. Oh, and wait, any minute now they'll…never mind. You'll see."

"What?"

He touched a finger to his mouth in a hushing motion. "It's better as a surprise."

They strolled silently along the path as the deepening dusk made it difficult to see. Instantly, hundreds of variegated lanterns leaped to life in perfect unison. Leticia breathed out an *oooh* and the crowd let out a collective gasp. Nobility and shop boys alike exclaimed over the sight.

"Remarkable," Leticia breathed. "How do they do that?"

Kensington said, "I assume with an army of servants and practiced timing."

Following Tristan, who now escorted Isabella, the group strolled along the Grand Walk through rows of whimsical pavilions all representing Chinese, classical and gothic styles of architecture.

As their group gathered in two neighboring dinner boxes and chattered about the sights, musicians played a selection of Handel. Leticia found herself seated between Tristan and Captain Kensington, and across from Lord Bradbury. Isabella sat between Lord Bradbury and another gentleman. Servers brought out platters of food including an assortment of biscuits, thinly sliced ham, and some of the best wine she'd ever tasted. She glanced at Tristan, whose eyes sparkled with pleasure.

"You're enjoying yourself," she commented.

"I am indeed." Tristan sipped his drink, then held it out to her. "Care to try some arrack punch?"

"What's in it?"

"Rum mixed with other things including the grains of the Benjamin Flower. Quite a heady liquor." He grinned.

She held out her hands to ward it off. "Er...no. One of us should keep our wits about us."

He raised his glass to her in silent homage, then sipped it. Toward the end of the meal, a bell sounded. Several people sprang to their feet including Tristan. His glass of arrack punch remained half full.

"What is it?" she said.

"You don't want to miss this." Tristan offered his arm, exchanged meaningful glances with Lord Bradbury. "If you don't mind?"

Bradbury's eyes narrowed briefly, but waved him off. "Not at all. Miss Isabella, if I may have the pleasure?"

Her face lit with pleasure, Isabella took Lord Bradbury's arm and disappeared into the magical garden.

Leticia wound her arm through Tristan's. "Where are you taking me?"

Tristan looked over his shoulder. "My apologies, but I wanted to be the one to show you this. It happens at nine o'clock and lasts just a few minutes." He walked on, glancing sideways at her. "What do you think of Lord Bradbury?"

"He was an attentive companion, but I'm confident he has no designs on me."

"I'm confident he does, especially after that look he gave me when I wanted to spirit you away." He grinned at her. "Of course, nothing quickens the chase more than healthy competition."

Leticia scoffed. "If I thought either of you were competing for me, I'd be a foolish green miss indeed."

"Admit it; men find you attractive."

"The only men interested in me are the ones you've put up to it."

He affected a wounded expression. "Not true. I've done nothing but make introductions. Their interest is genuine."

"Tristan…I appreciate what you're trying to do but you must see what a futile effort it is to bring me to the attention of a man like Lord Bradbury. No one of his rank would have any interest in the daughter of a simple country squire."

"Have faith in your feminine allure, Tish. You're

well-respected in the *ton* and lovely to boot. He'd be mad not to consider you. Besides, people have crossed bigger social lines than those between you and Bradbury."

She turned to him in surprise. "Why, Tristan, I believe there was a compliment in the midst of that."

"Don't sound so shocked. Have I been so inattentive that I never compliment you?"

"I can honestly say I don't recall you ever paying me any such thing. Although I do seem to recall that you admired my neck once. Of course, at the time, you were threatening to bite it because I'd made some kind of reference to the possibility that you were a vampire."

He chuckled. "I do admire a pretty neck."

"I refer to your habit of keeping late hours and sleeping away the daylight."

They passed underneath a bower, which blocked them from the prolific lanterns and cast a shadow over them. Couples strolled past without taking note of them.

He stopped and turned to her, and the intensity in his eyes glimmered in the shadowy light. "I apologize for being remiss in my compliments to you. I shall make an effort to rectify that omission." He cupped her cheek with a gentle hand.

Too startled to move, she went still, all her focus captured by Tristan. His touch induced strange stirrings deep inside, both soothing and exciting. Her heart thudded an unsteady rhythm.

His voice took on a tone he'd never used with her, achingly soft. "You are lovely, Leticia. You have skin like a porcelain doll, and eyes like the sea—mysterious and passionate, yet as innocent as a new leaf in spring. And your lips"—he brushed the pad of his thumb over her lower lip, sending spirals of tingling warmth outward—"they are like rosebuds waiting for a touch to release their sweetness." His voice turned sultry. "They would tempt any man."

His gaze lowered to her mouth. His hand cupping her cheek made slow caresses, his thumb tracing her cheekbone. Every nerve in her body quivered. Her heart flailed against her ribs and her breath came too fast. His aftershave curled around her, drawing her in closer in a blend of familiar bay rum and some other, more exotic, scent. His hand slid along her cheek to her chin. With one finger, he gently lifted her face toward his.

She leaned into him and rested a hand on his chest over his heart. He drew closer, leaning down toward her. His lips parted and came nearer, nearer still. The nervous excitement in her stomach tightened, building up a pressure that must surely shatter her any moment. Her mouth yearned to touch his. Her body craved his arms around her. He closed his eyes. She held her breath, aching, burning for his kiss. The world held its breath in expectant wonder.

No. This was wrong. Tristan was a friend; nothing more. Besides, for all she knew, he presently engaged in an affair with Mrs. Hunter, or someone like her.

She drew back with a strangled laugh and put a shaking hand on her forehead to check for fever. "No wonder you're such a master seducer. You almost fooled me with that one."

Tristan opened his eyes, but they were heavy lidded as if coming awake. "Hmm?"

With that sleepy-eyed, slightly bewildered look, he looked so much like the sweet Tristan of her youth that she longed to guide his head to her lap and stroke his hair and listen as he read poetry to her.

Not quite. She wanted nothing more in that instant than to kiss Tristan, either as he appeared now, flushed and confused, or in that magical bubble of desire that had unexpectedly engulfed her a moment ago. She almost laughed. Such an act with Tristan would be foolish on every possible level.

No wonder Elizabeth had fallen so hard for Tristan before she married Richard. No doubt every woman of Tristan's acquaintance had succumbed to his spell and threw themselves at his feet.

Tristan's eyes seemed to focus. Stepping away, he dragged his fingers through his hair and blew out his breath. If she didn't know better, she'd think he was as stunned as she. After clearing his throat, he chuckled and shook his head. "Just checking to see if you're woman enough for these men I'm considering for you."

"Woman enough?" She lifted a brow.

He winced. "Ah…"

"Don't move," rasped another voice. A ragged man holding a knife crouched in the darkest part of the shadows, poised to spring. "Gimme yer valuables, gov'nah. You too, missy."

Leticia gasped, her heart skittering to a stop. Cold chills spread across her arms.

Tristan stepped in front of Leticia, blocking the man from her view. "We don't want any trouble."

"No trouble," the knifeman said. "Jes gimme yer purse and that there fancy ring and you'll never see me again."

Leticia gripped Tristan's shoulder with both hands and peeked out at the thug.

Tristan stood, calm and courageous. He held out

his hand wearing his signet ring, which bore the Barrett family crest, and turned it so the filtered light made the rubies sparkle. "The money I could part with, but this ring has been in my family for generations. It is one of five, which are worn by descendants of the very first Lord Averston dating back to William the Conqueror. If you think I'm going to hand it over because you wave a puny knife at me, you are unforgivably stupid."

Leticia gasped at his audacity, her gaze darting to their assailant. Surely the thief would be furious.

Tristan reached back and placed a hand on her hip, an intimate, soothing gesture.

The knifeman scowled and brandished the knife. "'and it over, fool, along with yer money, or I'll carve ye up first and then I'll 'ave a go at yer ladybird." He leered at Leticia.

Tristan's shoulder tensed under Leticia's hands but his voice remained calm. "Very well. I can see you won't be reasonable." He reached into his back pocket underneath his tailcoat and pulled out a small pistol. With a steady hand, he leveled the pistol at the thief. "You will not touch this lady. You aren't fit to look at her. Now back away and leave us in peace or I'll be forced to shoot you."

The thug's eyes widened and he held up his hands. "No trouble, sir, no trouble. I'll jes' be on me way." He faded back into the shadows.

"Back away, Tish." Tristan took a step back and Leticia followed his lead as if they were dancing in reverse position. When they reached lamplight on a main path, Tristan peered again into the shadows, then guided Leticia forward.

He tucked the gun away and turned to her. "A bit

127

of adventure, now, eh?"

Now that danger had passed, Leticia began shaking. Tristan enfolded both of her hands inside his, strong and safe and steady.

"Come," he murmured. "We'd best find a constable before the blackguard tries that with someone else."

Leticia nodded. Tristan took her hand and they walked, hand-in-hand like children. Tristan hailed a constable, described the knifeman, and pointed out his last known location. The constable went to investigate. Leticia hadn't been able to utter a single word.

He turned to her. "Tish?"

She looked up into Tristan's concerned eyes and tried to pull herself together. "You were amazing. When did you start carrying a gun?"

"Since those men snatched Richard last year. I rather like defending myself and others."

She let out a shaky breath. "My hero."

He kissed the top of her head. "Come, Love. Let's find the others."

Love. He'd never called her "love" before. Perhaps he frequently addressed women of his acquaintance by that term of endearment, but it enfolded her in joyful bliss. Grandmama had called her "beloved" with such sincerity that Leticia never doubted that she meant it. That same sincerity rang in Tristan's voice now. Could she trust that he meant it?

Walking on Tristan's arm, Leticia straightened her shoulders and released the last of her fears. She was safe with Tristan. Her friend. Her champion.

Chapter Twelve

A week after the unforgettable excursion to Vauxhall Gardens, Tristan arrived at Averston House in Mayfair a few minutes early for the ball. He found Elizabeth flitting about, giving final instructions to the footmen and adjusting flower swags adorning the room. Maids lit the remaining candles in the ballroom while the chalk artist packed away a pallet of chalks next to an ornately decorated floor. Tristan studied the chalk drawing on the parquet with a practiced eye—cherubs and flowers intertwined the Averston family crest, giving the fierce falcon a decidedly tamer look. Fitting, considering how Elizabeth had tamed Richard, transformed him from an unyielding, pompous stuffed shirt into a man of warmth.

Tristan shook his head. No woman would tame him. He liked himself as he was, thank you very much—free and unfettered.

"Tristan." Elizabeth smiled and held out both hands as she came to him. "You're early."

"I thought I might lend a hand, if needed."

"How kind, but I believe everything is in readiness." His sister-in-law fluttered her hand above her head in a gesture that encompassed the room. "What do you think?

"I've never seen anything grander."

Her eyes widened in alarm. "Is it too much?"

"Oh, no. All the biggest snobs will be green with envy and they'll fall all over themselves to try to match what you've done here." He looked around again. "My mother used to throw balls and such, but nothing on this scale."

As a child, he'd peeked out through the railings, awed by the glittering display. Mama had always kissed him good night before going downstairs to join her guests. Tristan had always followed, and sat watching until his nursemaid had shooed him back to the nursery. Mama had been so beautiful and seemed happiest the day of a party. If Tristan hadn't been such a misbehaved boy, she might have loved him enough to stay.

"Tristan?"

He remembered himself. "It's perfect. All the Averston ancestors are nodding in approval." He turned away from her probing gaze.

Leticia and Isabella arrived, so deep in conversation with their aunt, Mrs. Tallier, that none of them saw him. "...don't want any kind of censure to touch your name," Leticia said.

"If Lady Averston says it's acceptable, I'm sure it is," Mrs. Tallier said.

Leticia frowned, a familiar mulish look in her eyes. "It's all well and good for old maids and widows and married women, but I'm not sure it's proper for a young miss newly out."

"What do you think, Tristan?" Isabella said.

Four pairs of eyes turned to him. Leticia's glance slid away and a faint blush touched her cheeks. The memory of his hand on her soft cheek sent his heart racing. He couldn't believe he'd almost kissed her.

Leticia, of all people—his oldest and most trusted friend! What had he been thinking?

Would she have enjoyed his kiss?

"You ought to call him Mr. Barrett," Mrs. Tallier gently chided.

"I do in public, Aunt, but I've known him most of my life so it seems overly formal to do so in private," Isabella said. She addressed Tristan. "Do you think it would be wrong for me to take part in the auction?"

Leticia let out a sharp laugh. "It's futile to ask Tristan anything about propriety. I doubt he knows the meaning of the word."

Tristan took a step back under the force of her verbal blow. Did she have such a low opinion of him? Or did she bear some belated anger over their near kiss at Vauxhall? She hadn't seemed upset at the time, or later in the evening. It would be like a woman to think about it later and get all riled up over a small thing.

He bristled. "Just because I have a reputation, doesn't mean I am not a judge of what's proper. I know the rules of society."

Instead of looking apologetic, Leticia set her mouth in a challenging glare. "Then tell my sister and aunt that Isabella should not put herself on the auction block."

Before Tristan could open his mouth, Isabella let out a huff of annoyance. "I'm not selling myself as a slave; it's a supper dance."

"She'll be viewed by every man in attendance," added Mrs. Tallier, "which could be of great advantage, especially if the bids climb as high as I suspect."

"Oh, dear." Elizabeth looked between all four of them, her eyes wide with alarm and her chin quivering as if she were about to burst into tears. "You don't think this will create a scandal, do you?"

"Certainly not." Mrs. Tallier turned to Leticia. "You, young lady, ought to trust your elders. Lady Averston would never do anything outside of the pale. If she did, I would not support it."

Tristan almost pointed out that Elizabeth, younger than Leticia, could not rightfully be her 'elder', but thought it a moot point.

Leticia's mouth worked, visibly torn. Tristan hooked his arm through hers. He walked forward, forcing her to walk backward until they reached the far end of the ballroom away from the others. With his hand on each of her shoulders, he turned her to him.

"Tish?"

Leticia's eyes grew shiny as if she were fighting tears. "I don't want this to hurt Isabella; I couldn't bear it if it did."

His ire melted under her rare show of emotion. "It won't. Everyone knows this is for charity. Elizabeth and your aunt are pillars of society and etiquette; everyone respects them. As they said, this is for the supper dance and supper. What could possibly happen?"

She let out a half sob and shook her head, her hands coming up in a helpless gesture.

He lowered his voice into soothing tones. "I'm sure the guests are the picture of propriety. Richard and Elizabeth were very selective with their invitations."

Leticia drew a labored breath and nodded. "I suppose you're right."

He squeezed her arms. "I know you've taken some abuse about this school idea, but you're doing the right thing. I admire your passion."

She looked up at him with those large green eyes, so trusting, so lovely. "Do you really?"

"Indeed. If anyone dares speak out against you or Isabella, I'll take them out and thrash them." He smiled to soften his words, though he meant them.

She laughed ruefully. "To tell you the truth, I was tempted to crack my umbrella over Lord Petre's head when he was so rude."

"I'm sure you were. You are downright lethal with umbrellas."

They shared a smile remembering when she'd done that to him years ago.

Tristan looked over his shoulder as voices filled the ballroom. "It looks as though your guests are already starting to arrive. Shall we?" He held out an elbow.

She placed her hand on his arm. "I'm sorry I impugned your honor. I didn't mean it."

He opened his eyes wide in mock surprise. "You impugned my honor?" He donned a fearsome scowl. "That's it, woman; choose your weapons. I'll meet you at dawn."

She smiled at his idle threat. "Of course you know what is and isn't proper. I merely…"

He waited, not certain he wanted to hear the rest. She shook her head and never completed her sentence.

He finished for her, "You hate what a rake I am and you think me incapable of anything exemplary." He couldn't keep the bitterness out of his voice.

She looked up at him, but he refused to meet her gaze. He was starting to hate what a rake he had become, too. It was all so meaningless. Maybe it would become fun again when he had Leticia wedded and his obligation to her ended. Or maybe it had been so long since he'd been with a woman that he had forgotten how well it helped fill his emptiness—temporarily, at least. Perhaps he needed a bracing drink. Or a smack to the side of his head.

The evening began in earnest, guests arriving, gentlemen paying their subscription, greeting, laughing, drinks flowing. Music began and soon dancers obliterated the chalk drawing on the floor. Tristan did his part, dancing with as many wallflowers as he could find and flirting with proper older ladies until they cracked a smile. He didn't realize until his dry throat drove him to the lemonade table that he hadn't touched a glass of champagne. He rather became accustomed to having a clear head. Odd, that.

For Leticia's sake, he kept an eye on Isabella but she had no shortage of partners. Rather, they seemed to be stumbling all over each other for the opportunity to partner her. Overall, the evening progressed flawlessly, which reflected well on Elizabeth as well as for The Cause.

After the quadrille, Richard stepped forward and held up his hands. The string quartet silenced. Voices died down.

"Welcome, esteemed guests." His brother's voice rang in authority—probably the same voice he used when addressing Parliament.

"As you know, this evening is to benefit a school for orphans, to teach them basic skills so they may become respectable working class instead of thieves and pickpockets and worse. With that end in mind, the supper dance will be an auction. Every lady who feels inclined to do so may come to the front of the room and we gentlemen will auction for the privilege of waltzing with her, and then, of course, enjoy her company throughout supper."

Lady Brinton, Elizabeth's sister, stood up first. "I will volunteer."

A collective sigh came from the guests as the beauty made her way to the middle of the room. Toasted as a diamond of the first water when she arrived on the scene two Seasons ago and later made a match with Lord Brinton, she would surely create a heated bidding.

Richard bowed to Lady Brinton, took her hand, and called out, "What is your offer for the charming Lady Brinton?"

"Ten pounds," called the Duke of Suttenberg.

"Twenty." And so the bidding continued. The Duke bid for a dance with his daughter, no doubt to help drive up the bids, as did her husband, Lord Brinton. One lady after another stood next to Richard, smiling as gentlemen caught the spirit of the game proving how generous and deep in the pockets they were. Elizabeth brought in three hundred pounds.

Richard's chest puffed in obvious pleasure that his bride had fetched such a handsome sum from another gentleman. Tristan grinned. Elizabeth had thought herself plain next to her beautiful sister; perhaps the bid tonight would help dispel that belief.

When Isabella stood, several young bucks bid, each growing more and more reckless. Three hundred pounds also won the supper dance with Isabella. Tristan craned his neck until he spotted the winning bidder, a friend of Richard's known as a kindly, respectable gentleman. Tristan could trust him not to take advantage of the sweet young lady. Tristan breathed a sigh of relief. Next to him, a young man muttered as he watched Isabella take the man's hand and stand next to the winner until the bidding ended.

Lady Tarrington stood, wife of the Earl of Tarrington. The bidding heated as men vied for the attention of the lady whose beauty had not diminished with age. Her husband won her bid, paying nearly as much for Lady Tarrington as Elizabeth's bid had fetched.

Leticia stood. Tristan's stomach tightened. Wearing a stunning gown of ivory trimmed in leaf-green, almost the shade of her eyes, she smiled out at the crowd but he recognized that nervous pull to her mouth. Surely she didn't fear she would fail to bring a high bid, did she? He must make an effort to compliment her more. Without the near kiss, of course.

She would bring the most money of all, if he had to pay it himself.

"Twenty pounds," he said at the exact same time as another voice. He glanced around to locate the other voice.

"Thirty," called someone else.

"Fifty," bid a third.

Unexplainably annoyed and unable to locate the other voices calling out, Tristan shouted, "Two hundred pounds."

A brief silence followed his jump in the bidding.

"Two hundred fifty." Ah. Kensington. Good man to keep his word to help to drive up the bids.

"Three hundred." Lord Bradbury.

Tristan glared at the back of the lord's head. "Three hundred twenty-five."

Bradbury stood. "Four hundred." His focus fixed

upon Leticia who looked stunned.

A collective gasp arose.

"Why, she's not that beautiful," a woman whispered to another behind her fan.

"Someone must love her," said her companion in reply.

"Or be trying to woo her."

Tristan would not be outdone by the smooth Bradbury. He fisted his hands. "Four hundred twenty-five."

"Five hundred pounds." Lord Bradbury's voice rang out.

Tristan growled. Five hundred pounds? How dare that encroacher step in Tristan's territory! As he opened his mouth to bid higher, he caught himself. What had gotten into him? He wanted Leticia to spend time with Bradbury. Tristan had picked out the lord for her because he matched all of Leticia's criteria. Bradbury was perfect for Leticia.

So why did his hackles raise at the thought of that man waltzing in—literally—and having supper with his Tish? Tristan laughed to himself and unfisted his hands. He had no designs on Leticia, and no urge to dig that deep into his pockets.

Richard glanced at Tristan to see if he would bid again, but Tristan made a wave of surrender.

Richard grinned, a regular occurrence since his marriage to Elizabeth. "Lord Bradbury, for the modest sum of five hundred pounds, you have won the supper dance with the incomparable Miss Wentworth."

Laughter and applause rang out. A few more ladies stood, received bids, then Mrs. Hunter arose and lifted her chin.

Tristan gaped. He'd forgotten how beautiful she was. Wearing a scandalously low-cut gown of icy blue silk, Mrs. Hunter stood looking out over the crowd. Her eyes met his boldly, daring him to bid.

The bids flew then, and Tristan called out a few, so as not to hurt her feelings, but her bid reached well over three hundred pounds. Mr. Wynn came in as the highest bidder. She smiled and took his hand, avoiding Tristan's gaze. Wynn grinned like the rake he was and in a scandalous move, kissed her hand, clearly hoping he'd won more favors than a dance and supper. She gave Wynn the same come-hither smile she'd used on Tristan a few weeks ago.

Tristan had probably ruined all his chances of ever taking the beautiful temptress as a lover. The thought should have bothered him—it had been too long since he'd had a woman in his arms. Instead, he felt as if he'd dodged a bullet.

The bidding ended and Tristan glanced about seeking Leticia. There. Next to Bradbury. She lit up all of London with her smile, no doubt delighted her evening had been such a successful venture. He couldn't blame her for being happy; she'd created a heated bidding war. Surely her delight had nothing to do with being won by Lord Bradbury. Surely.

Shaking his head over his own reaction, Tristan laughed it off. If all progressed as it appeared to be, Leticia would be as disgustingly happily married to Lord Bradbury as Richard and Elizabeth. Then Tristan's troubles would all be over. He'd be free to pursue whatever, or whomever, he wished. He'd be free.

Free and alone.

As the music began, Tristan moved off the dance floor while the winning bidders and their partners began the waltz. Leticia's face glowed as she laughed at something Lord Bradbury said.

Tristan had the sudden urge to plant a fist in the center of Bradbury's nose.

Kensington ambled over to Tristan. "A good bluff, Barrett. You took quite a chance, though."

Shaking off his irritation, Tristan raised a brow at Kensington. "Chance?"

"If Bradbury hadn't come through, you would've paid a pretty price for a dance with Miss Wentworth."

Tristan shrugged. "Ah, well, good cause and all that rot."

"You played the part of the outraged suitor."

"All part of the act, old man."

"You should take to the stage."

Tristan eyed him but Kensington wore a mild expression.

"You played your part well, too," Tristan said.

"As you said, a good cause. Since I didn't win the hand of a fair maid for the supper dance, I shall have to make my donation in private."

"Good of you."

"She is pretty."

Tristan followed his line of sight. Leticia waltzed by in the arms of Bradbury, blast the man.

Wait. Kensington admired Leticia now, too? "What about your being uninterested in marrying?"

Kensington's mouth quirked. "Not saying anything about marrying—merely that she's a pretty lady. She has the kind of quiet beauty that grows on a man, like a flower opening up from a bud into a vibrant blossom."

Oh, so now Kensington waxed poetic? Perhaps Kensington's nose ought to be rearranged as well.

Kensington seemed to come back to himself. "How is your sister? Selina, isn't it?"

"She's well."

"Italy, right?"

"Last I heard. She's been to France and Greece, too. She is supposed to come home this summer but her last letter indicated no interest in returning."

The waltz ended and they went into supper. Tristan kept quiet and consumed enough food to impress a horse. After a few minutes, he realized his rudeness to those sitting near him, so he donned his famous charm like a suit of armor and flirted with all the females within earshot.

Wynn and Mrs. Hunter appeared to enjoy each other's company, as did Leticia and Lord Bradbury, blast him. Tristan made a renewed effort to avoid the couple and focus on the ladies he presently slayed with his wit and charm, not to mention his dangerous good looks, of course.

After dinner, Tristan sauntered along the terrace to take in some air. Mr. Seton stood looking out over the gardens lit with Chinese lanterns. Tristan wandered over to him and offered the quiet man a smile. The cold air turned their breath to puffs of smoke.

Tristan tilted his head at Seton. "How are you enjoying London this Season?"

"Well enough."

"Odd weather we've been having, eh?"

"Yes. Nice enough for our day at Vauxhall, though." Seton took a pinch of snuff.

"Good thing my petition to the weather god wasn't

in vain."

Mr. Seton gave a start. "What?"

"A poor jest. Glad to hear you enjoyed it." Tristan clapped the diminutive man on the shoulder.

"I did. Thank you for including me."

They made small talk over the next few minutes until the conversation turned to people they knew.

Tristan saw his chance. "Say, what do you know about Lord Bradbury?"

"Lord Bradbury? I admit I don't know him well."

"Can you tell me anything about him?"

Mr. Seton looked thoughtful. "He thinks before he speaks. He's even tempered. Genuine."

"The type the ladies would like."

Seton nodded. "My sister admires him."

"Any public affairs?"

"None that I know of. I see him at *soirees* or the opera on occasion, often with a different lady, and all of them respectable."

"He never consorts with actresses or opera singers? No mistresses?"

"I haven't heard that of him. Why?"

Tristan shrugged. "He seems to have taken an interest in my friend Leticia. I don't want him to break her heart."

"I noticed that. At Vauxhall." He let out a sigh and stared down at his drink. "And tonight."

Tristan winced. He'd forgotten Seton had feelings for Leticia or he wouldn't have brought up the topic of Bradbury.

"Lord Bradbury isn't the type to break hearts," Seton added. "He is every bit as honorable as your brother; he'd never show interest in a lady and then walk away." Seton sounded unhappy rather than admiring. He let out another sigh. "I suppose I never had a chance with her anyway."

Tristan nudged him. "Come, let us get a drink. I'll bet you a guinea Mr. Wynn loses at cards tonight." He pointed his chin toward the game table visible through a window.

Seton shook his head, declining the bet. "Wynn always loses. You'd think he'd learn how to bluff."

Tristan grinned and mulled over what Richard and Seton had said about Bradbury. They both seemed to think the young lord worthy of Leticia. From what Tristan observed of him while they were at Vauxhall, they were right. Bradbury had behaved with upmost propriety without a trace of rakishness or recklessness. He'd be a perfect husband for Leticia.

The thought didn't quite ring of victory.

Chapter Thirteen

Leticia stood next to Elizabeth staring up at the ramshackle building that would soon become a school. "Are you sure it won't fall down around us?"

Elizabeth stared up doubtfully. "The agent said it's in good repair. The roof is new. And the improvements we are making are going well."

"Let's go inside."

They pushed opened the door. Inside, their solicitor stood examining the ceiling. The main hall echoed with their footsteps as they crossed the room.

The older man greeted them. "It's taking shape. The furniture will begin arriving tomorrow and the books and slates should be here any time."

"You've done a wonderful job," Elizabeth said. "I don't know where we'd be without you. And the teachers?" She turned to Leticia.

Leticia nodded. "I've been corresponding with the applicants. There are three I'm going to interview this afternoon. Are you able to attend?"

"Of course, but I trust your judgment."

"I hope one of them will be suitable," Leticia said. "The applicants all seemed to have a proper education."

The solicitor interjected. "Are they aware of the wages we can offer?"

"The three I'm interviewing today are."

"We hope to garner more supporters, then we can

give the teacher a raise if she works out." He made a gesture to the rest of the school. "Come, let me show you around."

They toured the kitchen. A broken-down table stood in the middle of the room with four rickety wooden chairs but the stove looked capable enough. A small room off the kitchen could board the kitchen help, if the need arose, and one of the rooms upstairs would board the teacher. Perhaps in time, they could house a few children, as well, as a type of charity boarding school. A large room near the main door could provide a place for the children to gather after their studies.

"This would be the perfect room for dancing." Elizabeth fell into a waltz pattern.

"Dancing would aid them in finding future spouses, since even among working classes, social activities involve dances," Leticia agreed. "Wouldn't it be wonderful if we could bring in a piano to accompany them, and perhaps teach some of them to play?"

The solicitor coughed into his fist. "I doubt teaching penniless orphans to play the piano would help them find employment."

"A piano to provide music so they could learn to dance would be nice." Elizabeth cast a guilty glance at the solicitor.

The man adjusted his spectacles. "I suggest you focus on the basis of reading and mathematics first before you consider things like dancing and music."

"We will. For now." Leticia and Elizabeth smiled like a pair of naughty children in perfect accord with their plans.

They completed the tour, discussing where to place the furniture. Leticia frowned at the small hearth in the schoolroom. "I doubt this will provide adequate heat. Do you think we could squeeze the cost of a second stove out of our budget?"

The solicitor frowned and made calculations. "I believe so, especially if we can find a used one. That would leave us with barely enough funding to keep the school open for a single year, and I don't recommend having less than a year's cushion for expenses."

Leticia imagined little fingers too cold to hold their slates and pencils. "At least they'd be learning. And we may yet receive more pledges."

The solicitor nodded and turned to leave. "Shall I remain here while you conduct your interviews?"

"No, don't bother." Leticia waved her hand. "Two of Lady Averston's footmen are here if we need anything."

"In fact, if you'd be so kind as to send one of them in on your way out," Elizabeth added.

He nodded, bowed, and took his leave.

One of Elizabeth's footmen came in. "My lady?"

"Oh, Cooper, do light a fire for us, please."

"Of course, my lady."

The former-thief-turned-footman, thanks to Mrs. Goodfellow's agency and Elizabeth's dogged belief in the man, worked a tinderbox. As he leaned forward, Leticia caught sight of a pistol tucked into his breeches. A pistol? She caught Elizabeth's eye and nodded toward the firearm in an unspoken question.

Elizabeth smiled down at the man. "Cooper always carries a gun when he leaves the house with me."

Cooper grunted. "Can't be too careful. Spec'ly after th' trouble las' year."

Leticia nodded, picturing the burly servant helping

Tristan and Captain Kensington rescue Richard from the terrible men who'd captured him. No doubt his caution sprang from a loyalty to his mistress who had given him a second chance, in addition to the scare they'd had when Elizabeth had nearly been captured as well. But then, Elizabeth's gentle nature inspired devotion from everyone who knew her, both servant and lord.

Cooper blew on a flicker in the hearth. A moment later, a flame crackled. A humble knock sounded at the door in the other room and Cooper hurried to open it. A girl barely out of the schoolroom entered and stood in the threshold. Golden-blonde hair peeked out of her limp bonnet and eyes as blue as a china doll's stared at them through a thin face. Her threadbare pelisse hung from her body. Leticia wanted to hire her to save her from starvation. The young woman gripped a ragged valise as if it contained all her possessions.

She curtsied and spoke in cultured tones at odds with her appearance. "Ma'am. I'm Matilda Harper—Mrs. Harper."

Leticia motioned her in. "I'm Miss Wentworth and this is Lady Averston. Do come in."

They sat on the hard wooden chairs and Leticia began. "In your letter, you mentioned you were a governess?"

"Yes, ma'am. After my husband died in the war, I worked as a governess. I have no children," she hastened to explain as if fearing having children would render her unsuitable.

"Have you references with you?" Elizabeth asked.

Young Mrs. Harper paled. "No, ma'am. I'm afraid I haven't."

"None at all?"

Mrs. Harper wrung her hands. "I left under…unfavorable circumstances."

"You were dismissed?" Leticia asked.

"No, ma'am—I left." She swallowed and kept her gaze on the floor.

"You left without giving notice?" Leticia exchanged looks with Elizabeth.

Elizabeth leaned forward and eyed the girl. Two bright spots appeared on the girl's cheeks and her shoulders fell.

"Mrs. Harper." Elizabeth's voice gentled. "Did you leave because you were handled roughly?"

The girl's mouth pressed together and her chin started quivering.

Anger roiled up inside Leticia. "Your employer took advantage of you?"

Mrs. Harper snuck a look up. "I rebuffed him. Over time, he grew so forceful that I felt I had no choice but to run."

Elizabeth clenched her hands in her lap. "Do you have anywhere to stay?"

"No, ma'am. I have no family."

"We can offer you a room in which to sleep, rent-free, until we've made a decision."

The girl looked up, hopeful. "Here?"

"No," Elizabeth said. "I wouldn't want you to stay here alone; our caretaker has not arrived yet. You'll come home with me. We aren't promising you a position yet; we have other applicants to interview, but I vow you won't sleep in the streets."

Leticia almost hugged Elizabeth. Fortunately, Richard owned many lucrative estates and investments, or he'd never be able to feed all the lost waifs his wife kept bringing home.

"Now, let's discuss your education." Leticia glanced at her notes with her interview questions.

During the interview, they learned the girl had a solid education and an infallible memory. She'd worked as assistant teacher at a factory school in the north where she'd received her education before she married. After her husband of two months died, she'd become a governess to seven children for nearly a year.

Upon completing the interview, Elizabeth said, "Wait in the main hall until we've completed the interviews, then you'll come home with me, at least for a time, until we've made a decision and you are able to make other arrangements."

The young woman nodded, her mouth working as if trying to hold back tears. "I'm so grateful to you, my lady."

After the girl curtsied and left, they looked at each other. Leticia spoke first. "She's well-spoken and well-educated, but I fear she may be too timid to control a large classroom."

"She has experience—limited, admittedly—but she does have some."

"Her experience is with girls who come from better circumstances. Street children may be much more unruly."

"We shall see," Elizabeth said.

Cooper announced their second applicant, and they repeated the process but found this one too stern. The third arrived, but after taking a look at the humble accommodations, announced she was no longer interested.

After the third applicant flounced away, Leticia glanced at Elizabeth who chewed on her lower lip.

"I like Mrs. Harper," Leticia said.

"A trial basis, perhaps, then." Elizabeth nodded. "If she isn't up to the challenge of a larger classroom, we can, at the very least, give her a good reference so she may find a position elsewhere, and it will buy us time to find a replacement."

Leticia pictured a brute trying to take advantage of that sweet slip of a girl in his employment. "Horrid man. I'd like to run him through."

"Things like that should never happen," Elizabeth agreed.

They stood and donned their gloves and hats. By then, the fire had died down to embers.

Cooper came in, banked the coals and turned to them. "Ready t' go 'ome, m'lady?"

Elizabeth nodded. "Yes, we're going home. The girl in the main hall is coming with us. She'll be our new teacher, but she shan't stay here all alone."

"O' course not," Cooper agreed. "Didn't ye 'ire a caretaker?"

"And a maid, but they won't arrive until after the furniture comes."

Cooper summoned the carriage, locked all the doors and windows, then escorted them to the main hall. Did other footmen consider themselves their mistress's personal bodyguards? Perhaps Richard had put him up to it. It would be so like him to be that protective.

The very young Mrs. Harper stood, chewing on her lower lip as she eyed them.

Leticia smiled. "Mrs. Harper, we'd like to offer

you the position of head school mistress. You'll begin next Monday."

Mrs. Harper let out her breath in what almost could have been a sob. "Oh, ma'am, my lady, thank you. I promise to do my very best to help the young ones."

"I'm sure you will," Leticia soothed. "We have every confidence in your ability. The class will be small at first, but it will grow as word gets out."

"Yes, ma'am. My last employer had seven active children, including twin boys. I may be small, but I can handle a class."

Elizabeth said, "Since the school isn't quite ready for boarders, you'll stay with me. When the furniture and the other staff arrive, you can move in."

"The carriage is 'ere, m'lady," Cooper said.

They boarded the carriage, lighter of heart now that they'd found a schoolteacher. Elizabeth dropped off Leticia at Aunt Alice's house and she practically skipped inside. The round table in the middle of the foyer groaned underneath the weight of the vases filled with flowers. Bouquets arrived each day for Isabella. What a triumph already!

Isabella entered the room and gestured to the flowers. "Aren't they pretty? And look; one is for you." She indicated a vase of red and white roses.

"Me?" Leticia picked up the card.

Dear Miss Wentworth,

I cannot recall when I have enjoyed the company of a lady as much as I enjoyed yours. Please consider doing me the favor of allowing me to call upon you in the near future. I look forward to spending time with you again.

Your humble servant,

Bradbury

"Oh, my," Leticia breathed. Though Lord Bradbury had been generous to donate an exorbitant sum of money on her supper dance, he had done so out of kindness, not any personal gesture. Hadn't he?

"Is it from Lord Bradbury?" Isabella leaned over her shoulder.

"It is."

Isabella let out a squeal, then composed herself, looking around to see if anyone had witnessed her loss of comportment. "I knew it. You didn't believe me, but I knew he liked you."

"Oh, good heavens, Bella, it's commonplace for a gentleman to send flowers to a lady with whom he danced."

"These are *roses*."

"It might be his signature. He might send roses to everyone."

Isabella huffed. "Sometimes you are no fun at all."

"It's pointless to get one's hopes up about a bouquet." Leticia inhaled the fragrant scent.

"Are you afraid to get your hopes up?"

"He's a kind gentleman, so yes I like him, but he's also a viscount, so no, I'm not entertaining any naive dreams that he has intentions other than courtesy because we shared a dance and supper for a charity."

"He singled you out at Vauxhall," Isabella reminded her.

Leticia shrugged. "Tristan put him up to it. I need to change for dinner." She turned away from her sister and climbed the curving staircase to her room.

Isabella followed. "What were the requirements on your list, the one you gave to Tristan when he made his wager with you?"

"I have no wish to discuss this."

"If I recall correctly, you wanted a husband who would be faithful, kind, have integrity…oh, and something about wit and intelligence, as I recall."

"Isabella…" Leticia warned. Clearly, relating to her sister the conversation she'd had with Tristan had been a lapse in judgment.

"Lord Bradbury is handsome, a viscount in possession of a great fortune, he seems kind, a witty conversationalist, doesn't have a reputation for gambling, did not drink at either social event where I saw him, and, according to Aunt Alice, he is a man of integrity who has never had any public affairs, which means he's either very discreet, or virtuous. Either way, he's not a rake. If you don't want him, you're hopeless."

Leticia stammered, unnerved by her sister's onslaught. Finally, she managed, "No viscount of his means will consider wedding a country miss with a feeble dowry and a passable face."

"Your face is beyond passable. As far as the rest— he will offer for you if he loves you."

"He doesn't love me."

"He might if you give him a chance." Isabella sighed. "If you don't want him, can I have him?"

"If you love each other, bless you both." Leticia turned away.

"What is this really about?"

At the doorway to her room, Leticia paused and leaned against the doorjamb. "I'm afraid to give him a chance."

"Why?"

Leticia gathered her thoughts and gave voice to her fears. "What if I do fall in love with him, and then he marries another? I don't think my heart would survive another blow of that nature."

Isabella made a sound of distress. "Oh, Tish." She wrapped her arms around Leticia and hugged her close. Leticia leaned against her sister, letting her love and warmth surround and comfort her.

After a moment, Leticia pulled away. "We need to dress for dinner."

Isabella didn't move. "You have so much love to give to a husband and a family. You are foolish not to give Lord Bradbury a chance."

Leticia smiled sadly. "If he calls, I will encourage him, but I won't hold out hope he has any designs on me."

"Then I'll hope enough for the both of us." Isabella waltzed out of the room.

Leticia shook her head. She used to have Isabella's innocence once when a future with Richard seemed certain. But not all dreams come true.

Chapter Fourteen

As Tristan arrived at Richard's London house, he followed Leticia's sweet voice to the front parlor where he found her ensconced with Elizabeth. Strange how he breathed easier in her company.

"The furniture arrived at the school moments ago," Leticia said to Elizabeth. "Shall we be there to ensure they put everything where we want it?"

Elizabeth stood arranging flowers in a vase. "Richard sent Cooper off on an errand so I will need to wait until his return. You know how they are."

Letitia's expression turned wistful. "I think it's sweet how protective they are of you." She straightened as if redirecting her thoughts. "I'd like to get there as soon as possible, but I understand."

Tristan stepped into the room. "I'd be happy to escort you. I've never seen this school of yours. I vow to guard your lovely selves as well as Cooper would." The weight of his pistol tucked into the back pocket of his coat gave him a sense of security.

"How kind of you to offer," Elizabeth said, "but I'm afraid we'll need some men to move the furniture."

Tristan pretended to be affronted. "I'm a man. I can move furniture."

Leticia laughed. "We weren't insulting your manliness, Tristan, but it might be dirty work." She gestured his clothes.

Tristan looked down at his attire—buff breeches, blue tailcoat, gray-and-white striped waistcoat. Nothing remarkable about his understated clothing. "Should I tie my cravat into a plainer knot, then?"

They laughed at his quip.

"No," Elizabeth said, "but your cravat might get dirty, along with the rest of your fine clothes."

"Good. It will give my valet something to do. He's getting too lazy by half. Shall I summon the carriage?"

"If you would, please." Elizabeth tucked another flower into her arrangement.

By the time Tristan returned to inform them that the carriage awaited, Leticia and Elizabeth had donned their pelisses, gloves, and hats. Inside the carriage, they chatted as a group until they reached a rather ramshackle building. New shutters and a new front door stood out in sharp relief against the weather-beaten wood of the structure. Did the whole building lean to one side?

When the carriage stopped, Tristan gaped. "*This* is your school?"

Two pairs of defensive eyes met his. "Yes, this is it," Leticia said with a challenge in her tone.

He huffed a disbelieving laugh. "A good, stiff wind could blow it over."

"It doesn't look like much but an engineer assured us that it was structurally sound." Elizabeth sounded hurt, as if he'd told her that her baby was ugly.

Leticia rushed to say, "It needed some fixing up, of course: a new front door, windows, shutters, repairs to the main stairs. We also decided to whitewash the main schoolroom."

Tristan nodded as if he agreed. At least no one

would try to rob such a poor-looking place.

Inside, furniture and crates lay strewn about in the small, dark foyer with doors leading off to each side. Two brawny men carried another box to the end of the room. They set it down with a thud.

Elizabeth spoke to them, gesturing. They both grabbed crowbars and started opening boxes.

Tristan removed his tailcoat, collar, and cravat, and set them on a box next to his hat and gloves. As he rolled up his shirtsleeves, he looked at Leticia and Elizabeth who stood looking at him with their mouths open. "Tell me what you need me to do."

Leticia put her hand over her mouth and pretended to be shocked at his state of *dishabille*. "Oh, my."

He offered her a rakish grin. "Is that a request to take off more?" He made as if to unbutton his waistcoat as well.

"No!" Leticia and Elizabeth shouted together.

Tristan chuckled. Sometimes it was too fun to tease very proper women. He gestured to the maze of furniture. "Shall we start at this end and work our way back?"

"Very well." Leticia nodded and removed her pelisse. "I'll show you where to put the bed frames. Elizabeth, do you want to start going through those crates?"

"Of course."

"Here." Tristan grabbed a crowbar leaning next to the nearest crate and pried off the lid. Inside laid a stack of primers. After he opened all the crates, he picked up a bed frame and nodded at Leticia. "Lead on."

She took him to the small bedchamber off from the kitchen and scullery. To his surprise, Leticia helped him set up the frame. He carried in the mattress and tossed it on the bed. As he stepped back, he caught Leticia looking at him, with an expression that, on any other woman, would have been called admiration. Desire, even. But on Leticia…

He grinned. "Leticia Wentworth, are you admiring my muscles?"

She flushed bright red. "No. I mean, of course I'm glad you're strong enough to help us with all this heavy lifting, but I'm not admiring you. You are such a vain creature!"

He couldn't resist teasing her a little more. "Come now, admit it; you want to see my muscles. You want to touch them."

"I most certainly do not. I'll leave it to all your ladybirds to feed your impossibly large vanity. I'm sure Mrs. Hunter does that quite well."

He blinked. "Mrs. Hunter?"

She made a sound of disgust that resembled a cat coughing up a hairball. "I don't care!" She marched out of the room.

Tristan stood, stunned. Leticia thought he was having an affair with Mrs. Hunter? And she was angry about it? Did this require further consideration?

Leticia returned a moment later with an armload of bedding. "One of the other bed frames goes in the room off of the servants' entrance over that way." She gestured. "I'll show you where the third one goes upstairs when I'm finished."

Clearly dismissed, Tristan went back into the main hall. Women were such perplexing creatures. And no, he did not want to think any more about the reason for her anger.

Elizabeth's footman, Cooper, and another man arrived. Cooper addressed Elizabeth. "I got yer message, m'lady. You oughtn't leave withou' me."

"I know, Cooper, but we wanted to get started, and Tristan is here with us."

Tristan acknowledged Cooper who gave him a nod of deference but his mouth still turned down as if he felt unneeded.

Soon, they had the whole group working, and Cooper's usual grin returned. Tristan kept up a series of quips, throwing out absurd poetry he made up as he went along, and keeping them all laughing. Working together, they got all three of the beds set up, as well as chests and a clothes press. Once the staff quarters were set up, they went to work on the schoolroom, setting up shelves, which Elizabeth and Leticia filled with books, and then bringing in the desks one by one. Tristan worked every bit as hard as the laborers, enjoying himself more than he would have suspected. When they'd finished, they stood back to admire their work.

"It looks like a school." Leticia's smile lit up the building. He half-expected her to clap her hands and jump up and down.

"It does indeed." Elizabeth beamed.

Leticia indicated the end of the room furthest from the small fireplace. "We found another stove to put at this end. It should arrive any day now."

"We hope to have a pianoforte, as well," Elizabeth added.

One of the men who came with Cooper brought in a bucket of water that he'd pumped from outside and they all washed off a surprising amount of dirt.

Tristan donned his discarded cravat and tailcoat.

"I'm starved. Anything to eat in the kitchen?"

"No. We'll have to go home."

Tristan worked at the knot in his cravat that would probably leave his valet weeping. "Very well. Home it is."

While Tristan handed Leticia and Elizabeth inside the Averston family coach, the workers perched outside. After settling himself in the rear-facing seat opposite the ladies, Tristan flexed his shoulders, trying to ease the tension and fatigue as if he'd spent hours boxing and fencing.

"Thank you for all your hard work, Tristan," Elizabeth said.

"Yes, you were wonderful." Leticia's smile turned impish. "I had no idea you were capable of lifting anything heavier than a riding crop or a hand of cards."

He raised his chin and assumed a lofty air. "I can lift a gun, as you'll recall."

Her smile turned soft. "So you can, for which I am so very grateful."

Tristan's mouth dried. If she turned too many of those enchanting smiles on him, he might be tempted again to kiss her, and this time, do a thorough job of it.

He almost smacked his own forehead. Kissing Leticia would be a mistake for more reasons than he cared to enumerate. This threatened to get too serious. He searched for a change of topic.

"How is your mother?" Elizabeth asked Leticia.

Tristan let out a breath of relief that a benign conversation had started.

"She's well," Leticia said. "She is growing weary of spending so much time in bed, but she's making the best of it. She's taking up sketching again. She says my sisters sit on her bed and read aloud, and they've even put on theatrical performances for her."

"I'm glad they're keeping her company," Elizabeth said. "Is she excited at the prospect of a new baby?"

Leticia smiled. "Very much. She's hoping it's a boy, of course. I'm sure my father is too, although he assures her he'll love a daughter as much as a son, but I know it would be of great comfort to them both to have a son to inherit the estate."

"When is she due?" Elizabeth asked.

"Late August or early September, she thinks."

Elizabeth smiled, but wistfulness touched her expressive face. "I envy her."

Leticia patted her hand. "I'm sure you'll be blessed with a family soon."

"I hope so. It's been a year since our marriage…"

Tristan tried to picture Richard as a father, getting his children out of one scrape after another the way he'd always done for Tristan.

The carriage stopped in front of Tristan's rooms. He bid them both farewell and stepped out of the carriage.

After consoling his valet, Bentley, on the sad state of his soiled clothing, Tristan ate, bathed, and changed, then took a hackney to Leticia's aunt's house. Why he felt so compelled to seek her out, he didn't dare consider. Perhaps duty drove him there to learn whether she'd enjoyed waltzing and dining with Lord Bradbury the other night. Never mind that she'd been smiling and laughing each time she'd danced with the man. Mere courtesy might prompt her pleased expression. But that sparkle in her eyes seemed genuine enough when she spent time with Bradbury. It appeared his plan was working very well.

Blast it all anyway.

Still, he ought to inquire about Lord Bradbury. He had failed to ask her earlier today; he might as well call upon her now.

During the drive, he entertained himself by fantasizing beating Lord Bradbury to a pulp, first at fencing, then at fisticuffs. By the time the hackney arrived at Mrs. Tallier's house, Tristan found himself whistling. Inside the drawing room where they received guests, Leticia stood conversing with two ladies, and Isabella held court in another corner with five young bucks who tried too hard to impress her and ended up coming across like over-eager puppies.

Leticia's aunt, Mrs. Tallier, greeted him. "Mr. Barrett. How kind of you to call upon us."

Tristan bowed. "It's always a pleasure, ma'am."

Mrs. Tallier turned to someone behind him. "Lord Bradbury. Do come in. How delightful to see you again."

Bradbury. Tristan ground his teeth.

Wait. What did Mrs. Tallier mean by saying "again?" How often had the lord been calling? The auction took place two days ago. Surely he hadn't called since then. Had he?

Tristan stepped to the side and turned, eyeing Bradbury who greeted Mrs. Tallier with a formal bow.

Donning his mask of urbane boredom that he used with the upper levels of snobbery, Tristan inclined his head and drawled, "Bradbury."

Bradbury's gaze flitted to him and he returned the nod. "Barrett."

Tristan made a grand sweeping gesture toward the

room in general, as if he were inviting Bradbury in, and took another step back. Folding his arms, he leaned against the wall and pretended to study the view outside. Bradbury strode to Isabella, greeted her, acknowledged the bucks, and chatted. A moment later, he moved to his true target—Leticia. Before he reached her, the Setons stood and bade Leticia good day.

Tristan tried not to watch as her face lit up when she spotted Bradbury or the way he sat as close to her as he could without breaching propriety. The dog.

Next to him Mrs. Tallier heaved a dreamy sigh. "Lord Bradbury. I can scarce believe it."

Tristan watched the woman and her look of pure rapture. "Do you know him well?"

"Oh, my goodness, yes. I've known him since he was in leading strings. His mother and I are great friends, and he went to Oxford with my son. One of the finest young gentlemen I've ever known. Of course, he's thirty now, but still young—especially compared to me." Her smile turned self-deprecating.

Thirty—the perfect age for a man to marry, so they say, confound it.

"To think he's considering my Leticia..." Mrs. Tallier's voice trailed off and her eyes took on a faraway look. She seemed to remember herself. "Well, time will tell."

Perfect. Three ringing endorsements for Lord Bradbury. Leticia would be married by summer and then all of Tristan's obligations to her would end.

He should be happy.

Why this knowledge made him want to challenge Lord Bradbury, he couldn't say. Perhaps because Bradbury too closely resembled Richard? Too perfect.

Too proper. Too loved by everyone.

Tristan cast one final look at Leticia and Bradbury. Bradbury smiled and tapped her on the nose, and Leticia laughed. Very cozy. Intimate.

Nauseating.

"If he hurts her, I'll kill him," Tristan muttered.

Mrs. Tallier looked at him in shock.

"Good day." He stalked out of the house.

Visions of his mother riding away without looking back flashed into his mind. He had an appalling urge to weep.

Chapter Fifteen

Sitting next to Lord Bradbury on the settee, Leticia looked up as Tristan left. How odd. He hadn't spoken to her.

"I hear your school is almost in readiness," Lord Bradbury said.

She returned her attention to Lord Bradbury. "It is. We got everything moved in and arranged. Thanks to the success of the fundraiser, we purchased another stove. The schoolroom has one small fireplace and we feared it wouldn't be adequate. We also dream of getting a pianoforte someday so we can teach dance but that may not happen for some time."

Bradbury's eyes took on a thoughtful stare. "I might be able to help you with the pianoforte. One of my properties has one. It resided in the vicar's house but the new vicar's wife didn't want it taking up room in the parlor, so we stored it in the main house. No one is using it. I don't know what kind of condition it's in, but I can arrange to have it shipped to you and see to any repairs."

Leticia clasped her hands together. "Would you do that?"

A slight curving of his lips softened his features and warmed his blue eyes. What a handsome gentleman, and so kind.

"If doing so puts that beautiful smile on your face

again, then yes, I would consider that a small price to pay."

Looking down, Leticia laughed, unaccustomed to such flattery. Only Tristan said such ridiculous things, and he did it to put on an act. "Then on behalf of the school, I do most humbly and gratefully accept."

"Excellent. I'll make the arrangements." He met her gaze. "By any chance, do you enjoy visiting museums?"

"Very much, but I have not had a chance to do so this year."

"Have you ever visited Bridgewater Collection at Cleveland House?"

"Oh, no." She'd never imagined receiving an invitation to view such a private collection.

"It's worth seeing. Would you do me the honor of accompanying me tomorrow?"

Surprised by his continued attentiveness, Leticia faltered for a moment. "Yes, of course. I'd be delighted."

"Excellent. I've already received permission to view it. May I come for you at four o'clock?"

"I'll be ready."

He glanced at the clock on the mantel. "I fear I must take my leave."

Leticia followed his gaze. He'd stayed precisely twenty minutes. Lord Bradbury always did everything right.

He took her hand. "Until then." As he held her hand, his blue eyes darted between hers as if he were trying to read her thoughts, then he released her hand, stood, and bowed. After another smile, he took his leave of her aunt and left.

Donna Hatch

Leticia sat alone. Could a man of his rank and means be interested in a frumpy little country miss like her? Tristan would chide her for calling herself frumpy and would no doubt come up with all kinds of ridiculously flowery adjectives to use instead.

Why had Tristan left so soon?

This morning as they'd labored side-by-side at the school, he'd been a hard worker and had hefted heavy objects without complaint. It had seemed easy to him. More than once, she'd caught herself admiring the breadth of his shoulders or his toned muscles underneath his linen shirt. Tristan joked with the men, his aristocratic accent at odds with the comfort with which he interacted with the low-born. He gave no indication that he felt any class distinction. Within minutes, the workers were joking with him as if he were an old friend.

She wondered if Lord Bradbury would have helped in such a personal way, or been so amiable to men of a class so far beneath him. She failed to conjure that picture.

"Leticia," Isabella called. "We're going to the milliner's. Would you care to join us?"

Leticia looked up. While she'd been lost in thought, their callers had all said their goodbyes and taken their leave. "Yes. I'll change into my half boots and get my wrap."

Moments later, their carriage fell into the usual London traffic. Isabella chattered on about all the young men who'd called on her, relishing the attention. As well she should.

A pair of young men trotted by on horses, their voices carrying to Leticia. "My bet's on Tristan Barrett.

He's fearless—never lost a race that I've seen."

Leticia's heart stopped. Tristan? She put a hand on her chest and drew steadying breath, trying to calm her fears. Tristan had been steeplechasing for as long as she could remember. An accomplished rider, he loved it and excelled at it. She had no reason to fear for his safety.

"Yeah, but Appleton's got a new curricle that flies."

"I'll bet one hundred quid Barrett beats Appleton."

"Hurry. We don't want to miss the race." Their voices faded away.

Curricle. Tristan wasn't racing on horseback; he was curricle racing. Her heart did a slow, backward crawl.

"Leticia, my dear. You look as if you're about to swoon." Aunt Alice's voice broke in through the fear squeezing Leticia's lungs.

Every muscle in her body screamed to run after those men and find out the location of the race. She had to stop it. "Aunt. We must follow those riders." She pointed to the two young men.

"What is it?" Isabella laid a hand on her arm.

"Tristan's going to be in curricle race right now."

Isabella paled and put her hand over her mouth.

Aunt Alice clucked her tongue. "Good gracious. Is that boy trying to get himself killed?" She barked out orders to the driver and the carriage lurched forward the instant they were seated.

Hurry, hurry, hurry, Leticia willed the carriage. If only she could get there in time to stop the race.

The longer she rode, the more her cold fear heated to anger. Selfish, stupid Tristan. Didn't he know if he got himself killed, the blow might kill Richard? Didn't he know how many people loved him and would mourn his death?

By the time they reached the outskirts of town, the carriage had to stop. Dozens of horses and carriages lined the highway as spectators all crammed in to watch the dangerous race.

Leticia got out and hailed a nearby man. "Excuse me, do you know where the starting line is?"

"Up that way a few miles." He pointed. "The finish line is by that hedgerow."

A ribbon fluttered in the breeze, marking the ending point. Since the carriage couldn't get through, Leticia picked up her skirts and ran toward the starting line. In the distance, two tiny objects blocked the highway. Curricles. A gunshot crackled and the objects sprang forward.

Too late! She could only watch as Tristan risked his life for a meaningless race.

Chapter Sixteen

Standing next to his horses, Tristan eyed his opponent's sleek, new curricle. Well-sprung and designed by a master, it gave him pause. Still, the curricle made up only one part of the formula for a winner. The horses and the driver made up the rest. Tristan had no fears on that regard. A skilled driver, he had never lost a race. His well-matched team ran synchronously. Appleton posed no threat.

His stallion snorted and stomped, tasting the energy of an upcoming race. Tristan ran a soothing hand over the steed, speaking in low tones. "You'll get your chance. Just run like you always do, and we'll take home another victory."

Next to him, Appleton grinned. "Not this time, Barrett. My new curricle is like the wind. You don't stand a chance."

Tristan gave him his best curled lip of disdain. "Your cattle aren't as experienced as mine, and you don't have the heart of a winner."

Appleton snickered, his eyes alight in excitement. "I will today. Then you can see what it feels like to lose. Don't worry, I'll buy you a drink out of my winnings."

They grinned at each other, both posturing as much as their horses.

Tristan pointed up ahead. "Watch that curve. It

comes up faster than you think."

"Try to stay on your side of the road."

"Good luck." Tristan held out a hand.

Appleton gripped it. "You, too." Appleton looked ahead and let out a breath, his one sign of nervousness.

"Good luck, Barrett," Palmer said as he hefted the starting gun.

"My bet's on you," called another voice. Wynn strolled up with Mrs. Hunter on his arm, both wearing expressions of smug amusement.

Tristan tensed. "Thank you."

"I wagered a hundred quid on you, so I hope you win." Wynn glanced at Mrs. Hunter.

"I hope I win, too." Tristan eyed them.

Mrs. Hunter released Wynn's arm and slinked over to Tristan, her lithe body moving with the grace of a cat. "Perhaps a kiss for luck would be in order," she purred.

He raised a brow. "Are you offering?"

She moved so close that her body touched his. "Good luck, Tristan." She rose on tiptoe and kissed him.

He tried to pull away, but she entwined her arms around his neck and deepened the kiss. For a moment, Tristan succumbed. He'd been so lonely. It had been far too long since he'd touched a woman.

No. He wanted more than a meaningless dalliance. His breath rasped. He pushed her away. Though obviously an enthusiastic participant, she failed to ignite the flames he thought she would.

Why did he feel so confoundedly guilty?

She looked at him from underneath her lashes, her lips curving into a smile. "A skilled kisser. No doubt skilled at other things."

Stepping back, Tristan cleared his throat and glanced at Wynn, but he leered at a woman who strolled by smiling at him over her shoulder. Wynn didn't seem to notice that the woman in his company had thrown herself at another man. This kind of thing never bothered him before. What the deuce was the matter with him? When had he started thinking like Richard?

Bold and confident, Mrs. Hunter smiled at Tristan and indicated Wynn with her head. "John and I have no special relationship. Do come by my house tonight and we can have our own private victory celebration." She slipped her calling card into his pocket.

There. The perfect, uncomplicated offer like so many he once enjoyed. He watched her saunter to the sidelines, all the while wearing her come-hither smile.

He should do it. He would do it.

No. He might have a few hours' pleasure but tomorrow he'd wake up as alone as ever, and wondering if he'd put another stain on the family honor. Or disappointed Leticia yet one more way.

He wouldn't do it.

He'd be alone forever.

Maybe he should get involved in some kind of cause, something to occupy his time instead of all these meaningless pursuits.

"Ready, Barrett?"

He glanced at his opponent. "Ready." He slipped a foot into the stirrup at the outer edge, took the second small step, and swung the rest of the way into the open curricle. He checked to ensure the top was folded all the way back and securely fastened.

A rush of nervous energy filled him, clearing his thoughts, sharpening his mind. He focused on the road, the motion of the horses through the reins in his hands. Each breath the horses took, each stomp of their hooves, crackled in his head. He sat forward and braced his feet into a wide stance. He nodded at Palmer holding the gun in the air.

"Gentlemen, ready."

Excitement swept through Tristan and his muscles tensed. A gunshot split the air. Tristan snapped the reins. Two pairs of horses leaped forward, their hooves moving in a blur. Trees and people flew past him in a colorful smear like an impressionist's painting. Aware of every movement of the team, he eased them into a flat out run. Born winners, they responded, their necks stretching out and their legs moving in unison.

Over the rutted highway they flew. Exhilaration replaced Tristan's blood until he was born of wind and speed. He slipped into a state of tranquility where he lived to move at one with his team, where leather and metal and animal blended with man until they were one, unified force.

A shout to his side snapped him out of his nirvana. A sickening bump shuddered through him, then an ear-splitting crash. His carriage lurched to one side. The horses stumbled and went down. All the world slowed into one horrifying motion.

The horses dragged down the pole attached to their harness, converting the two-wheeled curricle into a springboard. The curricle launched Tristan into the air. Helpless to stop himself, he flew, limbs flailing. He landed hard on the ground and rolled.

Tristan disintegrated in an explosion of pain.

Chapter Seventeen

Mute with dread, Leticia stood, her hands over her cheeks, as the curricle racing against Tristan spun out of control. Horse and carriage and rider went down in a tangled mass right in the path of Tristan's team. Tristan's lead horse stumbled and went down, dragging the other with it. The entire curricle tipped forward, throwing Tristan out and upward.

Leticia screamed. Disbelief swirled with horror into a dark maelstrom.

Tristan's body sailed through the air, his arms thrashing as if he were trying to swim. He hit the ground with a sickening thud and rolled a few times. Leticia's heart dropped. He lay still. Stunned silence fell over the crowd.

Leticia ran. Focused on the motionless form in the road, she raced as if her body became pure motion. She dodged the other curricle, trying to shut out the screaming of the horses, and stayed focused on Tristan. Others in the crowd snapped out of their shock and moved to aid injured men and horses.

A crowd formed around the twin wreckages. Leticia pushed through the people and dropped to her knees next to Tristan. He lay on his back, still and pale. Dirt and blood smeared his white face.

"Tristan?" Kneeling next to him, she reached for him but her hands stopped mid-air.

What to do? What if he were…

Urgent, she called again. "Tristan!" She bent over him and put a hand on either side of his face. "Open your eyes."

His eyelashes lay close to his cheeks, fanned out dark and long like a child's. Still no response.

She pressed her hand on his chest over his heart but the thumping of her own racing heart prevented her from finding a heartbeat. Oh, please let there be a heartbeat!

"Is he breathing?" asked someone in the crowd.

She held her cheek next to his nose and closed her eyes, concentrating, searching for any sign of breath. "Please, Tristan. Give me some hope."

There. A tiny movement of air. She held her breath, hoping she hadn't imagined it. Once again, a puff of air blew across her cheek. She sucked in a gasp and rested her forehead on his chest. He lived.

One of Tristan's friends pushed through the crowd. He stopped short at the sight of Leticia's head on Tristan's chest.

He gasped a few times before speaking. "He's dead?"

She lifted her head. "No. He's breathing." She stroked Tristan's dark hair as she had when they were very young. Still as thick and silky, but this time blood matted his hair.

The other man let out his breath. "All right. Let's get him back to his rooms."

"No," Leticia said. "We'll take him to his brother at Averston House in Mayfair." She looked back down at Tristan's face. If he weren't so pale, he might have been sleeping but for the awkward angle of his limbs.

Urgency rippled through her. "Tristan, wake up!"

One of Tristan's horses lay lifeless on the road; the other continued to scream. Both his forelegs hung at sickening angles. Leticia wanted to throw something. All of this loss for sport—so senseless. So foolish.

Aunt Alice found her and took command. "You, you, and you," she pointed to three able-bodied men. "Pick him up—carefully—and take him to my carriage over there." She looked back at her coachman and nodded. "Take care of that poor horse."

The coachman nodded. Grim and silent, he pulled out a gun. After rubbing his hands over the horse's neck to soothe it, he placed the barrel behind the horse's ear.

Sickened, Leticia looked away. The crack of the gunshot ripped through her as if the ball had struck her. The horse's screaming stopped. All the world fell silent.

Leticia focused on Tristan. His pallor faded to a ghostly hue.

Men carried Tristan as if he were a bowl of milk they were determined not to spill. The somber crowd parted to let them through, talking in low tones, or not talking at all. Some wept.

As the men lowered Tristan onto the floor of the carriage, Leticia glanced back at the tangle of the other carriage. The crowd parted enough to give her a glimpse of the other man lying with a coat over his face. Two horses sprawled in crumpled heaps on the road.

Leticia swallowed a sob. She climbed in and sat on the carriage floor with Tristan's head in her lap. The men laid him crosswise, then bent his knees to allow the door to close.

After a command from Aunt Alice, the carriage

started. No one spoke. Silently, Isabella sobbed and rested a hand on Leticia's shoulder. Silently, Aunt Alice sat with her handkerchief pressed over her mouth. Silently, Leticia held Tristan's head, her heart as still as Tristan. The silence drove a wedge of pain deep into her soul. Each bump, each jostle of the carriage, tore through Leticia, no doubt inflicting further damage to Tristan's battered body.

They arrived at Averston House after an interminable drive. Aunt Alice left the carriage but Leticia sat cradling Tristan's head, stroking his hair, searching for any more sign of life, terrified that his heart would stop. Faint, uneven breathing gave the one indication that he lived.

The front door of Averston House opened and two footmen darted toward the mews, no doubt sent to bring the doctor and notify Richard of his brother's injury. Cooper and the two men who'd helped them move furniture in the school—had that been today?—dashed down the stairs toward the carriage.

Cooper nodded at Leticia. "Miss."

Leticia opened her mouth, but couldn't speak. Elizabeth's footman and bodyguard slid a hand underneath Tristan's back. The other men got into position, lifted him, and carried him so smoothly he appeared to glide up the stairs. Leticia followed them in. Calm and in command, Elizabeth called out orders as she led the way. Servants scurried to obey her. Leticia followed them to a room in the family wing. Inside, they laid him on the bed. Without flinching, Elizabeth unbuttoned his clothing and removed his cravat, still calling commands. Her words faded to meaningless noise in Leticia's head.

Leticia held back, uncertain what to do. Tristan's family would care for him. But she couldn't leave. Not yet.

There must be something she could do. She looked around. A pitcher and bowl sat upon a bureau. Water. She could bathe his face. Her hands shook as she poured the pitcher of water into the bowl. After throwing a linen towel over her arm, she carried the bowl of water to the nightstand and set it down. Using the towel soaked in water, she bathed Tristan's face. The removal of dirt and caked blood revealed purple bruises and a raised bump surrounding a gaping cut on his forehead. It started bleeding again as she washed it.

While Leticia cleaned his face, Elizabeth felt along his arms and legs, her eyes narrowed in concentration. Leticia moved to the open V of his shirt, trying to overlook dark hair and rounded muscles on his chest.

They finished and sat back, unsure what to do now.

Elizabeth spoke. "I can't feel any broken bones, but that doesn't mean there aren't any. There may be much worse damage that I cannot feel. We'll know more when the doctor arrives. How long has he been unconscious?"

Leticia shook her head. "Almost an hour, I think."

Elizabeth looked down at Tristan. "From what I know, the longer he stays out, the worse it is." She moistened her lips. "We should—" She stopped, breathed, tried again. "We should prepare ourselves…"

"No." Leticia gripped Tristan's hand, willing him to open his eyes.

Hushed, Elizabeth said, "I sent word to Richard."

Leticia gripped Tristan's unmoving hand with both of hers. Now, with nothing for her to do, the full impact of what had happened settled into her. Over and over, she relived the accident, slower than before, as the other man's horses stumbled, crashed into Tristan's curricle, his horses going down, their screams, the shattering of curricles, the crashing noises that rent the air, Tristan flying, falling, landing. Lying still.

She folded in half, resting her elbows on her knees and her forehead in her hands. A sob shook her body. And another. Elizabeth sat next to her and put an arm around her.

If she lost Tristan, she didn't know what she'd do. How would she ever live without his teasing smile? He'd been her playmate, her dearest friend, her confidant, and of late, her hero.

"Leticia." Aunt Alice's voice sounded hollow. "There's nothing you can do here, child. Come home. I'm sure Lady Averston will send word as soon as they know anything."

Leticia lifted her head. "No, Aunt, please let me stay here."

Elizabeth arose. "I'd appreciate her company, if you don't mind."

Aunt Alice's expression softened. "Very well. I'll have a change of clothing sent over."

Leticia looked down at the front of her dirty, muddy pelisse. A large stain smeared across the front. Tristan's blood.

She looked back at his face, the color of the pillowcase…except the linen developed a stain, spreading outward.

Alarm knifed through her. She stood. "There's an injury on the back of his head, too."

They rolled him over. Sure enough, blood matted

his hair and spread over the pillow. With Elizabeth holding Tristan by the shoulders to keep him on his side, Leticia cleaned the gash so thoroughly she feared she'd hurt him even in his unconscious state. She wrapped his head with bandages, and sat with her hand pressed over the wound to slow the bleeding. Elizabeth propped pillows around him to keep him on his side.

Footsteps approached. "The doctor is here, milady."

They turned as a silver-haired man wearing horn-rimmed spectacles entered and ordered them out.

Leticia paced the length of the corridor, her heart thudding for a prognosis as if she awaited a verdict on a life or death trial. At the end of the corridor, she stood by the window and stared out, unseeing. She turned and paced back the other way toward the main staircase.

A servant held out a valise in her line of vision. "This arrived for you, Miss Wentworth."

"Put it in the lilac room," Elizabeth said. "Then fill a bath for Miss Wentworth."

"Yes, milady."

"Elizabeth!" Richard's voice boomed from downstairs.

"Up here," called Elizabeth.

Leticia watched Richard charge up the stairs, taking them two and three at a time. Sheer panic, uncharacteristic for Richard, clouded his expression. "How bad is it?"

"The doctor arrived a moment ago," Leticia said.

Elizabeth's breath hitched. "It's bad."

Richard enfolded her into his arms. Normally, Leticia would have turned away, unable to watch the sight of them embracing. Now, she averted her eyes to give them a moment of privacy. Strange, it no longer bothered her to see Richard with another woman. With his wife. With Elizabeth. Whom he loved. Leticia felt nothing except a vague relief that Richard had someone to whom he could turn for comfort. Either she no longer loved him at last, or her alarm over Tristan deadened the pain.

"What happened?" Richard asked, his gaze darting between them.

Leticia moistened her lips. "It was a curricle race."

Richard let out his breath in a long, exasperated exhale.

Leticia continued, "The other driver appeared either to have lost control, or one of his horses misstepped, and they rammed into Tristan's curricle. He was thrown." Her voice cracked.

"You saw it?" He released Elizabeth and grabbed Leticia by the arms. Grief and terror and fury in his dark eyes, eyes so like Tristan's, spilled onto her. "You were there and you didn't stop it?"

She shrugged off his hands. "I went to stop them but I was too late—they'd already started."

He released her, dragged both hands through his hair and collapsed onto a settee in the corridor, hunched over. Elizabeth sat next to him, her hand on his back.

The doctor came out, fingered his hat, and looked up, with apology in his expression. Richard leaped to his feet. Leticia held her breath.

The doctor said, "The good news is that there doesn't appear to be any broken bones, and there's no swelling in his abdomen to suggest internal injury."

They waited for the inevitable bad news his tone suggested.

"The head injury is serious. But don't lose hope. It's too soon to tell…" The doctor looked down at his hat.

Leticia fisted her hands so tightly that her fingers ached. A low, rushing noise filled her ears.

Richard drew himself erect, as expressionless as a stone, his arms straight, hands fisted, clearly bracing for the worst. "Don't mince words, doctor. I want the whole truth."

"I've done all I can for now. Time will tell. The longer he is unconscious, the worse it will be. You must prepare yourselves for the possibility that he may not recover."

His words hit Leticia like a blow to her stomach and her knees buckled. She felt her way to a chair and fell onto it.

The doctor continued his horrifying prognosis. "If he does awake, he'll be in severe pain and very disoriented. He may not remember the accident or other events—even people. The effects may last a matter of days…or be permanent. These things are difficult to predict. I'll come back tomorrow to check on him." The doctor left.

Richard, pale and grim, turned around. He spoke in flat, unemotional tones. "I should send word to Selina."

"I'll do it," Elizabeth offered. She tugged on Leticia's hand. "I'll show you where you can clean up."

Numb, Leticia followed her friend to a room and let a maid undress her and guide her to a bath. After redressing in the comfortable gown Aunt Alice sent, Leticia returned to Tristan's room. She pushed the door open, her attention fixed on the figure in the bed. He lay on his other side, propped up by pillows, a bandage wrapped around his head the same whiteness as his pallid skin.

She crossed the room and sat on the edge of the bed. "Tristan. It's time to wake up now."

She laid a hand on his cheek, careful not to touch any bruises or cuts. Numb, she sat motionless with her hand on his cheek. He lay as if lifeless except for the slight rise and fall of his chest. Outside, the sun sank and darkness enshrouded the room, emptying it of color. A pall fell over the city.

Elizabeth came in and sat next to her. Putting an arm around her, she rested her head on Leticia's shoulder. "I sent a tray to your room."

"Thank you." Leticia's voice sounded as if it belonged to someone else, someone without hope.

"Shall I bring it to you here?"

Leticia shook her head, too weary to reply.

"Don't say good bye yet," Elizabeth said. "Richard refuses to send for the bishop to give him Last Rites. Tristan may yet pull through."

Helpless anger roared inside. Shaking with fury, Leticia leaped to her feet. "Of course he's going to pull through. He's going to be fine. He's not going to die. He's not."

Elizabeth held up her hands and spoke to her as if she were talking to a skittish mare. "I know, Tish, I know. I hope and pray he'll be whole and well."

"Don't call me that. Tristan calls me Tish. Richard called me Tish. You don't call me Tish." Unable to look at the naked hurt on Elizabeth's face, Leticia whirled around and fled the room. At the end of the corridor, she ran into Richard so hard that she staggered backward. Wearing nothing more than his shirtsleeves and breeches, he steadied her.

She shrank from him. He was someone else's husband. She oughtn't see him in such a state of undress. A small part of her registered that the sight of him stirred nothing in her heart but a sense of familiarity.

"Tish?" He reached for her again, that almost constant look of apology in his expression, the same one that had been there ever since he found himself engaged to be married to Elizabeth returned in his eyes.

His pity raised her ire. She stepped back. "Stop. Don't touch me."

His hand fell away. "Forgive me."

"I don't love you," she blurted out. "You can stop looking at me with pity and apology. I'm quite well."

In a quiet voice, he said, "I know."

"Lord Bradbury has been courting me. And Captain Kensington—both fine men."

"Yes, I heard, and yes, they are."

That melancholy compassion remained in his expression, his tone. She fisted her hands. "Lord Bradbury is much like you, but that is not why I have a preference for him."

Serious and intense, but now less apologetic, he nodded. "I am gratified to hear that."

She said nothing further.

He waited.

What had she hoped he'd say? She turned away as shame sank into her that she'd felt a need to make that point. Knowing he watched her, she marched back to Tristan's room with her back ramrod straight and her chin high. Yet, she'd spoken honestly. Every word rang of absolute truth.

Inside Tristan's room, she found Elizabeth rocking back and forth, sobbing.

Cold horror blasted through her. "No!"

Leticia raced to the bed to lean over Tristan. He lay unmoving, his chest still rising and falling. Her relief hit her so hard that she had to sit down.

"He still lives." She let out a half sob of relief. Why was Elizabeth weeping?

Elizabeth lifted her face. "I'm sorry. I'm so sorry. I didn't realize you still hated me for taking Richard from you. I thought you were over him. I am so sorry."

Leticia closed her eyes as remorse flooded her. She'd been thoughtless and cruel and had lashed out at a dear friend. "No, Elizabeth, I'm sorry. I don't hate you. Not at all. I never did. And I *am* over Richard."

Again, the truth of her words hit her. She no longer loved Richard, not as she once did. Seeing him and Elizabeth console each other no longer caused her pain. Running into him in the corridor failed to set her heart racing, only vague sense of impropriety over his *dishabille*. No longing or aching. No sorrow. No regret. He was familiar and dear, but like a brother rather than a man she once planned to marry. The knowledge cleansed her, healed her.

She took her friend's hand. "Forgive me, Elizabeth. I'm worried about Tristan and angry that I didn't get there soon enough to stop the race. I'm furious at him for being so reckless and foolish. A man was killed today, and four horses—it was awful. I can't get it out of my mind. And now Tristan is…" She gestured to him. "Forgive me for lashing out at you. I need him to be all right." Her throat closed over and tears ran down her cheeks.

Elizabeth put an arm around her. "Of course I forgive you. You are my very dearest friend."

They sat together, letting their shared sorrow cleanse them of hurt. Richard came in. He leaned over Tristan and watched him for a moment. Elizabeth slipped a hand into his and he squeezed it, then took a chair near the bed where he sat staring. Night fell. A maid came in and lit the lamps.

As Leticia watched Tristan's face, his eyelashes moved. She straightened. His eyes squeezed more tightly closed, then he blinked. She held her breath. He opened his eyes, blinked several times, and squinted up at the ceiling.

She leaned over him. "Tristan?"

His eyes slid to hers and he looked at her without moving his head. "Tish?" He blinked again. "Did you hit me over the head again? With a brick?"

His speech slurred, but at least he spoke. What a beautiful sound! She wanted to shout *huzzah!*. She settled for enjoying the warmth and gratitude that flowed over her like bathwater.

Elizabeth clasped her hands together. Richard leaped to his feet and dashed to the bed. "About time you woke up. Get better fast because I'm going to thrash you."

"What did I do now?" Still squinting, Tristan pulled his hand out of the covers and put it to his head. "My head…"

Leticia tried not to notice his bare arm and shoulder, how beautifully formed, how the sight sent strange warmth to her face.

Richard scowled at his brother. "You raced a curricle, you idiot."

Leticia poured a glass of water and cradled Tristan's head so he could drink. A few drops ran out of the corner of his mouth and she wiped it dry.

Tristan moaned. "Why are you so angry? The race was weeks ago and I won. Palmer was furious."

"You've curricle raced more than once?" Richard demanded. He let out his breath in disgust.

"Stop shouting." Tristan put his hands over his eyes and moaned again.

"I suppose I shouldn't be surprised you'd take up such a dangerous pastime," Richard grumbled. He drew a breath and softened his voice. "Do you remember the race today?"

"Today?" Tristan squinted. "Who won?"

Leticia touched his shoulder. "You and the other driver, someone named Appleton, were in an accident."

"Appleton?" Tristan scowled. "He doesn't have a curricle."

"He had a new one. You don't remember what happened today at all?"

He rubbed his head, sucking in his breath when his fingers touched the lump on his forehead. "I remember moving things in the school. Later, I paid you a call. You were with Bradbury, and your aunt sang his praises. I don't remember leaving her house." He closed his eyes. "My head hurts."

Leticia measured a small amount of laudanum into a glass. "This will help with the pain."

He tried to sit up but had no strength. She held his head and pressed the glass to his lips.

After drinking, he winced as the back of his head touched the pillow. "Accident? Was anyone hurt?"

Richard gripped his shoulder. "Appleton." He

swallowed. "He didn't make it."

Tristan's eyes widened and narrowed and filled with horror. "I killed Appleton?"

Leticia brushed his hair back from his face. "No, Tristan. He lost control and tipped his curricle. It crashed into yours and you all went down. It wasn't your fault."

Tristan's throat worked. "I shouldn't have raced him. He was inexperienced." He closed his eyes and turned his head away.

He undoubtedly needed to be alone to work out his grief. Though she longed to hold him, comfort him, he would rather grieve alone.

Leticia pressed her lips to his brow. "I'm glad you're awake. You frightened me."

He looked up at her, his eyes shiny with unshed tears and his face lined with anguish. "I'm sorry. I've let you down in so many ways."

"Nonsense. Rest and get well." She almost added, 'and no more racing,' but thought better of it. He'd lost a friend today, and nearly his own life.

Tristan's eyes fluttered closed and his chest rose and fell in sleep.

Leticia stood. "Perhaps I should go home now."

Richard stood. "I'll call the carriage to take you."

Leticia moved to the doorway, then turned back to watch him a moment longer. Tristan lived. She hadn't lost him. She could not have borne it if he'd died.

Chapter Eighteen

Tristan existed in a fog of agony and blurry vision. Laudanum helped with the pain, and made him sleepy enough to escape the alternating anger and sadness that his friend had died in a curricle race he didn't remember. But when the medicine wore off, the ache in his head and heart returned. One night, after an indeterminable number of days, Tristan lay still, resisting the urge to ring for help as Elizabeth had instructed. Instead, he let the pain come, let it punish him. He'd killed Appleton as surely as if he'd put a gun to his head.

No wonder Richard thought him a wastrel. The thrill of a race meant nothing compared to the life of a man. In fact, a great deal of his life up to that moment had been frivolous, stupid, risky. Gambling, racing, drinking, blithely permitting young widows to seduce him—for what? A few moments of pleasure. A few moments of forgetfulness. A few moments of feeling alive.

That wasn't living. Living meant helping Leticia find happiness. Living included finding a cause, searching for ways to make a difference. He'd found purpose searching for the perfect man for Leticia, aiding her to raise money for the school, getting the school set up. Through most of his youth, he'd tried to feel alive in all the wrong ways.

In the middle of the night, a dark form matching Richard's build padded in. Tristan pretended to be asleep so he wouldn't have to talk to his brother. He didn't want to hear the well-deserved accusation in Richard's voice. Tristan already couldn't escape the accusing voice in his own head.

Wastrel. Libertine. Rake.

All were true. And he hated them. Hated what he'd become.

As Richard's soft footfalls neared, Tristan kept his breathing deep and steady. Richard laid a hand on his forehead as if testing for fever. After a heartbeat, his brother brushed a strand of hair from Tristan's face, a shockingly affectionate gesture. A moment later, he left, closing the door behind him.

Richard loved him. No matter what, his brother always had his back. Sometimes his help felt suffocating, but Tristan had never doubted that Richard would always be there for him.

Tristan stared at the ceiling. Richard had always understood the purpose of his life. It was time Tristan found the purpose of his own. When he was well enough, he'd throw himself into helping others. He'd do more for the school. He'd announce his intention to run for the House of Commons so he could aid people on a larger scale. He'd stop having meaningless affairs.

He had raced his last.

By the time gray light slid into the room between the bedcurtains, the pain in his head expanded to sheer agony. He moaned and writhed, each moment of torture was penance for his life, for the disgrace he brought to the family name, the grief and despair he'd caused Richard, the men who lost fortunes to him because he was better at bluffing and counting than they, the life he took at the race. He considered all the hearts he might have broken when he'd deluded himself in his belief that they shared a mutually pleasurable moment. And worst, he relived the many ways he'd hurt and disappointed Leticia. Each throb of his head, each ache in his body, represented another stripe of punishment.

He fingered his signet ring, vowing to be a better Barrett, to live by a higher code of honor—if the pain in his head didn't kill him first.

A fuzzy version of Elizabeth came into his room. "Oh, Tristan, why didn't you ring for help?" She placed a cool hand on his head.

He moaned in reply. She poured a dose of laudanum and held his head so he could drink. Moments later, the pain dulled but the clouds in his vision remained.

Elizabeth sat in a chair next to his bed. "Does anything else hurt besides your head?"

"I feel like I was trampled by a herd of elephants and then beaten with a tree trunk."

"Any place in particular?"

"It all hurts, especially my head."

She folded her arms. "Well, you might want to complain more because Richard is ready to thrash you as soon as you've recovered."

"I know."

"You scared him. All of us."

"Trust me, it won't happen again. I'm done with racing. I guess I'll…" He trailed off as a new thought struck him. "Were my horses injured?"

"I'm afraid neither of them survived."

He blew out his breath in a long exhale. Perfectly

matched, well-behaved horses who loved to win. Gone. He'd killed them, too.

A blurry Richard came in and leaned over him.

Before Richard could say anything, Tristan announced, "I'm never racing again. And I've decided to run for the House of Commons."

Richard paused. "You must have hit your head worse than we thought."

"I'm in earnest," Tristan said. "I'm finished with all the meaningless parties, women, games, racing. None of it matters. I want to make a difference like you do in Parliament, and like Elizabeth and Leticia do with their school."

Richard's fuzzy outline sat down hard. "I should have thrown you from a moving curricle years ago."

Richard might have been smiling, but the clouds that surrounded everything made it impossible to see detail. Fatigue overcame Tristan again. He awoke to his valet, Bentley, rousing him to take care of physical needs and to bathe and shave him. Sitting up brought on waves of nausea and dizziness, so he did everything lying down. Though bruised from head to toe, nothing appeared to be broken.

After Bentley got him changed into a clean nightshirt and tucked back into bed, the doctor returned.

"I'm glad to see you awake." He listened to Tristan's breathing, checked his heart, and looked into his eyes. "Any dizziness or blurred vision?"

"Yes—especially blurred vision."

"Memory loss?"

"I can't remember the accident, or anything that happened in the hours leading up to it."

"All normal. The dizziness and vision issues

should pass in a few days. Stay in bed until it does." The doctor felt his chest and stomach, as well as all his limbs but found nothing that pained him enough to be broken. "Extreme emotion is also a common side effect of a hard blow to the head. If that happens, know it's normal and it, too, will pass soon."

Tristan murmured, "A friend of mine died that day. I doubt that will pass soon."

The doctor patted his shoulder but didn't offer patronizing advice about how that, too, would fade. He changed the bandages on Tristan's head and bade him a good day.

"If there's any sign of fever, send for me at once," he said to Richard and Elizabeth at the door.

A servant brought Tristan a cup of broth but he drank little more than half before he fell asleep.

When he woke, Leticia sat next to him holding his hand. With his blurred vision a halo surrounded her entire body and her face glowed with ethereal beauty. She smiled and squeezed his hand. Beams of afternoon sunlight streamed in between the draperies like sparkling stripes of gold.

He drew in a deep breath, inhaling her fragrance. "You smell good. That's not your usual perfume."

She let out her breath in an amused exhale. "No. Isabella and I picked out some new scents."

"I like it. The violet undertones are very provocative."

She laughed softly. "You find everything provocative."

"Not true. Horse manure does nothing for me."

She laughed again, the sound of it washing over him like sweet, cool water. "I mean, everything that involves a woman, silly."

He entwined his fingers with hers. "You may be surprised to hear that I have refined taste in a great many things, especially women."

She grew serious. "I know, Tristan. I do."

She did know. In spite of her sometimes-snide comments about his debauchery, she understood him a great deal—better than anyone. While others assumed he seduced other men's wives and preyed on the innocent and frequented brothels, Leticia knew somehow that he had always been selective. Little did she know he had recently become extremely selective. Could a man of his previous nature become celibate—at least temporarily? The thought left him wanting to gasp for air. But he was finished with meaningless affairs with meaningless women. The past year had almost fit the bill for celibacy, anyway, and he'd survived that.

She shifted but left her hand in his. "Can I get you anything—water or medicine?"

"Water."

While she poured a glass, he rolled over onto his side and propped himself up with his elbow, grateful his valet had dressed him in a nightshirt so Leticia wouldn't have to see more of his skin than she should. The compassion in her expression sent another bolt of guilt through him.

Softy she asked, "Are you in pain?"

"I think I'd rather have gotten shot in the shoulder again. That hurt in one place instead of my entire body." He drank from the glass.

"You're lucky you're alive. A fall that bad should have broken every bone in your body."

After handing her the glass, he lay back and closed

his eyes. Had Appleton suffered or had he died in an instant? His family must be overwhelmed with grief.

"I know." His throat tightened.

Leticia enfolded his hand in both of hers. He hung on to her as if she alone protected him from his demons. While she remained near, those demons stayed in the farthest shadows instead of surrounding and overwhelming him. He must do what he could to keep her untainted by his darkness.

"You shouldn't be alone in my room, Tish."

"You? Lecturing me on propriety?"

He opened his eyes and shot her a baleful glare. "As I seem to keep pointing out to you, I am aware of proper behavior."

She smiled, her expression gentle. "The door is open. Besides, I doubt anyone considers you a threat in your condition."

"I don't want you to suffer any more because of me. I've been a great disappointment to you." He gave up the struggle to keep his eyes open.

She laid a hand over his, so soft, so warm, so comforting. "That's no way to talk. Right now, you concentrate on getting better. We can discuss your many sins later."

Grimly, he said, "I don't want to talk about them. I want to stop committing them. I'm doing things differently from now on."

"Very well," she soothed. "Hush now; don't worry about it."

She didn't believe him; she was humoring him. He'd have to prove it to her. He had a great deal to prove to a great many people. He would change. He would show everyone he could be a better man.

Her voice sounded very near his ear. "Tristan, stop worrying. All will be well."

He released a long exhale and kissed her hand. "I'm glad you're here. You heal me." Holding her hand next to his cheek, he relaxed. The pain eased with her touch.

She wiggled her fingers out of his. "I should go and let you rest."

He gripped her hand. "Stay. Please stay."

She huffed her amusement. "A moment ago, you said I shouldn't be in your room."

"You shouldn't." He kissed her hand again and pressed it against his face.

"I'll check on you later this evening." Her clothes rustled as she arose, and she leaned over to kiss his cheek.

He lifted his head and turned his face to allow her easier access but at the last second, she turned her head the opposite way than what he'd anticipated. Their lips touched—an accident, of course, but shockwaves from the kiss nearly knocked him out of bed.

She didn't move away. He kissed her in earnest then. To his surprise, she responded. The softness of her lips, the gentleness, all wrapped up in her sweetness, filling him with a thrilling energy unlike any he'd experienced. He'd shared similar moments with scores of women, but none came close to the purity, the happiness, the safety of kissing Leticia. She embodied warmth and beauty and love. At last he'd found that missing piece of his life.

She gasped and drew back. He tried to focus on her face but the halo-like glow surrounding her blurred her expression. Was she shocked? Horrified? Repulsed?

He reached for her like a blind man reaches for a guide. "Leticia?"

She let out her breath hard, then laughed. "Oh, dear. I'm sorry about that. I didn't mean to do *that*."

She was sorry. But she didn't sound angry or repulsed. Encouraging, that. Her voice took on a faintly accusing tone. "Did you do that on purpose?"

"No. Well, not that first kiss. But I'm beginning to think I should have. A long time ago." He grinned.

"Oh, no, that would have been a very bad idea."

He hesitated, suddenly as terrified as a fifteen-year-old. "Did you like it?"

She let out a strangled laugh. "I've had better."

He jerked back which sent a bolt of fiery pain through his head. Better? She'd had better? Whom had she kissed? Richard? Kensington? Lord Bradbury? He'd call out them all, one by one. Pistols at dawn.

He moistened lips that ached—craved—to kiss her again. "How much better? Who?"

She took a few steps back until all he could see was the glowing whiteness of her gown. "I'll come visit you again tonight. Rest well."

Pain closed in around him, sending jagged, dark spikes into his vision. Fear engulfed him. If she left, he would die. "Don't leave."

"I have to go…I'm…"

Panic and agony stabbed at him from every direction. His breathing turned to gasping. He had driven her away. She feared he would try it again and couldn't stand to touch him. She personified purity and light, and he was filthiness. And they both knew it. But without her, he would drown.

"Tish!" Desperate, he gasped. "Don't leave."

"Here, drink this." She slid a hand behind his head, careful not to touch the bump in back and pressed a cup to his lips.

He gulped down the laudanum and reached for her, blinded by pain. "Stay. Please stay."

"Very well." She sat at the edge of the bed and let him hold her hand.

He fell asleep with her cool, soft hand in his, and dreamed of holding her in his arms.

Chapter Nineteen

Leticia left Tristan sleeping and hurried back to Aunt Alice's house to prepare for Lord Bradbury's arrival. She couldn't seem to keep her mind on the upcoming opportunity to view Wellington's private art collection. Every time she tried to put that kiss out of her mind, the touch of Tristan's lips burst back into her memory. An accident. Meaningless.

He'd seemed to enjoy it. Of course, as a rake, he doubtless kissed any willing female and enjoyed it.

She sighed at the unkind and untrue thought. Despite the jabs she sometimes poked at him, he didn't accept every offer that came his way. Even he had his scruples, after all—no barmaids or brothels, and he turned down other men's wives, so at least he respected those boundaries.

Still, if he took half the women for lovers that rumor suggested, he was a philanderer of the worst kind. His kiss meant nothing. He hadn't instigated it. Even that second time could be explained away by pure instinct. It meant nothing to him. It should mean nothing to her.

So why did she keep recalling the silky, sensual gentleness of his lips? Why did her body spring to life each time she remembered it as much as it had when their lips had met for that briefest of instants? A dull ache built in her stomach each time she relived it. A current swept her away, too strong to fight. She must at least keep her head above water.

All she wanted to do was run back there and kiss him again.

No, that path led to heartache. If she kissed Tristan again, she ran the risk of caring for him beyond their comfortable friendship. She'd best avoid all temptations regarding Tristan.

Perhaps her reaction sprang from her concern over his wellbeing. After all, seeing him in that terrible accident stirred up her emotions. Surely she ought not to trust any sort of passion until she'd recovered from the trauma of Tristan almost dying. Once that happened, all would return to normal and their association would once again be mere friendship.

With her maid's help, she changed into a pale pink walking gown and sat while the maid did her hair. She reached for her favorite blue pelisse, then remembered it had been ruined when Tristan had bled on it. The memory of his limp body, his closed eyes, the pallor of his skin, made her stomach lurch. She pressed a fist into her abdomen.

Calm down. He'd awoken, well, and with his wit intact…and with the softest lips she'd ever imagined.

She let out a growl. She should not think of Tristan this way. Lord Bradbury, a fine man who offered much, including a sterling reputation, ought to occupy her thoughts. She turned her mind to finding a pelisse to put on over her walking dress.

"The purple one, miss?" asked the maid.

"Yes, the purple one will do."

She buttoned the rich plum pelisse trimmed with gold cord that Aunt Alice had insisted on buying for her. After selecting a simple, understated bonnet, and picking up her kid gloves and reticule, she glanced in the mirror one last time. Her cheeks bloomed with more color than usual, as if she were feverish. Who would have thought kissing Tristan would have thrown her into such a state?

A footman appeared. "Lord Bradbury to see you, miss."

"Tell him I'll be right down."

She took a steadying breath, shutting out all thoughts of Tristan. Instead, she brought to mind Lord Bradbury's handsome face, the blueness of his eyes and the way they crinkled at the corners when he smiled. With a regal carriage that would have pleased Aunt Alice, Leticia descended the stairs, gliding one hand along the railing.

Lord Bradbury waited in the foyer, examining a painting. His tall, lean form, so fashionable in the clothing styles of the day, brought a smile to her lips. It was odd, really, how things had progressed between them in so short a time. She'd seen him every day this week. If that didn't qualify as courting, what did? Courted by a viscount. She almost laughed. Who would have thought that it would happen to a simple country miss? Her parents would be in raptures.

Leticia reached the bottom step and crossed the floor to him. "Lord Bradbury."

He turned with a smile that softened imposing features. "Miss Wentworth, you are a bright spot in my day."

She curtsied. With an impish playfulness she asked, "Oh? Difficult day at the House?"

"Not at all. However, the day has notably

improved." He lifted her hand to his lips.

Startled that he'd kissed her hand before she'd had a chance to put her gloves on, she withdrew from his touch. Gentlemen didn't usually go around kissing ladies' hands unless they had some sort of understanding...unless, of course, people did things differently in London than in the country. Though Lord Bradbury hadn't done anything shockingly wrong, it still seemed improper. Forward. Shallow. When Tristan had kissed her hand and held it to his cheek, there had been such sincerity, such need.

Of course, he suffered from a blow to his head, so she'd be a fool to read more into that than existed. There she went again, thinking of the wrong man.

After pulling on her gloves and bonnet, she took Lord Bradbury's arm and let him lead her to his waiting coach. A fine family crest adorned the door of the older but beautifully maintained landau.

"It's a lovely day for having the hood down." She smiled up at him.

"Yes, fortunately for us, there have been a few rare sunny days despite these strange, cold temperatures. I wished to take advantage of today's fine weather." He helped her in and swung up beside her with practiced ease. The liveried driver snapped the reins and they were off.

They chatted like old friends and she had the distinct impression that she'd known him for years—perhaps it sprang from his resemblance in manner to Richard.

Inside Cleveland House, they read about exhibits and Lord Bradbury told her about the ones on loan from Egypt, his animated expression endearing. He hadn't shown that much spark about anything else. As she strolled along on his arm, she caught several admiring glances cast by other women nearby. She wanted to smile smugly and walk a little taller. Still, his handsome looks and charm and title were all superficial reasons to want to be with him. She liked him. He was kind and attentive. She imagined marrying him and spending her days with him, cozying up by a fire reading or talking. A life of safety and comfort lay down that path. He'd even shown support for the school, so her cause didn't seem to bother him. Could she really educate the children and have a home and family of her own, too?

After a few hours, they found a bench and rested. He turned to her. "I've made arrangements to have that pianoforte shipped to your school but it may be a few weeks before it arrives."

"Oh! That's so very generous of you. How can I ever thank you?"

"Your smile is thanks enough."

She looked down. How could such a perfect man have come into her life?

"Is anything on your mind, Miss Wentworth?"

She looked up into his kind face in surprise. "Am I poor company?"

"Not at all but you're not quite as lively as usual." He paused. "I heard about the mishap with Mr. Barrett. Is that what ails you?"

The terror that had paralyzed her as she'd watched him fly over the horses and land in a broken heap overcame her again. She fisted her hands. "A frightening experience, to be sure, but he's conscious now."

"You're close friends, as I understand?"

"Yes, I've known him all my life. We played together as children." She winced. Discussing Tristan with Lord Bradbury felt wrong somehow, as if it were too intimate a subject.

"Is there anything more?"

"Between us? Oh, no. We're friends." Her face heated as their accidental kiss, and their not-so-accidental kiss, invaded her mind. Shockwaves shot straight down to her toes from the memory.

"He seems to hover around you, acting rather like a jealous lover."

Uneasy, Leticia waved off his words and huffed a forced-sounding laugh. "No, he's playing matchmaker. He has it in his head that I won't be happy until I'm married."

"You don't agree?"

"Well, of course I'd like a husband and a home and a family, but I can be happy without those, too. Not everyone marries, you know."

"True. I have an unwed sister and she's happy enough, I suppose. She sometimes laments children she never had."

"I'm planning to love all the children in our school."

He turned to her in surprise. "You'll be the teacher?"

"No, of course not, but I plan to be involved enough to become acquainted with them. Perhaps I'll teach them to play the pianoforte."

He nodded and fell silent for a moment. "So, you and Barrett don't have any sort of relationship beyond friendship."

"No, he's like a brother to me." Her cheeks heated

again as she recalled his kiss and the strange rush that flooded her body and soul. "Besides, I could never love a libertine. I want a husband who will be faithful. Is that selfish?" She watched his reaction. Most gentlemen of the *ton* seemed to view it as acceptable to keep a mistress even after marriage.

Without removing his focus from her face, he shook his head. "Not at all." He placed her hand against his, lining up their fingers as if measuring the difference. "Your hands are small." He curled his fingers around hers.

She should not hope a fine man like him had plans for a future with a girl like her. Her words came out in a rush. "My lord. I'm an outspoken person and I've never been very good at holding my tongue. The truth is, I very much fear to continue spending time with you if there's no future for us. I'm not asking for any promises, but if you would never consider marrying the daughter of a gentleman farmer from the country, I beseech you to stop calling on me."

He said nothing.

She continued, "It's not for my sake, alone, that I speak. If people see us together, they will draw conclusions and think you've raised my expectations. Then, if nothing comes of it, our reputations might be called into question, and that might also adversely affect my sister's prospects." Finally, she snuck a look up into his face.

He smiled, the kind of indulgent expression people often wear when they watch children at play. "My dear Miss Wentworth, if I were that shallow, I would never have called upon you in the first place. I spend time with you because I enjoy your company. I do not yet know if we have a future together, but I'm willing to explore that option. If our path lies down that road, marriage would be the ultimate destination."

"Oh." Chastened, she looked down at their hands. "I didn't mean to besmirch your honor by implying your intensions were, well, dishonorable but our difference in rank—"

"I'm well aware of our differences, and while my family hopes I'll make an advantageous match, I seek the kind of love my parents had. I'm willing to overlook an inferior status. Besides, your aunt's status may be enough to please them."

Overlook an inferior status ? He acknowledged her lower rank, yet accepted her, a country bumpkin with a paltry dowry, if he decided they would suit. Her cheeks burned at his reminder. At least he didn't balk at her forwardness. And he did give her a candid answer.

"Forgive me for being so direct, my lord."

"Not at all, Miss Wentworth. I find it refreshing. I find everything about you refreshing." He smiled with unmistakable fondness.

Her embarrassment faded. They spent the rest of the afternoon laughing and sharing memories, hopes, dreams, and even a few fears. A new layer of intimacy opened between them. By the time he took her home, she had already mentally composed the letter she'd write to her mother about her diverting afternoon.

Inside the foyer of her aunt's house, Lord Bradbury bowed. "A pleasure as always, Miss Wentworth."

A footman hurried up to Leticia and held out a note. "Miss Wentworth, the messenger said it was urgent."

She took the note. The seal bore the Averston

family crest and she recognized Elizabeth's graceful handwriting. Tristan! She glanced at Lord Bradbury, torn between wanting to read the message and not wishing to be rude.

Bradbury gestured to it and took a few steps back to allow her privacy. "Please." He turned away and pretended to study the view out the window.

Her heart thumping, she broke the seal and read.

Leticia,

I need you most urgently. Tristan is feverish and delirious and calling for you. Please come post haste.

Yours,

Elizabeth

"Oh, heavens. Tristan has developed a fever. Elizabeth wants me. I must go at once."

"Elizabeth Averston?"

"Yes." She turned to the footman. "Call the carriage."

"I'll take you," Lord Bradbury said.

"Thank you." To the footman, she said, "Please inform my aunt I've gone to Averston House."

In the ride over, she sat in the open landau with clenched hands and racing heart. Lord Bradbury slid both of his hands around hers. His touch should have comforted her but instead added to her jitters. When they arrived, he saw her in and waited while the footman summoned the lady of the home.

Elizabeth rushed in. "At last! Oh, forgive me, Lord Bradbury. I fear we're in a state here."

"Fever due to injury?" he asked.

"Yes, the doctor wanted to bleed him, but I rejected that." Elizabeth twisted her hands. "His injuries bled so much already that I couldn't stand the thought of him losing more. The doctor thinks I'm mad."

"If I may," Lord Bradbury said. "I know of a doctor who's a bit unconventional. He uses herbs, much like healers of old, and has had great success. He saved my sister's life last year."

Elizabeth glanced at Leticia as if seeking her counsel. Leticia nodded. She could never abide the practice of bleeding a sick patient, either.

"Very well," Elizabeth said. "Send for him, if you will."

Lord Bradbury nodded. "Right away."

Leticia bade him a good day and accompanied Elizabeth upstairs. As she pushed open the door to Tristan's room, a blast of heat met her. Tristan lay moaning and writhing on the bed. Running the last few steps to him, Leticia tore off her gloves and touched his face. The dry heat of his fever nearly burned her skin. He mumbled something but his words were intelligible.

"Oh, no. This is bad." After removing her bonnet and pelisse, she poured water into a bowl and bathed his face with a towel. "Elizabeth, have someone put out the fire and open a window."

Elizabeth put a hand to her face. "The doctor told me to keep it warm in here to burn out the fever."

"That's an old-fashioned practice." Leticia immersed the cloth and squeezed it out. "When Isabella had influenza two years ago, our doctor said we had to cool her, to bring down the fever, or it would keep burning. It worked. She improved right away. Trust me, this is better."

Elizabeth rang for a servant and opened a window near the bed. The cool evening air blew in, cooling the perspiration on her face. Tristan babbled in delirium.

Leticia bathed his face and rinsed the cloth over and over. Then she bathed his neck and chest, as far open as she could push the open neckline of his nightshirt, pushing up the sleeves of his shirt to reach his arms and hands. The cloth dried quickly under the heat of his fever.

"This isn't going to do enough for him."

A gentle knock at the door admitted the young Mrs. Harper.

Surprised to see the soon-to-be-school teacher, Leticia straightened. "What is it?

"I beg your pardon, but I heard my lord's brother is very ill."

"Yes, he is," Elizabeth said, her face pinched.

"May I help in some way?"

"That's kind of you to offer, but there's nothing anyone can do. We're trying to cool him, and we've sent for a different doctor. I don't see how you can help."

The petite young woman took another few steps into the room, her gaze moving to the bed. She faltered. "Oh, my, he's very handsome. He looks much like my lord Averston." An expression of horror crossed her face, and she shot a frantic look toward Elizabeth. "Forgive me, my lady. I meant no disrespect."

Elizabeth smiled. "You're right; my husband is a very handsome man. So is his brother."

The young teacher drew a breath. "My mother was something of a healer back home. In the old days, people would have called her a witch. Anyway, the whole village came down with scarlet fever. She saved them with a combination of herbs, and immersing their bodies in cool water. She learned that if the water is too cold, like that of a river, they sometimes die on the spot—I suppose it's too much of a shock. If she put them in a warm bath and then added cold water at little at a time, it brought down the fever."

Leticia stared at the girl. She'd said more in that explanation than she had during her interview. "Is that so?"

"Yes, ma'am. I'd bet my life on it. She saved nearly everyone in the village. I don't know what herbs she used, but I do know the cool water made a difference."

Leticia looked to Elizabeth who had already strode to the door. She summoned a servant and barked out orders. "Have a bath brought up and filled with tepid water. Then send in Tristan's valet and Cooper. You return, too. You're going to bathe an unconscious man." She eyed the large, capable-looking footman.

The footman paused, nodded, and ran to obey. Within minutes and after a flurry of movement and explained instructions, Elizabeth, Leticia, and Mrs. Harper stepped out of the room to allow the men to work. Mrs. Harper slipped away but Leticia sat with her hands clenched in the same chair she'd used the night she had waited for the other doctor to examine Tristan as he lay unconscious. Elizabeth paced. The minutes dragged on, and each tick of the clock in the corridor seemed to echo in her head. Elizabeth sank into a chair, folded her hands, and closed her eyes as if praying.

The head housekeeper approached carrying a tray. "I brought you some tea and bread, my lady, Miss Wentworth." She placed the tray on a table nearby and dragged a few chairs lining the walls to the table.

"Thank you," Elizabeth murmured.

They sat but Leticia had no appetite.

"I wish the doctor would hurry," Elizabeth said.

"I hope the cool bath helps."

Cooper came out then. "'e's cooler now. I don't know 'ow long it'll last, though. We took off th' bandages afore we put 'im in th' water." He paused, then added. "Th' wounds are sickenin'.'"

Icy pinpricks stabbed Leticia's skin.

Elizabeth stood. "They're septic?"

"Don't look good, milady."

Elizabeth paled. In a faint voice, she said, "Thank you for your assistance."

Leticia went cold all over. One by one, the men left the room. Leticia ran to Tristan and touched his face. Though cooler and no longer ranting, he lay so still and pale that she had to touch his chest to reassure herself that he still breathed. With the bandages off, the exposed gash on his forehead turned her stomach. With black stitches holding the open skin together and thick green liquid oozing from between the black threads, it looked ghastly. Leticia wanted to tear open the stitches and clean out the green sickness. But that might make him worse. They kept their vigil, bathing his face, praying for his recovery. What delayed the doctor?

Richard arrived and Elizabeth filled him in. He nodded. "I've heard of Dr. St. Ives. By all means, let him try." White-lipped with concern, Richard lay on the bed next to his brother and watched him as if willing him to get well.

A young man strode in, all confidence. "I'm Dr. St. Ives. Lord Bradbury sent for me."

Richard sat up. "Come in."

The doctor went straight to Tristan. With long,

slender fingers that reminded Leticia of a pianist, he gently probed the wound in his head, then began a thorough examination.

"Carriage accident, I understand?" The doctor ran his hands over every inch of Tristan's head, then turned Tristan so he could see the wound in back.

Richard watched everything the doctor did. "He was thrown clear."

Leticia stood, expecting to be ordered from the room but the doctor didn't acknowledge her or Elizabeth's presence. She pressed her hands together against her lips and held her breath.

"Any other major wounds?" Dr. St. Ives pushed back Tristan's eyelids and looked at his eyes.

Richard said in a low voice, "The head wounds are the worst."

The doctor continued his examination, then slid Tristan's shirt up to feel along his abdomen.

Leticia averted her gaze.

Dr. St. Ives looked up as if realizing others were in the room. "Ladies, perhaps you ought to step out, unless one of you is his wife?"

"Er, no." Leticia, with Elizabeth at her heels, left and closed the door behind them. "We seem to be doing an awful lot of waiting while others tend to Tristan."

"I know." With a heavy sigh, Elizabeth sat next to her. "They virtually imprisoned me here in this house while Tristan, Captain Kensington, and Cooper rescued Richard last year. I waited in pure torture."

"I cannot imagine." She took Elizabeth's hands and they sat in shared worry.

Tristan let out an agonized cry that brought them both to their feet, and sent Leticia's heart galloping.

From the other side of the door came voices. "Hold him."

"I'm trying," said Richard.

Tristan screamed. Elizabeth fell to her knees and prayed. Leticia put a hand over her mouth, fearing she'd cast up her accounts. What were they doing to him? More cries, then silence. Her heart thundered in her ears and her legs shook.

Unable to stand it another moment, she went to the door. "Richard?"

"Stay out!" Richard roared.

Tristan screamed again. Leticia's knees wobbled and she had to sit down. More screams and moans. She put her hands over her ears but couldn't shut out the sound.

The cries ceased. All fell silent.

Chapter Twenty

Tristan awoke, disoriented. His head throbbed. How much had he had to drink last night? He hadn't been this jug-bitten in...how long?

No, wait; he lay in his old room at Averston House in London. He'd know those bed curtains anywhere. Mother always liked *fleur-de-lis*. What had he drunk last night? He felt like a horse had trampled him.

Not a horse. A race. An accident. A fall.

The death of a friend.

He closed his eyes, willing himself back into oblivion, but remained awake. Heavy breathing next to him caught his attention. To his right, Richard lay curled up next to him, almost touching Tristan's shoulder. Funny, how he always thought Richard would sleep on his back like some kind of monarch, not curled up like a child. Elizabeth slept on a chair next to the bed.

Off to the left, someone sighed. Tristan turned to that side. Pain spiked at the motion. Leticia sat in a chair scooted up to the bed, the upper half of her body resting on the mattress next to him, her head lying on her arm, her hand resting on his stomach. Her relaxed face reminded him of a painting of an angel. Her perfect rosebud lips parted as if she awaited a kiss.

He relived their kiss, shocking in its sweetness. Every muscle in his body screamed at him to repeat that act. The next time, he wouldn't surprise her with it. He'd woo her and kiss her when he was sure she wanted it. She may not want it now, but he'd pursue her until she did. And he'd do a proper job of it next time.

She said she'd had better kisses. Well, he'd make sure she got better—from him.

Whom had she kissed? The thought nagged at him but he shut it down. It didn't matter. He'd make sure their next would convince her she never wanted one from another man.

The old Tristan waited for beautiful, experienced widows to pursue him and offer themselves to him. The new Tristan would do the pursuing. He would court Leticia. He'd be proper and persistent until she said yes.

A bolt of alarm shot through him. Say yes to what? More than a kiss, surely. But what? Marriage? Good heavens, did he truly contemplate marriage? He stumbled over that thought.

If he ever were to marry, Leticia would be the one he'd want for a wife. She had been the one constant in his life, next to Richard. Tristan liked Leticia. He trusted her. She'd be a faithful and loving companion.

With one finger, he traced the curve of her cheek, admiring the perfection of her ivory skin like a finely-crafted porcelain figurine created to portray an angel. He ached to encircle her with his arms, to guide her head in the hollow of his shoulder, feel the length of her body against him, love her as a man loves a woman.

He loved her. He loved Leticia.

All those other women had been small, pencil sketches compared to the real, larger-than-life, living color of Leticia.

He caressed her skin with the pad of his thumb,

then traced the curve of her lips. She stirred and he let his hand fall away. He'd have to move with care, take his time. He must prove his sincerity, that he had changed from the callow rake of his past. She would be hard to convince. Still, she alone knew him. If anyone would believe in him, she would, in time.

She turned her head, and yawned. Her eyes fluttered open. She blinked as if trying to focus. As she met his gaze, she smiled and raised her head.

What a beautiful sight—Leticia smiling! He wanted to wake up to that glorious smile every morning. Her smile inspired him. He could do anything. The possibilities took flight.

"Good morning," she whispered.

He grinned at her but the motion tore at his cracked lips. "Good morning yourself, you hussy, spending the night in a bedchamber with two men."

Smiling, she reached out a hand and touched first his cheek, then his forehead. He held his breath, loving her touch, but afraid to move lest he frighten her off.

"You're cool, at last." She cradled his head while she steadied the glass so he could drink. "You gave us another scare. I hope you're finished having fun at our expense."

"I make no promises." He paused. "Did I have a fever? I felt like I might set the bed on fire."

"Your wounds sickened but Dr. St. Ives came and cleaned it all out and applied herbs. Unconventional, but effective."

"I remember being cold, too, and feeling like I was drowning."

"We gave you a cool bath to help bring down the temperature."

He lifted a brow. "We? So…you bathed me?"

She let out a snort. "Yes. I bathed you. I got in the hip bath with you and we frolicked in the water like a couple of mermaids."

His grin broadened. "I'm sorry I don't remember that. You must have been glorious, all naked with your hair floating all around you."

"Shh! Gentlemen are not supposed to think naked thoughts about nice young ladies, much less use the word." A twinkle in her eye revealed the playfulness hidden behind her rebuke, and a blush bloomed in her cheeks.

Tristan portrayed the picture of contrition. "You're right. Forgive me. I vow from this moment on to be the perfect gentleman."

"That, I'd like to see."

He sobered. "You will, just wait. I am in earnest. I've considered my life, and I vow to be a better man. No more meaningless activities. I will no longer be Tristan the Rake, but I will be Tristan the Paragon."

"Paragon of what?" she teased.

"You may laugh now, but you'll see. I'm going to settle down and run for the House of Commons and push to help the poor. I may buy an estate of my own and become a responsible gentleman farmer."

"You?"

"I've made some very lucrative investments over the past year so I could do it."

"I see." She grew thoughtful, no longer teasing, but clearly unable to believe his words as anything more than idle talk.

He added, "And one day, I plan to marry."

She choked out a laugh and touched his forehead

again. "You *have* been very ill."

"I'll show you."

"I can't wait."

"He's been talking like that ever since that blow to the head." Richard's voice rumbled next to him, amusement lacing his gruff tones.

"I thought you'd be happy," Tristan said.

"I am happy." A rumpled Richard propped himself up on his elbow and smiled. "I hope you're in earnest. But don't do those things because that's what I want you to do; do them because you're really committed."

Leticia touched his arm again. "I think you'd be wonderful serving in the House of Commons. You're a natural leader and you're so good managing people and seeing to their needs. It's about time you embraced your potential."

"Thank you, Tish. I appreciate your faith in me." Did she believe he'd do it or merely being supportive? It didn't matter. He'd show them all he could be a better man.

****

Over the next few days, his vision cleared and the pain in his head subsided. Leticia visited him each day, bringing him news, and sometimes staying long enough to beat him at backgammon or chess. When his strength returned, he returned to his bachelor's rooms, which ended Leticia's visits. Her absence opened a void inside him.

With the return of his health, he turned his mind to the unpleasant task of calling upon Appleton's family. He dressed with care in all black except for his white cravat. He left off his usual stickpin, his signet ring his one adornment. After his valet, Bentley, finished,

Tristan checked his appearance in the mirror, frowning at the purple, green and yellow bruise on his forehead surrounding a large black scab. At least the lump had gone down. It resembled a large grape instead of an orange. The rest of the bruises on his face had faded to a greenish yellow-brown. Fortunately, he had not knocked out his teeth. He was lucky to be alive.

"Shall I have your…er, shall I hail a hackney?" Bentley asked.

Tristan shot his valet a look of sympathy. The man had been about to call for Tristan's curricle but it had been destroyed in the accident. Tristan would need a replacement, not to mention a new pair of carriage horses; his rider and his hunter were unsuitable for pulling a carriage. Tristan let out his breath and stared out the window. His last pair had been the finest, most perfectly matched team he'd ever seen. Good-natured, too, for racers. How sad to lose them.

"Sir?" Bentley prompted.

Tristan cleared his thoughts. "I'll walk to the mews and have a horse saddled."

The valet opened his eyes wide in alarm. "Are you sure you should walk that far, sir?"

"I'm well enough for a little stroll, thank you." He headed for the door but stopped and turned around. "Bentley…"

"Sir?"

"Thank you for your aid during my incapacitation. I'm most grateful."

"Oh, sir, I would have done more, but your family insisted on caring for you 'round the clock."

"I appreciate your faithful service. I fear I've taken you for granted."

Bentley bowed. "You are a kind master, sir, and it's my pleasure to serve you."

Uncomfortable with all the emotion, Tristan nodded and left. After walking to the mews, which left him surprisingly fatigued, he had to sit down while a groom saddled his favorite riding horse. Once astride, Tristan made his way to Appleton's family home. After handing the reins to a lad to take care of his horse, he stood on the steps, looking up at the *façade*, sick with dread and remorse.

He didn't have to do this. He could leave now and no one would be the wiser. The Appleton family did not expect him. They may not welcome his visit. Would he meet with blame? Hostility? Undiluted grief?

He must do this. He owed it to the Appleton family.

Tristan sucked in a ragged breath and wiped the perspiration off his brow. It was like marching to a firing squad. With another deep breath, he strode up the steps, tugged firmly on the brass knocker, and let it fall.

A butler opened the door, took one look at Tristan's obviously battered face and blinked. Understandable. Tristan looked like he'd gone twenty rounds with the champ in fisticuffs.

The butler glanced down at Tristan's attire and opened the door a little wider. "May I help you, sir?"

Tristan handed him his card. "I'm Tristan Barrett—a friend of Ronald Appleton. I was in the accident with him." His voice failed him. He cleared his throat. "I wish to convey my condolences to the family."

The butler opened the door wider. "Come in, Mr. Barrett. I'll inquire if the family is receiving."

Black cloth covered all the pictures, and a pall

hung in the air. As Tristan waited nervously in the foyer, he brushed an imaginary speck off his sleeve and resisted the urge to adjust his perfectly tied cravat.

Footsteps neared. "This way, Mr. Barrett."

Tristan steeled himself and followed the butler into a front parlor. Inside, a gentleman stood, dressed head to toe in severe black. He bore a striking resemblance to Appleton but with silver hair and a little extra thickness around the middle. He eyed Tristan, making careful note of every inch of him.

Tristan swallowed against a dry mouth, half expecting the man to pull out a gun and start shooting.

The gentleman spoke. "You were in the accident with my son, Mr. Barrett?"

"Yes, sir. I came to express my deepest regrets. And my condolences." A bead of perspiration ran down his back and he fisted trembling hands.

The man continued to take measure of him. A muscle in his jaw twitched.

Tristan tried to fill the silence. "I'm sorry for what happened."

Finally, the senior Mr. Appleton spoke. "Please sit." He gestured to a settee. "I understand you nearly lost your life, as well."

"I still don't know how I survived." Tristan looked the father in the eye. "I am so sorry about your son, sir. Truly I am."

Mr. Appleton met his gaze, his expression blank. "Did you challenge him?"

Tristan let out his breath in exasperation. "I don't remember that day or the events leading up to it at all."

"I see."

"In fact, I don't remember him having a new

equipage and team. He used to say when he got a good carriage and cattle that he'd put an end to my winning record, but I do not know if I challenged him or he challenged me. Regardless, I should not have raced him. He was inexperienced. I should have known better." Tristan resisted the urge to sink his head into his hands, and instead remained sitting upright.

The other man let out an uneven breath. "He loved to race. He once said he felt most alive then. He usually steeple chased. I had no idea he had ambitions for racing curricles, but it doesn't surprise me. He was always looking for a new challenge, something new to conquer."

"I shouldn't have let him race in a new curricle. I don't know what I was thinking..." Tristan cleared his throat. "I vow, if there were any way I could go back to that day and do it over..."

Mr. Appleton nodded. "I'm sure you do."

They sat in awkward silence until Tristan spoke again. "I didn't mean to intrude, sir. I wanted to tell you that your son was a good friend and...I'm sorry." His throat thickened, and his voice shook. He stood to leave.

Mr. Appleton stood with him and took a step closer. "I don't blame you, not really. If it hadn't been you, it would have been someone else. And from what witnesses told me, he lost control and ran into you."

Tristan nodded. "So they say."

"A piece of advice, young man; let go of the blame and live."

Let go of the blame and live. Could he?

"Thank you, sir..." Tristan's voice trailed off as emotion closed over his throat.

They shook hands, Tristan blinking back tears, and he left the Appleton home.

Let go of the blame and live.

Yes. That's exactly what he would do—live. Live the way he should. He paused halfway down the steps. With a final, long breath, he released the guilt and self-loathing and set off to become a brother worthy of Richard's good name. And Leticia's paragon.

Chapter Twenty-One

Flattening herself against the wall outside the door so as not to be too visible, Leticia peeked into the classroom of the charity school. Mrs. Harper's voice rang out with calm authority as she taught the alphabet to a classroom of seven children, and one girl in her teens, while the pot-bellied stove warmed the room. The girl from Mrs. Goodfellow's organization who'd asked to be taught her letters sat at the back of the classroom, gazing at the teacher as if she'd never seen anything so wondrous. Next to the letter A on the chalkboard, Mrs. Harper drew a picture of an apple and an angel with wings and a halo. Her artistic skills and unconventional approach had the children enraptured. Smiling, Leticia tiptoed away so as not to disturb them.

In her office near the foyer, Leticia sat at a desk. She glanced about, remembering Tristan moving furniture with confidence and strength and cheer. She sighed happily and went over the latest figures from the solicitor. She nodded in satisfaction. They still had their year's worth of cushion, so they had plenty of time to garner more pledges before they'd need money again.

The door swung open and footsteps crossed the wood floor. Curious, she arose and went out into the foyer.

Tristan stood there, looking around as if he'd never seen the place. Crossing the room to him, she frowned.

"What are you doing here? Shouldn't you still be abed?"

He grinned, despite his drawn and pale face. "The doctor said as soon as the pain in my head passed and my vision cleared that I could get up."

"You've been up too much today; you look like you're about to swoon."

"I never swoon." His outrage came out fainter than he intended.

She took his hand and gave it a tug. "Come sit."

"Weren't the walls red?"

She almost laughed until she realized he was in earnest. "No."

"I remember them being red."

Leticia eyed him in concern. She led him to the nearest chair and tugged on his hand until he sat. From a nearby tea service, she poured him a cup of tea and added two lumps of sugar the way he liked it. "No, we had them whitewashed before the furniture arrived, but they were unpainted before."

He frowned. "Huh." He sipped the tea.

She waited to see if the color came back into his face. "How do you feel?" She resisted the urge to touch his face.

"Better." He finished the tea and set down the cup. "Where did you find that doctor? He seems to know what he's doing."

"Lord Bradbury recommended him. He practices in the country but comes frequently to London to help children in an orphanage. We're lucky he came to town."

"Bradbury." Why did his tone sound more like a grumble?

"Before Dr. St. Ives came, your head wounds were festering and you were burning up with fever. He cleaned out the sickness and applied herbs to the wounds."

"I'm indebted to Bradbury, then." His expression slumped.

"Well, yes, I suppose in a way since he sent Dr. St. Ives who, as I understand, was a doctor in the war but where he learned about herbs, I can't imagine."

Tristan hunched over and rested his head in his hands.

Leticia studied him. "Why have you come today?"

"I…" He paused. "I went to see Appleton's family today, to pay my respects."

Oh, poor Tristan! What a kind and thoughtful—not to mention courageous—gesture to make to the family. She put a hand on his arm. "That must have been difficult."

He let out a long exhale. "His father forgave me. He told me to stop feeling guilty. I didn't expect that."

Leticia kneeled in front of him. "He's right. Stop punishing yourself. You didn't cause the accident."

He nodded, his head still in his hands. A lock of dark hair tumbled over his brow, so much like the Tristan of her youth.

"Are you in pain?" She brushed his hair back away from his face and admired the way his curls caressed her fingers.

"My head hurts a little." His gaze moved to a vase of flowers Lord Bradbury had sent her, his card nestled among the blooms. Pain flitted over his expression but he cast it off with a lazy smile. "So, you and Bradbury?"

Donna Hatch

She looked down. Why did discussing Lord Bradbury with Tristan feel so awkward? She'd never had trouble sharing her thoughts with him before. Since they'd kissed, everything changed. The mere mention of Lord Bradbury to Tristan resonated like an insult or a betrayal…to Tristan. But that made no sense. Tristan was not, could not, be a suitor. He would never settle down, much less be constant to any one woman.

Tristan waited, watching her.

Leticia shrugged. "He has called upon me. I have no true expectations at this point." Marrying Lord Bradbury seemed a glamorous dream, but empty of true meaning, or joy.

She shook herself. He was perfect. She should be enthusiastic at the idea, not wishing he made her feel the way Tristan did. She should cast off these unfair comparisons. She knew Tristan. Lord Bradbury represented a mystery. That had to be the explanation for her conflicted loyalty.

"He seems to fit your criteria." Tristan stared out the window.

"Yes, he does."

His eyes narrowed, but when he returned his gaze to her, something akin to urgency entered his expression. "Don't rush into promising yourself to him, Tish."

His words took her aback. "I won't."

"I mean it. I know he seems a good match, and he's a lord, but you have time and you have plenty of other prospects."

"Captain Kensington, you mean?"

He winced. "And others. Please don't hurry into accepting him because you think he's your one

226

chance."

She took his hand and held it as warmth and friendship and something unexpected came over her. "I promise I won't rush into anything." She smiled. "I know you're against the institution of marriage, but I seem to recall you encouraging me to find a husband."

"I'm not against marriage. I...I might do it...someday."

"Really?" she drawled. "You? I don't believe it."

He looked away. "Do you have any idea how it feels to believe you'll be alone for all of your life?"

At his tone and expression, her teasing mood evaporated. She whispered, "Yes. I do."

He put a hand over hers. In a hushed voice, he said, "I don't want that for you."

"I don't want that for you either."

He met her gaze. A new intensity she'd never seen in him overtook his features. "I know you think I'm a wastrel, Tish, but I—"

She put a finger over his lips. "Shhh. I think you're a good man who's a little lost."

His eyes shifted back and forth as if searching for something. "I don't think I'm lost anymore. I know what I want; I want my life to count for something, to have meaning."

She smiled. Perhaps he truly walked the path to finding himself, after all. "I know you do."

"Have faith in me, Tish."

"I always have."

The color drained out of his face and he slumped over again.

She put a hand on his back. "Come. Let's get you back home."

He lifted his head. "I wanted to see the school now that it's open."

"Another day. Did you come in a hackney?"

"My horse is outside."

With his pallid skin and wilting posture, he didn't look strong enough to ride a horse. "Wait here." She found the school caretaker and asked him to hail a hackney. When she returned to Tristan, he had nearly folded in half. "Come, there's a hackney outside."

He didn't resist as she helped him stand and put an arm around her. She snatched up her pelisse and reticule on the way out. Outside, she instructed the boy tending his horse to tie it to the back of the hackney. Though she ought to put Tristan inside and send him off alone, Leticia climbed in with him. Surely no one would know if she had taken a short ride in a closed carriage with him. Besides, this was Tristan; he was like a brother to her.

Tristan gave his direction to the jarvey and then leaned back against the seat with his eyes closed and his mouth drawn in pain.

Leticia pursed her lips. "You overdid it. You need to pace yourself."

"Don't scold. I wanted to see the school. And you. Maybe I should move back in with Richard and Elizabeth so you can visit me again." His gaze slid her way.

"You probably should have stayed with them until your recovery is complete."

"Yes, I should have, for more than one reason. Will you visit me if I do?"

"Technically, a lady never calls on a gentleman, but yes, I'll come visit Elizabeth if you wish while you're there."

Smiling, he leaned his head back and closed his eyes. "I can live with that. I'll call on you, too."

What he meant by that, she refused to guess. After seeing him home, she returned to the school. The children had already gone. Upon completing her paperwork, she bade Mrs. Harper a good day and stepped outside.

A dark figure leaped out of the long shadows. He grabbed her arm and put a knife to her throat. Leticia's cry of alarm choked her.

"No one wants yer school, ducks," he hissed. "It ain't righ', teaching girls t' read. Shut it down or I'll do it myself, got it?" Eyes blazed underneath a hat drawn low over his face.

"Wh-who are you?" she managed through terrified gasps.

"Close the school, ya 'ear me?" The knife pressed against her neck.

Frantic, she nodded.

He removed the knife and slipped away. Leticia's legs wobbled. She staggered back inside and shut the front door. Her knees buckled and she slid down to a seated position. With her hand over her eyes and her back against the door, she sat gasping while her heart thundered in her ears. She couldn't think or move. Focusing on breathing, she sat until Mrs. Harper found her.

"Miss Wentworth!" Footsteps and rustling skirts hurried toward her. "Are you feeling poorly?" Mrs. Harper asked.

Did she dare tell her? It might have been an idle threat. If that were the case, Leticia would worry Mrs.

Harper for no good reason.

Leticia moistened her lips. "I got set upon…by a thief." Her fright crashed down on her, the reality of her peril and own vulnerability. A sob burst out of her.

Mrs. Harper gasped. "Did he hurt you?"

Leticia shook her head. When she could speak again, she managed, "No, I'm not hurt—only a bit overset."

"I should say so. Come into the kitchen and we'll get you a cup of tea."

Grateful to allow Mrs. Harper to fuss over her, Leticia sat at the kitchen table while Mrs. Harper fixed tea all the while shooting worried glances in Leticia's direction.

Leticia pulled herself together. "Forgive me for alarming you."

"What did he take?" Mrs. Harper set the sugar and creamer on the table.

"Take?"

"The thief. What did he take?"

Blink. "Er, nothing."

"A thief took nothing?"

Leticia let out a sigh. She couldn't mislead Mrs. Harper. "I'm not certain he was a thief. He seemed to be more interested in warning me. About the school. There are some in the community who do not approve of what we do here."

Mrs. Harper nodded, her expression thoughtful. "Ignorance breeds fear. Not so long ago, men believed women should never learn to read—forbidden in most places."

"Perhaps they feared we'd no longer want families if we got an education."

"Or that women would no longer submit ourselves to brutality," Mrs. Harper said darkly.

Intrigued, yet almost fearful at what she would learn, Leticia eyed her. "Is that your experience?"

"The strong always prey upon the weak. Reading gives one strength, a power most don't understand. When one is kept ignorant, he or she is easier to dominate. A lot of men feel women should be ruled. If we learn to read, we might decide we deserve honesty and respect. Not all men are willing to give that."

Fortunately, all the men close to Leticia valued women's minds and hearts. Not everyone did, as evidenced by the scene in the tea shop when Lord Petre tried to bully her, and the man with the knife today.

They sat sipping tea while outside a church bell rang and a child sang off key. Leticia's nerves smoothed over, her fear giving way to anger. How dare people try to stop something as wondrous as reading! A proper education may very well be the key to reducing poverty and despair.

Leticia set down her teacup. "If you are to stay here, you need more protection than one caretaker and a maid-of-all-work."

"Surely his was an idle threat."

Leticia touched her throat. "No, I'm certain he was in earnest."

Mrs. Harper straightened. "I refuse to be intimidated."

The young teacher possessed admirable spirit. "Being intimidated would be closing the school, which we shan't do. All I'm asking you to do is exercise caution. Come home with me tonight, and stay until we can arrange for other accommodations where you will have better protection."

Mrs. Harper nodded. "Perhaps you are right."

Within minutes, Mrs. Harper had packed a portmanteau and they took a hackney home. On the way, the teacher related the children's progress and their delight in learning, all the while her face glowing with pleasure.

Leticia vowed to do whatever it took to continue the school and bring hope to the downtrodden.

Chapter Twenty-Two

Inside the London study of the Duke of Suttenberg, Tristan shook the duke's hand. "I thank you, Your Grace, for your guidance, and will give that serious thought."

"My pleasure." Grinning, the duke eyed him. "I must say, I am a bit surprised you are considering serving in Parliament. I admit, I don't know you well, but your reputation does not paint you as that sort."

Tristan winced. "I admit I had a few wild years, but I have grown dissatisfied with the emptiness of it all. I had a rather eye-opening experience that has given me reason to consider my purpose. I wish to do something that matters. This may be what I seek."

The duke regarded him with thoughtful eyes. "Serving king and country is a great place to start. There are other ways one can find meaning—small and simple ways."

"Like the school my sister-in-law and Leticia Wentworth have funded."

"Yes, a worthy cause to be sure. Also, simply placing another's wishes ahead of your own can be strangely gratifying."

Tristan considered. Aware of a hovering servant who no doubt bore a message for His Grace, Tristan bowed, thanked him again, and left the ducal residence with clearer goals and a knowledge of requirements he must meet in order to serve as a Member of Parliament. He had only to decide now if he should take this path.

Wordsworth said:

"...And what in quality or act is best
Doth seldom on a right foundation rest,
He labours good on good to fix, and owes
To virtue every triumph that he knows... "

Leticia would, no doubt, approve if he went into Parliament. However, he refused to take a position simply to impress her or prove to her he'd changed. No, he must be certain he wished to serve in order to make a meaningful contribution.

"Barrett!" Armand Palmer called and waved.

Tristan looked up at the familiar voice. "Good afternoon, Palmer."

"I haven't seen you in an age. Where've you been?"

Did he not know? "Recovering from the accident." Not that Palmer or any of his friends had paid him a call.

Palmer sobered. "Oh right. Bad luck, that. Appleton was a good egg—miss the bloke. Miss you, too. Good to see you up and about. You looked half dead when they carried you off. Do join me. Catch up, and all that rot."

"Where are you bound?"

"The White Stag." Palmer launched into a favorite drinking song.

Tristan glanced around in the event anyone might have overheard the bawdy song, but no one of polite company seemed to be nearby. "Thank you, but I have another engagement. Perhaps another time."

"As you wish. Good to see you. Truly."

"You, as well."

They bade farewell and parted. Odd, but Tristan hadn't missed his old friends. He'd been so involved in finding prospects for Leticia, then recovering from his accident, he had failed to notice their absence. Still, he should have jumped at the opportunity to enjoy the comfortable familiarity of their friendship. Time in their presence held little appeal at the moment, however. Perhaps the group held less interest without Appleton.

How sad that he didn't remember those last few moments of Appleton's life. It seemed too cruel that fate snatched away their last moment as friends.

Or perhaps fate had given him a gift. Memories of Appleton's laughing face as they steeple chased, their outrageous dares, bets and other tomfoolery, remained untainted by the scene of his death.

Tristan rode through the streets under a cloudless sky, passing St. James Park as a balloon rose from the trees like a silvery sunrise. As a child, he'd ridden a gas balloon, a rare, cherished memory with his father and brother. His mother had declined, choosing to wave at them from the ground. She'd been happy then, giving no indication she would one day leave.

Richard had hung on to the basket with one hand and to the back of Tristan's coat with the other—always protecting Tristan. Tristan had laughed and leaned out as far as he could, exhilarated at the sensation of flight. As he grew, he considered such past times mundane. Still, racing and drinking and carousing had not eclipsed sweet family moments such as balloon rides.

He arrived at Mrs. Tallier's house, but paused at the front steps. Was today their at-home hours? Did it matter? He and Leticia had been friends so long that

Donna Hatch

they never used to stand on ceremony, but now that he sought to be respectable, should he observe social niceties such as a lady's at-home hours?

If Tristan were to win Leticia's heart away from either Captain Kensington or Lord Bradbury, he must use any advantage. Moreover, he was already here.

Leticia, Isabella, and Mrs. Tallier greeted him in the parlor. Tristan's focus narrowed on Leticia.

She eyed him. "Are you feeling better?"

"Yes, yes, no need to worry. I am feeling quite the thing."

She smiled and all seemed right with the world. If only that smile could greet him every morning and be the last thing he'd see at night.

She approached him. "Are you sure you're well?"

He grinned and took her hand. "Never better. It's a sunny day. Come enjoy it with me. We could ride to the park. Go on the balloon, if you so desire."

"The gas balloon?"

"Have you ever done it?"

She faltered, cast a glance in the direction of her sister and aunt. "No, but I can't today."

"No? You aren't afraid of heights, are you?" he teased.

"I can't go today. I…already have plans."

"Oh? It's too late for shopping. What are these plans?" He gave her his most charming smile.

She hesitated again. "I'm going riding with Captain Kensington."

He deflated. Kensington. Curse the man. He had claimed no interest in marriage, so why take Leticia riding?

Tristan mustered on and collected his smile. "No

236

matter. How about the theater tomorrow? Richard and Elizabeth will be there, too. You are all welcome." He spread his arms to encompass the other two ladies.

A pained expression overcame Leticia. "We are already going with Lord Bradbury."

He swallowed. His brilliant plan to find her a respectable husband appeared to be paying off...too well.

She squeezed his hand. "I'm sorry, Tristan. I can go with you Friday afternoon, if you wish."

He clawed at his composure and summoned a *savoir faire* expression. "Of course, Tish. No matter. The weather may dictate our actions. If the weather is clear again, we shall brave the gas balloon. If not, perhaps..." he had no clear social calendar and could think of nothing to suggest.

"I have yet to view the Parthenon Sculptures," she suggested.

He raised a brow. "I didn't realize you were a connoisseur of art."

"Not necessarily, but I do enjoy seeing items of historical interest and taking in sights unique to London."

"Your wish is my command, fair lady. We shall view the marble sculptures at the British Museum." He released her hand, stepped back, and made a low, flourishing bow. Turning to Leticia's aunt and sister, he bade them all good day and left.

Outside, Tristan let out a huff. So much for his plan. At least he had Friday. He toyed with the idea of joining Palmer and his other friends at the White Stag and drinking away his cares. The lure of mind-numbing drink and laughing with his old friends called to him like a siren's song.

That would put him back on that same path leading to the same dead end where he'd wallowed far too long. People counted on him. Cared about him. He had a reason to live—not exist for the next mindless pleasure.

Taking advantage of the clear, cloudless day, he walked, not paying attention to his direction as he scrambled to find his own place in the world. Richard had always known his place; as a child, he'd been groomed to be the next earl and he excelled at his duties. When they were younger, Richard had taught Tristan some matters of estate as a side-thought in the unlikely event something happened to Richard, but Tristan had never paid much attention to the instruction, instead studying literature and poetry for his own enjoyment. He got his degree at Cambridge almost by accident.

But now, now he wanted—needed—more. An identity. A purpose. Perhaps he could help Richard by taking over the management of one or two of the properties. It would have the dual purpose of lightening Richard's heavy load so he could focus on his wife. Helping Richard could be a gesture of gratitude for all the years that he'd watched over Tristan, and it might help in Tristan's search for his own purpose.

He sent a note to Richard, asking to meet him outside of Parliament tomorrow after the next session. Richard's reply came promptly.

The following afternoon, he dressed in fashionable yet understated clothing and set out for Parliament. Outside, he gazed up at the timeless structure that had helped shape British history and law. To be a part of that felt a sobering responsibility.

Members of Parliament left the building in small groups and Tristan wandered up the long sidewalk to the front steps, staring like a gawking child at the graceful spires pointing heavenward. He felt small. Yet, to be connected with something that grand, that important appealed to him.

Richard strode down the steps between the Duke of Suttenberg and Lord Bradbury, their expressions light. Richard's laugh rang out and he shook his head. Tristan grinned at the contagious sound. Since his marriage, Richard smiled and laughed more often. He gave all the credit to Elizabeth.

The moment Richard caught sight of Tristan, his posture changed—not tense, but...what? Wary? Expectant?

"Tristan," he called. "Come to White's?"

Tristan nodded and waited for them to approach. They exchanged greetings, the other two lords declining an invitation to accompany them, and Tristan joined his brother in Richard's waiting coach.

Seated across from Tristan, Richard eyed him. "What is on your mind?"

Tristan clasped his hands together. "Don't laugh. And don't faint. But I am here to ask you if I can help with the estate. Or anything."

Richard's eyebrows shot up.

Tristan added, "I could take over some small detail. Perhaps manage one of the properties, or help with a specific aspect that affects all of them. I don't know much about crops, but I have a passing knowledge of structures, bridges..." He shrugged. It had all sounded better in his head. Now that he had voiced it, it seemed paltry.

Richard cocked his head to one side. "You want to help? Why?"

"I want to do something to pay you back for all the times you've been there for me. I'd like to try to ease your burdens. To be honest, I don't know what to suggest, except..." an idea came to him as he spoke. "I could visit some of the properties, inspect the house and the tenants. Speak with the stewards. You wouldn't have to travel as much. You could spend more time with your wife."

Richard's disbelief transformed to speculation and then serious consideration. "I could have you view the property in Northumbria—I haven't been there in years. And I have never visited the property in Cornwall that came as part of Mama's dowry. It's fallen into a fair state of disrepair with only an aged caretaker."

Tristan nodded. "I'd be happy to see what it needs. I could go to both places."

Richard studied him. "What's on your mind?"

Spreading his hands out, Tristan searched for an answer. He shook his head, rejecting every poetic phrase that entered his mind. Richard hated when Tristan waxed poetic. Finally, he settled with, "I owe you much, so I thought you were the one I should try to help first."

A pause. A long one. Richard went still, a sign of deep thought. At last, he shifted and gave a loose wave. "Very well, I welcome the assistance. Cornwall is a higher priority. It will take you at least a week to get there, and this time of year, the roads could be bad. Perhaps visit this summer, but in the meantime, open a correspondence with the caretaker?"

A week. If he left town to oversee that property,

he'd be gone two and a half to three weeks, which would take him away from Leticia for far too long. But if that's what Richard needed, Tristan would see to it.

He nodded. "I'll begin at once."

Richard's mouth quirked to one side. "You're serious about this."

"I am." Tristan looked him straight in the eye.

As if realizing the reason for Tristan's change in behavior, Richard sobered. "You don't have to do this as penance, you know."

Tristan studied his hands before spreading them wide. "I want to do more. I want to *be* more."

Richard leaned forward and placed a hand on his shoulder. "Then let's help you find more."

"Thank you."

For the first time in who knew how long, Tristan had goals; learn all he could about the possibility of running in the next election for the House of Commons, ease some of Richard's burdens, help Elizabeth and Leticia with their school, and become a man who could hold up his head in polite company, the kind of man Leticia deserved.

If he were to crowd out Kensington and Bradbury, he must get more creative. No matter. He excelled at creativity. He looked forward to the challenge of winning the heart and hand of his dearest friend, whom he could never let out of his life.

Chapter Twenty-Three

Leticia fastened the frog closures of her plumb-colored pelisse, and donned a bonnet before she went to the morning room to await Tristan. She sank into a striped armchair and put on her kid gloves.

Why on earth had Tristan been so insistent on taking her somewhere? And why did he seem so crushed when she explained her plans with Lord Bradbury and Captain Kensington? The idea that Tristan would be jealous…no, a ludicrous thought.

What would it be like to be pursued by a man like Tristan, though? She almost sighed at the thought. Memory edged into her mind of her lips accidentally brushing his. The shock of that contact had sent alternating hot and cold chills straight down to her toes. Then he'd kissed her a second time and…oh my…

Instinct must have prompted that second kiss—nothing more. Heaven help her if he ever kissed her on purpose!

Perhaps all kisses were so exhilarating. She tried to imagine sharing such a moment with Lord Bradbury, a remarkably handsome man, as well as kind and attentive, with a wry sense of humor. She'd enjoyed viewing the Bridgewater Collection at Cleveland House with him. How would his kiss affect her? Somehow the idea fell flat. Perhaps she would not know until she shared such a moment with him.

Or Captain Kensington? He had not actively courted her, but he'd sought her out on occasion. Also handsome and kind, with a lively, albeit dark humor, the captain would make a desirable husband. In moments, she detected an underlying sorrow, the source of which she had yet to learn. He was mysterious. What would it be like to kiss him? That thought also failed to invite any excitement.

The idea of kissing Tristan—a real, purposeful kiss, left her breathless.

No. No. *No*. She must not think of a notorious *roué* in such a way. She remained safe as long as he stayed in the realm of her friend. Anything more would be a dangerous, foolhardy risk to her heart and peace of mind.

The front door knocker echoed through the foyer, and Leticia rose to greet Tristan. His smile met her. Stylish as usual but wearing grays and blues instead of his usual, more vibrant colors, he stood, tall and lean. His eyes, clearer than she'd seen in years, sparkled.

"Good afternoon, Tish." His grin warmed her all over.

"Good afternoon, yourself. The weather appears to have bent to your will."

"Because I asked for your sake, I am sure." He affected a bow. "Are you prepared for a balloon ride?"

The nervous quiver in her stomach increased to that of a small cyclone. Still, it would not do to appear as frightened as a kitten in a den of wolves; Tristan would surely tease her for years.

She lifted her chin and gave a negligent wave of her hand. "Oh, certainly. I always do such things. They're hardly exciting any more. Perhaps I'll go on safari next."

Grinning, he offered his arm. "I hope elephants and tigers don't bore you. You might want to bring a warm cloak—it's much cooler up there."

Up there. Heaven help her.

Tristan smiled, so handsome and steady, that she squared her shoulders and grabbed a cloak.

Tossing the cloak over her arm, she said with false courage, "Lead on, good sir."

Outside, an elegant barouche bearing his family coat of arms awaited them, complete with a driver and four horses. Battling back her nervous anticipation, she forced cheer into her voice.

"A barouche. How stylish."

"It's Richard's. I know it's ostentatious but my curricle was irreparable." He drew a breath, his expression grim. The knot of his cravat moved as he swallowed. "I've ordered a phaeton and am having it built lower than the usual style so it would be more stable, and not require a ladder."

"Sounds reasonable." Still fashionable, but safer with four wheels instead of two like his curricle, a phaeton would be much steadier, especially if he had it lowered. The accident appeared to have instilled a sense of Tristan's own mortality.

He glanced at her as if searching for a meaning behind her words. "I will never race again."

His earnest, sorrowful expression tugged at her heart. A pity he must cast off a pastime that he clearly loved. Still, his recognizing the folly of engaging in such danger meant he'd be less likely to repeat it.

She touched his arm. "I look forward to seeing your new phaeton."

His grim expression softened. "I'll take you for a drive as soon as it's completed."

"I've never ridden in one."

"Good. Then I look forward to being your first."

A glint touched his eyes as he handed her into the luxurious conveyance and she sank into seat cushions softer than a feather bed. The folded down hoods made the vehicle perfect for seeing the sights of London. Being seen with Tristan made her want to sit up a little taller.

"Have you purchased a new team of horses?" she asked.

He shook his head. "I didn't see any I liked at Tattersalls, but I'll go again next week. My phaeton won't be ready for another two weeks at least; I have time." His dark eyes carried a luster in them she had not seen in years, and his steadiness gave him a new maturity.

She gazed at him, amazed at his transformation. "I've never seen you so bright-eyed. At least, not in years."

He quirked a brow.

She searched for an explanation. "The more dissipated you grew, the more your eyes dulled. And then when you were hurt... Well, I'm glad to see you looking so well."

His expression took on a far-away look that reminded her of the poetic romantic he'd been as a youth. "Too much drink has lost its appeal. I rather like having a clear head."

She touched his hand where it rested on the seat between them. "I like it, too."

The coachman turned into the park entrance. As

they went deeper inside the haven of green, the noises of the city faded. The balloon rose above the trees like a giant, silver sun.

A quiver of excitement raced through her. "I've always wanted to ride in one of those."

"Why haven't you?"

"Our schedule is busy. Besides, my aunt thinks they are dangerous." She finally admitted, "I'm a bit frightened at the thought."

"It's very safe, I promise." Tristan looked ahead. "We're here."

In a wide expanse of grass, a small crowd formed a circle underneath an airborne balloon tethered by ropes. A shimmer of silver wrapped up in an elongated ball soared overhead. The coachman drove them closer, revealing the balloon's immensity, though it floated perhaps a hundred feet above the lawn.

Awed, Leticia craned her neck. "It's huge."

As Tristan helped her down from the barouche, she could hardly keep her eyes off the magical-looking craft.

"I'm happy to have impressed you." A chuckle touched his rich voice.

Dragging her gaze away, she eyed Tristan who stood half a head taller than she. His hand, still on her arm, warmed through the fabric of her clothes to her skin. His scent, familiar but somehow more masculine-than-ever, burrowed deep inside her.

His eyes danced over her face, an odd combination of intensity and joy. "Your eyes look very green today, Tish." The intensity vanished and her childhood playmate returned. He tapped her underneath the chin, snapping her out of whatever madness had seized her.

"Shall we ride your balloon?"

She pushed back the quiver in her stomach and wound her arm around his. "Have you ever ridden one?"

"A few times as a child."

She nodded and swallowed, but the nervousness only grew. Tristan paid their fare and led her toward the balloon. As they approached the send-off point, several men pulled on ropes as thick as their wrists to bring the balloon back to its starting place. The balloon sank to the earth, bringing a large basket filled with passengers. Workers tied the ropes while others attached large bags of sand to keep the balloon down. Starry-eyed adults and a few wide-eyed children climbed out of the large wicker basket using stepladders. Excited chatter filled the air as the passengers related their experiences. None of them looked terrified. She gulped.

A couple in line in front of them got in next, and the balloon rose, soaring effortlessly above them. Her nerves eased at the awe-inspiring sight.

"Amazing." Leticia breathed.

Tristan stood next to her, letting her experience it without interruption. Strange how he always seemed to know what she wanted. Richard had never been in such harmony as she was with Tristan. Her love for Richard must have muddied her connection to Tristan.

What if the feeling she had always harbored for Richard had, in fact, been some form of hero worship instead of a healthy love between potential man and wife? She would have to give that further thought. It might help her identify her feelings with regard to Lord Bradbury and Captain Kensington.

Several minutes later, men with arms the size of

pugilists hauled the air craft down using its ropes.

"The balloon stays tethered the whole time?" Leticia asked.

"It does," Tristan said. "We can't go flying all over London looking in people's windows, you know."

She tried to give him an answering smile but it probably came out wobbly.

"Almost our turn," Tristan said.

Leticia donned her heavy cloak. Her fingers trembled as she fastened the frog closures.

Tristan's sure hand held her steady as she mounted the stepladders on either side of the wicker basket. Her legs shook so badly she had to grasp the other pair of hands outstretched to help her. As Tristan climbed in after her, she peered around tanks and handles and gazed up at the balloon over her head. Harnesses connecting to ropes attached the basket to the ornate balloon, covered by some kind of netting, created an intricate network.

"Welcome," the balloon operator said. "I'm your pilot. It's a clear, still day—perfect for a balloon ride." He grinned, his craggy face and missing teeth reminding her of an old sea captain.

"Excellent," Tristan said.

"Release the ballasts," the pilot called out.

As he opened a valve and pulled on a lever, workers removed the sand bags. They lifted off in a smooth, effortless rise. The ground fell away. Trees and people and buildings shrank below her. Fear arose and cut off her breath. Nothing seemed connected to her. What if she fell out of the basket? What if the balloon caught fire? What if the tethers broke and they floated away and never came back down? Her breath came in harsh bursts.

"Nothin' t' worry about, miss," the pilot said. "All very safe. I've been doing this for ages."

"If memory serves, this is powered by a type of gas called hydrogen?" Tristan asked the pilot.

"Aye. Makes the balloon lighter than air so it can go up."

Up. Up and away from the ground. So far up...

Tristan touched her shoulder. "Tish?"

She turned to him, unable to speak.

Without a word, he drew her into his arms and held her while she trembled. He rubbed circles on her back, slow and soothing. "We're safe. Hold onto me."

Burrowing into him, she clutched him as if he alone protected them all from a horrible death. He held her, steady, strong. The mint in his clothes mingled with his bay rum aftershave and that uniquely adult Tristan scent, calming her fears—familiar and yet different in a way that left her baffled. His strong arms held her against his solid chest.

His beloved voice rumbled through her. "Look Tish—you will want to see this."

Without moving, she opened her eyes. London Bridge, the spires of Parliament, the Thames winding like a shining pathway sprinkled with stardust—all of London lay before her like a detailed, colored map. Ships and other watercraft dotted the river like a child's toys. The ocean's great expanse shimmered in the distance. Land formations she never knew existed now revealed themselves in the layout below. Absolute silence reigned in this world above the land.

A cold breeze blew a strand of hair over her eyes. She pushed it back, mesmerized by the view, and by the singular experience of enjoying the flight within the safe harbor of Tristan's arms. She looked up at him, her motion catching his attention. He slowly smiled, and her heart opened up like a flower to the sun.

A sublime transcendence settled into her heart. Tristan. Her dearest friend. And yet, something more, something encompassing friendship but carrying it to a new level of joy, peace, safety.

"It's magical, isn't it?" He spoke almost reverently as if reluctant to break the beauty of the moment.

She nodded, too awed to reply.

He looked back out at the panorama. "I'd forgotten what it's like up here."

The view. Of course. She rested her head against him, no longer afraid but absolutely craving more of him, more of his touch, more of...

She didn't allow herself to finish the thought. Instead, they spoke in whispers, pointing out landmarks to each other. She could happily die here, in this quiet, surreal world, enfolded in Tristan's arms.

The pilot pointed out some sights Leticia had not noticed, and she admired the scene.

"Here we go, now," the pilot said. "Time to go back down."

Tristan watched the pilot's every movement, clearly fascinated. "Do you ever fly without a tether?"

The pilot nodded. "Oh, aye, but not in London. I go out a ways before I lift off—it's easier to find a landing spot. Better visibility, too. Always an adventure flying untethered. No two flights are the same."

They began the descent, so gradually that it seemed as if the ground rose to meet them. Tristan loosened his hold on her and she moved away from him. The closer they came to the ground, the greater the distance she put herself from Tristan.

They hit the ground with a soft thump and Leticia shifted her feet to stay balanced. With her hands folded, she waited as the land crew placed the stepladders. She drew a breath, ashamed for her panic, and for the unseemly way she threw herself at Tristan.

Some inner glow filled Tristan's eyes and the smile he offered her eased the tension inside her. His glance reassured her as surely as if he'd reached out and touched her with his hand.

He held her steady as she climbed the stepladders up and over the basket, and joined her on the ground. As she wound her hand through his arm and they strolled to the waiting carriage, a new awareness of him tingled her senses—surely the euphoria of the balloon ride caused her unexplained reaction.

She met his gaze. "What an unforgettable experience. Thank you."

His familiar grin, yet warmer somehow, appeared. "It was most assuredly my pleasure." Tristan the rake resurfaced with a teasing light glimmering in his eyes. "If I'd known all I had to do to get you into my arms was take you in a balloon or some other great height, I would have done it years ago."

Her world righted itself, and she whacked his arm. "Tell anyone about that and I'll tell your cook to put mushrooms in your favorite stew."

He shuddered dramatically. "No need to resort to cruel threats. Your secret is safe with me." Grinning, he led her up the rise to a walking path. "Shall we take a walk or do you need to return right away?"

"I have no engagements."

They walked and talked, and their familiar friendship returned. Yet, that underlying awareness of Tristan remained, each breath he took vibrating through her, each smile bringing an answering one to her lips, each mood, every expression echoing in her heart.

The sunlight flirted with the leaves overhead, sending shafts of light on his face, his hair. As they walked, a cat drowsing in the sun startled and slunk off into shrubbery, and Tristan quoted a poem by Keats about cats.

"Does everything remind you of a poem?" she asked.

His mouth curved upward on one side. "I suppose a great deal does."

Elizabeth loved poetry too—something that had drawn Tristan and Elizabeth together for their brief fling in a time that now seemed so long ago. Perhaps time did heal all wounds, for the wound of losing Richard to Elizabeth had vanished.

As they completed their walk and boarded the carriage, Tristan cocked his head. "An ice from Gunther's?"

"How well you know me." She smiled.

As they sat in the carriage enjoying ices, Tristan devouring his, he put a hand on his head. "Ow."

A bit smug, Leticia shook her head. "You ate yours too quickly; eating cold that fast always causes head pain."

He winced. "I'll be sure to remember that."

"Not much experience with ices, I imagine?" she said sweetly.

"No, my friends and I preferred to take refreshment in other ways, as you well know, you saucy wench."

"I hope you don't still call me that when we're old and gray."

He leaned back, that gleam coming back into his eyes. "Perhaps I'll have a new nickname for you by then—if you stop acting like a saucy wench."

"Never. You wouldn't know me then."

"True. Very well, let's think of a new one. How about...pet."

She made a face.

"Ducks?"

She made a gagging sound.

"Dear?"

"Hmm." She pretended to consider.

The gleam turned to a hot, sultry glower she'd never seen before. Very slowly, his lips and tongue moved forming, "Love?"

Every drop of moisture in her mouth evaporated under the heat of his stare. Leticia, the proper young lady, the friend, the rational being, collapsed and incinerated. Out of the ashes flew a new creature, one born of instinct and need. Her focus fixated on his mouth. Her lips starved for his kiss. Her arms ached to wrap around him. Her body craved his arms to enfold her. A temptation assaulted her to cast off her dish of ice and throw herself at him and do more than seek comfort in his familiarity.

The spoon cut into the edge of her fingers, snapping her out of such madness. Cold realization hit her like an icy wind.

This, then, must be the reason why every lady, proper or not, threw themselves at Tristan's feet. He need only give them *that look*, and they lost all reason. No man should have that much power.

Anger that he'd had so much control over women all these years raced through her. If she'd been made of paper, the heat of her rage would have blackened her.

She tossed her head. She tried to make her voice sound teasing, but her brittle anger hurled her words at him like darts. "Don't look at me like that, you rake. That obviously works with others, but you can be assured that I'm impervious to such a cheap ploy."

He jerked back. Blinked. Confusion and hurt flitted over his features. "What?"

A Gunther's waiter who passed by the carriage caught her eye. "I'm finished." She handed her half-eaten dish of lemon ice to him. Tears burned her eyes but she blinked them back. She would not cry in front of Tristan. The shameless womanizer! To think she almost fell for his game. How many he had seduced with such a look, she hoped she never knew.

"Please take me home." Her voice cracked. She swallowed and grappled at her tattered composure.

Tristan handed his dish to the waiter and spoke to the coachman. As the carriage pulled into traffic, neither of them spoke.

His hand enclosed hers. "Tish?"

She stared straight ahead. If she looked at him now, she'd lose control and yell or cry.

"What did I do?"

She clamped her mouth shut. So much for him knowing her so well.

"I promise you, whatever look you thought you saw, was not some tool in my seduction repertoire. Contrary to popular belief, I don't have an arsenal of weapons to use on women. Even if I did, I'd never use it on you."

She sighed. "I know—you use them on women you find attractive." She removed her hand from underneath his. Why, then, had he used it on her?

"Is that what this is about?" He leaned over and peered at her face from under the brim of her bonnet. "Tish?"

She sighed again and looked at his face. Her smile probably came out sad. "'Tis of no consequence."

"Don't you know how attractive you are?"

"It doesn't signify. Do forget I said anything about it."

He took her hand in his and pulled it against his chest. She half expected him to start spouting outrageous sonnets or something, but his expression remained serious, despite the fondness in his eyes. "Leticia Wentworth. You are one of the prettiest ladies I have ever seen. Every man who sees you knows it. I didn't refrain from flirting with you all these years because I found you unattractive; I never flirted with you because it felt wrong. I have known you all of my life—loved you as a friend all of my life."

Which did make sense, curse him.

"I would never attempt to trifle with your heart or your sensibilities. Things have changed between us. We've survived many difficulties, you and I." He enfolded her hand with both of his, still holding it against his chest. "Don't you know how much you mean to me?"

His dear, familiar face filled her vision, eclipsing all else. He had loved her as a friend all of his life. Of course he did. Therein lay the blessing. And the curse.

Bittersweet, she smiled. "Forgive me for overreacting. I know we are good friends, you and I, and I know why you never flirted with me."

His eyes narrowed as he studied her. "Do you? In truth?"

As they approached the house her aunt had let out for the Season, Leticia looked up at him. He sat so very near that she wouldn't need to move much to kiss him. Just lift her head and…

She cleared her throat. "Thank you so much for the balloon ride. It was unforgettable."

"It was for me, as well." That lazy glint returned. "Do feel free to pretend we're way up high any time."

She let out a scoff and whacked his arm again.

"We can still view the Elgin's Parthenon Sculptures if you wish. I've never seen them and would love to see them with you."

He hadn't taken other women there? Where did he take women he courted? Of course, now that she thought of it, he had never courted a lady before. She stopped that line of thought before she ground her teeth into powder.

"Thank you. I would like that, too." Now why had she agreed to it? Spending more time in Tristan's company was a pointless exercise. And quite possibly dangerous. Lord Bradbury would take her to see the famous marble sculptures if she asked him. However, viewing them with Tristan appealed in ways she couldn't begin to explain.

He grinned. "Tomorrow?"

She nodded. "I am engaged for the evening, but I'm available all day."

A slight pause, curiosity brightened his eyes and he opened his mouth to ask her something, but with a slight shake of his head said instead, "Until tomorrow then."

If she were of an inclination to place wagers, she would have wagered that he wanted to ask her about her evening plans, and with whom. Since when did he refrain from expressing his thoughts?

For some reason, she needed him to know she would not see Lord Bradbury tomorrow night. "I'm attending a small dinner party hosted by Mrs. Goodfellow."

His gaze slid her way. "Bradbury or Kensington invited?"

"Not to my knowledge."

His posture relaxed. Puzzling. Why the sudden dislike of her spending time with the gentlemen he'd previously been so happy for her to meet? Again, flared a faint suspicion—hope?—that he was jealous. Ridiculous.

He handed her down from the carriage and escorted her to the front steps. The noise from the streets seemed loud and busy, as if everyone in the district were nearby.

She made a loose gesture to the door. "I'd invite you in but my aunt is likely still gone with Isabella."

"Of course." He bowed low over her hand, then continued to hold it as he straightened. "Tomorrow."

She nodded. "Tomorrow."

He held fast to her hand. Her focus fixed on his as if somehow every muscle in her body had frozen in place. He swallowed. Twice. Then he released her hand and backed away. As he strode down the stairs, he glanced over his shoulder, smiling, and looking almost triumphant.

Released from whatever spell she'd been under,

Leticia went inside.

What a confusing situation! She should have refused to see him on the morrow. Spending so much time in Tristan's company had both an unexplained and uncomfortable effect on her sensibilities.

Chapter Twenty-Four

Tristan finished his correspondence with the caretaker of the property Richard had turned over to his care, and signed his name with a flourish. How gratifying this undertaking had been! The caretaker clearly enjoyed someone taking an interest in the "old place" and had plenty of suggestions for restoring it to its former glory. Tristan had half a mind to hire a coach and view the property immediately. But not now. Roads were difficult in the best of times, but this year produced the coldest spring he'd ever seen. He might hit torrential rain or even snow in places. No, he'd best wait until summer.

Besides, he didn't dare leave now with Bradbury and Kensington competing for Leticia's affection.

Yesterday, the balloon ride had been turbulent at best—at least in her heart. Heated glances, a few blissful moments in his arms, the exhilaration of flight, comfortable friendship, and that moment when she'd grown angry with him—all creating a confusing combination. Why had she grown so angry with him? Had she felt overlooked as he flirted with every other lady or woman whose paths he crossed?

That didn't make sense. She'd never shown any signs of desire for him, until quite possibly these last few days, and she still viewed him as a shameless rake.

He craved the love of a faithful woman. To such a

woman, he would give everything—his heart, body, and soul. To Leticia, he would give it all. Would she ever see him for who he'd become, or always view him as a dissipated rake?

There must be a way to prove himself to her.

He set the pen in its holder and capped the inkwell. After sanding the ink, he folded and sealed the letter and handed it to a servant to have it posted.

Richard's barouche arrived and Tristan practically skipped out to it and tapped his toe during the drive as if the cadence would speed his arrival to Leticia. Inside the foyer of her aunt's house, already prepared to leave, Leticia waited.

His heart sang at the beautiful sight. "Leticia love, you look exquisite."

She faltered and made a point of adjusting her gloves. "Er, thank you."

He grinned to put her at ease. "And how refreshing that you are always ready when I come for you."

It worked. Her eyes took on a playful glint. "I know it's terribly unstylish not to adhere to the custom of ladies making a gentleman wait. However, I assume he tells her what time to expect him so she knows when to be ready."

Bowing, he took her hand and kissed it. If only her gloves could vanish. As he straightened, he tucked her hand into the crook of his arm. "I am delighted, as always to benefit from your superior good sense."

She let out a slight chuckle. "You don't have to play the part of a besotted suitor, Tristan."

"What makes you think I'm not a besotted suitor?"

She huffed. "You? I'm hardly your type."

"Perhaps my type has changed."

She shook her head, disbelieving. He pursed his lips. He had much to do to convince her.

He made a gesture. "Your carriage awaits." Walking taller with Leticia on his arm, he led her outside. He glanced at gathering clouds. "I hope the weather holds."

She looked up. "Didn't you pay homage to the weather god?"

"Of course, but he may not grant me two requests in a row."

"Perhaps you need to make a better offering," she suggested.

"Perhaps...but I rather frown on virgin sacrifices—"

"For which I am grateful."

"—but I suppose I could offer something else." He handed her into the barouche.

"Such as?"

He lifted an eyebrow. "Do you have any suggestions?"

She pretended to think as the carriage rolled over the streets. "You could sacrifice your wild ways."

"I already have. Or haven't you noticed?"

She laughed. "Oh, of course. How could I forget?"

He sobered. "I'm serious."

Patting his hand, she gave him an almost matronly shake of her head. "A few weeks may not be an adequate sacrifice."

"You believe me un-genuine?"

Still smiling, she shrugged. "I think your changes will be short-lived."

"I think you will be surprised."

Her eyes turned soft and her smile embodied

Donna Hatch

everything affectionate and lovely. She made no comment.

Mentally, he sighed. He couldn't blame her. He had years of bad conduct for which he must atone, and it might take a decade of good behavior to prove to her he had changed in truth.

In front of the British Museum, they climbed the stairs, passing between the enormous columns, to the entrance.

He paused in the main area. "Do you wish to view other displays as well as the sculptures?"

She retrieved a guide from her reticule and studied it. "Let's see the sculptures first, then browse as we have time." She smiled, a genuine warmth that he hoped she gave no one else. Reading aloud from the guide, she gestured. "I think it's this way."

Inside the Elgin Room, a curator gave them a bland description and brief history of the famous and controversial Parthenon Marble Sculptures, which some called simply the Elgin Marbles.

Tristan breathed a sigh at the mind-numbing narrative. "I don't think they could have found a more coma-inducing guide if they searched the entire world."

Leticia chuckled. "What do you think of Lord Elgin bringing the marble sculptures from Greece to England?"

"I think he was a self-serving vandal."

Her eyes opened wide. "Surely not."

"Even Lord Byron disapproves. In *Child Harold's Pilgrimage*, he lamented that 'the antiquities of Greece had been defaced by British hands.' I'm inclined to agree."

Her eyes sparkled the way they did when she

262

embarked on a debate. "If he protected them from destruction, then he saved valuable works of art. He did bring them here for the world to enjoy. John Keats wrote a sonnet that celebrates the Elgin Marbles."

Taken aback, Tristan stared. "Since when do you read poetry?"

"I don't, as a rule, but I read about this one. It's what piqued my curiosity about seeing the marbles in the first place." She nodded to the art in question.

Tristan gestured to a sculpture of a horse's head nearby. "Is it everything you'd hoped?"

"I admit I prefer the images carved into a frieze over the statues—they are more intact. All those headless and armless statues are a bit disconcerting. They must have been spectacular in their prime, though, don't you think?"

Tristan eyed them. "I'm sure." Wickedly, he asked, "Your feminine sensibilities aren't offended by all the male nudes?"

With exaggerated delicacy, she cleared her throat. "I'm trying not to look."

He laughed at her partially pained, partially playful expression.

They browsed a few minutes longer, reading from the paper guide before they wandered to other rooms and other displays. Leticia strolled on his arm, her delight in exploring, and the tones of her voice, sometimes playful, sometimes awed. Tristan let out a sigh of contentment. A missing piece inside him returned and fell into place. Without moving his head, he looked at her as she admired a painting.

Her lively face, so familiar, and yet more dear than ever, entranced him. How had he missed what a beauty she'd become? How much time he had lost looking for a sense of belonging when she had been here, practically under his nose, all his life! He ached to gather her into his arms, press his mouth to hers. That very moment. In public. Or better yet, haul her off to some vacant room and do a thorough job of kissing her in private.

He must resist. He must move slowly to gain her trust and prove to her, and to himself, he had changed, that his intentions truly were honorable—but not so slowly that Kensington or Bradbury had a chance.

Upon leaving the museum, Tristan glanced at the sky again. Though still early yet, the gloom had deepened to near darkness as storm clouds thickened.

Leticia eyed the heavens and said in mournful tones, "Your offering may prove inadequate."

Straight-faced, he said, "I suppose I could still try that virgin sacrifice."

She gave him a withering glare.

He shrugged. "The rain may hold off yet, until we can get home."

The coachman arrived with the barouche to take them home, and Tristan steadied her as she climbed in. How many times he'd done such a simple act without appreciating the gift of her presence. What a blind fool he'd been.

He leaned back in his seat and affected a casual air. "What else would you like to do while you're in London?"

"Are you trying to help me see all London has to offer since this will be my last time to town?"

"Your last trip to town?" He turned in his seat to face her.

She looked down. "I may come for the school, or to visit Elizabeth, but I won't be back for another Season. I'm here at my aunt's insistence and because it comforted Isabella for me to come with her for her first Season."

He eyed her. "I doubt very much this will be your last visit to London."

"Well, I…I suppose if I were to marry a Member of Parliament, I would return." She lifted a shoulder.

Did she refer to Lord Bradbury, then? Had she developed a preference for him over Kensington? He didn't know whether to be alarmed at the thought or relieved that she'd eliminated a contender.

Still, she chose to spend time with him today. He refused to give up.

"How is the school proceeding?" he asked.

Her expression softened. "It is most satisfactory. We gather new students almost every day. Although, we appeared to have lost one." A shadow passed over her face but she cast it off with her usual cheer. "I have begun teaching some of them to play the pianoforte. You never know when a skill may aid in obtaining employment normally closed to members of their social status. Oh!" Her eyes sparkled. "Elizabeth and I want to teach them to dance."

"Dance?"

"Yes, people of almost every class dance, and public dances are an effective way to meet prospective spouses as balls are for members of our social circles. If these girls know how to dance, they have a better chance of marrying a man with a good position."

He thought it over. "That's a good idea."

"I asked the servants at my aunt's house to tell me

when and where the working classes gather for these public dances, but I don't want to send the children unprepared. I thought a few practice sessions would be wise."

Tristan leaned back and eyed her hand. Would she allow him to hold it? "I didn't see much of the school the last time I went there. Perhaps you could show me around now that it is in full operation?"

"Would you like to go now?"

"There is nothing I'd rather do." He called out the direction to the coachman, who turned the carriage at the next intersection. "So, your pupils will not only read and do arithmetic, but play piano and dance."

"Such skills will help them find gainful employment and rise above their circumstances," she said.

"If they don't, it won't be for a lack of trying on your part." Unable to refrain from touching her, he took her hand and raised it to his lips.

"And Elizabeth. She and I hatched this plan together, and it would never have reached this point without her." Did he imagine her voice grew unsteady?

He wrapped his fingers around hers, rubbing his thumb over the back of her hand.

She looked down at their hands. "That's distracting, you know."

"Is it?" Surely a good sign.

Her eyes locked with his and she nodded. Her pupils dilated. She swallowed. Moistened her lips.

Leticia's feminine, passionate reaction to his touch warmed him with unholy pleasure. Good thing they were in an open carriage or he might be tempted to cast off his determination to woo Leticia properly, and kiss her until she pledged herself to him alone.

She removed her hand from his. The absence of her touch hit him like a cold stream. Oh wait. He looked up as more rain hit his face.

"We'd best raise the canopy," she said.

Surprised she'd make such a suggestion, he stared at her. "We can't do that; it would turn the barouche into a closed coach. It would ruin your reputation."

She let out a huff of exasperation. "Tristan, it's raining. Concessions can be made."

As if in reply, the heavens opened up, and rain drove down on them. Rain fell in torrents and blew across the street in sheets.

Still, he shook his head. "I won't have anyone call into question your purity."

"So, you'll get drenched—and I will, as well?" She stared at him as if he'd lost his mind.

"If anyone saw us hiding behind a canopy, they could claim I'd compromised you."

Her expression changed from incredulous to hurt to anger. "Oh, that would be terrible, wouldn't it, with no one to save you from having to marry me the way Richard saved you from having to marry Elizabeth!"

Tristan rocked back. "The Duke of Pemberton refused to allow me to marry his daughter and insisted on Richard."

As he spoke, his anger grew. How could Leticia bring that up again? The entire episode had been a nightmare for everyone concerned. It had been a miracle that Richard and Elizabeth had found happiness together considering the circumstances that facilitated their marriage. To think that Leticia still blamed him...the thought opened an old wound and poured in salt.

She folded her arms and glared at her feet while her clothes and bonnet went from water-spattered to drenched.

The coachmen cleared his throat. "Sir." He handed back an enormous black umbrella.

"My thanks." Tristan opened it and held it over them both, although they were already soaked. Leticia retrieved a handkerchief from her reticule and wiped her nose.

He drew two steadying breaths. "How many ways must I apologize for the fiasco with Elizabeth?"

She shook her head. "You don't."

"Then why are you so angry?" When had she become so short-tempered?

She sniffed and her lip trembled.

"Leticia? Are you crying?"

"No."

As he peered at her face, tears fell from her eyes and streaked her cheeks. The sight hit him like a punch. "Tish?"

He should have raised the hood and spared them both the argument, but he had a feeling they argued over more than the rain hood.

Though tempted to put an arm around her, he settled for sliding his hand down her arm to her hand. He tried to put a teasing note into his voice. "You know, if you don't explain yourself to me, I might be tempted to think you want me to ruin you."

She let out a scoff.

He painted on a lazy grin in case she looked at him. She didn't. He opted for a drawl, "Perhaps all along you've been wishing I'd carry you off and ruin you.

Then you'd have to marry me."

She did look at him then. Her accusing stare wiped away his smile.

"You mean, *you'd* have to marry *me*." Her huff of breath carried the weight of a sob. "That would make us both miserable."

She considered marriage to him miserable? "Why would you say that?"

"Because a man ought to be attracted to his wife as you have never been attracted to me. Most of all, it would break my heart if my husband were a rake."

He sagged. He would never prove himself to her. "Can't you see that I am not a rake anymore? I have changed." He tightened his grip on the umbrella's handle and steadied it over them.

Frowning, she shook her head. "Temporarily, I am sure—a natural reaction to your accident."

"No, Tish. I had already changed. I admit that the accident did cause me to look deeper within myself to find what really matters—to seek out more worthwhile pursuits such as helping Richard with estate business, and considering Parliament. However, I began to change long ago. I haven't done anything that would justly condemn me as a rake in a very long time."

She gave him a patently disbelieving stare. "You have completely given up gambling and drinking and—the most difficult to believe of all—loose women?"

Defensive, he said, "Yes. All. I haven't gone near a woman in nearly a year." Not since Richard accused him of seducing his wife and threw him out of the house. "I haven't been intoxicated in several months—I told you this—I have grown to dislike the sensation of being out of control. Since the accident, I haven't had a drop of alcohol except for a glass of wine at dinner. It's been longer than that since I placed a single wager—not that I gambled much anyway even in my former life." With the umbrella behind her like a backdrop, her eyes danced between his, searching. He'd never in his life wanted so badly for her to believe him.

"Why?" she asked, her voice hushed.

"It lost its appeal. I want to do something that matters. Be worthy of the love of a good woman. A lady."

Still she gave him that searching gaze.

He pulled off one of his gloves and wiped moisture from her cheeks, more rain than tears, he hoped. "Come now, you've known me all our life. Have I ever lied to you?"

A small, sad smile came in reply. She shook her head.

"You are lovely. Desirable." He traced her lips with the pad of his thumb.

She studied him, a smile of wistful disbelief. If they were alone, he'd kiss her until she stopped doubting his sincerity.

The carriage pulled up to a stop in front of her aunt's house. Still holding the umbrella over her head, he helped her down.

"Perhaps you'd best come in," she said. "You can wait until the rain stops."

Tristan called to the driver. "Go on to the mews at the end of the street. We can wait until the storm passes to return home."

"If it's all the same, sir, I'd best get back to the earl. He will need me tonight."

Waving him off, Tristan nodded. "I can take a

hackney home. Thank you."

"Sir." The coachman touched his cap and drove off.

Holding the umbrella over them both, Tristan trotted up the stairs next to Leticia. Inside, they stopped in the foyer. Leticia's bonnet drooped, water dripping off the brim, and her clothes stuck to her body in a way that should not have been so provocative. She gave Tristan a sideways glance, her mouth quivering and her eyes crinkling. He probably looked as drowned as she.

Her mouth compressed and then a bark of laughter erupted. He stared. Tears a moment ago, and now laughter? When did Leticia become so driven by her sensibilities?

"Oh, Tristan, you should see yourself. You look like a drowned cat."

He affected a lordly air. "Madam, I believe the words you seek are devilishly handsome."

"Oh, right. A devilishly handsome drowned cat." Her peals of laughter undid him, and he joined in.

"You, my dear, look like a…" He couldn't think of an appropriate insult with her wet clothes clinging to her delicious curves.

The butler arrived and cleared his throat. "A towel, miss?"

"For Mr. Barrett. And show him to a room where he may change. Do what you can for him. I'll go to my room and change. Send for my maid, please."

She vanished up the stairs. By the time Tristan had changed into some borrowed, but ill-fitting clothing from a decade ago, and warmed himself by the fire with a cup of tea, Leticia re-emerged. Her aunt and sister accompanied her, thus preventing a continuation of their earlier conversation. Her Aunt Alice chatted, amiable as always, and Isabella contributed, but Tristan said little as he watched Leticia. Though her earlier emotional state vanished, she continued to send occasional long looks his way.

Again, came that suspicion that she'd misread his intentions. Somehow, over the years, she'd made up her mind that he found her unattractive—the reason why he'd never flirted with her.

He'd have to clear up that misunderstanding.

What if he were wrong? If he declared himself to her, he risked rejection.

Still, if she could love him…

He would take that risk.

Chapter Twenty-Five

Leticia sat next to Lord Bradbury in his private box in the Theatre Royal on Drury Lane, and peered through her aunt's lorgnette at the stage. From the box, the actors appeared healthy and attractive. However, the magnifying lens of the lorgnette revealed the young and handsome hero as a man twice her age wearing garish make up. Still, their comical facial expressions made up-close viewing enjoyable, and the music exceeded anything she heard back home.

Lord Bradbury shifted and draped his arm across the back of Leticia's chair—not touching her but still too…close. She glanced at her aunt, who murmured something to Isabella. Both kept their focus riveted to the stage.

The murmur of voices from other boxes as well as from below gave evidence of how many came to the theater to see and be seen rather than to enjoy a comedy production. Tuning them out, Leticia returned her focus to the stage and paid attention to their dialogue, laughing at the mishaps, jests, and expressions.

When the curtain fell at intermission, Isabella clasped her hands together. "I've never seen a production so grand. What impressive costumes, and the set is glorious! Oh, and when the prima donna sang, I thought I would weep. I don't know how I'll sleep tonight."

Glancing behind him at Leticia's sister, Lord Bradbury let out a low chuckle that bordered on paternal, as if he enjoyed the antics of a child—a rich chuckle, but nowhere near the infectious laugh Tristan often released. "I'm gratified you are enjoying yourself, Miss Isabella." He turned his focus on Leticia. "And you?"

Leticia toyed with the lorgnette. "It's very diverting, my lord. I share my sister's enthusiasm. Although, I admit, I wish the peanut gallery would be quieter so I could hear better." She indicated those in the pit who created the most noise. The chandeliers filled with candles illuminated them almost as brightly as the stage lights illuminated the actors. She expected Lord Bradbury to laugh at her peanut gallery comment, or rush to their defense that they were not as unfortunate as those who attended plays during Shakespeare's time and had to stand.

He shrugged. "Many come for pleasures other than to enjoy a theatrical performance."

Leticia decided to tweak him a bit. "Why do you attend?"

A charming smile touched his lips. "To spend time with you and your delightful family, of course."

It should have pleased her that he'd taken her to the theater with the express purpose of spending time in her company. Instead, the compliment fell short.

Lord Petre and his mother, the ever-present dowager, stopped by the box. Leticia tried to keep a smile in place despite their rudeness to her in the teashop. Lord Petre's wife, Lady Petre, always a silent shadow, stood next to her husband who never gave any indication that he noticed her existence. Poor thing.

"Bradbury," Lord Petre said by way of greeting. "I haven't seen you here in an age. You, usually rent out the box, eh?"

Bradbury stood in greeting. "Er, no, I let friends borrow it when I don't attend a production."

"Oh, of course." Petre said. "I guess you don't need blunt, eh?"

Bradbury stiffened. "I derive pleasure from letting others receive enjoyment without quibbling over cost." He glanced at Leticia. "Forgive me, Miss Wentworth, Miss Isabella, are you acquainted with the Petres?"

She toyed with the idea of giving them the cut, but for Lord Bradbury's sake, resisted. She smiled at Lord Bradbury, managing more warmth for him than for their visitors.

"Yes, we are. Lord and Lady Petre." Leticia glanced at the lord's silent wife who fixed her gaze on the floor. Leticia turned her gaze to the poor creature's mother-in-law and inclined her head. "My lady."

Aunt Alice had drawn herself up and stared at the visitors with open distain but they appeared oblivious of her.

"Dear Mrs. Tallier," the dowager viscountess said with false friendliness. "You are looking well. You must be enjoying showing off your nieces to everyone."

"Of course." Aunt Alice gripped her fan with white fingers.

The dowager made a loose gesture to Leticia and Isabella. "I'm sure it must be vastly rewarding to do so since you never had children of your own. Such a pity."

Aunt Alice's mouth pinched.

"Let's hope the younger one fares better than the elder, eh? What is this—your fourth Season, dear?" The dowager gave a patronizing smile to Leticia.

"Third," Leticia said through clenched teeth. She refused to volunteer that her first Season had been years ago. Until Richard got married, another season had never been deemed necessary since her future seemed certain.

Aunt Alice drew a breath, but before she could give the dowager the scathing set-down she deserved, Lord Petre broke in. "Ah, yes, Miss Wentworth. Hardly noticed you. I hope you gave up on that foolish rot about a school for the poor."

"Certainly not." Leticia lifted her chin. "It is progressing in a satisfactory manner."

"No good will come of it, mark my words."

"I hardly think it is any concern of yours," she shot back.

In a dismissive manner, Petre turned away and fixed his gaze on Lord Bradbury. "Bradbury, you'd do well to put a stop to such foolishness before you consider giving that girl another moment of your time."

Bradbury went still. "On the contrary. I applaud the efforts she and Lady Averston have expended for the school and I have given them my full support."

Lord Petre frowned. "Short-sighted, lad. Don't lose your head over a female or you'll grow to rue the day. Put your foot down from the start and she won't give you any trouble." He nodded once to punctuate his point.

If Leticia had a drink in her hand, she would have been tempted to throw it in Lord Petre's face. His poor wife!

Bradbury's hands fisted but his expression remained polite. "You are entitled to your opinion,

Petre, but do not presume to counsel me."

"That's no way to speak to your elders."

"Good evening." Bradbury gestured to the doorway in a clear invitation to leave. The highest-ranking person in the box and unconcerned about offending an elder, Bradbury turned his back on Petre.

Sputtering, the unwelcome guests left.

Bradbury let out his breath as if he'd been holding it. "I hope you don't think me ill-mannered for the way I dismissed them, but I might have been tempted to say or do something drastic to that boorish oaf if he and his mother had remained another moment."

"I think you handled it quite well," Aunt Alice said. "They deserved no better. If this had been my box, I would have cut them dead."

Leticia nodded. "Indeed."

Isabella, who'd been quiet throughout the entire exchange stood. "I believe I shall go for some refreshment."

Aunt Alice stood. "Excellent idea. I could use some lemonade." A chorus of agreements followed.

During their descent on the grand staircase to the floor below their box, Leticia tried not to gawk at the beauty of the grand saloon and its sumptuous décor. Lamps hanging from the ceiling provided adequate light and cast a warm glow over the wide array of visitors of all classes who flirted, laughed, and sized up one another.

Inside the retiring room decorated with crimson paper and carpeting, Leticia checked her reflection to be sure nothing was amiss.

Isabella joined her by the mirror. "Well?" Isabella nudged her. "Isn't he wonderful? Aren't you falling madly in love with him?"

"With whom?" Leticia felt along her chignon for loose hairpins.

Isabella laughed as if she found Leticia thick in the head. "Lord Bradbury, you goose."

Leticia found herself at a loss for a moment. "Well…"

"Come now, Tish, you can tell me. Hurry before someone comes in."

"He is…a very pleasant gentleman." She pushed a loose hairpin back into place.

"Pleasant?" Isabella's mouth twisted into an incredulous moue. "That's hardly flattering. Aren't you violently in love with him?"

Leticia let out a weak laugh. "Not violently, no. I may be starting to have…feelings for him. These things take time. I hardly know him."

"Oh, come now. Mama and Papa fell in love at first sight."

"It doesn't happen that way for everyone. Most people must be better acquainted." Satisfied with the state of her hair, Leticia inspected her gown in the mirror.

Isabella shook her head and smoothed her gown. "I don't understand you. He's perfect."

"He is pleasant," Leticia admitted. "And polite."

Isabella waved her hand. "Hardly words of adoration. Does his nearness make your heart go all aflutter? Does his smile make you weak in the knees?" She clasped her hands together dreamily.

"Well…I do like to spend time in his company."

Isabella peered at her in disbelief. "What is wrong with you? He's a lord with a long and respected lineage. He is handsome and witty and intelligent. He's also *kind*. He treats you like a princess."

Leticia chuckled. "You mean he wants to marry me off to someone I've never met to strengthen England's alliance with Spain or Nigeria?"

Isabella let out a sound that might have been interpreted as a snort on anyone less lady-like. "You know what I mean."

Leticia affected a mournful tone. "I always felt sorry for princesses getting sent away to some new land to marry a stranger—pawns in the games of power and politics."

"Honestly!" Isabella turned away from the mirror.

Sobering, Leticia said, "Forgive me, Bella. I don't know what to say. You are right; Lord Bradbury seems to be the perfect man. I should be in raptures at his attention."

So why didn't she love him? Why didn't his presence set her heart aflutter the way it did in Tristan's company? In fact, her heart did more than flutter; it often pounded harder the closer she came to him.

Surely, her reaction centered around that accidental kiss in his sickroom. Every nerve in her body had exploded. And during the balloon ride, he'd chased away her fears and turned the experience into a lovely memory that brought a smile each time she thought of the sight of London all laid out below them like a colored map. Perhaps her initial and unexpected fright had prompted such a strong response. She closed her eyes and shook her head at her own foolishness. Her reaction lay squarely on Tristan's skill as a master seducer, nothing more.

Isabella turned a penetrating stare on Leticia. "Do

your feelings for Tristan Barrett impair your feelings for Lord Bradbury?"

Leticia's face heated and she laughed, making a point of looking down at her gown and smoothing it as if she found a multitude of wrinkles. "What a foolish notion! Tristan has always been rather like a brother to me."

"He's not your brother. He's lauded as one of the most handsome bachelors in all of England, and pursued by women and ladies of all ages. He is interested in you beyond mere friendship."

"Hardly. Besides, I would never consider a rake, and he knows it."

"I hear rakes make the best husbands," Isabella sang out.

"No. They don't. They break their wives' hearts and bring their family to social and financial ruin." Leticia shut out images of Tristan's smile and the earnest expression when he swore he'd changed.

Aunt Alice joined them, then. "Very sensible of you, Leticia. I would not encourage you toward a rake. However, I caution you to remember not to judge people too harshly; they seldom fit into neatly labeled boxes."

Before Leticia could question her further, a group of chattering young ladies filed in, probably from boxes in the upper levels. Aunt Alice led the way to a circular alcove at the one end of the salon. Though small, the room's domed ceiling and Corinthian columns gave it a spacious appearance.

Lord Bradbury stood talking with Richard and Elizabeth. As they reached the others, Bradbury smiled. She returned the expression, searching for any sign of excitement. Nothing. What was the matter with her? She should be quivering for Lord Bradbury.

Bradbury gestured to the refreshment table. "May I get you something? Wine? Champagne?"

"Those oranges are tempting," Leticia said.

"Of course." He excused himself.

Richard took Elizabeth's hand. "And for you, darling?"

"Surprise me."

They shared a look that seemed to contain a private joke before he joined Bradbury. Within moments, a crowd of young gentleman surrounded Isabella, peppering her with questions and showering her with compliments. Aunt Alice kept a sharp eye out on the bucks vying for Isabella's attention.

Elizabeth drew Leticia aside. "I haven't been to the school all week. How is Mrs. Harper?"

"She's a fine teacher—doing wonderfully well with the children."

"Is she unhappy traveling to the school from your aunt's house?"

Leticia shook her head. "Not that I am aware. I send a footman with her every day to keep watch over her."

"Do you think the threat on you was an isolated incident or do you believe Mrs. Harper is in danger?"

"It was probably an idle threat but I rest easier with Mrs. Harper protected."

"I hope he does not take more drastic measures," Elizabeth said grimly.

"Who will take drastic measures?" Richard returned and handed Elizabeth a slice of cake.

Lord Bradbury offered Leticia a small plate with

several neatly peeled orange slices and a napkin. His eyes brightened in curiosity over Richard's question, but he remained silent.

"The man who attacked Leticia," Elizabeth explained.

"What?" Lord Bradbury stared.

Leticia shot Elizabeth a warning look. "It wasn't an attack, exactly. Someone told me no one wanted the school and that we should close it. It was nothing—the ramblings of the ignorant."

"He had a knife," Elizabeth said as if determined to exaggerate trouble.

Lord Bradbury's eyes widened. He put a hand underneath her elbow. "Miss Wentworth, if you are in any danger, perhaps you should reconsider…"

"No." Leticia shook he head. "As a mere precaution, the teacher is staying with my aunt, and we send a footman with her to the school, but surely nothing more will come of it. I refuse to disappoint the children. In fact, I'm teaching them to play the pianoforte—thanks to your generous donation—and we will also teach them to dance in the hopes of giving them access to potential husbands in the working class when they are old enough."

Bradbury's expression turned from concerned to incredulous. "Dancing as well as music? Don't you think that's raising their hopes too much?"

Leticia stared at him. "I thought you supported our efforts."

"I do. It's commendable. But thinking that they will rise very far above the situation of their birth—that's not likely."

Disappointment turned the tangy orange in her

mouth to dust. How could he not understand? "Then why did you help us raise money at the ball? Why give me the pianoforte?"

A sheepish smile touched his mouth. "To impress you. Besides, I figured this would be a passing fancy and that you'd eventually realize the poor will never make anything of themselves."

Stung by his dismissal of her cause, Leticia studied the last orange slice on her plate. "You never know."

Tristan had been so supportive—excited, almost—that it never occurred to her that Bradbury felt differently.

He paused. "No, I suppose not."

Intermission ended and they returned to their box. Leticia stared at the farce on stage while her mind turned over the new knowledge that Lord Bradbury had revealed a major flaw. Could she overlook it? Some husbands curtailed their wives' involvement in causes. Would Lord Bradbury eventually forbid her to pursue such a noble cause if they married?

Chapter Twenty-Six

In the mews near his bachelor's rooms, Tristan eyed his new phaeton and broke out into a sweat. He hadn't driven since the accident that claimed Appleton's life, and nearly his own. The horses stood as if awaiting his courage. Tristan had been driving since he was barely out of leading strings. One accident should not leave him quaking.

To take his mind off his almost paralyzing fear, he rubbed the noses of his new team. Their soft nickers soothed him. The gelding, Willow, gave Tristan's neck a lippy kiss, the hairs of the horse's chin tickling. Tristan ran a hand along their necks and backs. He checked the harness, and continued down the side of the carriage, admiring its graceful lines. The phaeton, built to his exact specifications, gleamed shiny black despite the dull light. New paint combined with leather and the warm scent of horses created a heady aroma.

He swallowed. He could do this.

After taking a bracing breath, he climbed inside the carriage and settled in the cloud-soft seat. Another swallow. He picked up the reins. Perspiration trickled down the side of his face. Dancer stamped and blew out her breath. Right. Get on with it.

He threaded the reins through his fingers, and took a firm hold. Another breath. He clicked to Willow and Dancer, and flicked his wrists. The horses stepped forward in near-perfect unison. As he guided the team onto the street, a rush of panic shot through him. The team responded to his tension by side-stepping.

"Easy," he said. "Go easy." He might as well have been speaking to himself.

The horses swiveled their ears back to listen to him. He drew another breath and relaxed his arm muscles, his shoulders. "We can do this, Dancer. Work with me, now, Willow."

The horses fell into a comfortable walk. If Tristan hadn't been so terrified, he would have shaken his head at the thought of him walking a team hitched to a beauty like his new phaeton. One step at a time. Literally. So early in the morning, a few people and the occasional cart rumbled along the street. He drove without a direction, following the streets to get a feel for the team and carriage. He calmed. He could do this.

He urged the team to a trot. They responded, matching their strides to one another. In the well-sprung conveyance, the bumps in the road were of little consequence. Exhilaration shot through him. How long he drove, he could not have guessed, but the roads soon filled with other carriages and riders on horseback, many heading toward Hyde Park. The team trotted with matched strides, responding to his guidance, and ignoring the chaos of the London streets around them.

He had to show Leticia. He arrived at Mrs. Tallier's house as Leticia stepped out of the front door, accompanied by a familiar-looking woman and a brawny footman.

He pulled up in front of the house and called out, "Where are you bound so early today?"

Leticia's expression lit up and she waved as she

descended the steps. "To the school. Is that your new rig?"

"Do you like it?" He puffed out his chest.

"It's beautiful!" She moved up alongside the carriage. A teasing glint entered her eyes. "I'm surprised it's black. How understated."

He grinned. "You expected bright yellow with red wheels, no doubt."

"Something like that."

After securing the reins, he leaped down and gestured. "Well, I did get green seats. Too dark to match your eyes but…"

"Very elegant." She walked up to the horses and rubbed their faces, missing his comparison.

Actually, ever since he discovered her eyes were green, he'd begun choosing that color more and more often. How had he not noticed the particular beauty of the color green?

She cooed at the horses. "Are you going to introduce me?"

"The mare is Dancer and the gelding is Willow."

"They're charming."

Willow gave her a nibbly-horsey kiss. Leticia giggled.

"*Oi!*" Tristan pretended to scold the gelding. "For shame, Willow. You can't go around kissing every pretty girl you see."

Leticia grinned at him as she rubbed Willow's nose. "Why? Are you the only one who can do that?"

"Leticia, Love, if I kissed every pretty girl I saw, I would have kissed you years ago." He rested an arm against Willow's back and eyed her.

She laughed, but did a double take as if searching

for his sincerity. Her green bonnet brightened the green of her eyes, and little curls next to her cheek and temple framed her face. She was so lovely. She sobered and looked back at the horse as if unprepared to see the admiration in his expression.

She seemed out of reach today, as if the connection between them had been stretched. He dropped the flirtatious guise and settled for some honesty.

"Today is the first time I've driven since the accident," he said quietly.

She touched his arm, looking into his eyes. "Are you...well?"

Her hand on his arm warmed him by degrees all the way to his heart. "It took a bit of courage at the beginning, but it feels comfortable now."

She removed her hand and ran it along Dancer's perspiring back. Lucky Dancer. "You've been driving for a good long while, now."

Tristan nodded. "Since early this morning. I wanted to get the feel of the team and carriage, see how they handled, before the traffic started."

Leticia glanced over her shoulder at the young woman and a footman who murmured to one another, sending darting glances at Leticia.

"I'm keeping you from your plans," Tristan said. "Can I give you all a ride? There's enough room in the footman's seat if they are willing to sit close."

"Thank you." She gestured to the pair. "Mr. Barrett will give us a ride, if you don't mind squeezing into the back. Oh, forgive me; Mrs. Harper, have you met Tristan Barrett?"

Mrs. Harper nodded. "I have, indeed. Thank you for all your help with the school," the teacher said in a cultured accent at odds with her position and plain attire.

"My pleasure." Tristan helped the teacher up and stepped back to let the footman climb in.

Mrs. Harper gestured to the footman. "This is Peter. He's been kind enough to watch over us at the school."

Peter touched his forelock. "Sir."

Tristan nodded a greeting at the footman and offered a hand to Leticia. Leticia climbed in, somehow managing to make it look graceful despite her skirts. "The lower height certainly makes it easier to get in."

"Would you believe I decided to lower it for that very reason—so you could get in easier? And it's safer." If Tristan's plans played out, she would be the only woman who ever rode next to him in his new carriage.

Leticia smiled. As she settled on the seat, she gave a little bounce. "Oh, my, I don't recall ever sitting in such a soft seat."

He grinned. "I'm glad you like it."

As he drove, Leticia's presence comforted him. His tension faded and his confidence strengthened. Dogs barked, vendors called, men strolled, and carts rattled, all in a familiar orchestra of the symphony of London. Mrs. Harper and Peter sat in the back, conversing.

He glanced at Leticia sitting in comfortable silence next to him. "Does Mrs. Harper double as a chaperone for you when your aunt or Elizabeth are not with you?"

"My aunt approves. Mrs. Harper is very respectable and genteel. Circumstances have…not been kind to her of late."

"Young."

"Widowed." She glanced sharply at him and he could almost hear her condemning thoughts.

He'd once had a preference for widows, but now he had eyes for Leticia alone. Time would prove his intentions to her.

"Why do you need someone to watch over the teacher?" Tristan asked.

Leticia's brows lifted before a light of understanding came into her expression. She glanced at the footman. "To ensure her safety."

"Has there been trouble?"

Her gaze slid his way. "Nothing we couldn't handle."

"Tell me," he coaxed.

She waved her gloved hand in a dismissive gesture. "Someone..." she glanced anxiously at him. "Well, a man waved a knife at me and told us to close the school."

A cold bolt shot straight through him. "What!"

The horses danced and sidestepped. He swallowed and relaxed his shoulders.

She touched his arm again. "I'm sure it was nothing more than the idle threat of an ignorant man who fears what he does not understand. Still, Elizabeth and I felt it prudent to have Mrs. Harper stay with me and to send someone to keep watch over her in case there's any real trouble. Really, it's nothing."

The idea of someone threatening Leticia twisted his gut. He opened his mouth and then snapped it shut, censoring the first thing he wanted to shout at her. He fought to keep his voice steady. "You are unharmed?"

"Yes, of course."

If he ever got his hands on that despicable villain

who dared pull a knife on a lady—on his Tish…

He drew another breath. "When did this happen?"

"Oh, a few weeks ago."

"And you didn't see fit to tell me?" His attempt to keep his voice down failed.

Her tone turned defensive. "You were hurt, and had other things on your mind. And then later, well, an opportune moment never presented itself."

He let out a sigh. "Oh, Tish. Don't wait for an opportune moment to tell me something like that." He glanced at her. "Please."

The brim of her bonnet hid her face too much for him to see her expression. "I'm sure nothing more will come of it."

"Still, don't keep things like that from me." Anger and hurt knotted in his gut. She must have been terrified when it first happened. Yet, she had failed to tell him.

Softly, she said, "I didn't want to add to your worries."

"True friends don't keep secrets."

"I wasn't keeping it a secret…oh, very well. I see your point." Again, that touch. "I'm sorry, Tristan. Please don't be angry. Don't worry; nothing has happened since. I'm sure that's the last we've seen of that man."

His anger dissipated, but the hurt remained. Had she told Bradbury? Kensington? Did everyone know except him?

He pulled up in front of the school and helped her out. The teacher and footman leaped out and mounted the steps, leaving Tristan alone with Leticia.

She put a hand on his face, her expression apologetic. "I wasn't shutting you out." As she lowered her hand, her mouth curved upward, part rueful, part sad. "Do you remember that summer you were so angry and hurt that I wouldn't let you inside the tree house?"

A faint memory surfaced of standing at the bottom of the tree calling up to her and being denied admittance. The sting of rejection had cut him. He nodded.

"When I went to apologize, I offered you a piece of peppermint candy, but you didn't truly forgive me until after I had hugged you."

"Sometimes I wish we were still children." Perhaps he could arrange another balloon ride so as to once again have her in his arms.

She took his hand and tugged. "Come inside."

He gestured to the horses. "I can't leave the cattle standing. They're tired and need a rubdown."

"I will be but a moment."

He allowed her to lead him inside. She closed the door, removed her bonnet, and turned to him. The voices of the teacher and footman echoed to them from another room. Leticia threw her arms around him and held him. The air rushed out of his lungs. Her soft body pressed against him, creating alternating hot and cold tingles racing down his backbone. He wrapped his arms around her and held her close.

The sweet, pure pleasure of holding Leticia shone light deep inside his soul. Dark, shriveled parts of his heart opened up to receive her light.

He could no longer resist. He loved Leticia. Loved her! He would do whatever he must to ensure her happiness, her safety. If he ever lost her, every good and wholesome part of him would surely perish.

He swallowed. "If something ever happened to

you…"

She pressed a hand to the nape of his neck. "I'm unharmed."

With her comforting, intoxicating scent enfolding him, he squeezed her, basking in her touch, the sensation of her arms around him, her body pressed against him, filling him with hope.

"Um, Tristan? I can't breathe very well."

He loosened his grip.

She stepped back, her breath unsteady and her cheeks flushed. He cocked his head. There it was again; signs that Leticia felt an attraction for him as a man, and not merely as a friend.

She glanced up at him with enlarged pupils and her breathing sounded like a series of sighs. Yes, she wanted him. Satisfaction curled inside. They'd taken a step in the right direction.

"Forgiven?" She offered an unsteady smile.

He shrugged. "I might need another embrace to make sure."

She swatted his arm. "Don't leave poor Dancer and Willow out there too long."

The horses. Right. But the thought of leaving her side… "I'll take them home and return."

"Oh." She blinked. "Very well. I should be done with the music lessons by the time you return. In fact, after luncheon, we will have our first dance class. Do you think you could help us teach a country dance? We could use some males to act as partners."

"I would be honored." After bidding her good bye and promising to return soon, he danced out to the gig and sang all the way home, mentally penning sonnets to Leticia.

Chapter Twenty-Seven

Leticia peered inside the classroom at the street urchins-turned-students. Thin bodies, ragged clothing, unkempt hair and shabby shoes, and in some cases, bare feet proclaimed them the poorest of the poor, the cast offs, the ones no one acknowledged that they existed. Yet their eyes lit up with curiosity and delight. They had hope for a better future. They'd even recruited other students. The school now had over two dozen eager learners. How could anyone not see the value of this effort?

While she let her gaze rove over their happy faces, she gave a little start. Molly, who had been missing the last few days, had returned. As the girl turned her head, Leticia let out a gasp at the swollen, bruised face.

Poor thing. No wonder she'd been absent. She must have met with an accident and needed time to recover. If Leticia had bothered to check, perhaps she could have been of some assistance. Perhaps she still might help the child in some way.

As Mrs. Harper ended her lesson and invited the students to practice their reading, Leticia leaned in and caught her eye. Mrs. Harper nodded.

"Molly," Leticia beckoned. "It's time for your music lesson."

The girl stood and came to her, not quite meeting her gaze. As they left the classroom together for the smaller front room they'd taken to calling the music room, Leticia eyed the girl.

They sat and Leticia smiled. "I've missed you, sweeting. How did you get hurt?"

Gaze downward, Molly mumbled, "Fell."

An inner warning sounded inside Leticia. "What happened?"

The girl's breathing grew rapid. "Oh, nuthin'. Jes' clumsy. Tripped an' 'it a table."

Leticia touched her arm. "Sweeting, did someone hurt you?"

Molly shook her head.

"You can tell me if someone did."

Molly nodded. Letting it go for the time being, Leticia pulled out the simple etudes she'd brought for the children to learn, and began the lesson. In the background, children's voices rose as they repeated lessons in unison. Leticia corrected Molly's hand position, reminding her to curl her fingers and sit up straight, and reviewed counting the rhythm.

At the music lesson's conclusion, Leticia sat back. "Very good. You may tell Sarah it's her turn and return to your seat."

"Yes, miss."

As the girl stood, Leticia said, "Molly, you can tell me if something is amiss. I will do anything I can to help you."

Again, the nod. Leticia sighed. Did some neighborhood boy hurt her? They tended to travel in packs and sometimes got rough, even with girls. Leticia must keep a sharp eye out.

Throughout the day, the music lessons continued, crowding out other thoughts. As the last music student left, a shadow drifted into the room.

"You're very good with them." Tristan's voice, rich and low rumbled, and a spot inside her heart warmed.

He stood leaning a shoulder against the doorjamb, handsome and smug, but with a softness in his clear eyes that had never been there before. Wind-tossed dark curls tumbled over his brow invitingly. A bottle-green tailcoat gave his handsome looks an exotic slant. Had he always looked so good in buff breeches that fit him like a second skin?

Her pulse leaped and pounded double time.

But this was Tristan. Her childhood friend.

She stood and made a point of gathering her music. "Your arrival is timely. We will be stopping for luncheon soon. Then we'll begin our first dance lesson. Are you still willing to help us demonstrate?"

"Of course." He pushed off the wall and strode to her, all fluid grace. "What are you going to teach them?"

"My aunt's servants said reels are popular. I thought we'd start with a Scottish Reel."

"Good idea." In the main entryway, he stopped and picked up a large basket. "I brought luncheon."

"Oh, that's kind of you. I only have a bit of fruit and cheese. We can eat in the kitchen. Mrs. Harper will let the children have a recess soon, so they can eat as well. You know, I suspect what little we feed them here is more than they get any other time."

"You're providing food?"

"Not much. Bread and milk in the morning, apples and bread and sometimes cheese at noontime. We found that they are more alert and learn better."

Tristan nodded. "It's difficult to concentrate when one is hungry."

"Exactly!" She smiled.

Tristan always understood. She hugged her music and led the way to the kitchen. Tristan's presence filled the room. As he strode next to her, again came that fluttering sensation. His bay rum aftershave tickled her senses, familiar, and yet more, as if his unique scent had shifted subtly, from one that reminded her of their long-standing friendship, to a sensation of, well, something entirely uncomfortable. And yet, she wanted to bury her face into his neck and inhale.

All her senses sharpened and focused on him, magnifying his breathing, the rustle of his clothes as he set out food, each shift of his arms and shoulders, the thickness of his lashes, the tumble of his hair over his forehead.

Good gracious. Whatever ailed her?

In the kitchen, while Leticia cut slices of crusty bread and placed them on a plate to take to the classroom, Tristan spread out the contents of the basket, enough to feed four grown men. After she delivered the food, she returned to share her meal with him. He sat across from her, casting occasional glances at her as they ate and chatted of inconsequential topics.

Mrs. Harper entered but stopped short. "Oh, forgive me if I've interrupted."

Tristan stood as if a lady had entered. "Not at all. Please join us." He indicated a chair at one end of the table. "Does the footman—er, Peter was it?" At her nod, he continued, "Would he like to join us as well?" At Mrs. Harper's surprise, he added, "We're in a school kitchen. I'm not one to stand on ceremony."

The young teacher smiled at him, then turned her head to the doorway. "Peter," she called. "Do join us. Mr. Barrett has enough to feed a small household."

Tristan grinned at the teacher in friendliness and a touch of humor—no sign of the rakish flirt. Had he really changed so much that he would not show a trace of interest in the pretty young widow?

The footman appeared. They ate luncheon together, Tristan including all three of them in the conversation as if they were great friends. She watched Tristan, again lost in the admiration of his handsome face. A new maturity had settled over him, making him more handsome and dynamic than ever before. In many ways, he had transformed into the man Leticia had always believed he could be. Of course, this new lifestyle may be temporary as a way of dealing with the accident and the loss of his friend, and nearly the loss of his own life. She should not place too much hope in his behavior becoming permanent.

But oh, if it did…

What? What did that mean for her?

She'd never considered Tristan as anything more than a friend—until lately. No, she would be wise to focus on Lord Bradbury and Captain Kensington as potential husbands. They were steady and reliable.

Yet they did not add the same excitement to her life as Tristan, the same sense of belonging. That sense of belonging probably arose from her lifetime friendship between them—not because of a future as a couple. Didn't it?

After luncheon, Mrs. Harper returned to the classroom. Peter divided his time between lounging in the back of the classroom, patrolling the exterior, and casting adoring glances at the teacher.

Tristan and Leticia settled in the front parlor in a pair of chairs next to a small pot-bellied stove opposite the pianoforte Lord Bradbury donated. He had proven himself a kind and supportive man. She should not judge him too harshly based on one conversation.

Leticia pulled her shawl more closely around herself. "I hope you don't mind waiting a bit. Mrs. Harper has a firm schedule. Today, she made some alterations to create time for the dancing lesson, but not until they finish mathematics."

"There is nothing I would rather do than spend time with you." That soft smile reappeared, flirty and …affectionate? Yes. Affectionate. He'd been unusually affectionate of late in a way that transcended their usual friendship.

Did her interpretation of his affection arise from the strange, womanly attraction she'd developed for him over the last few weeks?

Footsteps pounded up the front stairs and the front door banged open. "Where is she?" A male voice roared. A bearded man in a coarse coat burst inside, his face purple and his fists held upward on either side of his body. "Molly!"

Leticia and Tristan leaped to their feet, Tristan stepping in front of Leticia protectively.

"Molly, you stupid wench, come! Now!" shouted the man.

Mrs. Harper stepped out of the classroom, her eyes wide. Molly peeked her head outside the doorway, surrounded by other faces.

Leticia drew herself up and stepped around Tristan. "You are interrupting our school, sir. Please leave."

The man turned his gaze her way. "My girl will 'ave no part of this. Molly! Come 'ere. Now!"

With a whimper, Molly shuffled to him. He cuffed the back of her head. "I tol' ye to stay away."

Molly shivered. "I wanna read, Papa."

Oh, dear. Surely this vile man wasn't this sweet child's father?

"No! I forbid it!" He boxed her ears.

"Stop!" Leticia rushed forward but Tristan caught her by the arm.

"Sir." Tristan's voice, filled with authority, caught the man's attention. "There is no cause to strike the child."

"She disobeyed me. I won't 'ave a willful girl, getting' no 'igh falutin' ideas." He spat on the floor and grabbed Molly by the arm.

Molly burst into tears. "Please, Papa, please let me stay."

As the girl's father raised his hand to strike her again, Tristan grabbed the man's arm. "If you hit that child in my presence again, I will flatten you."

The man swung at Tristan who neatly dodged it and landed a punch of his own. The man staggered back but as he lunged, Tristan pulled out a pistol. The sight checked the man's step.

The girl's father stared hard at Tristan. "Molly. Out."

Molly shuffled toward the door.

Leticia called. "Molly, wait. You don't have to go with him. Remember when I said I would help you? You can stay here, or…"

"Shut yer trap, woman!" the girl's father snarled. "My girl. Not yours. She goes wit' me." As if remembering the pistol trained on him, he snapped his mouth shut.

"No," Lectica said. "I won't allow you to take her. You—"

Tristan's voice cut across hers, gentle but decisive. "He's right. As her father, he has a legal right to keep her."

She turned to Tristan, angry and helpless. "He hurts her."

Tristan kept his focus on the man, steady, grim. He flicked his gun toward the door. "Go. Do not return."

The man cast a sneering glance at all of them and dragged his hapless daughter by one arm. He left the door wide open behind him.

Peter closed and bolted the door. "Sorry, Miss. I'll keep better watch."

Mrs. Harper shepherded the children back to the classroom and instructed them to recite sums aloud.

Leticia rounded on Tristan. "I can't believe you wouldn't let me—"

"Keep her?" Tristan supplied. "Then what?"

She struggled to come up with an answer. "I don't know, but I can't stand the thought of her living with such abuse."

Tristan tucked away his gun and put a hand on each of her shoulders. "If you tried to take her from her father, you would be in danger of the law."

Leticia struggled against anger, helplessness, sorrow.

Gently, Tristan pulled her in close and held her. "I know, Tish." He let out his breath. "Fathers should love and protect their children, not hurt them."

Enfolded in the soothing comfort of his arms, her

distress faded. She held on to him as a deep place inside her sighed.

He let out a caustic laugh. "Although, I suppose some children are full of the devil and deserve a few beatings."

She pulled away to look at him. "No child deserves any beating."

"Not like that." He glanced at the door through which Molly and her father exited.

"Not like what your father did to you, either."

Memories surfaced of, as a child, often finding Tristan, grim and teary-eyed but trying not to cry, curled up in the hollow of the oak near the brook after his father had whipped him. She had always put an arm around him and tried to reassure him that he was a good boy. Eventually, he stopped believing her. Now, as it did then, the idea of the gentle, dreamy-eyed Tristan she knew as a child being subjected to harsh punishment sent pain through her.

His eyes took on a faraway look, his expression unbearably sad. "I was such a disappointment...the reason my mother left."

"No, of course not." Did he really believe his mother ran off because of him?

His lips tightened. "I would never treat my children that way. There are more effective ways of punishing a misbehaving child and ensuring discipline than inflicting welts and bruises."

"Of course there is." She smoothed back that curl that always tumbled over his brow and let her fingers slide along his smooth-shaven cheek.

His eyes became intensely focused on her. With deliberate slowness, he slid one hand up her arm, over her shoulder, up her neck to her face. His thumb grazed her cheek in a feather touch. The air around them thickened, and all her nerve endings tingled as if a thunderstorm raged nearby. His gaze focused on her mouth. Her lips heated in response. He lowered his head, paused, met her eyes. A question lay there, open and honest.

She didn't know the answer. Her heart throbbed and a slow, burning tightness coiled in her stomach. He moved his other hand, slow and sensuous, up her shoulder to her other cheek. He stood, warm hands on her face, his eyes hot. He lowered his head again but paused a breath away.

Is this what she wanted?

He brushed his lips over hers, warm and unbearably soft. Someone let out a sigh. Or a moan. The pressure of his mouth increased to a gentle tug, asking, testing. It returned with renewed heat, no longer asking but offering. Unimaginable pleasure crept over her. The slow burn intensified.

Footsteps outside the room neared. "Stay in line, children." Mrs. Harper's voice rang out.

Leticia leaped away from Tristan. The warmth of his touch, his kiss, remained. While Tristan moved to stare out of the window, Leticia sank into one of the armchairs facing the stove. She pressed a finger over her lips. They throbbed. Burned. Delicious warmth inside her made her want to stretch like a cat. No wonder mothers and chaperones kept such wary eyes on young girls. Everything proper inside her crumbled under the power of Tristan's skillful kiss. The reckless behavior of so many women now made perfect sense.

She was a fool to venture there, especially with a

libertine of Tristan's caliber. She would do well to remember that he was not the sweet, sensitive child she'd comforted, confided in, played with, loved as a brother but most of all as a friend. Over the last several years, he'd become a rake in every sense of the word. He claimed to have changed, and indeed appeared to have done so, but this newly reformed side of him may not be here to stay.

If she gave her heart to him, only to have him eventually resume his life as a rake, she may never survive the heartbreak.

Chapter Twenty-Eight

Staring out the window of the front room in the school while every muscle in his body screamed at him to carry Leticia off to a dark corner, Tristan took several steadying breaths and ran through the latest figures the land steward had sent to him until his heartbeat returned to normal. Later, he would pull out the memory of kissing her, and revel in it, but for now, he needed to appear perfectly circumspect. He almost snorted at the idea of linking the word perfect with any part of himself. Too far away to touch, Leticia sat shuffling sheets of music with shaking hands.

Footsteps reached them. "Ah, here you both are." Mrs. Harper's voice cut through his thoughts.

Tristan turned and gave her a bland smile. Leticia looked up and held up sheet music as if indicating she'd found something she sought. All appeared innocent—if no one noticed Leticia's flushed cheeks.

"Form two lines please," Mrs. Harper instructed the children. "Mr. Barrett and Miss Wentworth will help us. Right here, Mr. Barrett, if you please."

The footman, Peter, entered, and the four adults helped teach the reel to the children. Throughout it all, Leticia refused to look Tristan in the eye. At first, he assumed the kiss flustered her, perhaps even embarrassed her. As the dancing lesson progressed, however, it became apparent something truly distressed her.

He must address her concerns before they festered. For now, he focused on the dancing. He guided girls ranging from barely tall enough to reach his elbow to adolescent. Engrossed in his assignment, he guided and complimented until they managed a reel. At the end, as they all bowed and curtsied, Tristan glanced at Leticia. She met his gaze and smiled.

Perhaps whatever concerned her could be assuaged more easily than he first feared.

Mrs. Harper dismissed the students, reminding the older ones of the public dance.

Leticia moved toward the room's doorway but Tristan called her. "Miss Wentworth, a word if you please?"

Mrs. Harper called as she headed to the schoolroom, "We will wait for you outside."

"I'll hail a hackney." Peter unlocked the front door and held it open for the children and the teacher, then followed them all out.

Alone with Leticia, Tristan moved to her side and peered into her downcast face. Very softly, he said, "Tish."

She stiffened, staring at the floor. He put a finger under her chin, lifted, and waited until she looked him in the eye.

A teary gaze met his. "Please don't make me fall in love with you."

He blinked. Fall in love with him?

"I won't do it," she said with a fierceness at odds with her usual demeanor. "I won't risk you breaking my heart. You say you've changed, and I think you believe it, but I don't know if..." She pinned him with a stare.

"Have you changed in your heart, or are you temporarily adjusting your behavior out of some idea of paying penance—or worse—as a way of adapting your seduction repertoire for me the way you adapted it for Elizabeth?"

All the wind left his lungs. If she'd driven a blade through his heart, it could not have caused worse agony. His throat and eyes burned. The pain heated to indignation, to anger. "This has nothing to do with Elizabeth. When will you stop flinging that in my face? I have changed. Why can't you see that?"

She folded her arms and looked down. Her condemnation knifed though him.

He fisted his hands. "You are so eager to give another chance to those who live in the streets, to champion change for them. It seems I don't get that same opportunity." He whirled around and rushed out, nearly trampling Peter outside.

"Y-your carriage is here, sir," Peter stammered.

Tristan said, "Drive it home. I'll walk."

He headed down the street and walked and walked until he found himself in a secluded area of a park. Alone, he broke into a run and ran until his legs weakened and his lungs ached. Twilight fell, enshrouding the city. At least, the growing darkness would help conceal his state of dishevelment. His anger and pain faded to an empty hopelessness.

She would never forgive him. To her, he would always be a rake.

A drinking song serenaded him, guiding him to a tavern. Lights shone from the windows and laughter beckoned. What did he have to lose?

He opened the front door, seeking its familiar,

mind-numbing diversion. Inside the tavern, the blend of tallow candles, smoke, unwashed bodies, and beer greeted Tristan like an old friend—familiar, and yet somehow foreign. Men gathered in groups, drinking, singing bawdy songs, and playing cards. Women of loose morals and an abundance of cleavage wove among them, some sitting on laps, offering samples of wares they were willing to sell.

In a nearby table, a man in a drunken stupor snored and drooled on the table while one of his companions relieved him of his purse. Others traded jests and far-fetched stories while laughing at their own wit. The general gaiety should have slid on him like a familiar coat. Instead, it shifted, unreal, strange, and distant, like revisiting a painting he'd viewed years before and finding that the truth didn't quite match his memories—the colors brash instead of bright, the subjects hideous instead of handsome, their games tiresome instead of titillating, and their intent calculating instead of congenial.

Had he changed that much, or did he merely see the truth now that he viewed the scene with a mind undimmed by the fog of alcohol and a devil-may-care attitude? And worse, did Tristan appear this way to Richard all those years? His conscience shouted a resounding *yes* to all.

Disgusted by the revelation, Tristan returned to the quiet outside. A lamplighter worked his way down the street, chasing away the shadows with his light. Fog crept through the streets, sending a chill through Tristan. He reached to turn up his collar but his fingers encountered a tailcoat, not a greatcoat. He paused to get his bearings. White's would be closer than his bachelor's rooms, and he could find warmth and food there.

After a brief ride in a hackney, he strode into the club and paused. Gentlemen sat in small groups or alone, talking quietly, sipping port or brandy. Some sat alone reading the newspaper. Two wrote in the famous White's Book where gentlemen logged their wagers both great and small. From the dining room came the aroma of savory meat, the clink of glasses, and the scrape of silverware. The scene felt wholesome and serene in comparison to the tavern. He found a seat and ordered a beefsteak.

"Dining alone tonight?" Captain Kensington appeared next to him. "Do you mind if I join you?"

Kensington. Another painful reminder of all the ways Tristan fell short. His appetite fled. Still, he gestured to the empty seat. "Please."

Kensington sank into the chair and made small talk for a few minutes, all the while, Tristan trying to quell his irritation at facing a rival for Leticia's affection. Tristan used to genuinely like the fellow, and they'd certainly enjoyed some good times, as well as a few scrapes, together. But now, with so much at stake...

Kensington had spent his last ten years serving King and Country, not as a wastrel. Perhaps he deserved Leticia. Still, Tristan had no intention of stepping aside. He was nowhere near that noble.

After a few minutes, Kensington fell silent, toying with the stem of his wineglass. "Tristan..." He let out his breath. "When you suggested that I court Leticia..."

Tristan stiffened. No. No, not yet. Not before Tristan had a chance to prove himself to Leticia.

Kensington continued, "I did it as a favor to you,

for the most part. She is a delightful girl. But…"

Tristan raised a brow and held his breath.

"I do not wish to pursue a courtship with her."

Tristan leaned forward.

"It's not that I couldn't be happy with her. I probably could be content, but I do not love her, and after knowing—" He broke off and then tried again. "It is inappropriate to continue to see her and raise her expectations. Since Lord Bradbury is also calling upon her, I think it best that I step aside."

Tristan let out a sigh of relief. "I see."

Kensington's next words came out rushed. "I have not given her any reason to believe my heart is engaged, nor do I believe hers is, either, nor did I kiss her, or…anything."

"I should hope not." If Tristan learned Kensington had kissed Leticia, he might have to rearrange the man's face.

But no, her kiss, while sweeter than anything he'd ever experienced, revealed without a doubt that she'd never had such an experience, despite her earlier taunt. That thought made him want to puff out his chest, as well as give her more experience in the art of kissing.

"I know you are old friends," Kensington said, "Rather like a brother to her, I should think. Since the idea of my courting her was yours, I thought it best to tell you my intention, or lack thereof."

Tristan tried to affect a calm demeanor. "Very sensible of you. I appreciate your candor."

Kensington eyed him. "You aren't angry with me?"

"No, of course not. You seemed to have treated her well, made her feel admired, and you showed others she was desirable, which, no doubt, boosted her view of herself. Withdrawing now before expectations are raised is a wise course of action."

"I'm relieved to hear that."

Tristan took a leap of trust. "Just so you know, I don't view her as a sister."

Kensington tilted his head to one side. "I see."

"She is…special."

Kensington toyed with a small gold band he wore around his little finger, a ring Tristan had not noticed before. "I have business in the continent. I depart Tuesday next."

"Will you be in Italy, by chance?"

"Yes, as a matter of fact, I will." Kensington eyed Tristan.

"Perchance you could look in on my sister Selina? She's been gone a rather long time and seems reluctant to return home. Perhaps you can reassure me as to her safety."

"I'd be happy to."

Their food arrived, and they spent the remainder of the time talking like old friends. Warm and fed, and with one obstacle to Leticia's heart now cleared away, Tristan turned over new possibilities as to how to convince her that he truly loved her and that she could trust him with her heart.

Chapter Twenty-Nine

Inside her bedchamber at her aunt's house, Leticia fastened her garters and smoothed wrinkles in her silk stockings. As she stood to allow her maid to lower her ball gown over her head, Isabella entered.

"Do I look well enough?" her sister asked, turning.

Leticia glanced at her. "Bella, you always look perfect."

Isabella gestured to her ivory gown with tiny aqua flowers and trimmed in matching ribbon. "I don't think this color suits me."

With a sigh, Leticia gave her a closer look. "Come in by the light so I can see you better."

Isabella came closer and stood near the tall candelabra where beeswax candles flickered. With her dark hair styled meticulously, and her large, darkly lashed, blue-green eyes more vibrant with the matching aqua of her gown, and the creamy perfection of her skin, she created a stunning image.

"The gown is a perfect complement to your complexion, and it brings out the color of your eyes."

Isabella's smile was pained. "Truly?"

Leticia studied her. There seemed to be a deeper issue here than Isabella's appearance. "Whatever is amiss, dear?"

Isabella sank down on a nearby chair. "I want to look well tonight."

The maid finished pinning Leticia's gown and departed without a sound.

"Any particular reason why?" Leticia asked.

"Oh…not really." Isabella stared off into space for a minute. "May I ask you a question?"

"Of course." Leticia stepped into her carriage shoes.

"If Lord Bradbury offers for you this season, will you accept him?"

Leticia hesitated. "I do not know. As I told you before, I do not fancy myself in love with him. He's all that is charming and good and…I should be madly in love with him. But…"

She pictured herself kissing him, but the memory of kissing Tristan leaped into her mind. So gentle, so passionate, his kiss introduced her to a whole new realm of pleasure. The idea of sharing such a moment with Lord Bradbury felt flat and colorless. Yes, she wanted to be kissed again, but not by Bradbury—by Tristan. Her body ached to be back in his arms again, to press her lips against his, to bask in the warm smoothness of his voice, to laugh with him, to tease him, too see him smile at her in that slow, heart-melting manner of his.

She didn't dare, did she?

Her eyes burned. Why couldn't she have remained mere friends with Tristan? Why did she start seeing him as a desirable man?

When she'd thrown her parting words at him, he'd stepped back as if she'd slapped him, and for a moment, his carefree, flirty exterior crumbled, leaving a wounded child in his place. The pain in his expression—pain she caused—nearly broke her heart.

She'd hurt him. She, who used to comfort him when he'd needed solace as a child, and when Richard's disappointment had stung him, she'd always offered him healing without censure.

How ironic that the moment she began seeing him as a mature man who created grown up stirrings in her, that her affection became conditional, judgmental.

Isabella put an arm around her. "Tish, what is it?"

She let out a weighted sigh. "I'm so confused. I should love Lord Bradbury for the honorable, virtuous man that he is. Instead, I can't stop thinking about Tristan. But that's absurd; he has always sworn he'd never marry, and besides, he'd make a terrible husband. Probably half the widows of the *ton* under the age of forty have seduced him. How could I be so foolish as to think of him as anything other than a shameless rake?"

"Because he's changed."

"So he claims, but has he really?"

"It's all over London. Everywhere I go, people are whispering about how respectable he's become."

"They are?"

Isabella nodded. "Some matrons say it often happens when young men grow up and begin thinking of their future. I heard Lady Tarrington say most young gentlemen don't do that until about the time they reach their thirtieth year. It seems Lord Tarrington was something of a rake in his youth, too. Tristan seems to be changing rather younger than normal."

Leticia gaped at her. "Isabella, no young lady such as you should be hearing those things, and you should not know what that all means."

Isabella rolled her eyes. "I have eyes and ears and a brain."

Leticia groaned. When did her innocent little sister grow up?

Looking around as if about to divulge a secret, Isabella lowered her voice. "When our maid went away because she was in a family way, I asked Mama for details of how that happens, and she explained—enough that I understand when people talk behind their fans, now." She grabbed Leticia's arm, her eyes wide. "Oh, don't worry, it hasn't incited my imagination. I'm no more interested in any of that than before. In fact, I was so disgusted that I could barely look at men for weeks and weeks."

Aunt Alice peered in. "Ladies, the carriage is here."

"Be right there, Aunt." Leticia stood and picked up her dancing slippers.

Rising, Isabella looked Leticia in the eyes. "You should give him a chance. Tristan has changed, and he is in love with you." With that, she marched away, leaving Leticia standing, awestruck, in the room.

Tristan in love with her?

She stood grappling with the possibilities until Aunt Alice summoned her. Almost dizzy with conflicting memories both old and new, she picked up her reticule and shawl, and joined the others. When they arrived at the home of their host, they removed their wraps and changed from carriage shoes to dancing slippers. After greeting the hosts in the ballroom, Leticia stood with Isabella and Aunt Alice. Moments before the first set began, almost simultaneously, two gentlemen approached and asked Isabella for a dance.

Isabella smiled at the contenders. "Oh dear. I would be pleased to stand up with each of you fine gentlemen. Perhaps one of you might be willing to reserve the next set for me?"

The gentlemen eyed each other. One said, "I would be delighted to await your charming presence for the next set, Miss Isabella." He bowed, cast a meaningful glance at the other, and strode away.

The victor inclined his head, looking rather too smug for Leticia's preference, and held out a hand. Isabella glanced at Leticia before taking his hand, amusement dancing in her eyes and left with her dance partner.

Leticia cast a glance around, admiring the finely tailored suits and pretty ball gowns of the assembly. Tristan's familiar form caught her eye. He stood conversing with none other than the incomparable Duke of Suttenberg and a gentleman Leticia did not know. Though society hailed the duke as one of the most handsome bachelors in all of London, and the other man a distinguished older gentleman, neither compared to Tristan's stunning perfection. Her heart began a rapid acceleration, building with every beat. How handsome he was! And how dear he'd become to her—more than ever.

Nearby, a sultry, feminine laugh caught Leticia's attention, as well as Tristan's. A beautiful lady about Leticia's age with golden curls held her fan in front of her, looking in his direction. Leticia searched her memory for the lady's name but could only recall that she'd been widowed during the war. The widow shifted her hold and tapped the edge of her fan with her finger. Leticia almost gaped. Using the language of fans, the woman invited Tristan to come speak with her.

Tristan's mouth froze, as if he'd stopped mid-sentence. Leticia held her breath. Tristan returned his gaze to his companions and resumed his dialogue. He hadn't approached the beauty despite her invitation.

"Shall we take a seat, my dear?" Aunt Alice's voice drew Leticia's attention.

"Of course." No need to stand so close to the dance floor looking desperate while a set had already begun. Nor would it do to keep watching Tristan.

They moved toward the edge of the ballroom and found a settee. Leticia sat and spoke with everyone who stopped to chat.

Lord Bradbury arrived. "Mrs. Tallier." He bowed. "Miss Wentworth, how splendid to see you again. Please do me the honor of standing up with me."

Lord Bradbury failed to have the slightest effect on her heart beat. Still, she always found dancing a pleasant diversion, and one did not refuse an earl.

As he led her to the dance floor for the next set, complimenting her on her gown, she glanced again at Tristan. He stood alone, staring out the French doors as if he were lost in thought, his expression pensive. The blonde widow stood nearer him, but he failed to even glance in her direction. What had him blue-deviled this evening? Did he regret the kiss? Did rakes ever regret kisses? She almost let out a sigh. She'd never imagined that act could be so singularly beautiful or devastating.

"Miss Wentworth, have you already promised the supper dance to someone?" Lord Bradbury asked.

"Er, no, not yet. But I'm not certain we ought to dance a second time in one evening."

He cocked his head. "No? Why ever not? It isn't as if I've asked you for a third. That would be scandalous." His eyes twinkled.

Three other couples joined them to make up a square for the quadrille, so Leticia lowered her voice. "No, of course not, but…I don't want people to draw conclusions. The opera a few nights ago, two dances tonight…it might imply a relationship we do not have."

"Are you concerned people might view that as us showing a preference for one another?"

"Aren't you?"

The quadrille started and she curtsied to him as he bowed to her.

"No. I want people to know." He looked her in the eyes.

A bold declaration. Leticia flushed and looked down. She turned to take the hand of the gentleman next to her and circled. She and the other ladies changed partners, taking her away from Lord Bradbury.

If Lord Bradbury's heart were truly involved, she needed to give serious thought to a future with him. As she circled, holding hands with the gentlemen on either side of her, she glanced up at Lord Bradbury across the circle from her. He stared at her rather too intensely.

He deserved a truthful response. A second dance would not qualify as a true declaration of her devotion to Lord Bradbury, but somehow, it felt too intimate, considering her tepid feelings toward the gentleman. Still, such a fine man would make an exceptional husband. Perhaps she should let her head, rather than her heart, rule her decisions. If she discouraged Lord Bradbury, she may not get any offer. Without the means of having another London Season, this may be her last chance for a home and family of her own. Going back to the country would leave her without prospects. She faced a life of being a burden to her parents and continuing to help various relations with their health needs or their children for the rest of her life.

Of course, she had the school. But loving and helping those children would not give her a home of her own, nor fill her home with children. Nor would it fill her heart with the love of a husband—but that sweet dream faded away.

She continued circling and twirling in the dance pattern as she made her way through successive partners until she came back around to Lord Bradbury. She admired his lean figure and his handsome face. More importantly, he was kind, attentive, and had a reputation for being every bit as upstanding as the Duke of Suttenberg, the paragon of gentlemanly behavior. Did Bradbury offer her the happy companionship of a good man, or a life of dissatisfaction?

His earlier question lingered in his eye as he took her hand and they circled. She would be happy with him, surely.

Making up her mind, she said, "If you aren't reluctant, then neither am I."

Still he waited as if he had not received the confirmation he sought.

"I would be honored to save you the supper dance, Lord Bradbury."

He smiled, his eyes lighting up—not the blast of cheer that Tristan's eyes did, but still a charming expression. The rest of the intricate dance passed in a blur, as did the following dance in the set. Leticia, breathless from the vigorous exercise, and her promise to Lord Bradbury, returned to her aunt who sat with the Countess of Tarrington.

"I'm sure it's nothing," the countess said with a wave of her hand. "I'm tired, nothing more." Lady Tarrington, though of an age similar to Leticia's mother, bore the beauty of a much younger lady.

Aunt Alice turned to Leticia and gestured to her. "Lady Tarrington, may I introduce my niece, Leticia Wentworth?"

Leticia curtsied. "I believe we were introduced at the subscription ball, Aunt."

"Ah yes, Miss Wentworth," the elegant older woman said. "You drew a rather flattering sum for the privilege of a supper dance."

"All in the name of charity," Leticia said.

The countess looked her over. "My, you are lovely. I must introduce you to my son, Cole. A few months ago, he returned from the sea where he served as a lieutenant in His Majesty's navy."

Leticia smiled. "You must be very proud."

"Of course, but I'm happier that he returned home. He was gravely wounded, but at least he's back and well again."

The distinguished older gentleman Leticia had spotted speaking with Tristan earlier appeared. He took the countess's hand and kissed it, all the while his eyes fixed on her face.

Lady Tarrington smiled. "I'm quite well, never fear, my love."

She introduced him as Lord Tarrington who greeted them all with a nod. He bowed, kissed his wife's hand again, offered her an affectionate smile, and left.

What a loving and devoted husband. Oh, what Leticia wouldn't give for someone to look at her like

319

that. She sighed.

Lady Tarrington gazed after her husband. "He does worry over me so. But if the doctor can't find anything wrong, it's probably nothing."

"I'm sure you're right," Aunt Alice replied.

Leticia glanced back at the place where she'd last seen Tristan but he had moved on somewhere, hopefully not into the arms of the widow trying to attract his notice. Near the doorway, a movement caught her eye.

Tristan stood near the blonde, their heads close together, their postures intimate. It appeared Tristan the Rake had returned. Clearly, he had not changed so much. Her eyes stung and her vision blurred.

Leticia bit her lip and squared her shoulders. Lord Bradbury caught her gaze from a few feet away. As he led another lady out to the dance floor, he smiled at Leticia, a slow, private smile.

Lord Bradbury. Kind. Attentive. Well behaved. A respected peer of the realm. She would have him if he asked her. And she'd be happy about it. Lord Bradbury would not break her heart. In time, she would learn to love him.

She gave him her most brilliant smile before lowering her gaze, the picture of a demure lady. Let Tristan have his loose women. She would have a home of her own and a family with a man who understood the meaning of constancy.

Chapter Thirty

Tristan swore under his breath. How did he get himself into such entanglements? He looked down into Henrietta's enchanting face. He must not weaken. Yes, she was beautiful, and yes, he was lonely, but he no longer sought such empty pleasure. He ached for meaningful, lasting pleasure. Joy. Love. With Leticia.

He edged back. "I'm sorry, Henrietta."

The blonde widow smiled coyly at him and wound her finger around a long curl skimming her collarbone, a provocative motion he once found irresistible. "You don't have to pretend with me, Tristan. Now that I'm back in England, we can resume where we left off…"

"No, we can't," he said. "I'm sorry."

Her blue eyes searched his, her expression sobering. "I never asked you to wait for me when we last parted, you know. If there's been someone else, well, I'm not so maudlin as to expect any sort of fidelity. You know that, don't you?"

He looked away. "I've changed. I want something…permanent."

She laughed. "Oh, Tristan. You aren't thinking of asking me to marry you? You know how I feel about that."

This was not going well. "No, I mean to ask someone else to marry me."

There, he'd said it. Of course, he still had a great

deal of work ahead, but he would not give up.

Her smile faded. "You're in earnest."

"I am."

That irrepressible spirit, born of supreme confidence returned, but her tone took on a mocking edge. "Are you doing this to satisfy your brother? Oh, wait, I know, you've met an heiress."

Tristan shook his head. "I'm courting her because I love her."

She folded her arms and gave him a disbelieving frown. "I don't believe you. Not you, of all people."

"It's true. I love her and I plan to marry her as soon as I've convinced her I've changed. Being seen with you won't help that endeavor. This is goodbye, Henrietta." He offered an apologetic smile and walked away from the passionate beauty from his former life who now tempted him no more than Mrs. Hunter had at the house party.

He glanced at his pocket watch. He'd been certain Leticia would be here tonight but he had yet to have spotted her. Of course, in this crush of humanity, he might never find her.

A footman appeared with a tray of drinks, but Tristan declined. Having a clear head made it easier to read people, outwit opponents, appreciate a subtle joke, and resist women best left in the past.

Winding his way through the crowd, Tristan found his sister-in-law conversing with Miss Seton. "Elizabeth. Delightful as always."

Turning, Elizabeth smiled. "Tristan. I didn't know you were here tonight."

They made all the correct pleasantries before he asked the question burning him. "Have you seen

Leticia?"

"Why, yes. She's dancing." Elizabeth gestured to the dance floor.

At the far end of the room, a radiant, smiling Leticia danced with—Tristan ground his teeth—the Duke of Suttenberg. Perfect. Another paragon for competition. In the same circle danced Lord Bradbury and Captain Kensington. Tristan almost cursed. Hours after telling Tristan he was an unforgivable rake, Leticia danced with his main competitors, none of whom had behaved in a rakish manner in their entire lives.

Of course, Kensington hadn't been a saint in his younger years, but his exploits never labeled him a rake. He'd come home from the war decidedly subdued, so of course the *ton* viewed him as a mysterious and well-mannered war hero. At least Tristan didn't have to compete with him any longer. Practically tapping his toes in impatience, he waited until the set ended. Before Suttenberg returned Leticia to her aunt, Tristan stepped up. He gave Suttenberg a polite if curt nod and focused on Leticia.

Tristan held out a hand and gave her his most disarming smile. "Dance with me, I beg you, or I might expire on the spot."

Suttenberg chuckled and faded into the background.

Leticia's expression turned from startled to amused. "You needn't be so theatrical, you know."

He grinned. "Sometimes I cannot help myself."

Returning his smile, she looked into his eyes. "It pains me to tell you this, but the next one is the supper dance, and I've promised it to Lord Bradbury."

Bradbury! Tristan faltered. If he'd found her sooner, but no, he'd been walking the streets of London, almost succumbing to the lure of his old ways before he came to his senses. Then he'd had to change into his evening attire and dancing shoes before he dared appear at the ball. To top it off, he'd had difficulty finding her in this crush.

"I see," he managed.

The image of Leticia waltzing with Bradbury, in such an intimate position, and then bathing him with her smiles and favoring him with her company and her rich laughter all through dinner made him want to hunt down Bradbury and challenge the man for a fisticuffs match. As satisfying as that sounded, such measures would not win Leticia's favor. A more subtle approach, then.

Her smile faded. "I'm sorry, Tristan."

He drew a steadying breath and focused on everything he loved about her, which made it easy to smile at her with sincerity. "The last dance of the evening, then. Or I really will expire on the spot."

She seemed breathless and she looked down. "Of course—for the sake of your life."

Bradbury arrived then, slipping in between them and taking her hand. He cast a dismissive glance at Tristan. "Barrett." Then he turned his back on Tristan and held out his hand as the first notes of a waltz filled the ballroom.

The proverbial gauntlet landed at his feet. Tristan said under his breath, "May the best man win."

With his brows raised, Bradbury glanced over his shoulder at him. Tristan stared back, all boldness. After a startled pause, Bradbury swept Leticia into his arms in waltz position though the music had yet to start. Grinding his teeth, Tristan moved back to Elizabeth standing in the company of several ladies. Tristan singled out the shy young Miss Seton, offered a proper bow, and invited her to dance. As they waltzed, he teased a smile out of her by making wild claims of their winnings at whist and becoming a formidable partnership. It helped him to keep from staring at Leticia as she waltzed and later dined with another man.

After supper, Miss Seton thanked him for being her dining companion, adding, "I know you would rather have been with someone else, but you were kind to spend this time with me."

As he tried to deny it, Miss Seton added, "You're a fine gentleman, Mr. Barrett. I hope you get your heart's desire."

Sheepish, Tristan took his leave of her. Back in the ballroom, he sought out the hostess and begged a favor. With a smile, and a wink, she agreed. Tristan danced every set with wallflowers and each time placed himself near enough to dance with Leticia as the formation moved. Once, Henrietta caught his eye, and she gave him a puzzled, hurt frown. He did his best to avoid looking at her.

At last, the final dance began. A waltz. Tristan grinned at the hostess for agreeing to his wish. He wound through the crowd to Leticia. Bradbury stood next to her, close and possessive. That must be Tristan's cue.

Tristan tugged at the end of his waistcoat, and stepped up to her. "I believe this last one is ours." He held out a hand.

With an apologetic glance at Bradbury, she put her

hand in Tristan's. As the music began, she lifted her brows. "Another waltz?"

"How fortunate for us," he murmured.

She cocked her head to the side. "Did you arrange that?"

"Of course I did. I refused to be robbed of an opportunity to waltz with you."

"And why is that so important?"

"A chance to hold you close." He held her gaze, willing her to see the truth.

Her eyes widened. She took a step back, but he caught her hand and led her to the floor, drawing her into waltz position. Her breathing quickened as they danced. He held her no closer than he ought, no closer than strictly proper, but every breath, every rustle of her skirt, every motion, heightened his senses until he expected to shatter into a hundred pieces.

"Come riding with me tomorrow, Tish. Early in the morning."

"I-I can't. I have calls to make."

"You don't make calls that early."

She let out a huff. "You don't get up that early."

"Yes, in fact, I do, and have been for most of the Season."

She leaned back to look at him. "Why?"

"Because, as I keep trying to tell you, I don't stay out all night anymore—unless I'm dancing with you, that is." No longer willing to resist, he drew her closer—not so much as to scandalize chaperones, but enough to make his point. In a low voice, and allowing his breath to stir the little curls by her ear, he murmured, "Come riding with me tomorrow, Tish."

She shivered and her hand trembled. "I-I shouldn't.

I mean, I don't know if a groom will be available to attend me."

"No groom necessary. I will see that you come to no harm."

"Alone?" her brow furrowed.

"No less proper than riding unchaperoned in an open carriage."

"No, I mean, yes, I mean, I realize that but—" She broke off and her mouth tightened.

He put a slight distance between them. Perhaps that would ease her distress. Very gently, he asked, "When did you become reluctant to spend time in my company?"

She remained silent so long that he feared she would never answer. After a hard swallow, she whispered, "You know why."

He whispered back, "Because I kissed you?"

Her cheeks pinked, and she held her lower lip between her teeth.

Tristan put a husky, teasing quality into his voice. "Was it so bad?"

She let out a shaky breath and turned her head away.

His stomach clenched. "Don't fear me, Tish. I would never ruin you."

"I know." Her eyes brightened with gathering tears.

The sight of her tears sent a bolt of alarm through him. "Trust me. Please trust me."

She refused to look at him. He needed to fix this. Now.

The waltz ended. He led her off the dance floor, but instead of returning her to her aunt, he took her outside to the far edge of the terrace, still within view of the open doors but out of earshot. With lights from the ballroom falling upon them, he stood near enough that they could converse. Though craving the contact, he refrained from touching her.

"Then please believe me when I say that I have changed. I know you have other prospects, but I ask you to allow me to court you. Don't agree to an offer from anyone else—I beg you—until I have had a chance to prove to you that I am what I claim."

She turned and leaned on the stone balustrade, gazing out over the moonlit gardens.

Unable to resist touching her, he also leaned on the balustrade and rested his crossed arms next to her, letting his fingers brush her elbow. "Let me prove to you my intentions. Let me show you my heart."

She closed her eyes as if his words inflected pain. At last, she nodded.

"Come riding with me tomorrow?"

Another nod. "I'll be ready."

A steady stream of couples passed by on their way from the garden into the French doors leading to the house.

"Leticia dear," Mrs. Tallier called from the doorway. "I believe Isabella is rather fatigued."

"Coming, Aunt." Leticia glanced at Tristan.

Trying not to allow his desperation to show, he said, "I'll call for you at seven o'clock."

For a moment, the Leticia he knew and loved emerged and cast him a disbelieving smile. "My, so early for Town hours."

"Even owls are capable of being awake early mornings—with the proper motivation." He grinned.

She awarded him a faint smile in return, still two-parts disbelieving. "It's almost three o'clock in the morning. Let's make it eight, shall we?"

"Agreed."

After another smile, she joined her aunt inside. Tristan took a long exhale. He still had much damage to repair, but at least she'd agreed to give him a chance.

A sultry feminine laugh caught his attention. Mrs. Hunter ascended the steps on the arm of a gentleman. Upon reaching the terrace, they shared an intimate smile and parted ways. The gentleman slipped in first, while Mrs. Hunter smoothed a hand over her hair and her gown. As she strode past Tristan, she glanced at him, and paused mid-step.

"Well, Tristan Barrett," she purred. "You are looking absolutely delicious this evening." She sauntered to him and draped herself against the balustrade, looking up at him with a sultry glint in her eyes. "I hope you'll be a gentleman and rescue me from a lonely ride home tonight."

Tristan stiffened and took a step back from her. How had he ever found such women desirable? "I believe you have already found relief from loneliness this eve."

"An appetizer. I'd love to make a main course of you." She touched his lapel and ran her hand up along it to his cravat.

He stiffened. "I must decline."

Her lazy sensuality increased. "Come home with me for a glass of champagne. Talk to me."

Tristan pushed off the railing. "I'm sorry, Mrs. Hunter, but I am not looking for a dalliance." He affected a brief bow and strode away as quickly as possible without breaking into a run.

Inside the doors, he ran straight into an older gentleman prowling along the perimeter of the ballroom as if searching for something.

"Forgive me," Tristan said, stepping back.

The gentleman, elegant and distinguished, with blond hair fading to silver, glanced at him. "No harm done, young man." He narrowed his eyes at him. "I say, have we met?"

Tristan searched his memory. "I believe so. I'm Tristan Barrett. We were introduced at the benefit ball, I believe."

"Ah yes. You are the very image of Lord Averston—brothers?"

"Yes, my lord. And you are Lord Tarrington, as I recall."

"The same. Say, have you seen a bracelet hereabouts? My wife lost hers."

Tristan drew a breath and collected himself. "No, sir, but I'd be happy to help you search."

Tarrington nodded. "Good man."

"Where have you looked so far?" Tristan indicated the floor.

The earl made a gesture. "I started at that far corner."

Servants also hunted in the near-vacant ballroom, their gaze fixed on the floor.

"The servants might find it if I don't hurry, and I want to be my lady's hero, even if I am getting old and gray." Lord Tarrington winked.

Tristan smiled and joined the search. A moment later, a glittering object caught his gaze. Tristan hurried to it and picked up an emerald bracelet. He carried it back to the earl. "Is this it?"

Tarrington broke into a broad grin. "By jove, it is! Many thanks."

"My pleasure, sir. Tell your lady you found it so you can be her hero." Tristan pressed his finger to his lips.

The earl chuckled. "I owe you, son."

"Not at all."

"I know it isn't my business, lad, but you seem a bit blue-deviled. Is there anything I can do to repay you?"

Tristan sighed. "No, sir, not unless you can change a person's reputation or win a heart."

A blond brow raised. "Whose reputation? Yours or another's?"

"Mine, more's the pity."

"Ah. Your last few years as a rake are now hindering your wooing of a lady?"

Tristan blanched. Did everyone know of his wild ways?

"I had the same problem. I found the lady of my dreams but she wouldn't hear of letting a known *rouè* court her."

Tristan stilled. "What did you do?"

"First I took a hard look at myself to determine if I were changing to please her, or if I wanted to change. Once I realized that I wanted to change for the very reason I lost my heart to her—because my life, as I'd been living it, was meaningless—I turned my energy to bettering myself and my life; I took a greater interest in our estate, followed political concerns, took up some good causes, did everything I could to make myself into the kind of man that would attract a lady of her level of excellence."

Tristan nodded. "And then?"

"It wasn't easy, I feared it was too little too late for her—others were courting her. But I refused to give up."

"Did it work?"

His blue eyes danced as he fingered the bracelet . "After thirty two years of marriage, I'm still her hero."

"I'm glad. I hope it works out as well for me."

The older man nodded. "I wish I were having this conversation with my son, Cole. At first I was proud of his exploits, but he's doomed to suffer from the same mistakes I did. I hope he doesn't wait until it's too late." He clapped Tristan on the shoulder. "Change is not easy, but it's worth it."

"Did you find it?" a feminine voice called from the far end of the room leading to the great hall.

Tristan grinned at the earl. "Go impress your lady fair."

The earl held up the bracelet and called, "Right here, my love."

The countess, a stunning older lady with rich, dark hair, clasped her hands together. "My hero. You always manage to save the day."

Tristan bowed and crossed the wood floor, scuffed from dancers, on his way out. He must find a way to prove himself to Leticia.

Perhaps he could ask his man of business to provide a ledger, which would show his expenses were not extravagant, and that his gambling wins and losses were infrequent and never for exorbitant amounts. He could show that to Leticia to put her mind at ease in that regard. As far as drinking, she already noticed he'd virtually cut that out of his life. As to the more serious of all his past vices, he was at a total loss. He'd resisted all manner of temptations, with more ease than he ever would have imagined, but she had no way of knowing that. How could he prove his faithfulness?

Chapter Thirty-One

With the train of her riding habit draped over her arm, Leticia paced the length of the foyer. Morning light peeked in the windows, but failed to cast light on a wise course of action. She turned and paced back the other way, passing a table filled with flowers from both Lord Bradbury and Tristan. She continued into the open doorway of the morning parlor.

"Leticia?"

Leticia let out a yelp and jumped back. "Gracious, Aunt! You nearly put me into an early grave."

Aunt chuckled. "I didn't mean to startle you, dear." Curled up in a settee and wearing an ivory morning gown, Aunt Alice sipped tea.

"I didn't think anyone was up at this hour." Leticia sat in an armchair next to her aunt.

"I don't sleep much these days. I'm surprised to see you up after such a late night."

Leticia adjusted her riding gloves. "I'm going riding with Tristan."

"Ah. Has he declared himself to you?"

Leticia choked. "No. Well, not really." Although his words last night might have been taken for a declaration of sorts.

"I've never seen a more smitten young man. You are wise to consider a man like Lord Bradbury, and he's a fine catch, of course, but you are a very subdued version of yourself in his presence. When you're with young Mr. Barrett, you come alive."

Leticia hugged herself. "I'm comfortable with him because I've known him all my life."

Aunt Alice set down her teacup. "What is it that makes you disregard him as a prospect?"

"You know what."

"He comes from a long and distinguished family, he has a generous allowance, he's delightful, and clearly devoted to you. It doesn't hurt that he's hailed as one of this Season's most eligible bachelors. Why, all Season the gossip columns have been comparing Tristan to the likes of the young Viscount, Cole Amesbury, his youngest brother Christian Amesbury, Lord Bradbury, and even the Duke of Suttenberg. One of my favorite columnists is calling them The Five Incomparables, and declares they've put all of London into a collective swoon." She leaned forward. "Although, truth be told, I'd add Captain Kensington into that list."

Leticia waved her hand. "Yes, yes. Tristan's handsome face is not the issue."

"You're worried about his reputation." Aunt Alice clasped her hands and regarded her.

Leticia sank into a green striped armchair. "How do I know he won't revert back to his dissipated lifestyle?"

"If you are asking me how does one person know if another person has repented, that is for God to judge—not us. All we can do is believe by their words and their behavior that they are sincere, trust that they are strong enough to persevere, and offer encouragement when they weaken." She poured herself another cup of tea and sipped. "It sounds to me that you are afraid."

"I am. I'm afraid if I fall irrevocably in love with him, he'll eventually fall back into his old ways. That would break my heart."

Aunt Alice set down her teacup. "You cannot be so afraid of twisting an ankle that you never allow yourself the joy of dancing."

Leticia turned that thought over. "You're saying the joy of love is worth the risk of a broken heart."

"That's right." Aunt Alice leaned forward. "Do you believe his feelings are genuine?"

"I'm...not certain what, exactly, his feelings are. We've been friends forever. Now, there's something new between us. I'm not sure I understand fully what is happening, or what he wants to do about it. Even if I did, I don't know if I dare."

Last night Tristan had surprised her. Twice. She'd watched as he'd rejected not one, but two offers from women who he would normally... Well. She wouldn't go into details. Had Tristan's changes really become permanent? During the house party, Tristan had showed no signs of succumbing to the alluring Mrs. Hunter, if Mrs. Hunter's frustrated expression were any indication. Last night, she'd overheard two people commenting on how Tristan appeared to be growing out of his dissipated youth and turning into a steady young man. Did they all see something she failed to recognize?

Aunt Alice picked up her cup. "As his oldest friend, don't you think you, of anyone, should believe in him?"

Guilt wagged a finger at Leticia. She looked away. "As his friend, yes, I should be. But if I am to become more than a friend—"

"You need to decide once and for all; do you trust him? If so, give him a chance. And let Lord Bradbury know your heart is otherwise engaged. You cannot keep them both dangling."

"Dangling?" Leticia rocked back as if her aunt had thrown hot tea in her face. "Is that what I'm doing?"

"Some may view it that way."

Sinking down into her hands, she let out a moan. What to do? Lord Bradbury resembled a bed of coals, warm and steady and constant. Tristan reminded her of fireworks, bright and explosive and exciting. Would he vanish in a blink?

Leticia remembered the gun he carried, and the deadly calm with which he'd wielded it at the thug in Vauxhall. In the balloon ride, when she'd been frightened, he'd held her in a comforting embrace. She'd never experienced such a sensation of safety than she had with Tristan. Even his kiss had been respectful, an offer, a question, letting her take what she wanted, demanding nothing in return. She'd felt beautiful and cherished and...loved.

Did Tristan love her?

More importantly, did she love him?

The front door knocker broke the silence. Leticia stood as the butler opened the door and greeted Tristan.

"Good morning, Aunt," Leticia murmured.

"Have a wonderful time, dear."

As Leticia entered the foyer, Tristan's face, so familiar, so dear, and yet somehow different, guided her to his side like a lighthouse guides lost sailors. His lean, broad-shouldered frame filled out his riding coat in a way that no doubt drew envy from gentlemen and

Donna Hatch

admiration from ladies—far too handsome for his own good. If he'd been born plainer, perhaps he would not have been the object of every lewd woman who saw him. If only he'd had the wherewithal to have refused them.

He grinned and her heart leaped like a crazed circus performer. He met her halfway across the room, took her hand, and brought it to his lips. After kissing the back of her hand, he kept it nestled in his. The contact of his bare hand on hers gave courage to that crazy circus performer in her heart.

"You are radiant this morning, Leticia Love."

Love. Did he mean that? Did he love her?

His grin turned intimate. How long they stood there, hands intertwined, looking into each other's eyes, she could not have guessed. With his free hand, he touched her cheek. Did his touch mean he saw her as different, that he had never felt this way about someone else? That he had never treated anyone else as he treated her? That he would love her faithfully all his life?

"You seem to be taking very careful measure of me today."

She opened her mouth but no sound came out.

He leaned down and kissed her brow, a feather-light touch. Then he kissed her cheek. Finally, he leaned lower. She lifted her face upward, aching, craving, starving for another kiss from Tristan. His lips touched the hollow below her earlobe, then her cheek.

The kiss on her mouth never came. Instead, a soft rumble of his laughter brushed over her. She opened eyes she didn't remember closing.

Tristan whispered, "I'm very encouraged that you

want me to kiss you. I may grant your wish—later." A playful glint entered his eyes.

Her face burned that he'd read her so easily, and worse, denied her desire. How truly vexing man! He deserved a contemptuous set down—if only she could think of one.

His teasing grin reappeared. "I can't tell you how gratifying it is that you seem happy to see me today." He stepped back and spoke loudly enough to have been overheard. "It's a fine day outside and I have it on good authority that we will be blessed with a rain-free ride."

Still unable to speak, she picked up her riding crop and strode toward the door past the table of flowers. Tristan caught up to her before she'd stepped foot outside and offered his arm. She battled to regain control of her wits.

"You are a scoundrel," she muttered.

He chuckled softly. "Are you trying to tell me you are not happy to see me?"

She sighed. "You can be so aggravating."

"I hope there will be more happy times than aggravating times in store for us, Love."

There he went again, calling her "love." What was she supposed to make of that?

She waved toward the vases of blooms. "By the way, thank you for the flowers."

"You are most welcome."

A footman held two horses saddled and ready to ride. After greeting her mount and letting him get her scent, she accepted a boost up from Tristan and arranged the skirts of her riding habit. Still wearing that irrepressible grin, Tristan rode beside her to Hyde Park.

Inside the park, birds trilled and twittered like so

many prima donnas vying for center stage. Wind whispered in the trees bringing scents of freshly mown grass and spring flowers.

As they headed for the fenced-off riding trail known as Rotten Row, Leticia scrambled for something to say to this different Tristan. "I always thought Rotten Row was a strange name. I'm told it's named for *La Route du Roi,* or King's Road, although last week, someone said the row led to Eton College, so they called it *Rue d'Eton.* It seems it eventually got corrupted to Rotten Row." Oh heavens, she was rambling on about a boring subject.

He lifted a brow but drawled in a tone of cultured urbane boredom one normally reserved for a new acquaintance in a drawing room, "Oh? I thought it was named for the mix of gravel and crushed tree bark to create a pliable surface for the horses' feet and legs. Rotten also means soft, you know."

"I suppose we'll never know for certain." Her cheeks heated. Why did she start such a dull conversation with Tristan?

He glanced at her, mischief and challenge sparking in his eyes. "I know for certain that if I raced you there, I'd win."

His familiar teasing eased her tension. She scoffed. "Of course you would; I won't go running through the park like some wild little girl."

"Come now; there's no one about. Who would censure us?"

With a slight shake of her head, she smiled. "You're still stinging over my beating you the last time we raced."

He gave a dismissive wave. "That was years ago—

when you were a wild little girl."

"Getting beaten by a girl must have been a blow to your manly pride," she teased.

He shrugged. "I wasn't very manly then, so 'tis of no consequence."

"You have always been manly, and you know it."

His gaze slid her way and a secretive smile hovered at his lips as if he had tucked some surprise gift there and waited for the right moment to share it with her. If it were anything like his kiss, she ought to sit down first or she might not survive with her composure intact.

The gleam in his eye, two parts playful and one part sensual, had an adverse effect on her heartbeat. "Yes, I suppose I have always been manly. You, however have not always been so womanly—you were once a scrawny little brat."

"You oughtn't remind a lady of things like that," she said with exaggerated primness.

His rich, contagious chuckle warmed her all over and she had to smile.

They reached the end of the fence dividing Rotten Row from the rest of the park and guided their mounts into the riding pathway. No one else used the Row this morning, not even grooms exercising horses. They trotted at a comfortable pace, Leticia adjusting to her borrowed horse's gait, and Tristan riding as if he were born in the saddle.

For a time, the pathway followed the Serpentine River. Ducks glided over the surface like tiny boats leaving V-shaped wakes. The crisp morning air chilled Leticia's cheeks and filled her with exhilaration. Her horse strained against the reins, asking to run. Leticia let him increase to an easy gallop. Next to her, Tristan kept pace, grinning and rosy-cheeked. The ease of riding next to Tristan combined with the fresh air renewed her and quieted the questions in her mind. All too soon, they reached the end of the riding trail.

As they slowed to a walk, he took a deep breath and let it out. "A gratifying ride, due in part to the charming company."

"Flatterer."

"Honest."

Leticia's stomach rumbled. "Have you broken your fast yet?"

"No, I never have much appetite first thing in the morning."

"I find that hard to believe since you always seem to be hungry."

"It does indeed take a great deal of food to keep all of this"—he gestured to himself from head to toe—"so manly. I merely cannot begin feeding myself too early."

She huffed her amusement. "I'm not interested in feeding your conceit, but I haven't eaten yet, either. Care to join me for breakfast? My aunt won't mind."

"Thank you."

A feminine rider trotted toward them with a groom following behind. As the rider neared, the features of Lady Petre became clear. The lady glanced at them. Leticia sighed. The woman's husband and mother-in-law were odious but this lady seemed different, if a bit browbeaten.

"Lady Petre," Leticia called out by way of greeting.

The lady flushed, glanced at Tristan, and flushed deeper. The groom following behind her kept up close enough to attend to her should the need arise, but at a respectful distance to allow privacy.

Lady Petre slowed and nodded to them. "Miss Wentworth. Mr. Barrett."

"It's the perfect day for a bruising ride," Leticia said.

Lady Petre slowed as if to speak more, maneuvering her horse so she faced Leticia. "Miss Wentworth, I wish to apologize for my husband and mother-in-law. Their remarks in the teashop and at the opera were...unkind." She lowered her gaze and twisted her reins in her hands. "I hope you are not offended."

Leticia moved closer to her. "I assure you that I have quite forgotten. Think nothing of it."

A pained smile came over Lady Petre's face. "Thank you for being so gracious. And I..." She swallowed. "I applaud your efforts with the school. I wish I could lend my support."

"I understand, my lady." If she'd been able to reach the lady, Leticia would have grasped her hand. "Not everyone agrees with what we are doing, and of course I would not ask you to act against your husband's wishes."

The lady glanced up. "It isn't him; it's his mother. She has very strong opinions. If she weren't so set against it, he might be persuaded...perhaps..."

Poor thing. Living with an overbearing mother-in-law and a son who agreed with everything she said must be a trial. Leticia searched for something comforting to say. "I'm sure he's a good man deep down."

The lady continued to look down as she nodded. "Thank you. Good morning."

Tristan spoke. "Thank you for stopping to speak with us, Lady Petre. Your good opinion matters to us."

As Lady Petre looked up, her glance skittered away, but something in Tristan's expression captured her focus, and her smile grew, softening her features. "As does yours." She nodded a farewell and urged her mount forward.

"Delightful lady," Leticia murmured. "I hope she's right about her husband. I fear he dominates her."

"Do you think that's why she's so timid?"

"I used to think so, but now I wonder if she's timid by nature and allows herself to be ruled. Perhaps if she spoke up, she would receive more respect from her relations."

Tristan's eyes took on that unfocused look he got when he grew introspective. "Family matters are complicated. I used to think Richard was a thorn in my side. Now I understand he was trying to protect and help me."

Leticia bit back a teasing comment about how he must be growing up. In truth, he'd been maturing steadily—in more ways than one. Most of her life, she'd been too focused on Richard to realize how much Tristan had changed, especially over the past year. He had become a strong, capable, steady gentleman.

Chatting of inconsequential matters, they left the park and rode to Aunt Alice's house. After Tristan greeted her aunt, Leticia and Tristan went into the breakfast room and helped themselves to the buffet.

Leticia imagined sitting across a breakfast table from Tristan every morning, listening to the sound of his voice, of his laughter, admiring his handsome face, the two of them teasing each other, discussing interests and household or estate matters. She couldn't imagine anything more pleasant. Or more desirable.

Tristan leaned back and sipped his tea, eyeing her. That secretive smile returned.

In an attempt to appear unaffected, Leticia added cream to her chocolate and stirred the hot drink. "You look like the cat eying a canary. What wicked thoughts are you entertaining?"

"I'm thinking how lovely you are…how much I enjoy having breakfast with you."

She blushed. Had he known her thoughts mirrored his own? "It is pleasant."

"Are you going to the school today?"

"No, we are making calls."

He hesitated, seeming to choose his words with great care. "I may need to go to Suffolk for a few weeks to see about estate improvements."

"Oh? How soon are you leaving?"

"Next month."

A looming separation from Tristan for a few weeks left a hollowness inside. "I shall miss you."

"Will you?" he softly rumbled.

"Of course I will."

He leaned forward, then stood and took her by the hand, drawing her to her feet. Odd, but she always seemed to forget how much taller Tristan stood than she, and how broad. Her heart thumped at twice its usual tempo.

"I am reluctant to leave for that long."

"I…am reluctant for you to be gone so long." Her voice came out breathless.

He drew nearer. With his bare hand, he traced the side of her face. A place deep inside her sighed at his touch. He leaned in and kissed her, his lips every bit as warm and soft as the last time. However, this time, his kiss posed no question. It made a statement—of possession, of affection, of love.

All uncertainty about Tristan's sincerity dissolved. His heart thumped against her hand resting on his chest, and his caress grew firm. He slid his hand around the side of her face to the back of her head, guiding the angle, deepening the kiss. Under the power and majesty of their contact, her knees trembled. He looped an arm around her and held her against the length of him.

Tristan kissed her over and over, both hard and tender, demanding and gentle. His building passion fueled a longing inside her she never dreamed she possessed. Each moment, she lost another piece of her heart and became more joined with his until they were no longer two different people, but one stronger, more vibrant entity, whole and complete.

She knew then what she'd known all along but had been too stubborn to accept; she loved Tristan—not as a brother, nor a friend, but as a man with whom she would share her life.

Oh, how she loved him!

Chapter Thirty-Two

Tristan lost himself in the transcendent power of kissing Leticia. He had meant to convince her he loved her, but the strength of their passion and the depth of belonging that overcame him the moment he pressed his lips to hers took him by surprise. She sank against him and kissed him with all the tenderness and hunger also raging through him.

He'd never felt more complete or more certain of his path. Leticia loved him. She would never leave him.

Though his body screamed to stoke the fire blazing between them, he slowed the rate of their ardor to short, sweet kisses. Then he pressed his lips to her cheek, the hollow behind her ear, her brow, her forehead. He set a chaste kiss on her lips and cradled her face. With his uneven breathing—and hers—breaking the silence of the room, he rested his forehead on hers and grappled with his self-control. As he lifted his head, he gazed at her, admiring the curve of her cheek, the arch of her brow, the moist redness of her lips plump from kissing.

"I love you, Leticia."

She opened her eyes. Tears glistened her eyes and fell onto her cheeks. "Heaven help me, but I love you, too."

Using the pad of his thumbs, he wiped away her tears. "Heaven help us both, because I mean to marry you."

She smiled again, but something akin to pain dimmed the joy that should have been there. "I don't know if we should…"

"If I can trust you with my heart, you can trust me with yours, can't you?"

"Trust me with your heart." Her eyes widened. "You do trust me, don't you?"

"I always have."

She rose on her tiptoes and kissed him, the sweet kiss of promise. "Forgive me for doubting you. I do trust you."

"Marry me."

She let out a long breath. "It's not that simple."

"It's very simple." He enfolded both of her hands with his and tried to keep his tone confident and persuasive instead of desperate. "I will approach your father, vow to treat you like a queen and love you faithfully all my life, assure him that I have adequate means to provide a comfortable life for you and our future children, and beg him to let me marry you."

"Tristan."

"Then we will purchase a marriage license and get married—unless you'd rather post banns."

"Tristan."

"I'll carry you over the threshold…"

"Tristan."

"Then I'll show you why reformed rakes make the best husbands." He grinned rakishly.

"Tristan!"

He kissed the tip of her nose. "Yes, my love?"

She smiled at the term of endearment but looked down and squeezed his hands. "I…well, I…have an understanding with Lord Bradbury."

All the warmth inside him froze. "Has he formally asked for your hand?"

"No, not exactly."

"Did he speak to your aunt? Seek your father's permission?"

"No." She drew out the word.

He let out a pent-up breath. "Then you tell him that you came to the realization that you don't suit."

She sighed. "You know it's not that easy."

"It doesn't have to be complicated. You love me, and I love you, and we belong together. No two people were created for each other as perfectly as we are."

The front door knocker boomed and the butler's voice in the great hall carried to them. "One moment, Lord Bradbury, and I will announce you."

Tristan let out his breath in disgust. What timing!

"Oh, dear," she whispered.

He squeezed her hand. "Now is your chance. Tell him. It would be cruel to allow him to believe a minute longer than necessary that you will have him."

She drew a shaking breath and nodded. "You're right. I'd best tell him right away."

"Ah, there you are, dear." Leticia's aunt appeared in the doorway.

"Aunt." Leticia glanced at Tristan. Clear dread at the conversation she must have with Lord Bradbury halted her speech. At Tristan's reassuring look, she straightened as if finding her resolve. "Aunt, I must speak to Lord Bradbury as alone as propriety will allow."

Something in her tone must have revealed her intent, because Mrs. Tallier glanced at Tristan and she nodded with a knowing glint in her eye. "I understand, my dear. You may use the front parlor. I will be in the foyer, arranging the flowers."

Leticia greeted Lord Bradbury and, after a nervous glance over her shoulder at Tristan, invited him to join her in the parlor. Standing alone in the breakfast room, Tristan gripped the back of a chair lest he give into the temptation to rush to Leticia's side. She must do this alone, of course. Moreover, Bradbury deserved to keep his dignity while Leticia rejected him.

A commotion at the front door interrupted his thoughts. Her aunt's voice exclaimed, and a male voice replied, to which her aunt let out something akin to a shriek.

Tristan dashed to the foyer and pulled up short. The footman, Peter, who always accompanied Miss Harper, carried in the young teacher. With her arms wrapped around his neck, she buried her face in his neck cloth. Her shoulders shook and muffled weeping broke the silence.

"What has happened?" Leticia rushed to her side.

"She was attacked," Peter said grimly, oblivious to his own battered, swollen face.

Primal anger rose up in Tristan. "Who was it?" he demanded.

Peter said, "The bloke what showed up and dragged off his daughter a while back." The footman met their stunned stares with the ferocity of a savage.

"Are you hurt, Mrs. Harper?" Leticia put her hand on the teacher's back.

"He hit her," Peter snarled through clenched teeth. He swallowed, and added, "I think I killed him."

"Get the doctor," Leticia said to the butler. "And fetch a constable."

As the butler sent runners, Tristan patted his back pocket where he kept his pistol. It remained secure. "Send the constable to the school. I'll go there now."

Lord Bradbury stared at Tristan. "What are you doing here, Barrett?"

"I invited him to join us for breakfast," Mrs. Tallier said.

"Peter, take Mrs. Harper to her room," Leticia directed.

"I'll show you the way," Aunt Alice said.

Still cradling the teacher in his arms, Peter carried Mrs. Harper up the stairs behind Aunt Alice. Leticia put a hand on her head, as the full weight of what happened seemed to have landed on her shoulders. The thought of the gentle teacher suffering an attack left a sick heaviness in Tristan's stomach. Was Leticia in danger as well?

"That's it." Lord Bradbury drew himself up and addressed Leticia. "The school is closed. This has gone too far."

"No!" Leticia said. "We can't give up now."

"It's too dangerous," Lord Bradbury said.

Leticia spread her hands. "If we close the school, everyone who said we shouldn't do it will win. The children lose."

"I won't let you risk your safety for a bunch of street urchins." His voice left no room for argument, as if it were his decision alone to make.

Tristan took a step closer to Leticia, ready to back her up if she needed him. Though he understood the desire to protect her, he couldn't agree with Bradbury's solution or his heavy-handed approach. Instead of becoming angry, Leticia looked at Bradbury with beseeching eyes. With quiet determination, she said, "If we won't, who will?"

Bradbury opened his mouth then closed it. He glanced at Tristan as if seeking an ally.

Tristan shook his head. "No one cares for these children. If we don't help them, they will grow up unloved, unwanted, and unworthy. They will spend all their lives scrabbling for food and never have the self-possession to seek a better life."

Leticia had given that to them; she could give that to others. Tristan would help her any way possible.

Leticia's eyes shone as she gazed up at him, admiration so clear. His chest swelled in pride. He glanced at Bradbury who studied him.

Tristan slipped his hand into Leticia's and faced Bradbury, daring him to contradict. "We will hire more security, and perhaps look for a different neighborhood, but the school remains open."

Bradbury addressed Leticia. "I won't allow you to put yourself at risk."

Leticia shook her head. "My lord, this is a conversation for another time."

Bradbury went very still and glanced at Tristan warily. To Leticia, he nodded. "Of course."

Tristan squeezed her hand. "I'm going to the school to see what became of the attacker."

Leticia handed him a key. "Be careful."

Though tempted to kiss Leticia in front of Bradbury and thus stake his claim, Tristan nodded and left, vowing to do all he could to protect the school, its teacher, and most of all his beloved Leticia.

Chapter Thirty-Three

From the foyer of her aunt's house, Leticia watched Tristan leave and offered a wordless prayer for his safety as he returned to the scene of the violence.

"Miss Wentworth." Lord Bradbury's voice drew her attention. She'd almost forgotten his presence. "It appears I have come at an inconvenient time."

She steadied herself. "No. No, this is as good a time as any."

After exchanging a glance with her aunt, who moved to the flower arrangement on the table, Leticia led the way to the front parlor and left the double doors wide open.

Lord Bradbury approached and stood so close that his clothing brushed against her arm. "I have a matter I wish to discuss with you." He hesitated. "Perhaps I should have asked for an appointment. You are preoccupied, and seem to have returned moments ago from a ride?"

She glanced down at her riding habit. "Yes, Trista—er, Mr. Barrett and I went riding and he stayed for breakfast."

"I see." He paused.

She faced him. "There is something I should discuss with you without delay."

He gestured. "Very well. Perhaps you should speak your mind first."

"I…" Oh dear. How does one tell a kind gentleman—a lord—that one's feelings have changed without sounding like a fickle chit or a jilt? She sank down on the nearest chair. "Won't you please sit, my lord?"

He perched at the edge of the closest chair, his knees almost brushing hers. "My Christian name is Blake—I'd like very much if you would call me that."

Oh, no. This was serious. Leticia held herself in check lest she shoot out of the chair and force the gentleman to stand. She clasped her hands together. Drew a breath. Swallowed. "My lord, I find it difficult to tell you this, but it appears that I did not know my heart—have not been aware of my heart for quite some time now." A trickle of perspiration wandered down the back of her neck. "I implied…something that you might have understood as a promise. Indeed, that is how I meant it at the time, or at least, I thought I did."

He took her hand. "Miss Wentworth. I urge you to re-consider what you are about to say."

"Please…"

He rushed on, his expression urgent. "I know you and Mr. Barrett are lifelong friends, and you have understandably tender feelings for him. I am also aware of his appeal to ladies." His grip tightened. "Please consider the life I offer you. I offer you my title and my wealth, as well as my heart and my complete fidelity. I seldom drink or gamble and have always treated the fair sex with the dignity and respect they deserve—even those who do not respect themselves. I am not a rake— have *never* been a rake—and have always valued honor and fidelity."

Leticia's eyes burned. This was more difficult than

she had feared. "I admire that, and so much more, about you. But Tristan has changed. And he loves me."

He stepped closer, a breath away from an embrace. "*I* love you."

He was so handsome, so sincere. Oh, why had she not been more open to her heart regarding Tristan before engaging Lord Bradbury's affections? Her vision blurred and she focused on their clasped hands, his so warm and strong over hers. She blinked back her tears and returned her gaze to his face.

"My lord, I am honored, but—"

"Do not let yourself to be persuaded by the practiced flirtations of a rake. Allow me the chance to show you how I ardently love you."

Sorrowful but firm, she shook her head.

He arose and pulled her to a stand next to him. "Kiss me—once—and listen to your heart. If you feel nothing at all, then I will be a gentleman and step back."

"I can't do that."

The imploring in his eyes smote her straight to her heart. "I know I am asking much, but for once, let your heart rule your head. My words are inadequate; allow me to show you."

He lowered his head and kissed her, tender and soft. It was all for naught. His kiss awakened none of the love or passion that kissing Tristan had. None of the wholeness encompassed her the way it had when Tristan kissed her. Her heart remained unmoved except for a yearning for Tristan's touch.

Lord Bradbury drew back, his eyes sad. With almost desperate entreating, he said, "I'm willing to wait until your feelings…"

She shook her head. "I'm sorry. I love Tristan and will only have him."

Lord Bradbury released her hands and stepped back. He drew a long breath. "I hope he deserves you." He sketched a proper, if somewhat hasty bow, and left.

She had hurt a good man. Remorse stung her eyes. She hugged herself and bit her lip.

Nothing changed the fact that she loved Tristan, and she trusted him. Nothing would ever make her question Tristan's heart or devotion.

Chapter Thirty-Four

Shocked and numb, Tristan stood watching Leticia and Lord Bradbury kissing. Kissing!

He'd returned for his gloves, but instead found the unthinkable—Leticia betraying him. Leticia and Lord Bradbury stood, bodies pressed together, sharing a long, lingering kiss of lovers.

Tristan froze, alternating between rage and hurt. His first impulse hit like a blast of wind; to spin Bradbury around and punch him in the face. Then challenge him to a duel. But Leticia...

Leticia had made her choice. Tristan was a fool to believe he would be worthy of love—the kind of love promised by poets and songwriters and dreamers.

He stumbled backward and felt his way to the street. Somehow, he trudged through the fog around his vision and wound up in a hackney.

"Where to, guv'na?" sang out the cheerful jarvey.

Tristan rubbed a hand over his face and managed to croak out the school's location. He fell against the seat and sank into his hands.

It was like watching his mother drive away all over again. A familiar, aching hollowness swallowed him— the reminder that if he were a better person and not such a blatant disappointment, she would have loved him enough to stay with him. He had wanted to run after Mama, beg her to stay, vow to be good enough. In the end, it was not enough. He would never be enough.

He barely registered the jarvey's cheer as he paid the man and got out. The searing pain in his heart blinded him to all else but one horrifying truth; Leticia had kissed Lord Bradbury.

As he stood on the street, rain pattered him, waking him up to his surroundings. He rubbed his hand over his face to wipe off the rain dripping down his cheeks mingling with tears. The charity school stood in front of him. Darkened windows stared at him like the sightless gaze of a blind beggar hoping for a few meager scraps before he gave up and died. The front door hung crookedly and blew back and forth in a breeze. Broken. Abandoned. Forgotten.

Tristan let out his breath in disgust at his maudlin thoughts and pulled himself together. In case the assailant, should he be alive, was hale enough to put up a fight if he were reckless enough to have lingered, Tristan palmed his gun. He pushed the door open, squinting in the semi-darkness for any sign of threat. His ears strained for moans or breathing. All remained silent. He prowled the main floor and then went down to the ground level. Inside the kitchen, he found an overturned table, a broken chair, along with few drops of blood, but no signs of the intruder.

"Who's there?" An unfamiliar male voice echoed from the front of the school.

Tristan tensed, but chided himself. The attacker would not announce himself. More likely, the constable had arrived.

"I'm Barrett!" Tristan called, retracing his steps. "I'm here to help."

A lean young man wearing the distinctive scarlet

waistcoat of a Bow Street Runner stood framed by the doorway. "Ah, Barrett. Mrs. Tallier said to expect you."

"I didn't realize this was Bow Street's jurisdiction," Tristan said.

"Your friend is a most insistent old—er, lady." The Runner, who spoke with an accent that placed him as educated, if not of noble birth, grinned at him. A day's growth sprouted on his chin and hair black as coal curled around a hatless head. The man didn't look much older than Tristan but his world-weary eyes suggested he'd seen his share of hardship.

"Old lady?" Tristan asked.

The Runner clarified, "Mrs. Tallier sent a message to the magistrate demanding his assistance. Only Bow Street would do for her. It seems the magistrate, Lord Birnie, and Mrs. Tallier go way back."

Tristan said, "I'm here on behalf of Mrs. Tallier's niece. She's a...friend." No need to get into the details of what Leticia was, or was not, to him.

The Runner stuck out a hand. "Conner Jackson, at your service."

"Tristan Barrett." Tristan shook his hand and jabbed a thumb behind him. "The kitchen shows signs of a fight and there is a little blood but no body in the main floor or lower level."

Jackson nodded. "Show me." The Runner showed no deference to Tristan's higher rank, which suited Tristan just fine.

He led the constable to the kitchen and then showed Jackson around the school. They checked the upper floor, finding no intruder in any of the attic rooms, one of which they had set up for the teacher's bedchamber before she moved into Mrs. Tallier's house.

"There should be a caretaker," Tristan said. "Perhaps he went out."

Jackson pursed his lips. "I need to question the two people involved. A teacher and a footman, I hear?"

Tristan nodded. "They are at Mrs. Tallier's house. Share a hackney back?"

Jackson agreed and went to hail a hackney while Tristan locked the doors.

"Sir?" a child's voice called timidly from behind him.

Tristan located a girl of perhaps twelve standing in the street as if she were too frightened to draw near but couldn't make herself leave.

He peered at her. "You're one of the students here, aren't you?"

"Yes, sir." Her mouth quirked in a shy smile. "You 'elped me learn 'ow to dance."

He nodded.

She sobered. "Is Mrs. 'arper...? Is she 'urt?"

"Do you know what happened?" Tristan knelt to get eye level with the child.

The girl shook her head. "I only 'eard someone say that there was screamin' an' a fight and that the man wot loves Mrs. 'arper carried her out b'cause she were 'urt."

"Do you know who hurt her?"

She stared at the ground. "I think I 'eard tell it were Molly's father."

"I see. Do you happen to know where they live?"

She shook her head. "No, sir."

Tristan fished a shilling out of his pocket. "Thank you."

She took the coin and studied it as if she had never seen anything of its kind. Looking up, she turned beseeching eyes on him. "Are they goin' to close the school?"

"Not a chance."

Fisting her hand around the shilling, she nodded. "I sure 'ope not." She looked up at him, gave him a quick smile, and disappeared around the building.

A hackney pulled up and Jackson spoke to the jarvey. Tristan joined him as they both climbed in the carriage. At Mrs. Tallier's house, Jackson got out, but Tristan bade him farewell and took the hackney home. The last thing he wanted to do was see Leticia right now.

What would he say to her? Demand to know her intentions?

Had he been wrong about her all along and she was as faithless as he feared all women were, or had he only thought she'd pledged herself to him because that's what he wanted to hear, while instead, she was trying to tell him that she wanted Lord Bradbury instead?

He stood at a junction. He could step back and let her have the better man, a lord of unimpeachable character, a man she liked well enough to kiss. If Tristan loved her, that's what he should do.

He could give in to his selfish desire to fight for her, win her over, convince her they belonged together. But if she had already made her choice, could he do anything to change her mind?

He passed a sleepless night, revisiting the sight of Leticia in Bradbury's arms, trying to piece together what it all meant, agonizing over his choices and which path to take, and watching through a child's eyes as his mother left him over and over.

By morning, he could stand it no longer. He dressed in his most sober clothing and went to Mrs. Tallier's house, only to be informed that Leticia had left for the school.

Alarm quickened his pulse. "Did she go alone?"

"No, sir," the butler replied, "She went with Lady Averston, Mrs. Harper, and Peter. I sent along another footman for added security."

At least they'd taken that precaution. After thanking the servant, Tristan went to the school, no longer as concerned with getting answers from Leticia as much as to ensure her safety.

Inside the school doors, Peter stood as immovable and grim as the King's guard. Tristan exchanged a nod with Peter, and peered into the schoolroom. Children filled the desks. Mrs. Harper, who appeared unharmed except for a bruise under her eye and a reddened cheek, stood teaching with her usual calm efficiency. Her return to work only a day after suffering a frightening attack spoke volumes about her commitment. Tristan stole past the room and headed to the office where he'd found Leticia in the past. A footman the size of a pugilist stood with arms folded, leaning against the wall, his eyes alert. Tristan nodded to him and received an answering nod.

Inside the office, Leticia bent over the desk gathering together several papers and tucking them into a satchel. Elizabeth sat near a window, studying a ledger.

"Tish." His voice came out hoarse and grim.

She looked up and smiled. "Good morning."

She seemed pleased to see him. What did that

mean?

Her smile faded. "Is something amiss?"

Tristan broke out into a cold sweat. He tried to pull together his mask of flippancy but only managed to feel more desperate. He glanced at Elizabeth.

His sister-in-law stood. "I believe I am in need of a cup of tea." She glided out.

Tristan balled his fists. "Did I misunderstand you yesterday?"

Leticia's brow puckered and true confusion touched her eyes. "About what?"

He rubbed at the space between his eyes and pushed his fingers through his hair. "About…what we said…after we kissed."

Her expression softened, and though a faint blush pinked her cheeks, no shame revealed itself in her face. "About me finally realizing that I love you?"

The wind rushed out of his lungs. He struggled a moment to breathe. "Do you?"

She came around the desk and placed a hand on his chest, the other touching his cheek. "I always have. I was slow to realize it. I do love you, Tristan—so very much." Her eyes darted between his, searching, probing. Gently, she asked, "What is it?"

"Why did you kiss Bradbury after I left?" Giving voice to his question scraped out the inside of his heart, leaving him ragged and empty.

She paled. "Oh, heaven above. How did you find out about that?" True guilt wrote itself all over her face.

He stepped back out of her touch. "I saw you. I came back for my gloves, and I saw you…and him…"

She pressed her hand over her mouth and let out a strangled noise. "I'm so sorry you saw that. But—"

"Stop." He laughed sharply. "All this time you were so worried I'd betray you, and I was trying so hard to prove to you I wouldn't, it never occurred to me *you* would betray *me*. Or did you plan on leading us both on a merry chase until you decided which one you wanted? Have you been kissing Kensington, too?"

Her guilty expression stepped back and hurt took center stage. "You don't think I was leading you on?"

"Either that, or I have a different definition of the word love." His words came out bitter.

Leticia frowned and her gaze darted to the door. "Do you smell smoke?"

"Fire! There's a fire!" Peter's panicked voice boomed through the school.

Tristan rushed to the main room, Leticia next to him.

Peter bounded toward them, pointing to the narrow staircase leading down to the ground level. "The kitchen!"

Tristan and Peter, followed by the other footman, raced to the kitchen stairs, but smoke billowed up, too thick to breathe. Covering his mouth and nose with his sleeve, Tristan took the stairs two at a time. Squinting through eyes tearing from smoke, he glanced around. The entire kitchen burned from multiple locations. The back door stood open, the frame splintered as if someone had kicked it in, and an oily liquid moved across the floor leading from a broken lamp on the floor.

Coughing and blinking, his face burning from the blistering heat, Tristan backed up the stairs.

Peter pushed past him, using a blanket to try to put out the fire, but flames leaped up all around him.

"It's too late," Tristan shouted. "The whole thing is ablaze. We need to get everyone out of the building and organize a bucket brigade." He raced up the stairs.

Swearing, Peter followed. "Everyone out of the building. Get out now! Matilda! Get the children!"

Mrs. Harper sprang into action. Leticia raced to the schoolroom. Within minutes, they had collected the frightened children and ushered them to safety across the street. Elizabeth rushed out, her arms loaded with papers and a satchel. Outside, a small bucket brigade had formed with Peter at its head.

"Do you have fire insurance?" Tristan called to Leticia.

"Yes!" She pointed to a distinctive plaque on the outside wall.

"Someone already ran to fetch them!" the footman yelled.

Leticia, Elizabeth, and Mrs. Harper kept the children together and tried to calm them while Tristan, Peter, and several neighbors joined the brigade to douse the flames. Finally, a modern fire engine with a water pump arrived and poured water on the blaze.

To let the firefighters work, Tristan backed off and wandered to Leticia. She stood with her arms around two children, three more clutching her skirts, all staring in fascination at the billowing smoke. Silent tears streamed down Leticia's cheeks. A grim Mrs. Harper quietly comforted children gathered around her. Peter went to the teacher and stood next to her, not touching her but sending concerned and sympathetic looks her direction.

"It's all gone," Leticia said. "Everything— furniture, books...the pianoforte."

As the firefighters quenched the blaze, impotent smoke billowed into the sky. Volunteers wiped their brows, no doubt sighing in relief that the flames had not damaged their homes or businesses, and drifted away. The school children left one by one. Leticia, Elizabeth, Tristan, Mrs. Harper, and Peter remained alone but together.

"There's nothing left for us to do here," Tristan said.

No one had the heart to respond.

Again, Tristan spoke, "It's time to go home."

Elizabeth's coach carried the silent, ashen-faced group to Mrs. Tallier's house. Though Elizabeth offered to give him a ride home, Tristan declined. He walked. He still had not yet resolved anything with Leticia. Seeing her so bereft at the loss of the school had softened his heart toward her, but the truth remained; she had kissed Lord Bradbury after pledging herself to Tristan.

What did it mean? Had it been anyone less virtuous than Leticia, he might have dismissed it as a farewell kiss. But she'd looked so guilty when he confronted her that it could not have been anything so simple.

Chapter Thirty-Five

Leticia spent an agonizing day and night, sobbing until her head would surely split.

The school, the object of her hopes and dreams, had vanished—literally—in a puff of smoke because of one tragic, malicious act. Yet that loss paled compared to losing Tristan.

Oh, why had she been so foolish as to allow Lord Bradbury to kiss her? It had been a faithless act of weakness and betrayal. After that kiss, guilt had devoured her, and she'd spent a sleepless night wrestling with what to tell Tristan and how to convince him she'd never do anything of the kind again.

Now, Tristan not only knew, but had *witnessed* her perfidy. At least if she had found a way to tell him about it and to beg his forgiveness, she might have been able to salvage their relationship. But he wouldn't soon forget what he saw. He might never forgive her. Nor could she blame him.

He probably viewed her as selfish and dishonorable. Perhaps she was. Who professed her love to one man and kissed another? She deserved a lifetime of spinsterhood if she failed the first test of her faithfulness.

A horrifying thought brought her up short. Would the heartbreak she caused Tristan drive him to his former reckless behavior of drinking and debauchery?

Pain shot through her abdomen and she burrowed into her pillow. If she destroyed all the progress Tristan had achieved, she would never forgive herself.

Her judgmental, hypocritical behavior, and her selfishness stared back at her in all its ugliness. She'd constantly questioned Tristan's motives, his heart, his sincerity, and yet she had been the one to behave like a hoyden. If the earth swallowed her up now, nothing would make her happier.

Her aunt entered. "Leticia, dear. I know you are overset at the loss of your charity school. But surely you needn't go on so."

Leticia closed her eyes and tried to breathe through her shame. She should confess her kissing Lord Bradbury and allow all her aunt's condemning words to punish her. She deserved losing her aunt's good opinion. However, it might reflect on Lord Bradbury as well, and he didn't deserve that.

Instead, she said, "Forgive me, Aunt. I am sure you are right. But my head aches so badly, I cannot possibly attend a social event tonight."

Her aunt clucked. "I'll have a tray brought to you, along with some chamomile tea. Shall I send laudanum as well?"

"No, thank you." Every pain of her throbbing head served as punishment for her stupidity, her weakness, her betrayal.

Leticia's maid brought in a tray and cool compress, and slipped out. When Leticia's tears dried, she stared in numb desolation as shadows moved across the floor.

As darkness fell, Isabella entered, smelling of the new perfume she'd purchased and wearing a cream silk creation trimmed in pink that lent her a fragile, luminescent beauty. She called softly, "Leticia?"

"I'm awake, Bella," Leticia murmured, pillows muffling her voice.

"I heard about your school. I'm so sorry." She sat on the edge of the bed.

Leticia wrestled with whether to unburden herself on her sister, or carry her guilt in silence.

"I know it's a terrible loss." Isabella paused. "I'm surprised you aren't your usual stoic self. You were less overset when Richard married Lady Elizabeth."

Leticia shuddered in a breath. "It's not only the school. It's Tristan."

"What has happened?"

"I've ruined everything." A sob worked its way out of her.

Laying a hand on Leticia's back, Isabella leaned over. "Tell me."

Leticia did—everything from Tristan's proposal, to Lord Bradbury's kiss, to Tristan's discovery. "And now I've hurt him and he'll never trust me and I don't deserve him!" She burst into tears.

Isabella removed her hand and sat back. She said nothing while Leticia wept.

Pulling herself together, Leticia dried her tears and blew her nose. "Whatever am I to do?"

"Do?" Isabella let out a derisive huff. "I don't know if there is anything you can do. You have broken the hearts of two good men. I'm ashamed of you."

Leticia blinked at the condemning tones from her normally mild sister. "I'm ashamed, too. Although, to tell you the truth, I don't think I broke Lord Bradbury's heart. I'm not certain he truly loved me. I think he liked me, but we didn't have a deep emotional connection.

But Tris—"

Isabella stood. "You can tell yourself that if that makes you feel better."

Again, Leticia stared. "Lord Bradbury wasn't in love with me. He didn't support my involvement in the school, and I had the distinct impression that he hoped I'd give it up if I married him."

"He doted on you!" Isabella shouted. "He looked at you as if you were the most beautiful woman he'd ever seen. And he did support your school; he donated a pianoforte and participated in your auction. You were too blind to see how much he admired and loved you. I wish I'd known you would cast him aside—I would have encouraged him."

Stunned, Leticia pushed herself up to a seated position. "You have dozens of admirers."

"I suppose we all want the one we can't have." Isabella left the room, slamming the door.

Leticia gaped. Isabella's words knifed through Leticia.

Perfect. Through her narrow-mindedness, selfishness, and weakness, she had lost the good opinion of everyone who mattered to her. Worse, she'd ruined Isabella's chances with a man to whom she had formed a secret attachment. Leticia had been too selfish to see the truths in front of her.

She was the most wretched person in all of England. She deserved to live out her life in solitude and misery.

Chapter Thirty-Six

Tristan gave up on sleep and paced his bachelor's rooms. Perhaps he deserved nothing less. He'd been a rake of the worst kind. Leticia had no use for such men, and he had no finger of blame to point at her behavior.

The question remained: what to do now?

As morning dawned, he dressed and began walking. He walked for the better part of the day, coming no closer to a course of action. He could leave now for the country estates as he'd promised Richard he would do and let Bradbury have Leticia. He could stay and fight for Leticia—wrest her away from Lord Bradbury. If he succeeded, did he dare trust her to love a wretch like him—enough to be faithful to him? Or should he cut his losses, accept his loneliness as penance for all his past misdeeds, and immerse himself into helping Richard make the estate more prosperous than ever?

He found himself at the front steps of Averston House. Richard. Could he confide in him without giving away too many details that would reflect poorly on Leticia? As he stood on the steps, Elizabeth stepped out.

"Why, Tristan!" she exclaimed.

He faltered. "Is Richard home?"

"No, he said he planned to stop by White's for an informal gathering of some of his friends."

He nodded.

She fixed a searching gaze on him. "Is something amiss?"

"Nothing of import."

He backed away and continued on foot, ignoring his fatigue. Inside White's, Tristan squared his shoulders and mustered up enough dignity to greet his new friends with a smile and a few casual, light-hearted quips so as not to appear a kicked dog.

Deeper in the club, he spotted Lord Bradbury seated at a table alone. Tristan's blood heated. Torn between the desire to warn him that Leticia might be playing them both, and the urge to flatten the lord for pressing his advantage, Tristan marched to the good-for-nothing lord and glowered at him.

Bradbury raised his gaze and stared at Tristan as if he were a watercolor painted by an unskilled novice. "Barrett. Come to glo—"

"I should call you out."

Bradbury's expression went blank. Then pained. "She told you?"

"I saw you. How long have you been taking such liberties?"

Glancing around, Bradbury leaned forward. "Lower your voice lest anyone overhear and suspect who the lady in question is."

He was right, curse him. Regardless of what Leticia had done, Tristan had no desire to smear her reputation. He settled for wishing for the lord's demise.

Bradbury spread his hands. "I know it was beneath a gentleman. I assure you, that it went no further. You, of all people, should understand that sometimes a man—"

"I expect you to behave as a gentleman from this moment on," Tristan snarled. How dare that arrogant scoundrel throw Tristan's past into his face as a way of excusing his own bad behavior? Tristan planted his hands on the table and leaned in. "If I hear that you've insulted her or hurt her, I will call you out."

"You don't—"

"Be warned." Tristan strode away before he struck Bradbury in truth.

Tristan came within a hair's width of colliding with a waiter, and made his escape into another room.

The Duke of Suttenberg passed him. "Barrett." The duke inclined his head in a greeting.

"Suttenberg," Tristan managed.

The duke checked his steps. "I say ol' chap, you seem rather blue-deviled."

Tristan swallowed and grappled with his self-control. "Have you seen my brother, perchance?"

"I'm about to meet him in the coffee room. Care to join us?"

Tristan nodded and fell in step. In the coffee room, Richard sat surrounded by his peers in an animated discussion. Suttenberg took a seat at the table. Tristan had no stomach for conversation. Instead, he caught Richard's eye, turned on his heel, and walked out. He found an empty reading room nearby. A waiter came by with the offer of a brandy. Tristan almost accepted, but hesitated. A difficult decision lay ahead; having a mind numbed by drink would not help him. He declined.

He picked up something to read in the hopes that people would leave him alone, but the words blurred into nonsense.

"Did you wish to speak with me?" Richard's voice

drew him out of his fog of sorrow.

Tristan looked up, unable to give words to the pain crushing him.

Richard peered at him. "I promised Elizabeth I wouldn't be late. Care to join me in my carriage?"

Tristan dragged himself out of his chair and kept pace with his brother. Once inside the Averston coach, Richard settled back and eyed Tristan. "You look the very devil, little brother, but you're sober."

Tristan pushed his fingers through his hair. "I rather wish I were roaring drunk at the moment."

"Drinking yourself to a state of unconsciousness never solves anything—it only assures a 'roaring' headache on the morrow."

Tristan stared without seeing out the window and reached futilely at his stormy thoughts but they slipped away before he could name them. "I love Leticia."

Solemn and subdued, Richard said, "I know."

Tristan searched for words to identify his chaotic thoughts. "But she's…"

Richard supplied, "She's being courted by Lord Bradbury?"

Tristan closed his eyes but that brightened the haunting image of her in Bradbury's arms. "She told me she loved me, and that she was going to tell Bradbury they don't suit. Then I caught them…kissing…"

"Leticia?" Richard's surprise revealed itself in his tone.

"Either she's playing us both, or…"

"Stop." Richard said. "You know her better than that."

Rage knifed through him. "She kissed him!" he roared.

"Did she?"

"I saw them!"

"I know that's what you saw. But often that is not what really happened. You know her. She is not the kind of woman who plays men."

Tristan would not have thought so, either.

"Trust me," Richard continued. "I made the mistake of jumping to conclusions with Elizabeth, a great number of times, and it almost destroyed any chance of happiness in our marriage."

Tristan digested his words but they seemed to bang against each other in meaningless litany.

"Remember that night I thought you and Elizabeth had gone for a tryst during the ball?"

The reminder hit Tristan like a cold slap. He knew all too well how it felt to be so misjudged. Tristan rubbed his jaw to show Richard he remembered.

Richard fixed a pointed stare at Tristan. "Talk to Leticia again. This time, give her a chance to tell you what's in her heart. Listen."

Tristan leaned forward and rested his head in his hands.

"For all you know," Richard continued, "She didn't welcome Bradbury's kiss. You might have left before she spurred him."

Tristan lifted his head. What if it were true? What if she'd been the victim of an unwanted advance, and now the one person who should be defending her was instead condemning her?

"Go home and rest," Richard said. "Seek her out on the morrow when you have a clear head. Isn't she worth giving the her the benefit of doubt? Isn't she worth a second chance?"

Richard was right. Tristan owed Leticia the chance to explain. Either way, he, of all people, understood the concept of second chances.

Very well. He'd give her another chance. As Richard said: she was worth it.

Chapter Thirty-Seven

As dawn glimmered, gray and cold, Leticia picked her way through the rubble of what was once their charity school. Most of the outer brick walls remained standing, but all the rest of their dreams lay in charred timber and ash. She passed under what used to be the front door, stepping around holes in the wooden floor and heaps of rubble. At the smoldering remains of the pianoforte, she stopped. The wooden frame and keys had crumbled to little more than blackened dust. The metal harp inside remained like a skeletal reminder of slain hope.

Somehow, she would find a way either to rebuild the school, or start an orphanage, or...perhaps on a smaller scale, she might content herself with helping her sisters raise their children. She would make herself observe their happy marriages and children as a constant reminder of what she might once have had, and had thrown away. She would love her nieces and nephews with all of her heart.

For now, she'd allow herself this moment to mourn.

"Miss?" A child's voice broke through her haze of grief.

"Please leave me," Leticia said.

"We come to—*came*—to h-h-help, we did." the child emphasized the h in her word as if trying to make it a part of her speech. "Don't cry, Miss. We can rebuild, can't we?"

Footsteps approached. "She's right," Mrs. Harper said.

Leticia raised her head. One of the students held a homemade broom. Next to her, Mrs. Harper and Peter stood, their expressions hopeful. Behind them, scattered on the steps and spilling out onto the street, all the students, as well as several adults, held brooms or shovels or rags and buckets. Among the adults, she recognized a baker's assistant, several chimney sweeps, a blacksmith, and a fruit peddler.

Speechless, she stared at the army of support. She climbed to her feet. "Thank you all, but cleaning up is a small part of what we need. We'd have to rebuild, and replace all the books. We don't have the money for that, nor could we purchase desks…"

"You don't need desks to teach children, do you?" Tristan's familiar voice sent warm ripples all over her.

She resisted the urge to run into his arms. His expression, though not hostile, was still guarded. "It's only a building, Leticia."

So handsome, so solemn, and even vulnerable, he met her gaze. Her heart broke all over again. He was here. Had he come as a friend, or was he still willing to make a future with her if she managed the right apology? She owed it to him to try. If he rejected her, she'd be no worse off.

Tristan took another step toward her. "All you need for a school is a teacher and students. All of this"—he gestured at the remains of the building—"is nice but not necessary."

"I agree with Tristan." Elizabeth pushed her way

through the crowd with Richard helping clear a path for her. "We had grand hopes. One day, we can do all of that again, and more—have the charity boarding school as we dreamed. For now, we can concentrate teaching them their letters. I don't think they'd mind sitting on the floor to learn, would you, girls?"

A chorus of "no, m'lady" came in response.

"I spoke to our solicitor this morning," Elizabeth continued. "He ran the figures and said that we can rebuild the exterior of the structure and buy enough coal to get them through the winter. If we wish to add desks or anything else, we'd need to have another method of raising funds."

"We are here to help." Lady Petre called. "Excuse me." She wormed her way through. "When I heard of the fire, I informed my husband I intend to help."

Leticia gaped. "And he agreed to it?"

Lady Petre smiled. "I can be persuasive if I put my mind to it. He still disagrees with your venture, but allowed me to help as I wish."

Elizabeth took Leticia's hand. "Lord and Lady Tarrington donated a pianoforte."

Leticia looked at each face, overwhelmed.

Tristan stood near enough to touch if she stretched out her hand. "You are doing a good thing here, Tish. Don't throw it all away because of a setback."

If Tristan, of all people, still believed in her, she didn't dare quit now. She swallowed hard and blinked at tears stinging her eyes. She nodded. "You're right. If we have enough to restore the building, we can make do and add the rest a little at a time. I would never wish to throw away all we've worked so hard to achieve." She raised her voice. "Thank you all for coming. By all means, let's get to work."

All the volunteers got busy. Within a few hours, they'd made a noticeable improvement. By the time the adult helpers started leaving, making apologies that they needed to return to their places of business, the ground floor had been cleared of rubble. Much work remained to be done, but they had made progress.

"We've done all we can for now," she said. "We'll hire workers to finish the rest and to rebuild the main floor. Perhaps we should go home."

"I believe you're right," Elizabeth said.

"I have a meeting this afternoon with my steward," Richard added.

While Peter trotted off to find a hackney, Richard said, "The four of us can fit in our coach. Can we offer you both a ride?"

"Thank you." Leticia glanced at Tristan. "You're probably hungry. Would you care to come back with me and have luncheon?"

Again, that hesitance mingled with something else that she wanted to identify as longing but couldn't hope for that much. He nodded. "I would like that."

Dear Tristan! How badly she must have hurt him to put such hesitation in him. She wanted to throw her arms around him and hold him until his inner wounds healed. He might never forgive her enough to marry her now, but she couldn't bear the thought of Tristan living with emotional injury.

Peter returned with a hackney and helped Mrs. Harper inside. When the earl's crested carriage arrived, Richard handed in Elizabeth and took a seat next to his wife, leaving Tristan to hand in Leticia. He held out a hand, his gaze so shielded she couldn't begin to guess his thoughts. She looked into his eyes, hoping her regret and deep sorrow were revealed. He gave no reaction. Placing her hand in his, she stepped into the family coach. Tristan swung in and sat close enough that his thigh brushed hers.

As the carriage rolled along the streets, Elizabeth and Richard kept up a stream of conversation in a clear attempt to pretend they didn't notice the tension between Tristan and Leticia. Leticia focused on holding back her tears.

Once the carriage stopped in front of Aunt Alice's house, Leticia murmured her thanks to Richard and Elizabeth, and vacated. Tristan kept pace with her up the front steps. As they stepped inside, she turned to him. "May I speak with you in private before we join my aunt and sister?"

He nodded, his expression blank.

She led the way to the open front parlor, the exact place where she had foolishly allowed Lord Bradbury to kiss her. If only she'd been more decisive about her refusal, or pushed him away. If she'd slapped him, that would have removed all doubt about her feelings.

No, she couldn't fault Lord Bradbury for his intentions. Still, it had cost her Tristan's trust.

Leticia drew a breath. To give herself a moment, she removed her gloves and bonnet, and smoothed back her hair. Her words tumbled out in a breathless rush. "I owe you an apology. After you left, Lord Bradbury asked me to marry him. I refused—I told him I love you. He tried to discourage me from choosing you because of your past, and then he tried to show me how much he cared about me by"—she took another breath. Making herself say the words, she blurted—"kissing me. I never meant to do it; he caught me off guard. He hoped I'd enjoy the kiss enough to consider a life with him. He realized that my heart wasn't in it—I didn't reciprocate, I vow it—and he withdrew his offer. That doesn't change the fact that we did kiss, though."

She turned to him to let him see her desperate sincerity. "I don't expect you to forgive me, but please know that I never meant to play you false. I'm sorry. I'm so very, very sorry."

He said nothing. There was no forgiveness then. Perhaps at least he would no longer be so hurt.

She twisted her hands together. "I will always love you. I know you don't want me now. I've been such a hypocrite." Her eyes burned. "That's all I wanted to say. Thank you for giving me the chance to explain myself." Miserable, she turned to leave. Silently, she bade farewell at all hope of a loving marriage with Tristan, the only man she'd ever truly loved.

Chapter Thirty-Eight

After delivering her apology, Leticia turned to leave. Tristan should have known Bradbury was to blame, that Leticia had been innocent. Tristan should have flattened the blackguard in White's. There would surely be words—or more—between them in the future.

Tristan caught her arm. "Tish."

Leticia halted, looking at the ground. Tears dropped from her eyes, some falling to the floor, others carving out streaks on her cheeks.

He slid his hand from her arm down to her hand. "I love you. That hasn't changed."

Raising her head, she peered at him with tearful eyes.

He touched her cheek. "Forgive me for assuming the worst. I doubted you, not because you are untrustworthy, but because I doubt my own ability to be loveable."

She stepped closer, disbelief and sorrow in the narrowing of her eyes. "You *are* lovable."

"I don't deserve you. I don't meet the criteria you outlined when we first made our ridiculous wager. I can only do everything possible to make you happy within my limited ability, and hope it's enough…hope you will be happy enough to stay."

She put a hand on his cheek. "Your mother didn't leave because you disappointed her; she left because she was selfish."

Memories overwhelmed him and he was transported to when he was a small boy searching for his mother, running through the house calling for her. The head housekeeper had pointed out the window where his mother climbed onto a carriage. He'd raced outside, but the carriage had already begun rolling forward. Though Tristan had run as fast as he could, the carriage continued at a steady pace, more quickly than his legs could keep up. When the carriage with his mother disappeared from view, and he'd come to a crossroads with no way of knowing which direction they'd taken, he'd stopped, fallen to his knees, and sobbed.

Richard had found him then. Silent and grim, he'd picked up Tristan, hoisted him onto the back of the horse he'd ridden, and taken Tristan home.

"Can you ever forgive me?" Leticia pressed her lips together, studying him.

"If you'll forgive me for believing you could have played me false."

Leticia put her other hand on his chest and smiled so lovingly into his eyes that it almost undid him. Leticia. She was constant and driven by both duty and honor. No dutiful, honorable woman would leave her family, betray her husband, abandon her children.

Leticia was right. The realization struck him like a thunderbolt. His mother hadn't left because Tristan had been a bad child; she left for her own reasons. Perhaps she suffered from some form of mental illness. She may not have really loved her husband and had run off to be with another man. Whatever her reasons, she wasn't committed enough to stay—even for her children.

However, Leticia embodied selflessness and sincerity and honor.

She stood with one hand in his, the other on his chest, and so much love in her eyes that it nearly brought him to his knees.

With a tender smile curving her shapely lips, she said, "You do meet my criteria of an ideal husband."

With a huff of disbelief, he shook his head. "Hardly."

She pulled away, humor brightening her eyes. "Let's see. If I recall correctly, my list for a husband included monogamy, integrity, kindness, a sense of humor and a means of supporting me."

He managed a smile. "You're a very demanding wench, you know that?"

She grinned. "I am. But don't you see? You are that man."

He paused, working backward through her list. "Well, I do have ten thousand a year so unless you want to buy a castle, that would be adequate. We laugh a lot together. I hope I am kind more often than not." He stumbled over the remaining two qualities.

She finished. "You are a man of integrity. You always keep your promises and you act within your principles."

He swallowed, waiting for the final stumbling block, given his history.

"As far as monogamy, I have every faith in you. In your heart, you are a new man—a better man. You haven't changed much; you've always lived by your own code of honor. Recently, you've elevated that code. I know you would never betray me."

The trust and love in her eyes gave him courage. "I

vow it. I vow I will always be faithful to you. Only you." He leaned in and kissed her, full of promise and love.

She molded herself against him and wrapped her arms around him, kissing him with such pure love and passion that it healed him. Its strength and beauty reached through years of pain and isolation to that small boy who thought he'd disappointed his mother and driven her away. If a woman as remarkable as Leticia loved him, he was a worthwhile person—strong and noble and brave—and so very much in love that his heart expanded. The sensation washed over him, bathing him in light and joy.

In his heart, he sailed across an ocean to an island big enough for the two happiest people on earth.

Chapter Thirty-Nine

Leticia found her sister in the library working on a watercolor, humming a melancholy tune in a minor key. With the library windows framing her, and the pale gray, silver, and charcoal clouds behind her, she looked like a portrait painted with masterful strokes.

"Bella," Leticia murmured.

Isabella's gaze flitted to her but focused on her watercolor. After a moment, she tossed her brush into a tin cup, leaned back, and eyed Leticia with a weariness of an older woman.

"You look happy," Isabella said. "Am I to understand that you and Tristan have come to an understanding?"

"We have. He forgave me." Leticia let out a breath. "I only hope you will, some day. I am so sorry, Bella. I was too self-absorbed to realize you had formed an attachment to Lord Bradbury."

Isabella wiped her hands with a cloth. "Many gentlemen are courting me. Perhaps my feelings for one of them will change. Aunt assures me that if I do not find my heart's desire this year, she'll bring me back every Season until I do. I'm only sixteen—I'm not exactly on the shelf."

"It's true that you have plenty of time, but the fact is, I encouraged someone whom you preferred. That must cut you deeply."

Isabella poured mineral water onto the cloth, its pungent scent filling the room, and continued wiping her hands. "It matters not. He chose you."

Leticia let out a sigh. "I hope you will forgive me." She arose.

"Leticia." Her sister's voice halted her movement. "I am glad you and Tristan finally realized you were meant to be together. I know you will make each other happy." She offered a faint smile.

"I know it, too."

Isabella lifted a chin. "I don't believe I am in love with Lord Bradbury. I held him in high regard but I hardly conversed with him enough to form a true *tendré* for him. So really, it's not as if you wounded me so greatly."

"I'm sorry to have lost your good opinion."

Isabella's expression lightened. "You're my sister; I will always love you."

Leticia knelt at her side, and threw her arms around her. "I love you, too, Bella."

A servant arrived. "Mr. Barrett to see you, Miss Wentworth.

Tristan!

Leticia practically skipped to the front parlor where he stood grinning. Her knees went weak at the sight. He drew her into his arms and kissed her soundly. Her entire body turned to the consistency of lemon curd. When he lifted his head, Leticia hung on to his arms to keep upright.

Chuckling, he led her to a nearby Ottomane couch and they sank into its soft cushions together. "I love how flushed you get when I kiss you." He tapped her nose and wrapped his hands around hers. "I have two purposes for my visit today."

"Is one to kiss me?"

He grinned. "Very well, I admit it; I have three purposes."

"Oh, good. Then you'd best kiss me again."

He raised a brow. "Is that a request?"

"No. A command."

"Your command is my wish." As he lowered his head, she lifted her face and kissed him first. A low chuckle rumbled in his chest but he let her take the lead. She explored his lips as if finding them for the first time, each new sensation washing over her.

When she pulled away, he blinked, his face flushed, his breath as unsteady as hers. "Heaven help me," he muttered.

She swallowed to cover up her own breathlessness, and asked in an overly sweet voice, "What are the other two reasons for your visit?"

"I can't imagine..." He swallowed. He ran his fingers through his hair. "Right. Visit. I wanted to let you know that I am on my way to call upon your father."

She affected an innocent look. "Oh? What business have you with him?"

"There's a certain saucy wench with passionate kisses who I mean to hogtie and drag to the alter. I want his advice on what kind of rope to use."

She giggled. She, Leticia, a normally sensible young lady, was blushing and giggling like a silly schoolgirl. "I recommend something gold."

"Ah. Gold. Yes, I see, and perhaps smaller than a rope?"

"It only need be large enough to encircle a finger."

She held up her hand.

"I will take that into consideration." He kissed her hand.

The thought of his absence, if only a few days, left her oddly anxious. Besides, she couldn't pass up a chance to tease him a bit, and remind him of a certain promise. "You needn't rush off to speak to him now, you know."

"No?" he drawled, his eyes gleaming. "I rather felt the need for haste. Especially after your last kiss."

"Oh, no. The altar must wait until after Christmas."

Horror crumpled his face. "Christmas! I cannot wait that long."

Gleefully enjoying herself, she said in an overly serious tone, "I'm afraid you must. If you'll recall, you and I had a wager. You promised me that if I failed to marry by Christmas, you'd donate a hundred guineas to my charity school."

He blinked. "Er...no, I believe the wager was that if you didn't *accept* a marriage proposal by Christmas, I'd pay you a hundred guineas. You've accepted mine, so it counts."

"No, I'm quite certain that it was *marriage* that must occur by then."

"You can't be serious. Christmas is eight months away!"

"Are you afraid you will change your mind by then?" She shot him a look of challenge.

"No, of course not. I'm afraid I might ravage you before then."

She smoothed the lines from his forehead. Of course, ravishment implied a lack of willingness on her part, and nothing could be further from the truth. She grinned at the thought and didn't have the decency to blush.

He tilted his head. "Though I won this wager, far be it for me to deny support of your school. I'll draw up a bank note and deliver it to you on our wedding day. We could get married as soon as I purchase the license. I will get one next week."

Sobering, she entwined her fingers with his. "We can't marry that soon. My mother is in a family way and needs to stay abed lest the baby come too soon as the last two did. I want her at my wedding. We couldn't get married before September—maybe not until October, to give her time to recover."

He deflated. "That's still four months away."

"True." She almost laughed at his sad puppy eyes—except she shared the sentiment.

To his credit, he straightened. "Very well. I'm still going to ask your father's permission; he's expecting me and I want our engagement formalized."

She smiled. "I do, as well."

The worry lines returned to his brow. "Do you think your father will reject my suit?"

She smiled and kissed his cheek. "I have already written him and told him how much you've changed and how much I love you. I also informed him that I refused two other fine gentlemen because I will have no one but you, so unless he wants me to die an old maid, he'd best accept you."

He lifted a dark brow. "Two offers?"

She laughed guiltily. "I may have exaggerated Captain Kensington's interest in me."

He chuckled. "No one else believes you have a devious streak in you—it's small but it does exist." He smoothed a wayward tendril by her ear and skimmed his fingers along her cheek.

How she loved him! She leaned her cheek against his hand. "No one else knows me like you do."

She kissed him. Before she had time to worry if he thought her too forward for attacking him—twice—Tristan wrapped his arms around her and kissed her with such possessive tenderness that she melted.

He pulled away as flushed and breathless as she. "If it were anything less important than speaking with your father, I would not be going."

"If it were anything less important, I would take exception to your leaving me for so long."

Brushing a hand over her cheek, he grinned. "I have something for you. It belonged to my great-grandmother."

She brightened. "The one you called *Oma*?"

He nodded. "She taught me to love poetry. Despite their harsh-sounding language, Germans are extremely poetic and always speak with beautiful imagery." He retrieved a tiny package from a pocket in his tailcoat and unwrapped the handkerchief.

In his palm lay an exquisite brooch of delicate silver roses and leaves, and tiny rose cut diamonds. Her breath rushed out at the thoughtful gesture. "Oh my," she breathed.

With a hushed voice, he explained, "*Oma* often pinned it to her gowns. She said it reminded her how much she and her late husband loved one another." His face clouded. "She passed on a few months before my mother left."

If only his grandmother had been there to love and reassure her broken-hearted great-grandson abandoned by a thoughtless mother.

"I will cherish this always," Leticia said. She pinned it to her bodice and glanced up at him.

He kissed her, then held her close, his familiar scent embracing her as much as his arms. After another kiss to her temple, he stood. "I will be back in three days. I love you, Leticia."

She would never tire of hearing those words. "I love you, Tristan. Godspeed. Come to dinner when you get home."

He grinned. "Wild horses couldn't keep me away."

To say Aunt Alice was in raptures over Leticia's engagement to Tristan would have been an understatement. They embarked on a flurry of activity selecting a new gown for the ceremony as well as several new gowns and accessories Aunt Alice declared were quite necessary for a married lady. Isabella caught Aunt Alice's contagious enthusiasm and soon behaved as her old self.

When she wasn't shopping with her aunt and sister, Leticia met with their solicitor or contractors to begin rebuilding the school. In the meantime, Mrs. Harper taught her students in the park with only a few borrowed books and an ever-growing class size.

Leticia threw herself into the daily fray, all the while missing Tristan. On the third day, she arrived home later than she'd planned. With any luck, Tristan had returned and would be present for a small dinner party tonight. She'd invited Elizabeth and Richard as well. She'd toyed with the idea of inviting Lord Bradbury for Isabella's sake, but discarded the idea for fear both Tristan and Lord Bradbury would be uncomfortable. So, with little time to change for dinner, she headed for the stairs, unbuttoning her plum pelisse, and calling for her lady's maid.

"Miss Wentworth," called a footman from the foot of the stairs. "There's an urchin at the kitchen door asking to speak to you. He says he is here on behalf of one Molly."

Leticia put a hand over her heart. "I hope she's all right."

As she hurried to the kitchen, a second footman came from the front of the house. "Miss Wentworth. Mr. Barrett is here to see you."

She halted. Tristan was home! Forgetting herself, she trotted into the front parlor. There he stood, so beloved that her heart did a triple flip. He'd always been the kind of handsome that made her smile and sometimes covertly admire him, even when she'd been sure her heart belonged to someone else, but at that moment, he was so beautiful that the sight of him stopped her breath.

"You're home!" She launched herself into his arms.

Laughing, he caught her. All the nerve endings in her body let out a sigh as if getting a drink after a drought. He held her close. "Not quite, Love, but I plan to make a home with you soon."

She nestled in closer and kissed him, half laughing at his enthusiasm, then moaning as his mouth brought her to an edge she wanted to leap off.

When he ended the kiss, she fanned herself and managed, "Father said yes, I take it?"

"He did. Your mother said the doctor agreed to allow her out of bed in six weeks' time if all goes well, so we may have the wedding then—before the baby comes."

She let out a breath. "Oh, that's wonderful!"

His gaze moved downward. "You're wearing *Oma's* brooch."

"I wear it every day." She fingered his gift.

The first footman cleared his throat. "Shall I send the urchin away, miss?"

"Oh, dear. Molly. I almost forgot." She peeled herself off Tristan. "Molly is at the kitchen door. I'd best see to her. I fear what her father may have done now. I'll return in a moment."

Without taking time to remove her gloves or reticule still dangling from her wrist, she strode to the kitchen, passing servants bustling to prepare dinner, opened the door, and peered out.

A boy of perhaps six—with hair that looked as if it had never seen a comb—looked anxiously at her. "Miss Wentworth?" At her nod, he continued, "Molly wants you but she's too scared to come." He turned and gestured over his shoulder.

Leticia handed him a coin and followed him out. At the gate leading to the kitchen entrance, Molly slumped over, weeping and shuddering. A black bruise spread over her cheek and one eye swelled shut.

"Oh, no. Molly." Leticia rushed outside to the child.

Molly lifted her head and held up a hand as if trying to push her away. "No, miss. Go back inside."

"Oh, Molly. Did your father beat you again?"

"Meddling little tart," growled a voice behind her. Pain exploded from the side of her face and the ground slammed into her shoulder.

Dazed, she tried to breathe. A pair of arms threw a

rough bag smelling of horses over her head. She kicked and struggled but another heavy blow landed on her face. Black and white sparks blazed before her vision. A feminine voice cried out from far away and she floated backward in slow rolls.

When Leticia became fully coherent, a bumping, rocking sensation suggested she rode in some kind of cart. The coarse bag over her head scratched her face. She reached up to pull it away but her hands came up together, bound. Panic left her breathless. Think. How could she escape?

She lay on a hard surface, her head covered, and her hands tied in front of her. Her pulse pounded. She tried to move her feet but they were also bound. Working with care, she pulled the bag away from her face enough to see. Gray light illuminated her hands, still in their gloves, tied with a rough rope. Her pulse throbbed where a strip of cloth tied over her mouth bit into her skin.

Near her head sat several large metal containers like the kind used to transport milk. Between the metal containers, cloudy skies and fingers of fog met her sight. Voices nearby called out the last chance to purchase wares, and the scent of fish hung heavy in the air, mixing with damp, mildew smells nowhere but the waterfront could produce. Ship bells rang out, and water sloshed and gurgled.

A hundred questions bounced through her head. Yet a single clear course of action shone through the noise: if anyone were looking for her, she must leave clues to help them find her. She wiggled and strained but could not loosen her ropes. She managed to open the strings of her reticule and pull out a monogrammed handkerchief. Odds were high that someone else would find it first, but she had to try to let Tristan know where she was being taken. She stuffed the handkerchief through a large crack between the slats of wood in the cart and watched it fall.

The cart turned, shifting her body to the right. She pulled out a tiny throwaway bottle of perfume and shoved it through the cracks. It shattered on the cobbled streets, but hopefully the scent and the gold leaves painted on the glass would be a clue. The fan would be too big to fit. She stuffed everything else in her reticule down the crack. Still, the cart continued. What else could she leave in her breadcrumb trail?

Tristan's brooch winked in the fading light. No. She could not part with such a precious, and sentimental gift. Besides, urchins would likely find it before Tristan did.

Of course, if anyone but Tristan were looking for her, they wouldn't recognize her breadcrumb trail for what it was.

The cart stopped. Leticia toyed with the idea of pulling the bag back over her head and pretending to be out of her senses, but the need to see where her captor was taking her overruled that thought.

A face came into view. She let out a growl of disgust. Molly's father. She should have known. He'd used the perfect bait to draw her out of her aunt's home.

He narrowed his gaze at her. "Ye gonna come quiet-like or are ye gonna make me 'it you agin?"

Her face still ached from the last time he hit her. Besides, bound and gagged, she had little to offer in the way of resistance.

He grabbed her feet and hauled her out from

between the cans, pulled her to a seated position, and threw her over his shoulder. She let out a moan as his shoulder dug into her abdomen. As he carried her to a door and fumbled with the latch, she made a last, desperate attempt. She tore Tristan's brooch off her pelisse and tossed it to the side of the door. It landed facedown, covered by a piece of torn plum cloth. She prayed that her rescuer would find it before someone who would see it as an expensive bauble rather than her plea for help.

Her captor carried her inside and dropped her on the ground. Her breath left in a whoosh. For a moment, she couldn't breathe. The darkness in the room where she lay obscured her surroundings.

Panic stole her breath but she fought it back. Surely, if her captor desired her dead, he would have killed her already. Of course, there were worse things than death.

"If you were my wife or daughter, I'd beat ye about the 'ead and shoulders an' then take a belt to yer backside. But I suppose that wouldn't be decent to do wiff ye."

Decent. She let out a snort. Such a villain didn't know the meaning of the word. She was surprised it existed in his vocabulary.

He retrieved a knife and showed it to her. The sliver of light coming through the cracks under the door shone on the blade. Fear turned her cold.

He leaned over her. "I warn'd ye afore but y didn' listen, so listen now: close th' school an' ne'er open it agin."

She glared at him. What an ignorant fool!

As if seeing the defiance in her eyes, he grabbed

her by the hair and jerked her head back. The cold metal of his knife bit into her throat. A gasp worked its way out through her gag.

"I kin kill ye, see?" he continued. "It'd be easy. But I ain't no murderer. So, I'll give ye one final warnin'. If'n yous don' stop yer school, I will kill ye. I'll already be a murderer then so I migh' as well kill yer teacher. Then yer fancy friend with the fancy title. I'll take my time wiff 'er—I bet she smells real purty."

He grinned and the stench of rotten teeth gagged her. The thought of Miss Harper or Elizabeth in this villain's hands sent a shower of nausea raining down on her.

"I'll leave ye 'ere a while to think it over. Maybe I'll come back and let ye go if'n ye promise you'll leave off wiff this school business."

He opened the door and slammed it behind him.

She let out a half gasp, half sob. Were the lives of her friends worth the school? Would she live to see Tristan again? If only she'd realized sooner how matched she and Tristan were. Her affection for Richard all those years were a schoolgirl crush compared to the deep love she bore for Tristan. She'd wasted so much of her life pining away for the wrong man.

Tristan was probably searching for her with the same dogged devotion he'd used to rescue his brother last year—the rescue that had gotten him shot. Oh heavens, he might get hurt. Or worse. Panic left her breathless.

"Be safe, Tristan. Please be safe."

The gag muffled her words and they dissolved into silent prayer.

Chapter Forty

Gun in-hand, Tristan glanced back at Richard. His brother shook his head. A cart sat in the street, but who knew into which building the scoundrel had taken Leticia. She'd left a trail of clues for them—clever girl—as they'd followed, lost, and then found the cart again. But now?

In front of one in the endless line of doors, lay a piece of cloth. Was it purple? In the waning light, color faded.

He crept forward, bent down, and examined it. Purple. Unless he was mistaken, that purple cloth was the exact color of Leticia's favorite pelisse. He picked it up and found a hard object inside the soft fabric. When he turned it over, *Oma's* diamond brooch lay, still pinned, to the ragged scrap of cloth, glimmering in the twilight. He sagged in relief. She was here. Tristan tucked the brooch into his pocket and nodded at Richard. Stepping stealthily, his brother took up position opposite him with the door between them. From inside the building a male voice spoke.

As Tristan bunched his muscles, ready to spring, the door flew open and the man who'd stormed into the school and dragged out one of the students stepped out. Focused on tucking away a knife, the disgruntled father walked out.

Tristan leaped into action. A primal cry rang out.

He knocked the man down and leaped on him. Rage blinded Tristan to all but the need to punish Leticia's attacker for all the ways he'd hurt and frightened her. A pair of arms pulled Tristan off the man. Tristan struggled to continue to rain vengeance upon the scoundrel but the other arms held him fast from behind.

"He's had enough!" Richard's voice cut through the haze of fury consuming Tristan.

Tristan shook off his brother's arms. "Let go of me!"

"Leave off. Don't kill him." His brother's voice, calm and authoritative, peeled back another layer of the haze.

Tristan blinked. The cretin lay moaning, his face unrecognizable through blood and swelling. A knife lay several feet away. Tristan's gun lay in the opposite direction. Tristan looked down at his hands, bloodied and cut. How much of that blood was his and how much belonged to the other man, he could not guess, nor did he care.

"I'll watch him," Richard said, gripping his pistol. "Go inside and see to Leticia."

Leticia. Her name snapped him into motion. He strode into the dark room. "Leticia?"

A muffled whimper replied. What had that monster done to her? His heart pelted his chest and echoed in his ears. Cold perspiration trickled down his face. If she'd been harmed, he'd go back out and finish off the beast.

He took another step inside, wishing for all the world that he had a lamp. "Tish?"

Another wordless sound, more urgent this time, guided him a few steps to the right. Her perfume mingled with the scents of fish and dank rotting wood and jute. He could barely make out a dark form on the floor in front of him. He bent down and reached out. Something soft touched his gloved hands.

"Tish?"

Two more squeaks in quick succession. Was she so badly hurt that she couldn't speak? Or gagged? He tore off his gloves and felt around, finding soft fabric, an arm, a shoulder; lower down, with his other hand, he found a leg and a knee. He slid his arms underneath her back and legs, and lifted her up. Fighting the impulse to simply stand still and hold her close, he carried her outside where he could see to her better. He set her down on the cobbled street, leaning against the outer wall.

Gagged, white-faced and wide-eyed, Leticia looked back at him. Tristan worked the cloth's knot until it loosened enough to throw away. Red marks around her mouth testified of the tightness of her gag. A bruise purpled her temple and another darkened her cheekbone and eye. The brute had struck her. Tristan almost went for his gun. Instead, he worked at the ropes on her hands until Richard handed him a knife—the beast's knife—and cut her binds, freeing first her hands, then her feet.

"Oh, Tristan," she cried out.

Wrapping his arms around her, he held her close. "It's over. You're safe."

She nestled against him, gasping. He held her, murmuring reassuring words, and kissing her brow. If only he'd followed his gut and gone with her to the kitchen door to see about Molly. Instead, he'd hung back, not wanting to intrude.

"I'm sorry I didn't come sooner," he said.

She broke down and wept. He held her as helplessness and rage and tenderness warred, shredding his insides.

Her fingers curled around his lapels. "You came," she breathed. "You came."

"When I heard you scream, I rushed out, but he'd already carted you off."

She moved her hand to his cheek. In an unsteady voice, she said, "You found me. I knew you would."

"You left us a trail to follow. That was very resourceful."

She let out a huff, then sniffled. His heart ached to see her so shaken.

"I wasn't sure it was enough," she said. "Anyone might have taken them before you saw them."

"I wasn't far behind, but I was on foot. When I passed Richard on the street, I commandeered his coach, so we were never far behind. Each time we lost the cart in the traffic, we found another clue you left." He glanced at his brother. "I can't believe you came along when you did."

Richard met his gaze. "It appears providence was on our side."

Tristan sent him a look of gratitude. A half smile touched Richard's mouth and he nodded. A moan caught Tristan's gaze. The thug who'd attacked Leticia lay on his belly, trussed up like the pig that he was. Tristan wanted to roast him.

Leticia let out a shaky breath. Tristan fished a handkerchief from a pocket and handed it to her. She wiped her face and blew her nose.

"We need to get you home," Tristan said. "Can you stand?"

"I think so." Her voice came out stronger, more like the Leticia he knew.

Eyeing her with caution, he helped her up. She glanced at him and nodded, her gaze steadier. Still trussed up, the arsonist let off a string of curses at women in general and men who supported their madcap schemes.

Richard cuffed him. "Be silent." He dragged him to the carriage.

Tristan put an arm around Leticia. "He won't bother anyone, ever again."

Her eyes brightened with tears. She shook her head. "So senseless. One man's fear and resistance to change caused so much destruction and sorrow."

Tristan had a few other choice words he might have used but remained silent.

After delivering the criminal to the care of the authorities, Tristan took Leticia home. When they arrived in front of her aunt's house, no one got out of the carriage.

Leticia thanked them both like a proper lady, then burst into tears again and threw her arms around Tristan.

He held her, aching all over for what she'd suffered. What else had the monster done to her? "Did he hurt you?" he whispered in her ear.

He hoped she knew that he was asking if she'd suffered more than was apparent. "No. He struck me twice that I remember and threatened me with a knife, but nothing beyond that." She stiffened, pulled away, and eyed him. "I vow my virtue is intact. Does this change anything for us?"

"No, of course not. How can you think that?"

She bit her lip and glanced anxiously at Richard who should have looked uncomfortable witnessing such an intimate conversation.

Instead, he met Leticia's gaze with steady eyes. Richard spoke in firm, almost scolding tones. "No one of any conscience would blame you or question your purity. You don't know us very well if you think we're so shallow—and you don't know Tristan at all if you think this changes his feelings for you. Now, if you'll excuse me, I believe a stroll home is just the thing." He put on his hat and stepped out of the carriage.

Leticia glanced back at Tristan, a question still lingering in her eye.

He touched her face and smoothed her mussed hair back from her face. "I love you. Wild horses wouldn't keep me away from you, remember?" He tried for a playful tone but the horror of the day's events lay too heavily on him.

She attempted a brave smile. "My hero."

He wrapped his arms around her and held her until she relaxed against them and their hearts beat in unison. "I'll love you forever."

"I'll love you even longer."

Chapter Forty-One

Pausing on the church steps, Leticia smiled at Tristan and slipped her hand through the crook of his elbow. If it were possible for a person to perish from happiness, she would have been gone weeks ago. How she loved this man!

"Admiring me, Love?" Tristan drawled.

She smoothed the lapel of his tailcoat. "You look more dashing than usual."

Tristan grinned. "It's all those ungentlemanly thoughts in my head that make me so devilishly handsome."

"You shouldn't be thinking about the honeymoon until after the wedding takes place."

"I have news for you; I've been thinking about the honeymoon since before I asked you to marry me." He kissed her so gently, so full of love.

She shivered under the force of the warm tingles he never failed to evoke in her. "I do believe we ought to go inside and say our vows."

"Yes, let's do. Or I might do something to resurrect my scandalous behavior right here, right now. But first...."

He slipped a bank note into her hand. "As promised. I know the school means a lot to you."

"You mean much more."

If only she could capture that slow curve of his lips

and the joy brightening his eyes!

"I won the bet, too, you know," he said. "If you recall, the wager was that if I found you a husband before Christmas, you must name your son after me."

She pictured a little boy with dark curls and shining black eyes. "I will be happy to name our son after you."

He grinned. "With your maiden name. Tristan Wentworth Barrett. It sounds like the name of a visionary man."

"It does, indeed."

"Let's get married, you saucy wench."

"Very well, on one condition."

He waited, with a brow lifted.

"That you promise to take me in a balloon ride again."

He chuckled. "Your wish is my command. May that be the first of many diversions we enjoy together."

Grinning, she took his arm and walked into the church. In the pews, her mother, beautiful in a loose-fitting gown and decorative shawl smiled and dabbed at her eyes with a handkerchief. Her father cleared his throat and put his arm around her mother. Her sisters beamed. Aunt Alice positively glowed. All confidence, Leticia walked on Tristan's arm to the altar where the vicar pronounced them husband and wife.

After the ceremony, they went outside to a beautiful summer day and sat down to the wedding breakfast. Molly, who'd found a position with a baker willing to allow her to leave for school during school hours, as well as students from the charity school, helped serve food to the wedding guests. Molly made eye contact with Leticia, more steady and confident than Leticia had ever seen her.

Richard sat next to Tristan, teasing him as only a brother could, and offering wisdom if Tristan decided to make a bid for the House of Commons. Richard's pride shone in his eyes. Tristan basked in his brother's approval, but threw back good-natured insults all the same.

As they climbed into the carriage to take them away to their honeymoon, Tristan took her into his arms. "I love you, Tish."

"I love you." She nestled against him.

All those years she'd been wrong about him. She'd believed Tristan was her dear friend. Instead, he was truly the love of her life.